HOME BEFORE DARK

HOME BEFORE DARK

RILEY SAGER

THORNDIKE PRESS
A part of Gale, a Cengage Company

LIBRARY OF CONGRESS CIP DATA ON FILE.
CATALOGUING IN PUBLICATION FOR THIS BOOK
IS AVAILABLE FROM THE LIBRARY OF CONGRESS

ISBN-13: 978-1-4328-8047-7 (hardcover alk. paper)

Published in 2020 by arrangement with Dutton, an imprint of Penguin
Publishing Group, a division of Penguin Random House, LLC

Printed in Mexico
Print Number: 04   Print Year: 2020

For those who tell ghost stories . . .
and those who believe them.

Home's past.
Every house has a story.
Ours is a ghost story.
It's also a lie.

And now that yet another person has died
within these walls, it's finally time to tell the
truth.

Every house has a story to tell and a secret to share.

The dining room wallpaper might hide pencil marks charting the growth of children who lived there decades before. Under that sun-faded linoleum could be wood once trod by soldiers from the Revolutionary War.

Houses are always changing. Coats of paint. Rows of laminate. Rolls of carpet. They cover up a home's stories and secrets, rendering them silent until someone comes along to reveal them.

That's what I do.

My name is Maggie Holt. I'm a designer and, in many ways, a historian. I look for each house's story and attempt to coax it out. I'm proud of the work I do. I'm good at it.

I listen.

I learn.

I use that knowledge to design an interior that, while fully modern, always speaks to the home's past.

Every house has a story.

Ours is a ghost story.

It's also a lie.

And now that yet another person has died within these walls, it's finally time to tell the truth.

HOUSE
OF
HORRORS

A TRUE STORY

Ewan Holt

MURRAY-HAMILTON, INC.,
NEW YORK, NY

HOUSE
OF
HORRORS

A TRUE STORY

Ewan Holt

MURRAY HAMILTON, INC.
NEW YORK

PROLOGUE:
JULY 1

"Daddy, you need to check for ghosts."

I paused in the doorway of my daughter's bedroom, startled in that way all parents get when their child says something truly confounding. Since Maggie was five, I suppose I should have been used to it. I wasn't. Especially with a request so unexpectedly odd.

"I do?"

"Yes," Maggie said, insistent. "I don't want them in my room."

Until that moment, I had no idea my daughter even knew what a ghost was, let alone feared one was occupying her bedroom. More than one, apparently. I noticed her word choice.

Them.

I blamed this new development on the house. We had been in Baneberry Hall almost a week by then — ample time to have noted its eccentricities but not long enough to have gotten used to them. The sudden shifting of

11

the walls. The noises in the night. A ceiling fan that, when it spun at full speed, sounded like the clicking of teeth.

Maggie, as sensitive as any girl her age, was clearly having trouble adjusting to it all. At bedtime the night before, she'd asked me when we'd be returning to our old home, a sad and dim two-bedroom apartment in Burlington. Now there were ghosts to contend with.

"I suppose it can't hurt," I said, humoring her. "Where should I look first?"

"Under the bed."

No surprise there. I had had the same fear when I was Maggie's age, certain something awful hid in the darkness inches below where I slept. I dropped to my hands and knees and took a quick glance under the bed. All that lurked there was a thin coat of dust and a single pink sock.

"All clear," I announced. "Where next?"

"The closet," Maggie said.

I'd assumed as much and was already making my way to the bedroom closet. This section of the house — dubbed "Maggie's wing" because it contained not just her bedroom but also an adjoining playroom — was located on the second floor, under the eaves of the sloped roof. Because of the room's slanted ceiling, one half of the closet's old oak door slanted as well. Opening it made me think of a storybook cottage, which was one of the reasons we decided the space should belong to Maggie.

"Nothing in the closet," I said, making a show of yanking the chain dangling from the closet's single lightbulb and peering between hangers draped with clothes. "Anywhere else?"

Maggie aimed a trembling index finger at the massive armoire that stood sentinel a few feet from the closet. It was a relic from the house's past. An odd one. Over eight feet tall. Its narrow base gradually widened to a formidable midsection before suddenly tapering off again at the top. Crowning it were carvings of cherubs, birds, and strands of ivy that climbed the corners. I thought that, much like the closet door, it gave Maggie's room a touch of literary magic. It brought to mind voyages to Narnia.

But when I cracked open the armoire's double doors, Maggie sucked in a breath, steeling herself for whatever terror she thought waited inside.

"Are you sure you want me to open it?" I asked.

"No." Maggie paused, and then changed her mind. "Yes."

I pulled the armoire doors wide open, exposing a space occupied by only a few frilly dresses my wife had bought with the hopeful notion that our tomboy daughter might someday wear them.

"It's empty," I said. "See?"

From her spot in bed, Maggie peered into the armoire before letting out a relieved sigh.

"You know there's no such thing as ghosts, right?" I said.

"You're wrong." Maggie slid deeper under the covers. "I've seen them."

I looked at my daughter, trying not to appear startled, even though I was. I knew she had an active imagination, but I didn't think it was *that* vivid. So vivid that she saw things that weren't there and believed them to be real.

And she did believe. I could tell from the way she stared back at me, tears pooling in the corners of her wide eyes. She believed, and it terrified her.

I sat on the edge of her bed. "Ghosts aren't real, Mags. If you don't believe me, ask your mother. She'll tell you the same thing."

"But they are," Maggie insisted. "I see them all the time. And one of them talks to me. Mister Shadow."

A chill swept up my spine. "Mister Shadow?"

Maggie gave a single, fearful nod.

"What does Mister Shadow say?"

14

"He says —" Maggie gulped, trying hard to hold back her tears. "He says we're going to die here."

ONE

From the moment I enter the office, I know how things are going to go. It's happened before. Too many times to count. And although each incident has its slight variations, the outcome is always the same. I expect nothing less this go-round, especially when the receptionist offers me a knowing smile as recognition flashes in her eyes. It's clear she's well-acquainted with the Book.

My family's greatest blessing.

Also our biggest curse.

"I have an appointment with Arthur Rosenfeld," I say. "The name is Maggie Holt."

"Of course, Miss Holt." The receptionist gives me a quick once-over, comparing and contrasting the little girl she's read about with the woman standing before her in scuffed boots, green cargo pants, and a flannel shirt speckled with sawdust. "Mr. Rosenfeld is on a call right now. He'll be with you

17

in just a minute."

The receptionist — identified as Wendy Davenport by the nameplate on her desk — gestures to a chair by the wall. I sit as she continues to glance my way. I assume she's checking out the scar on my left cheek — a pale slash about an inch long. It's fairly famous, as scars go.

"I read your book," she says, stating the obvious.

I can't help but correct her. "You mean my father's book."

It's a common misconception. Even though my father is credited as the sole author, everyone assumes we all had something to do with it. And while that may be true of my mother, I played absolutely no part in the Book, despite being one of its main characters.

"I loved it," Wendy continues. "When I wasn't scared out of my mind, of course."

She pauses, and I cringe internally, knowing what's about to come next. It always does. Every damn time.

"What was it like?" Wendy leans forward until her ample bosom is squished against the desk. "Living in that house?"

The question that's inevitably asked whenever someone connects me to the Book. By now, I have a stock answer at the ready. I learned early on that one is necessary, and so I always keep it handy, like something carried in my toolbox.

"I don't really remember anything about that time."

The receptionist arches an overplucked brow. "Nothing at all?"

"I was five," I say. "How much do you remember from that age?"

In my experience, this ends the conversation about 50 percent of the time. The merely curious get the hint and move on. The morbidly interested don't give up so easily. I thought Wendy Davenport, with her apple cheeks and Banana Republic outfit, would be the former. Turns out I'm wrong.

"But the experience was so terrifying for your family," she says. "I'd surely remember at least something about it."

There are several ways I can go with this, depending on my mood. If I was at a party, relaxed and generous after a few drinks, I'd probably indulge her and say, "I remember being afraid all the time but not knowing why."

Or, "I suppose it was so scary I blocked it all out."

Or, a perennial favorite, "Some things are too frightening to remember."

But I'm not at a party. Nor am I relaxed

and generous. I'm in a lawyer's office, about to be handed the estate of my recently dead father. My only choice is to be blunt.

"None of it happened," I tell Wendy. "My father made it all up. And when I say all of it, I mean all of it. Everything in that book is a lie."

Wendy's expression switches from wide-eyed curiosity to something harder and darker. I've disappointed her, even though she should feel grateful I'm being honest with her. It's something my father never felt was necessary.

His version of the truth differed greatly from mine, although he, too, had a stock answer, the script of which never wavered no matter who he was talking to.

"I've lied about a great many things in my life," he would have told Wendy Davenport, oozing charm. "But what happened at Baneberry Hall isn't one of them. Every word of that book is true. I swear to the Great Almighty."

That's in line with the public version of events, which goes something like this: Twenty-five years ago, my family lived in a house named Baneberry Hall, situated just outside the village of Bartleby, Vermont.

We moved in on June 26.

We fled in the dead of night on July 15.

Twenty days.

That's how long we lived in that house before we became too terrified to stay a minute longer.

It wasn't safe, my father told police. Something was wrong with Baneberry Hall. Unaccountable things had happened there. *Dangerous* things.

The house was, he reluctantly admitted, haunted by a malevolent spirit.

We vowed never to return.

Ever.

This admission — detailed in the official police report — was noticed by a reporter for the local newspaper, a glorified pamphlet known as the *Bartleby Gazette.* The ensuing article, including plenty of quotes from my father, was soon picked up by the state's wire service and found its way into bigger newspapers in larger towns. Burlington and Essex and Colchester. From there it spread like a pernicious cold, hopping from town to town, city to city, state to state. Roughly two weeks after our retreat, an editor in New York called with an offer to tell our story in book form.

Since we were living in a motel room that smelled of stale smoke and lemon air freshener, my father jumped at the offer. He wrote the book in a month, turning the motel room's tiny bathroom into a make-shift office. One of my earliest memories is of him seated sideways on the toilet, banging away at a typewriter perched atop the bathroom vanity.

The rest is publishing history.

Instant bestseller.

Worldwide phenomenon.

The most popular "real-life" account of the paranormal since *The Amityville Horror.*

For a time, Baneberry Hall was the most famous house in America. Magazines wrote about it. News shows did reports on it. Tourists gathered outside the estate's wrought-iron gate, angling for a glimpse of rooftop or a glint of sunlight bouncing off the windows. It even made *The New Yorker,* in a cartoon that ran two months after the Book hit stores. It shows a couple standing with their Realtor outside a dilapidated house. "We love it," the wife says. "But is it haunted enough for a book deal?"

As for me and my family, well, we were everywhere. In *People* magazine, the three of us looking somber in front of a house we refused to enter. In *Time,* my father seated in a veil of shadow, giving him a distinctly sinister look. On TV, my parents being either coddled or interrogated, depending on the interviewer.

Right now, anyone can go to YouTube and watch a clip of us being interviewed on *60 Minutes*. There we are, a picture-perfect family. My father, shaggy but handsome, sporting the kind of beard that wouldn't come back in style until a decade later. My mother, pretty but looking slightly severe, the tightness at the corners of her mouth hinting that she's not completely on board with the situation. Then there's me. Frilly blue dress. Patent leather shoes. A black headband and very regrettable bangs.

I didn't say much during the interview. I merely nodded or shook my head or acted shy by shrinking close to my mother. I think my only words during the entire segment were "I was scared," even though I can't remember being scared. I can't remember anything about our twenty days at Baneberry Hall. What I do recall is colored by what's in the Book. Instead of memories, I have excerpts. It's like looking at a photograph of a photograph. The framing is off. The colors are dulled. The image is slightly dark.

Murky.

That's the perfect word to describe our time at Baneberry Hall.

It should come as no surprise that many people doubt my father's story. Yes, there are those like Wendy Davenport who think the Book is real. They believe — or *want* to believe — that our time at Baneberry Hall unfolded exactly the way my father described it. But thousands more adamantly think it was all a hoax.

I've seen all the websites and Reddit threads debunking the Book. I've read all the theories. Most of them surmise my parents quickly realized they'd bought more house than they could afford and needed an excuse to get out of it. Others suggest they were con artists who purposefully bought a house where something tragic happened in order to exploit it.

The theory I'm even less inclined to believe is that my parents, knowing they had a money pit on their hands, wanted some way to increase the house's value when it came time to sell. Rather than spend a fortune on renovations, they decided to give Baneberry Hall something else — a reputation. It's not that easy. Houses that have been deemed haunted *decrease* in value, either because prospective buyers are afraid to live there or because they just don't want to deal with the notoriety.

I still don't know the real reason we left so suddenly. My parents refused to tell me. Maybe they really were afraid to stay. Maybe nthey truly and completely feared for their lives. But I know it wasn't because Baneberry Hall was haunted. The big reason, of course, being that there's no such thing as ghosts.

Sure, plenty of people believe in them, but people will believe anything. That Santa Claus is real. That we didn't land on the moon. That Michael Jackson is alive and well and dealing blackjack in Las Vegas.

I believe science, which has concluded that when we die, we die. Our souls don't stay behind, lingering like stray cats until someone notices us. We don't become shadow versions of ourselves. We don't *haunt.*

My complete lack of memories about Baneberry Hall is another reason why I think the Book is bullshit. Wendy Davenport was right to assume an experience that terrifying would leave some dark mark on my memory. I think I would have remembered being hauled to the ceiling by an invisible force, as the Book claims. I would have remembered being choked so hard by *something* that it left handprints on my neck.

I would have remembered Mister Shadow.

That I don't recall any of this means only one thing — none of it happened.

Yet the Book has followed me for most of

25

my life. I have always been the freaky girl who once lived in a haunted house. In grade school, I was an outcast and therefore had to be avoided at all costs. In high school, I was still an outcast, only by then it was somehow cool, which made me the most reluctantly popular girl in my class. Then came college, when I thought things would change, as if being away from my parents would somehow extricate me from the Book. Instead, I was treated as a curiosity. Not shunned, exactly, but either befriended warily or studied from afar.

Dating sucked. Most boys wouldn't come near me. The majority of those who did were *House of Horrors* fanboys more interested in Baneberry Hall than in me. If a potential boyfriend showed an ounce of excitement about meeting my father, I knew the score.

Now I treat any potential friend or lover with a hearty dose of skepticism. After one too many sleepovers spent having a Ouija board thrust at me or "dates" that ended at a cemetery with me being asked if I saw any ghosts among the graves, I can't help but doubt people's intentions. The majority of my friends have been around for ages. For the most part, they pretend the Book doesn't exist. And if a few of them are curious about my family's time in Baneberry Hall, they know enough not to ask me about it.

All these years later, my reputation still precedes me, even though I don't think of myself as famous. I'm notorious. I get emails from strangers calling my dad a liar or saying they'll pray for me or seeking ways to get rid of the ghost they're certain is trapped in their cellar. Occasionally I'll be contacted by a paranormal podcast or one of those ghost-hunter shows, asking for an interview. A horror convention recently invited me to do a meet-and-greet alongside one of the kids from the Amityville house. I declined. I hope the Amityville kid did as well.

Now here I am, tucked into a squeaky chair in a Beacon Hill law office, still reeling from emotional whiplash weeks after my father's death. My current mood is one part prickliness (Thanks, Wendy Davenport.) and two parts grief. Across the desk, an estate attorney details the many ways in which my father continued to profit off the Book. Sales had continued at an agreeably modest pace, with an annual spike in the weeks leading up to Halloween. Hollywood had continued to call on a semiregular basis, most recently with an option that my father never bothered to tell me about to turn it into a TV series.

"Your father was very smart with his money," Arthur Rosenfeld says.

His use of the past tense brings a kick of sadness. It's another reminder that my father is truly gone and not just on an extended trip somewhere. Grief is tricky like that. It can lie low for hours, long enough for magical thinking to take hold. Then, when you're good and vulnerable, it will leap out at you like a fun-house skeleton, and all the pain you thought was gone comes roaring back. Yesterday, it was hearing my father's favorite band on the radio. Today, it's being told that, as my father's sole beneficiary, I'll be receiving roughly four hundred thousand dollars.

The amount isn't a surprise. My father told me this in the weeks preceding his death. An awkward but necessary conversation, made more uncomfortable by the fact that my mother chose not to seek a share of profits from the Book when they got divorced. My father begged her to change her mind, saying she deserved half of everything. My mother disagreed.

"I don't want any part of it," she would snap during one of their many arguments about the matter. "I never did, from the very beginning."

So I get it all. The money. The rights to the Book. The infamy. Like my mother, I wonder if I'd be better off with none of it.

"Then there's the matter of the house," Arthur Rosenfeld says.

"What house? My father had an apartment."

"Baneberry Hall, of course."

Surprise jolts my body. The chair I'm in squeaks.

"My father owned Baneberry Hall?"

"He did," the lawyer says.

"He bought it again? When?"

Arthur places his hand on his desk, his fingers steepled. "As far as I know, he never sold it."

I remain motionless, stilled by shock, letting everything sink in. Baneberry Hall, the place that allegedly so terrified my family that we had no choice but to leave, has been in my father's possession for the past twenty-five years.

I assume he either couldn't get rid of it — possible, considering the house's reputation — or didn't *want* to sell it. Which could mean any number of things, none of which makes sense. All I know for certain is that my father never told me he still owned it.

"Are you sure?" I say, hoping Arthur has

29

made some terrible mistake.

"Positive. Baneberry Hall belonged to your father. Which means it's now yours. Lock, stock, and barrel, as they say. I suppose I should give you these."

Arthur places a set of keys on the desk and pushes them toward me. There are two of them, both attached to a plain key ring.

"One opens the front gate and the other the front door," he says.

I stare at the keys, hesitant to pick them up. I'm uncertain about accepting this part of my inheritance. I was raised to fear Baneberry Hall, for reasons that are still unclear to me. Even though I don't believe my father's official story, owning the house doesn't sit well with me.

Then there's the matter of what my father said on his deathbed, when he pointedly chose *not* to tell me he still owned Baneberry Hall. What he did say now echoes through my memory, making me shiver.

It's not safe there. Not for you.

When I finally grab the keys, they feel hot in my hand, as if Arthur had placed them atop a radiator. I curl my fingers around them, their teeth biting into my palm.

That's when I'm hit with another wallop of grief. This time it's tinged with frustration and more than a little disbelief.

My father's dead.

He withheld the truth about Baneberry Hall for my whole life.

Now I own the place. Which means all its ghosts, whether real or imaginary, are mine as well.

MAY 20
THE TOUR

We knew what we were getting into. To claim Otherwise would be an outright lie. Before we chose to buy Baneberry Hall, we had been told its history.

"The property has quite the past, believe you me," said our Realtor, a birdlike woman in a black power suit named Janie June Jones. "There's a lot of history there."

We were in Janie June's silver Cadillac, which she drove with the aggressiveness of someone steering a tank. At the mercy of her driving, all Jess, Maggie, and I could do was hang on and hope for the best.

"Good or bad?" I said as I tugged my seat belt, making sure it was secure.

"A little of both. The land was owned by William Garson. A lumber man. Richest man in town. He's the one who built Baneberry Hall in 1875."

Jess piped up from the back seat, where she sat with her arms wrapped protectively around our daughter. "Baneberry Hall. That's an unusual name."

"I suppose it is," Janie June said as she steered the car out of town in a herky-jerky manner that made the Cadillac constantly veer from one side of the lane to the other. "Mr. Garson named it after the plant. The story goes that when he bought the land, the hillside was covered in red berries. Townsfolk said it looked like the entire hill was awash in blood."

I glanced at Janie June from my spot in the front passenger seat, checking to confirm that she could indeed see over the steering wheel. "Isn't baneberry poisonous?"

"It is. Both the red and the white kind."

"So, not an ideal place for a child," I said, picturing Maggie, rabidly curious and ravenously hungry, popping handfuls of red berries into her mouth when we weren't looking.

"Many children have lived quite happily there over the years," Janie June said. "The entire Garson clan lived in that house until the Great Depression, when they lost their money just like everyone else. The estate was bought by some Hollywood producer who used it as a vacation home for him and his movie star friends. Clark Gable stayed there. Carole Lombard, too."

Janie June swerved the car off the main road and onto a gravel drive cutting between two cottages perched on the edge of an imposing Vermont woods. Compact and tidy, both were of similar size and shape. The cottage on the left had yellow siding, red shutters, and blue curtains in the windows. The one on the right was deep brown and more rustic, its cedar siding making it blend in with the forest.

"Those were also built by Mr. Garson," Janie June informed us. "He did it about a year after the construction of the main house. One cottage for Baneberry Hall's housekeeper and another for the caretaker. That's still the case today, although neither of them exclusively works for the property. But they're available on an as-needed basis, if you ever get overwhelmed."

She drove us deeper into the forest of pines, maples, and stately oaks, not slowing until a wrought-iron gate blocking the road appeared up ahead. Seeing it, Janie June pounded the brakes. The Cadillac fishtailed to a stop.

"Here we are," she said.

The gate rose before us, tall and imposing. Flanking it was a ten-foot stone wall that stretched into the woods in both directions. Jess eyed it all from the back seat with barely concealed concern.

"That's a bit much, don't you think?" she said. "Does that wall go around the entire property?"

"It does," Janie June said as she put the car in park. "Trust me, you'll be thankful it's there."

"Why?"

Janie June ignored the question, choosing instead to fish through her purse, eventually finding a ring of keys. Turning to me, she said, "Mind helping an old lady out, Mr. Holt?"

Together, we left the car and opened the gate, Janie June taking care of the lock while I pulled the gate open with a loud, rusty groan. Soon we were in the car again, passing through the gate and starting up a long drive that wound like a corkscrew up an unexpectedly steep hill. As we twisted higher, I caught flashing glimpses of a building through the trees. A tall window here. A slice of ornate rooftop there.

Baneberry Hall.

"After the movie stars came and went, the place became a bed-and-breakfast," Janie June said. "When that went belly-up after three decades, it changed hands quite a few times. The previous owners lived here less than a year."

"Why such a short time?" I said.

Again, the question went ignored. I would have pressed Janie June for an answer had we not at that moment crested the hill, giving me my first full view of Baneberry Hall.

Three stories tall, it sat heavy and foreboding in the center of the hilltop. It was a beautiful structure. Stone-walled and majestic. The kind of house that made one gasp, which is exactly what I did as I peered through the bug-specked windshield of Janie June's Cadillac.

It was a lot of house. Far bigger than what we really needed or, under normal circumstances, could afford. I'd spent the past ten years in magazines, first freelancing at a time when the pay was good, then as a contributing editor at a publication that folded after nineteen issues, which forced me to return to freelancing at a time when the pay was lousy. With each passing day, Maggie grew bigger while our apartment seemed to get smaller. Jess and I handled it by arguing a lot. About money, mostly.

And the future.

And which one of us was passing the most negative traits on to our daughter.

We needed space. We needed a change.

Change arrived at full gallop, with two life-altering incidents occurring in the span of weeks. First, Jess's grandfather, a banker from the old school who smoked cigars at his desk and called his secretary "Honey," died, leaving her $250,000. Then Jess secured a job teaching at a private school outside Bartleby.

Our plan was to use the money from her grandfather to buy a house. Then she'd go to work while I stayed home to take care of Maggie and focus on my writing. Freelance pieces, of course, but also short stories and, hopefully, my version of the Great American Novel.

A house like Baneberry Hall wasn't exactly what we had in mind. Jess and I both agreed to seek out something nice but affordable. A house that would be easy to manage. A place we could grow into.

When Janie June had suggested Baneberry Hall, I had balked at the idea. Then she told us the asking price, which was half the estate's assessed value.

"Why is the price so low?" I had asked.

"It's a fixer-upper," Janie June replied. "Not that there are any major problems. The place just needs a little TLC."

In person, Baneberry Hall seemed less like a fixer-upper and more like the victim of neglect. The house itself looked to be in fine shape, albeit a little eccentric. Each level was slightly smaller than the one preceding it, giving the house the tiered look of a fancy wedding cake. The windows on the first floor were tall, narrow, and rounded at the tops. Because of the shrunken nature of the second floor, the windows there were less tall but no less majestic. The third story, with its sharply slanted roof, had windows reduced to the point where they resembled a pair of eyes looking down at us.

Two-thirds of the house were constructed as rigidly as a grid, with straight walls and clean lines. The other third was completely different, almost as if its architect had gotten bored halfway through construction. Instead of boxlike efficiency, that corner of Baneberry Hall bulged outward in a circular turret that made it look like a squat lighthouse had been transported from the Maine coast and attached to the house. The windows there were tidy squares that dotted the exterior at irregular intervals. Topping it was a peaked roof that resembled a witch's hat.

Yet I could sense the house's disquiet. Silence seemed to shroud the place, giving it the feel of a home suddenly vacated. An air of abandonment clung to the walls like ivy.

"Why did you say we'd be thankful for that gate?" said Jess, who by then had leaned between the two front seats to get a better view of the house. "Has there been a lot of crime here?"

"Not at all," Janie June said, sounding not convincing in the least. "The house gets a lot of looky-loos, that's all. Its history draws the curious like flies. Not townsfolk, mind you. They're used to the place. But people from out of town. Teenagers, especially. They've been known to hop the wall from time to time."

"And do what?" Jess asked.

"Typical kid stuff. Sneaking a few beers in the woods. Maybe some hanky-panky. Nothing criminal. And nothing to worry about, I swear. Now let's get you inside. I guarantee you'll like what you see."

We gathered on the front porch while Janie June removed the keys from the lockbox hanging on the door handle. She then took a deep breath, her padded shoulders rising and falling. Just before she opened the door, she made the sign of the cross.

We followed her into the house. As I moved over the threshold, a shiver of air sliced through me, almost as if we had suddenly passed from one climate to another. At the time, I chalked it up to a draft. One of those strange, inexplicable things that always seem to occur in homes of a certain age.

The chill didn't last long. Just a few steps, as we moved from the tidy vestibule into a great room of sorts that stretched from the front of the house to the back. With a ceiling that was at least twenty feet high and supported by exposed beams, it reminded me of a grand hotel lobby. An equally grand staircase swept upward to the second floor in a graceful curve.

Above us, a massive brass chandelier hung from the ceiling, its two decks of arms coiled like octopus tentacles and dripping crystals. At the end of each arm perched a globe of smoked glass. As we stood beneath it, I noticed the chandelier swinging ever so slightly, almost as if someone were stomping across the floor above it.

"Is someone else in the house?" I said.

"Of course not," Janie June replied. "Why would you think that?"

I pointed to the ornate chandelier over our heads, still gently swaying.

Janie June shrugged in response. "It's probably just a rush of air from when we opened the front door."

With a hand firmly on both Jess's and my backs, she guided us deeper into the great room. Dominating the wall on the right was a massive stone fireplace. A bonus during brutal Vermont winters.

"There's a matching one on the other side of the wall," Janie June said. "In the Indigo Room."

I was more interested in the portrait above the fireplace — an image of a man in turn-of-the-century garb. His features were harsh. Narrow, pointy nose. Cheekbones as sharp as switchblades. Dark eyes peered out from beneath heavy lids and eyebrows as white

40

and bushy as the man's beard.

"William Garson," Janie June said. "The man who built this place."

I stared at the painting, fascinated by how the artist was able to render Mr. Garson in such vivid detail. I noticed the faint crinkles of amusement around his eyes, the fine hairs of his arched brow, the slight upturn at the corners of his mouth. Instead of something reverential, the portrait instead depicted someone haughty, almost scornful. As if Mr. Garson had been laughing at the artist while posing for him, which in turn made it seem like he was also laughing at me.

Maggie, who had been holding my hand throughout the tour, stood on her tiptoes to get a better view of the portrait.

"He's scary," she whispered.

I had to agree. William Garson, at least in this artist's hands, seemed capable of great cruelty.

Beside us, Jess studied the portrait, her hand rubbing her chin. "If we buy this house, that painting is a goner."

"I'm not sure that's possible," Janie June said as she stretched an arm to tap the bottom corner of the frame — the only area she could reach. "It's painted directly onto the stone."

I took a closer look, seeing that she was

right. A rectangular section of the fireplace had been built with brick instead of stone, giving the painter a smoother surface to work with.

"So it's really a mural," I said.

Janie June nodded. "The frame's just for show."

"Why would someone do that?"

"I guess so Mr. Garson would always be a part of Baneberry Hall. He was, by all accounts, a possessive man. I suppose you could get the portrait removed, although the cost would be prohibitive."

"Is that allowed, you think?" Jess said. "Certainly a house this old and important to the town has been designated a historical landmark."

"Trust me," Janie June said, "the historical society wants nothing to do with this place."

"Why?" I said.

"You'd have to ask them."

At the back of the house, the great room emptied into a formal dining room meant for a family far bigger than just the three of us. Then it was on to the kitchen, accessed by a set of steps between the dining room and the great room. Much longer than it was wide, the kitchen sat in a sublevel that stretched the width of Baneberry Hall. Not quite house, not quite basement. Its décor reflected that uneasy limbo. Closer to the stairs, it was rather elegant, with tall cabinets, green walls, and a farmhouse sink large enough for Maggie to take a bath in.

Mounted on the wall were small bells attached to whorls of metal. I counted twenty-four in all, arranged in two rows of twelve. Above each one was a tag indicating a different part of the house. Some of them were just numbers, presumably remnants from when Baneberry Hall was a bed-and-breakfast. Others bore more lofty titles. Parlor. Master Suite. Indigo Room.

"Those bells probably haven't rung in decades," Janie June told us.

Farther into the kitchen, the décor began to shift, becoming darker, more utilitarian. There was a long butcher block table, its surface nicked by knife blades and darkened by stains made long ago. The cabinets ended, giving way to swaths of bare wall. By the time we reached the other side, all traces of the kitchen were gone, replaced by an archway of stone and a set of rickety steps leading farther into the ground.

"It's like a cave," Jess said.

"Technically, it's the basement," Janie June replied. "While it's definitely a little rustic, you could turn it into a very useful space. It would make a terrific wine cellar."

"I don't drink," Jess said.

"And I stick to beer," I added.

Janie June smiled wider. "Good thing there are so many other amazing things you could do with it."

Her cheery desperation told me this wasn't the first tour of Baneberry Hall she had given. I pictured young couples like Jess and me arriving with bright expectations that darkened with each room they saw.

I was the opposite. Each oddity the house offered only furthered my interest. All my life, I'd been drawn to eccentricity. When I was six and my parents finally allowed me to get a dog, I bypassed the shiny-coated purebreds at the pet store and went straight for a scruffy mongrel. And after being cooped up in an apartment so nondescript that it might as well have been invisible, I was eager for something different. Something with character.

With the kitchen tour over, we backtracked upstairs and to the front of the house, where the chandelier just inside the great room now glowed.

"That wasn't on earlier, was it?" I asked.

A nervous smile crossed Janie June's face. "I think it was."

"And I'm sure it wasn't," I said. "Does this house have electrical problems?"

"I don't think so, but I'll double-check."

Casting one more anxious glance toward the chandelier, Janie June quickly guided us into a room to the immediate right of the vestibule.

"Parlor," she said as we entered the circular room. It was stuffy inside, literally and figuratively. Faded pink paper covered the walls, and dust-covered drop cloths hung over the furniture. One of the cloths had fallen away, revealing a towering cherrywood secretary desk.

Jess, whose father had been in the antiques trade, rushed to it. "This has to be at least a hundred years old."

"Probably older," Janie June said. "A lot of the furniture belonged to the Garson family. It's stayed with the house over the years. Which is the perfect time to tell you that Baneberry Hall is being sold as is. That includes the furniture. You can keep what you like and get rid of the rest."

Jess absently caressed the desk's wood. "The seller doesn't want *any* of it?"

"Not a thing," Janie June said with a sad shake of her head. "Can't say I blame her."

She then moved us into what she called the Indigo Room, which was, in fact, painted green.

"A surprise, I know," she said. "The walls might have been indigo once upon a time, but

45

I doubt it. The room was actually named after William Garson's daughter and not the color."

Janie June pointed to the fireplace, which matched the one in the great room in size and scope. Above it, also painted onto a rectangle of smooth brick, was a portrait of a young woman in a lacy purple dress. Sitting in her lap, cupped in her gloved hands, was a white rabbit.

"Indigo Garson," Janie June said.

The painting was clearly the work of the same artist who'd done William Garson's portrait. Both had identical styles — the delicate brushstrokes, the painstaking attention to detail. But while Mr. Garson seemed haughty and cruel, the portrait of his daughter was a vision of youthful loveliness. All luminous skin and gentle curves. Radiant to the point that the faintest bit of halo circled her crown of golden curls. It wouldn't have surprised me to learn that the artist, whoever he was, had fallen a bit in love with Indigo as he painted her.

"The Garsons were a big family," Janie June continued. "William and his wife had four sons, who later formed big families of their own. Indigo was the only daughter. She was sixteen when she died."

I took a step closer to the painting, my gaze zeroing in on the rabbit in Indigo Garson's hands. The paint there was slightly chipped — a missing fleck directly over the rabbit's left eye that made it resemble an empty socket.

"How did she die?" I asked.

"I don't really know," Janie June said in a way that made me think she did.

Completely uninterested in yet another painting we couldn't remove, Jess crossed the room, fascinated by another image — a framed photograph that poked out from under a crooked drop cloth. She picked it up, revealing a picture of a family standing in front of Baneberry Hall. Just like us, there were three of them. Father, mother, daughter.

The girl looked to be about six and was the spitting image of her mother. It helped that both had the same hairstyle — long in the back and held in place by headbands — and wore similar white dresses. Side by side, they clasped hands and stared at the camera with bright, open faces.

The father kept his distance from them, as if he had been ordered not to stand too close. He wore a wrinkled suit a few sizes too large for his frame and a look on his face that resembled a scowl.

Unpleasant expression aside, he remained undeniably handsome. Movie-star handsome, which at first made me think these people had been visitors during Baneberry Hall's Hollywood years. Then I noticed how modern they looked, in clothes that could have been seen on the streets of any town in America. The only thing old-fashioned about them was the woman's glasses — a pair of spectacles with round frames that made her look a bit like Ben Franklin.

"Who are they?" Jess asked.

Janie June squinted at the photo, once again trying to act as though she didn't know, when it was clear she did. After a few more seconds of studied squinting, she said, "I believe those are the previous owners. The Carvers."

She gave a nod toward the photo, signaling to Jess to put it back where she had found it. We continued on, the tour speeding up, making me think Janie June didn't want us asking more questions. We were quickly shown the music room, replete with a grand piano with a wobbly leg, and a conservatory strewn with plants in various stages of decay.

"I hope one of you has a green thumb," Janie June said breezily.

She took us upstairs via an unassuming set of servants' steps between the dining room and the conservatory. The second floor was devoted to several bedrooms and a spacious bathroom at the end of the hall.

Jess, who for years had bemoaned the lack

of space in our apartment in Burlington, lingered in the master suite, which occupied the second-floor curve of the turret and boasted both a sitting room and an adjoining bathroom.

I was more taken with an area on the other end of the hall. The bedroom with the slanted ceiling and towering armoire seemed perfect for Maggie. I suppose it was the canopied bed that made me think that. It was just the right size for a girl her age.

"The armoire is one-of-a-kind," Janie June said. "William Garson had it made special as a gift to his daughter. This was her bedroom."

Jess examined it with the appraiser's eye she inherited from her father. "This is all hand-carved?" she said while running a hand over the cherubs and ivy that scaled the armoire's corners.

"Of course," Janie June said. "Very rare and, most likely, very valuable."

Maggie stood in the doorway, peeking inside.

"This could be your room, Mags," I told her. "What do you think of that?"

Maggie shook her head. "I don't like it."

"Why not?"

"It's cold."

I raised a hand, trying to detect a chill. The room's temperature felt normal to me. If anything, it seemed a little warm.

"I'm sure you'd grow to like it," I said.

The third floor, which was where Janie June took us next, was half the size of the second. Rather than an attic, we entered an open and airy study with built-in bookshelves covering two of the walls and two pairs of round windows that looked out over the front and back of the estate. They were, I realized, the tiny windows I had seen when we first arrived. The ones that resembled eyes.

"This was originally William Garson's study," Janie June said.

And it could now be mine. I pictured myself at the great oak desk in the center of the room. I loved the idea of playing the tortured writer, banging away at my typewriter into the wee hours of the night, fueled by coffee and inspiration and stress. Thinking about it caused a smile to creep across my face. I held it back, worried Janie June would notice and think she had the sale in the bag. Already I feared I had expressed too much excitement, hence the ever-quickening pace of the tour.

My wife's feelings were harder to decipher. I had no idea what Jess thought of the place. Throughout the tour, she had seemed curious if cautious.

"It's not bad," Jess whispered on our way back down to the second floor.

"Not bad?" I said. "It's perfect."

"I admit there's a lot to love about it," Jess said, being her usual careful self. "But it's old. And massive."

"I'm less concerned about the size than the price."

"You think it's too high?"

"I think it's too low," I said. "A place like this? There's got to be a reason it's listed so low, plus the furniture."

Indeed there was, which we didn't learn about until the tour was over and Janie June was ushering us back onto the porch.

"Are there any questions?" she said.

"Is there something wrong with the house?"

I blurted it out with no preamble, leaving Janie June looking slightly stricken as she locked the door behind us.

Tensing her shoulders, she said, "What makes you think something's wrong?"

"No house this big has an asking price that small unless it's got major problems."

"Problems? No. A reputation? That's another story." Janie June sighed and leaned against the porch railing. "I'm going to be up front with you, even though state law doesn't require me to say anything. I'm telling you because, let's face it, Bartleby is a small town and people talk. You'll hear about it one way or another if you buy this place. It might as well come from me. This house is what we refer to as a stigmatized property."

"What does that mean?" Jess asked.

"That something bad happened here," I say.

Janie June nodded slowly. "To the previous owners, yes."

"The ones in that photo?" Jess said. "What happened?"

"They died. Two of them did, anyway."

"In the house?"

"Yes," Janie June replied.

I made Maggie go play on the front lawn, within eyesight but out of earshot, before asking, "How?"

"Murder-suicide."

"Good God," Jess said, her face blanching. "That's horrible."

This prompted another nod from Janie June. "It was indeed horrible, Mrs. Holt. Shocking, too. Curtis Carver, the man in that picture you found, killed his daughter and then himself. His poor wife found them both. She hasn't returned since."

I thought about the family in the photograph. How happy and innocent the little girl looked. Then I remembered the father standing at a distance with that scowl on his face.

"Was he mentally unstable?" I asked.

"Clearly," Janie June said. "Though not in an outward way. Nobody saw it coming, if that's what you're asking. From the outside, the family looked happy as could be. Curtis was well-liked and respected. Same thing with Marta Carver, who owns the bakery downtown. And that little girl was just the cutest thing. Katie. That was her name. Little Katie Carver. We were all shocked when it happened."

"Poor Mrs. Carver," Jess said. "I can't imagine what she must be going through."

She meant every word, I'm sure. Jess was nothing but empathetic, especially to the plights of other women. But I also sensed relief in her voice. The kind that came from a bone-deep certainty that she'd never experience something as terrible as losing her husband and daughter in the same day.

What she didn't know — what she couldn't have known until much later — was how close she'd come to having that exact scenario happen to her. But on that May afternoon, the only thing on our minds was finding the perfect home for our family. When Janie June took Maggie for a walk around the grounds so Jess and I could confer on the porch, I immediately told her we should buy the place.

"Not funny," she said with a derisive sniff.

"I'm being serious."

"After learning *that*? People died here, Ewan."

"People have died in lots of places."

"I'm well aware of that fact. I'd just prefer it if our house wasn't one of them."

That wasn't an option where Baneberry Hall was concerned. Its history was its history, and we had no control over it. That left one of two options — look elsewhere or try to make it a place so happy that all the bad times in its past no longer mattered.

"Let's be rational about this," I said. "I love the house. You love the house."

Jess stopped me with a raised index finger. "I said there was a lot to love. Not that I felt that way."

"At least admit it's a great house."

"It is," she said. "And under any other circumstance, I would have already told Janie June that we're buying it. I'm just afraid that if we live here, what happened will always be hanging over us. I know it sounds superstitious, but I'm worried that it'll seep into our lives somehow."

I put my arm around her shoulders and pulled her close. "It won't."

"How can you be so sure?"

"Because we won't let it. That man — that Curtis Carver — he wasn't well. Only a sick man would be able to do what he did. But we can't let the actions of one disturbed person keep us from our dream house."

54

Jess said nothing. She simply wrapped her arms around my waist and pressed her head against my chest. Eventually, she said, "You're not going to take no for an answer, are you?"

"Let's just say I know that every other house we look at is going to pale in comparison."

This prompted a sigh from Jess. "Are you sure this is what you really want?"

It was. We'd spent years cooped up in a small apartment. I couldn't shake the notion that a fresh start in a house as big and ec-centric as Baneberry Hall was exactly what we needed.

"I am."

"Then I guess we're doing this," she said.

A smile spread across my face, wider than I thought possible. "I guess we are."

A minute later, we were back at Janie June's car, me giddy and breathless as I said, "We'll take it!"

TWO

I leave Arthur Rosenfeld's office in a daze, my legs unsteady as I move down the brick sidewalk to the restaurant where my mother is waiting. Despite it being a beautiful day in May, cold sweat sticks to my skin.

Although I had expected a swell of emotions during today's meeting — grief, guilt, a heap of regret — anxiety wasn't one of them. Yet a thick, heart-quickening fear about owning Baneberry Hall is my overriding emotion at the moment. If I possessed an ounce of superstition, I'd be worrying about ghosts and curses and what dangers might be lurking within those walls. Being the logical person that I am summons a different thought. One far more nerve-racking than the supernatural.

What, exactly, am I going to do with the place?

Outside of what's in the Book, I know nothing about Baneberry Hall. Not its condition. Not if anyone has lived there in the past twenty-five years. I don't even know how much it's worth, which makes me want to kick myself for being too stunned to ask Arthur.

My phone chirps in my pocket as I round the corner onto Beacon Street. I check it, guiltily hoping it's my mother canceling lunch at the last minute. No such luck. Instead, I see a text from Allie giving me an update about the duplex in Telegraph Hill we're remodeling. Two units means double the work, double the cost, and double the headaches. It also means double the profit, which is what drew us to the property.

Tile down in both master baths. Clawfoot tubs are next.

I can help, I text back, fishing for a good reason for me to cancel.

Allie replies that all is well without me. Another disappointment.

How did it go? she writes.

Surprising, I write back, knowing the morning's events are too much to discuss over text. I'll tell you all about it after lunch.

Tell Jessica I'm still available for adoption, Allie adds with a wink emoji. One of the many running jokes between us is that my mother would be happier if Allie, with her BeDazzled toolbelt and HGTV-ready smile, were her daughter.

It would be funnier if it weren't true.

I pocket my phone and continue to the restaurant, an upscale lunching spot with floor-to-ceiling windows offering a view of Boston Common. Through the glass, I can see my mother already tucked into a rear booth. Punctual as ever. I, on the other hand, am five minutes late. Since I know my mother will be sure to mention it, I wait to go inside, watching as she takes a sip of her martini, checks her watch, then sips again.

Although she was born and raised in Boston, living in Palm Springs for a decade now makes her look like an out-of-towner. When I was growing up, she had a more casual style. Earth tones, flowing dresses, cable-knit sweaters. Today, her ensemble can only be described as Late-Career Movie Star. White capris. A Lilly Pulitzer blouse. White-blond hair pulled into a severe ponytail. Completing the look are oversize sunglasses that cover a third of her face. She rarely takes them off, forcing her coral-lipsticked mouth to do the emoting. Currently, it droops into a disapproving frown as I enter the restaurant and make my way to the table.

"I almost ordered without you," she says, the words clipped, as if she's rehearsed them.

I eye her half-empty martini glass. "Looks like you already have."

"Don't be fresh. I got you a gin and tonic." She lowers her sunglasses to better study my outfit. "Is that what you wore to meet Arthur?"

"I was at a job site beforehand. I didn't have time to change."

My mother shrugs, unmoved by my excuse. "Dressing up would have been the respectful thing to do."

"It was a meeting," I say. "Not a memorial service."

That had taken place a month earlier, at a funeral home mere blocks from where we now sit. Not many people attended. In his later years, my father had become a bit of a hermit, cutting himself off from almost everyone. Even though they'd been divorced for twenty-two years — and since my father never remarried — my mother dutifully sat with me in the front row. Behind us were Allie and my stepfather, a kind but boring real estate developer named Carl.

My mother has returned for the weekend to, in her words, offer emotional support.

That means a gin and tonic, heavy on the former. When it arrives, the first sip leaves me dizzy. But it does the trick. The hit of the gin and the fizz of the tonic are a balm against today's surprises.

"So, how did it go?" my mother asks. "The last time I talked to your father, he said he was leaving you everything."

"And he did." I lean forward, accusingly. "Including Baneberry Hall."

"Oh?" my mother says, doing a terrible job of feigning surprise. She tries to cover it by lifting the martini to her lips and taking a loud sip.

"Why didn't Dad tell me that he still owned it? For that matter, why didn't you?"

"I didn't think it was my place," my mother says, as if that's ever stopped her before. "It was your father's house, not mine."

"At one time it belonged to both of you. Why didn't you sell it then?"

My mother avoids the question by asking one of her own.

"Are you sleeping?"

What she's really asking is if I'm still having the night terrors that have plagued me since childhood. Horrific dreams of dark figures watching me sleep, sitting on the edge of my bed, touching the small of my back. My childhood was filled with nights when I'd wake up either gasping or screaming. It was another game those bitches-in-training liked to play during grade-school sleepovers: watch Maggie sleep and scream.

Although the night terrors weren't as frequent after I hit my teens, they never fully went away. I still have them about once a week, which has earned me a lifetime prescription to Valium.

"Mostly," I say, leaving out how I'd had one the night before. A long, dark arm reached up from under my bed to snag my ankle.

Dr. Harris, my former therapist, told me they're caused by unresolved feelings about the Book. It's the reason I stopped going to therapy. I didn't need two sessions a month to be told the obvious.

My mother credits a different cause for the night terrors, which she states every time we see each other, including now.

"It's stress," she says. "You're working yourself ragged."

"I like it that way."

"Are you seeing anyone?"

"I'm seeing the duplex we're renovating," I say. "Does that count?"

"You're too young to be working so hard. I worry about you girls."

I can't help but notice the way my mother lumps Allie and me together, as if we're sisters and not co-workers turned business partners. I design. Allie builds. Together, we've flipped four houses and renovated three.

"We're growing a business," I tell my mother. "That doesn't happen without —"

I stop myself, realizing I've done exactly what she planned and veered wildly offtrack. I take a hearty swig of the gin and tonic, partly out of annoyance — at my mother, at myself — and partly to prepare for what's next.

Questions.

Lots of them.

Ones my mother won't want to hear and will try not to answer. I won't let her get away with it. Not this time.

"Mom," I say, "why did we really leave Baneberry Hall?"

"You know we don't talk about that."

Her voice contains a tone of warning. The last time I heard it, I was thirteen and going through a series of phases purposefully designed to test my mother's patience. Inappropriate makeup phase. Sarcastic phase. Habitual liar phase, during which I spent three months telling a series of outrageous fabrications with the hope my parents would crack and finally admit that they, too, had lied.

On that day, my mother had just found out I skipped school to spend the day roaming the Museum of Fine Arts. I got out of class by telling the school secretary I had contracted E. coli from eating tainted romaine lettuce. My mother was, obviously, livid.

"You, young lady, are in serious trouble," she said on the drive home from the principal's office. "You're grounded for a month."

I turned in the passenger seat, stunned. "A *month*?"

"And if you ever pull a stunt like this again, it'll be six months. You can't keep lying like this."

"You and Dad lie all the time," I said, angry at the unfairness of it all. "You made, like, a career out of it. Talking about that stupid book every chance you got."

The mention of the Book made my mother flinch. "You know I don't like to discuss that."

"Why?"

"Because that was different."

"How? How is the stuff you said different from what I'm doing? At least my lies aren't hurting anyone."

An angry flush leaped up my mother's

cheeks. "Because I didn't say things just to get back at my parents. I didn't say them with the sole intention of being a lying bitch."

"It takes one to know one," I said.

My mother's right hand flew from the steering wheel and cracked against my left cheek — a blow so sudden and stinging it jolted the breath from my lungs.

"Never call me a liar again," she said. "And never, under any circumstance, ask me about that book. Do you understand?"

I nodded, my hand pressed to my cheek, the skin there hotter than a sunburn. It was the only time I can remember one of my parents hitting me. Probably because it left a mark. For two days, the bruise from my mother's slap eclipsed my scar. Until today, I have never mentioned the Book to her again.

Thinking about that day always brings a pulse of memory pain. I touch my gin and tonic to my cheek and say, "We need to start talking about it, Mom."

"You read the book," my mother says. "You know what happened."

"I'm not talking about Dad's fictionalized account. I'm talking about the truth."

My mother downs the rest of her martini. "If you wanted that, then you should have asked your father when you had the chance."

Oh, I did. Plenty of times. Since my father had never backhanded me, I continued to try to get him to admit the truth about Baneberry Hall. I liked to spring the question on him when he was distracted, hoping he'd slip up and give me an honest answer. At breakfast, right before he dropped French toast onto my plate. At the movies, just as the lights dimmed. Once, I tried while we were at Game One of the World Series and Big Papi's three-run homer was whizzing toward our corner of the outfield.

Each time, I got the same answer. "What happened, happened, Mags. I wouldn't lie about something like that."

But he did. In public. On national TV.

Although I loved my father unconditionally, I also thought he was the most dishonest man I've ever known. That was hard for adolescent me to wrap my head around. It's still hard in adulthood.

Eventually, I stopped asking him about the Book. My late teens and twenties passed with nary a question. More than a decade of things left unspoken. It was easier that way. By then, I knew my family preferred tense silence over addressing the Book-shaped elephant in the room.

It wasn't until I was a week away from my thirties that I tried again. And even then it was only because I knew it was my last, best chance to get answers.

The end for my father had been in sight for days — long enough for me to get the idea that his passing would be marked by weather befitting our stormy relationship. Dark clouds in the sky and cracks of lightning. Yet his final breath emerged on a bright April day with the sun rising high in a flawless sky, its yellow glow matched by the forsythia blooming outside the hospice window.

I didn't talk much in the last hours of my father's life. I didn't know what to say and doubted my father would understand even if I did. He was barely conscious at the end, and certainly not lucid once the morphine drip had lowered him into a state of dreamlike befuddlement. His sole moment of clarity came less than an hour before he died — a shift so unexpected it made me wonder if I, too, was dreaming.

"Maggie," he said, looking up at me with eyes suddenly clear of confusion and pain. "Promise me you'll never go back there. Never ever."

There was no need to ask what he was talking about. I already knew.

66

"Why not?"

"It — it's not safe there. Not for you."

My father winced against a ripple of pain, making it clear he'd be slipping out of consciousness very soon, likely for good.

"I'll never go back. I promise."

I said it quickly, worried it was too late and that my father was already gone. But he was still with me. He even managed a pain-weakened smile and said, "That's my good girl."

I placed my hand on his, shocked by how small it was. When I was a girl, his hands had seemed so big, so strong. Now mine fit squarely atop his.

"It's time, Dad," I said. "You've been silent long enough. You can tell me why we really left. I know that none of it is true. I know you made up everything. About the house. About what happened there. It's okay to admit it. I won't blame you. I won't judge you. I just need to know why you did it."

I had started to cry, overcome with emotion. My father was slipping away, and I was already missing him even though he was still right there, and I was so close to learning the truth that my whole body buzzed.

"Tell me," I whispered. *"Please."*

My father's mouth dropped open, two

words forming among his labored breaths. He pushed them out one by one, each sounding like a hiss in the otherwise silent room.

"So. Sorry."

After that, all the light left my father. Even though he would technically remain alive for fifty more minutes, I consider that the moment of his death. He was in the shadowland, a realm from which I knew he'd never return.

In the days that followed, I didn't dwell on that final conversation. I was too numb with grief and too consumed with making funeral arrangements to think about it. Only after that draining ordeal had ended did it dawn on me that he never gave me a proper answer.

"Asking Dad is no longer an option," I tell my mother. "You're all I have left. And it's time we talk about it."

"I don't see why." My mother looks past my shoulder, desperately seeking out our waiter for another drink. "All that is ancient history."

A bubble of frustration forms in my chest. One that's been building since the night we left Baneberry Hall, inflated a little more each day. By their divorce, which I'm sure was caused by the Book's success. By every question deflected by my father. By the relentless taunting from classmates. By each awkward encounter with someone like Wendy Davenport. For twenty-five years, it's grown unabated, getting bigger and bigger, nearly bursting.

"It's our *lives,*" I say. "*My* life. I've been associated with that book since I was five. People read it and think they know me, but what they've read is a lie. Their *perception* of me is a lie. And I never knew how to handle that because you and Dad never wanted to talk about the Book. But I'm begging you, please, talk about it."

I down the rest of the gin and tonic, holding the glass with both hands because they've started to shake. When our waiter passes, I also order another.

"I wouldn't even know where to begin," my mother says.

"You can start with Dad's last words. 'So sorry.' That's what he said, Mom. And I need to know why."

"How do you even know he was talking about the book?"

Because he was. I'm certain of it. That final conversation had the feel of a confession. Now the only person who knows what my father was confessing to sits directly across from me, anxiously awaiting another hit of vodka.

"Tell me what he meant," I say.

My mother takes off her sunglasses, revealing a softness in her eyes that I've rarely seen in adulthood. I think it's because she feels sorry for me. I also think it means I'm on the verge of learning the truth.

"Your father was a very good writer," she says. "But he had his struggles. With writer's block. With self-doubt. He had many disappointments before we moved to Baneberry Hall. That was one of the reasons we bought it. To get a fresh start in a new place. He thought it would inspire him. And, for a time, it did. That house and all its problems and quirks — it was a treasure trove of new ideas for your father. He got the idea for a book about a haunted house. A novel."

"But Dad wrote nonfiction," I say, thinking about the magazine covers that had hung in his apartment, proudly framed. *Esquire. Rolling Stone. The New Yorker.* During his heyday, he had contributed to them all.

"That's what he was known for, yes. And that's the only thing his connections in the publishing world wanted from him. Facts, not fiction. Truth, not lies."

I implicitly understand where this story is heading. Since my father couldn't snag a book deal with a typical novel, he decided to go a different route. Make-believe masked as something true.

"Your father realized that in order for this to work, we'd need to make it look authentic. Which meant leaving Baneberry Hall and telling the police *why* we left." My mother takes a shy pause. "I know it all sounds so ridiculous now. But it felt like something that could be pulled off if done carefully. I agreed to it because, well, I loved your father. I believed in him. And, since I'm being honest, I hated that house."

"So, none of it was real?"

"There is some truth behind it. Baneberry's history. The stuff about the Carver family. And the kitchen ceiling, unfortunately. Although that was caused by a burst pipe and not, well, you know. As for the ghosts your father said you saw, they were nothing but your bad dreams."

"I had night terrors even back then?"

"It's when they started," my mother says. "Your father took inspiration from everything, even though the end result was mostly fiction."

I was right — the Book is a lie. Not all of it. But the important parts. The ones that involve us.

And Mister Shadow.

I always thought that if I was ever told the truth, it would feel like a weight lifting off my shoulders. It doesn't. Any relief I might have is tempered by frustration over all that useless secrecy. When I was a child, the Book made me an object of curiosity to some and an outcast to others. Being told the truth might not have changed that, but I sure as hell would have been able to handle it better. Realizing some of those growing pains could have been avoided fills my heart with an angry, gnawing ache.

"Why didn't you ever tell me?"

"We wanted to," my mother says with a sigh. "When the time was right. That's what we always said. 'When the time is right, we'll tell Maggie the truth.' But the right time never seemed to arrive. Especially when the book became more successful than we ever imagined."

"You were worried I'd tell someone?"

"We were worried you'd be disappointed in us," she says. "Your father especially."

She's assuming I wasn't already disappointed by years of lies and all the things left unspoken. But I was. Few things in life are more disappointing than knowing your parents aren't being honest with you.

"None of that matters." My voice cracks, and I realize I'm holding back tears. "You

72

should have told me."

"Everything you have is because of that book," my mother says. "It put food on the table and clothes on your back. *House of Horrors* paid for your entire education. Not to mention that inheritance you just received. We didn't know how you'd react if you found out it was all because of a lie."

"Is that why you and Dad got divorced?"

Something else we don't talk about. When they separated, the only thing my parents told eight-year-old me was that I'd be living in two apartments instead of one. They failed to mention that my mother would be in one of the apartments and my father in the other, never again living under the same roof. It took me weeks to figure it out on my own. And it took me years to stop thinking that the divorce was somehow my fault. Yet another youthful trauma that could have easily been avoided.

"Mostly," my mother says. "We had problems before that, of course. We weren't a perfect couple by any means. But after the book was published, I got tired of constantly lying. And fearing the truth would get out. And feeling guilty about all of it."

"That's why you refused to take money from Dad," I say.

"I just wanted to be free of it all. In

exchange, I promised your father I'd never tell you the truth." My mother sighs again. Sadder this time. A soft exhalation of defeat. "I guess some promises need to be broken."

The sunglasses go back on, a sign I've heard all she's prepared to say about the matter. Is it everything? Probably not. But it's enough to finally bring that sense of relief I'd hoped for. The truth at last, which ended up being just what I suspected.

Lunch progresses normally after that. Our new drinks arrive. My mother judges me from behind her sunglasses when I order a burger with extra bacon. She gets a salad. I tell her about the duplex Allie and I are trying to flip. She tells me how she and Carl are spending the entire month of June in Capri. When lunch is over, my mother surprises me with one last mention of Baneberry Hall. It's dropped casually as she pays the check. Like an afterthought.

"By the way, Carl and I talked it over, and we'd like to buy Baneberry Hall from you. At full value, of course."

"Seriously?"

"If we weren't serious, I wouldn't have brought it up."

"That's very nice of you." I pause, appreciative but also suddenly apprehensive. There's something else going on here. "But

I can't just let you give me money."

"We're not," my mother insists. "We're buying a property. That's what Carl does."

"But none of us know what condition it's in," I say. "Or how much it's worth."

"Just get the house assessed while we're away, and we'll give you the full value when we return. Quick and simple. We'll reimburse you for the assessment. You won't even need to set foot inside Baneberry Hall."

I freeze, my sense of relief gone in an instant. Because although their words differ, my parents' message is the same.

Never go back there.
It's not safe there.
Not for you.

Which means I still don't know the truth about Baneberry Hall. Maybe some of what my mother just told me is real, but I doubt it. If that were the case, why would she and my father both be so adamant about my not returning? They are still, after all these years, hiding something. The ache in my heart returns, more acute this time, as if my mother has just jammed the fork she's holding right through my chest.

"You have to admit it's a very generous

75

offer," she says.

"It is," I reply, my voice weak.

"Tell me you'll at least consider it."

I stare at the darkened lenses of her sunglasses, wishing I could see her eyes and therefore possibly read her thoughts. Can she tell that I know I've been lied to once again? Can she see the pain and disappointment I'm using all my willpower to hide?

"I will," I say, although what I really want to do is continue to beg for the truth.

I don't, because I already know she won't provide it. Not after all the begging and pleading in the world. If my father refused to do it on his deathbed, I see no reason why my mother would do it now.

It makes me feel like a child again. Not the odd, spooked girl in the Book, a characterization I never related to. And not the shy, mute version of me in that *60 Minutes* interview on YouTube. I feel like I did when I was nine and, having read the Book for the first time, thirsted for answers. The only difference between us is that I now have something nine-year-old me didn't — access to Baneberry Hall.

I plunge a hand into my pocket, feeling for the keys I stuffed there after leaving Arthur Rosenfeld's office.

There's a line I like to say to potential

buyers before they tour a renovated property. *Every house has a story to tell.* Baneberry Hall is no different. Its story — the real one — might still be there. Why we left. Why my father felt compelled to lie about it. What I actually experienced there. All of it might be hiding within its walls, waiting for me to find it.

"I'm glad," my mother says. "You're so busy. The last thing I want is for you to be burdened with some old house you don't want."

"I won't even think about that place until you and Carl get back," I tell her. "I promise."

I sip my gin and tonic and flash my mother a fake smile, realizing she gave me at least one snippet of truth during lunch.

Some promises do indeed need to be broken.

June 25
The Closing

"I need you to make a promise," Jess said as we drove to Baneberry Hall immediately after closing on the place.

"I promise you the moon," I replied.

"I need more than that. This promise has to do with the house."

Of course it did. We had ended up using the bulk of Jess's inheritance to buy Baneberry Hall outright. That seemed more sensible than being saddled with a mortgage that, between Jess's teaching salary and my meager freelance earnings, we might one day not be able to pay. And even though we got the house for dirt cheap, my hands shook as I wrote out a certified check for the full amount.

They were still shaking as I turned off the main road, on the way to our new home. Although we wouldn't be moving in until the next day, Jess and I wanted to stop by the place, mostly just to let it sink in that it was now really ours.

"What about it?" I said.

"Now that we're doing this — actually, truly, no-turning-back doing this — I need you to promise that you'll let the past stay in the past."

Jess paused, waiting for me to acknowledge that I understood what she meant. As a journalist, it was in my nature to poke around, searching for the stories that surrounded us. And it had certainly crossed my mind that moving into a massive estate where a man had murdered his daughter was one hell of a story. But I could tell from the stone-serious look on Jess's face it was a subject she didn't want me to touch.

"I promise," I said.

"I mean it, Ewan. That man — and what he did — is one story you don't need to investigate. When we move into that house tomorrow, I want us to pretend its past doesn't exist."

"Otherwise it will always be hanging over us," I agreed.

"Exactly," Jess said with a firm nod. "Plus, there's Maggie to consider."

We had already agreed not to tell our daughter about the fates of Baneberry Hall's previous residents. Although we knew there'd come a day when Maggie would need to know what happened, that could wait a few years.

Jess and I avoided talking about the subject until Maggie was either sound asleep or, as was the case that afternoon, staying with Jess's mother.

"I swear to you I'll never utter the name Curtis Carver in her presence," I said. "Just as I swear that I have no intention of trying to figure out what made him snap like that. I agree with you — the past is in the past."

At that point, we were pulling up to Baneberry Hall's front gate, which was already wide open. Waiting for us there was the caretaker, a scarecrow of a man wearing the state uniform of Vermont — corduroy pants and a flannel shirt.

"You must be the Holts," he said as we got out of the car. "Janie June said you'd be stopping by today. The name's Hibbets. Walt Hibbets. But you can call me Hibbs. Everybody else does."

He grinned, exposing an honest-to-God gold tooth. Fit and flinty and pushing seventy, he reminded me of a character out of a Stephen King novel. Still, I found myself charmed by his breezy manner and outsize personality.

"I got the grounds all cleaned up for you," he said. "And Elsa Ditmer gave the house itself a good scrubbing. So you should be all set. We know what we're doing, Elsa and me. We grew up here, the both of us. Our families have worked Baneberry Hall for decades. I just wanted to make you aware in case you find yourself in need of full-time help."

Honestly, we were. Baneberry Hall was too big for us to properly take care of on our own. But the purchase of the house meant there wasn't much money left for anything else. That included hired help.

"About that," I said. "From time to time, we might need the services of you or Mrs. Ditmer. But for right now —"

"You're a hearty young man who can do things on your own," Hibbs said with unexpected graciousness. "I respect and admire that. I envy it, as well. As you can see, I'm no spring chicken."

"But I'll be sure to call you if something comes up," I said.

"Please do." He jerked his head in the direction of the two cottages we had passed when we turned off the main road. "I live just over yonder. Give me a shout if you need help with anything. Even in the middle of the night."

"That's very kind, but I don't plan on disturbing you too much."

"I'm just letting you know." Hibbs paused in a way I can only describe as ominous. "You might need my help during the witching hour."

I had been on my way back to the car, but hearing that stopped me cold.

"What do you mean by that?"

Hibbs put a thin arm around my shoulder and pulled me away until Jess was out of earshot. Then, in a low voice, he said, "I just want to make sure Janie June told you everything you need to know about that house."

"She did," I said.

"Good. That's good that you know what you're getting yourself into. The Carvers weren't prepared for the place and, well, the less said about them the better, I s'pose." Hibbs gave me a genial slap on the back. "I've kept you long enough. Go on up with the missus and take another gander at your new house."

Then he was gone, turning his back to us as he strolled away to his cottage. It wasn't until we were back in the car and navigating the corkscrew of a driveway that I was struck by the oddness of the conversation.

"Hibbs asked if we knew what we were getting into," I told Jess as Baneberry Hall rose into view, just as grand as I remembered. "At first, I thought he was talking about the Carver family."

"I'm sure he was," Jess said. "What else could there be?"

"That's what I thought. But then he told me the Carvers weren't prepared for the place, and now I'm wondering what he meant by that." I brought the car to a stop in front of the house and peered upward at the pair of eye-like windows on the third floor. They stared back. "Do you think something else happened here? Something before the Carvers moved in?"

Jess shot me a look that was unmistakably a warning to drop it.

"The past is in the past, remember?" she said. "Starting now, we only focus on the future."

With that future in mind, I left the car, hopped onto the porch, and unlocked the front door. Then, with a flourish, I helped Jess out of the car, lifted her into my arms, and carried her across the threshold. A romantic gesture I never had the chance to do when we got married.

Our courtship had been a whirlwind. I was an adjunct professor teaching a class on New Journalism at the University of Vermont. Jess was there getting her master's in elementary education. We met at a party hosted by a mutual friend and spent the night discussing Truman Capote's *In Cold Blood*. I'd never met someone like her — so carefree and bright and *alive.* Her face lit up when she smiled, which was often, and her eyes were like windows into her thoughts. By the end of that night, I knew Jess was the woman I wanted to spend the rest of my life with.

We got married six months later. Six months after that, Maggie was born.

"You want to officially christen this place now or tomorrow?" I asked as I set her down in the vestibule.

"Now," Jess said with a wink. "Definitely now."

Hand in hand, we moved deeper into the house. I stopped a second later, caught short by the sight of the chandelier drooping from the ceiling.

It was on, glowing brightly.

Jess noticed it, too, and said, "Maybe Hibbs left it on for us."

I hoped that was the case. Otherwise it meant that the wiring problem Janie June had promised to look into had gone unattended. I didn't worry too much, because by then Jess was tugging me toward the curved staircase, her smile naughty and her eyes bright with mischief.

"So many rooms," she said. "Perhaps we need to christen all of them."

I willingly followed her up the steps, the chandelier suddenly forgotten. All I cared about was my wife, my daughter, and the wonderful new life we would have inside that house.

I had no idea what Baneberry Hall really had

in store for us. How, despite our best efforts, its history would eventually threaten to smother us. How twenty days inside its walls would become a waking nightmare.

Had we known any of that, we would have turned around, left Baneberry Hall, and never come back.

THREE

It's almost dark when I bring my truck to a
rattling stop in front of the wrought-iron
gate. The sky has the same purple-black hue
as a bruise. On the other side of the gate, I
can faintly make out the rise of the gravel
road as it begins its climb through the
woods. Atop the hill, barely visible through
the trees, is a patch of dark roof and a sliver
of glass reflecting the wan light of the rising
moon.

Baneberry Hall.

The house of horrors itself.

My father's warning echoes through my
thoughts.

It's not safe there. Not for you.

I chase it away with a call to Allie, announcing that I've made it safe and sound.

"How does the place look?" she says.

"I don't know. I still haven't unlocked the
gate."

Allie hesitates a beat before replying. "It's

okay to have second thoughts."

"I know."

"And it's not too late to change your mind."

I know that, too. I could turn around, head back to Boston, and accept my mother's offer to buy Baneberry Hall sight unseen. I could try to be okay with never knowing the real reason we left that long-ago July night. I could pretend my parents haven't lied to me for most of my life and that those lies haven't become part of who I am.

But I can't.

It's useless to even try.

"You know I need to do this," I say.

"I know you *think* you need to do it," Allie replies. "But it's not going to be easy."

The plan is for me to spend the summer getting Baneberry Hall in shape to be sold, hopefully for a profit. It won't be a complete renovation. Certainly not as extensive as what Allie and I do on a regular basis. I think of it as a major freshening up. New paint and wallpaper. Polishing the hardwood and laying down fresh tile. Restore what's usable, and replace what's not. The most ambitious I'll get is in the rooms that really sell a house. Bathrooms. Kitchen. Master suite.

"You make it sound like I've never fixed up an old house before."

This prompts a sigh from Allie. "That's not what I'm talking about."

She's referring to the other part of my plan — searching for snippets of truth that might be hiding in every nook and cranny. It's the main reason she's not joining me for the renovation. This time, as they say in the movies, it's personal.

"I'll be fine," I tell her.

"Says the woman who still hasn't gotten out of her truck," Allie replies, stating a fact I can't deny. "Are you sure you're ready for this? And not fabric-swatches-and-truck-full-of-equipment ready. Emotionally ready."

"I think so." It's as honest an answer as I can give.

"What if the truth you're looking for isn't there?"

"Every house has a story," I say.

"And Baneberry Hall already has one," Allie replies.

"Which was written by my father. I had absolutely no say in it, yet it affects me to this very day. And I need to at least try to learn the real one while I still have the chance."

"Are you sure you don't need me there?"

Allie says gently. "If not for moral support, then just for the fact that old houses can be tricky. I'd feel better knowing you had some help."

"I'll call if I need any advice," I say.

"No," Allie says. "You'll call or text at least once a day. Otherwise I'll think you died in an epic table-saw accident."

When the call is over, I get out of the truck and approach the gate, which dwarfs me by at least five feet. It's the kind of gate you're more likely to see at a mental hospital or prison. Something designed not to keep people out but to keep them in. I find the key for the lock, insert it, and twist. It unlocks with a metallic clank.

Almost immediately, a man's voice — as gruff as it is unexpected — rises in the darkness behind me.

"If you're looking for trouble, you just found it. Now back away from that gate."

I spin around, my hands raised like a burglar caught mid-job. "I'm sorry. I used to live here."

The truck's headlights, aimed at the center of the gate to help me see better, now end up blinding me. I scan the darkness behind the truck until the source of the voice steps into the light. He's tall and solid — cool drink of water poured into jeans and a black T-shirt. Although he could pass for younger, I peg him to be just north of forty, especially when he steps closer and I can see the salt-and-pepper stubble on his chin.

"You're Ewan Holt's girl?" he says.

A prickle of irritation forms on the back of my neck. I might be Ewan Holt's daughter, but I'm no one's girl. I let it slide only because this man seems to have known my father.

"Yes. Maggie."

The man strides toward me, his hand extended. Up close, he's very good-looking. Definitely fortyish, but compact and muscular in a way that makes me think he does manual labor for a living. I work with similar guys all the time. Taut forearms with prominent veins that crest bulging biceps. Beneath his T-shirt is a broad chest and an enviably narrow waist.

"I'm the caretaker," he says, confirming my first impression. "Name's Dane. Dane Hibbets."

My father mentioned a Hibbets in the Book. Walt. Not Dane.

"Hibbs's *boy*?"

"His grandson, actually," Dane says, either not picking up on my word choice or deciding to ignore it. "Walt died a few years back. I kind of stepped in and took over. Which means I should probably stop standing here and help you with this gate."

He pushes past to help me in prying it open, him pulling one side and me pushing the other.

"By the way, I was real sorry to hear about your dad's passing," he says. "Others in this town might have unkind things to say about him. His book is none too popular in these parts. None too popular at all. But he was a good man, and I remind folks of that on a regular basis. 'Few people would have kept on paying us,' I tell them. 'Especially twenty-five years after leaving the place.' "

A hiccup of surprise rises in my chest. "My father was still paying you?"

"He sure was. First my grandfather, then me. Oh, and Mrs. Ditmer. I mow the grass, do some landscaping, pop in once a week to make sure nothing's wrong with the house. Elsa — that's Mrs. Ditmer — came in every month to do a good cleaning. Her daughter does it now that Elsa's infirm, to put it kindly."

"She's ill?"

"Only in the head." Dane uses an index finger to tap his temple. "Alzheimer's. The poor woman. I wouldn't wish that on my worst enemy. But your father kept us all on and always made sure to check in on me whenever he was here."

Another surprise. One that makes me release my half of the gate, letting it swing shut again. "My father came here?"

"He did."

"A lot?"

"Not often, no," Dane says. "Just once a year."

I remain completely still, aware of the cocked-headed stare Dane is giving me but unable to do anything about it. Shock has left me motionless.

My father came back here once a year.

Despite vowing never to return.

Despite begging me on his deathbed to do the same.

These visits go against everything I was told about Baneberry Hall. That it was off-limits to my family. That it was a place where nothing good survived. That I needed to stay away.

It's not safe there. Not for you.

Why did my father think it was safe for him to return and not me? Why didn't he mention — not even once — that he still owned Baneberry Hall and came back here regularly?

Dane keeps on giving me that funny look. Part curiosity, part concern. I manage to cut through my shock long enough to ask a follow-up question.

"When was the last time he was here?"

"Last summer," Dane says. "He always came on the same date — July 15."

Yet another shock. A giant wallop that pushes me back onto my heels. I grip the gate for support, my numb fingers snaking around its wrought-iron curlicues.

"You okay there, Maggie?" Dane says.

"Yes," I mutter, although I'm not sure I am. July 15 was the night my family left Baneberry Hall. That can't be a coincidence, even though I have no idea what it means. I try to think of a logical reason why my father would return only on that infamous date, but I come up empty.

"How long would he stay?" I say.

"Just one night," Dane says. "He'd arrive late and leave early the next day. After the first couple of years, I knew the routine like clockwork. I'd have the gate open and waiting for him when he got here, and then I'd close it back up when his car drove by the next morning."

"Did he ever tell you what he was doing here?"

"He never volunteered, and I never asked," Dane says. "Didn't seem to be any business of mine. And not that yours is, either, but I gotta ask —"

"What the hell I'm doing here?"

"I was going to phrase it a bit more delicately, but since you put it that way, why the hell *are* you here?"

Dane shoots a glance toward the back of my pickup. Hidden under a canvas tarp are boxes of supplies, several tool kits, and enough power tools to supply a minor construction site. Table saw. Power saw. Drill. Sander. All that's missing is a jackhammer, although I know where to get one if the need arises.

"I'm here to check out the house, renovate the parts that need it, and prepare it for sale."

"The house is in fine shape," Dane says. "The foundation is solid, and the structure's sound. It's got good bones, as they say. It could use some sprucing up, of course. Then again, so could I."

He gives me a sly, self-deprecating grin, making it clear he knows how handsome he is. I bet he's used to making the women of Bartleby swoon. Unfortunately for him, I'm not from these parts.

"Do you think the house can sell?" I reply, all business.

"A place like that? With a bit of mystery surrounding it? Oh, it'll sell. Although you might want to be careful about who you sell it to. Most folks here wouldn't be too pleased to see it turned into a tourist attraction."

"The citizens of Bartleby hate my father's book that much, do they?"

"They *despise* it," Dane says, hissing the word like it's a bad taste he wants off his tongue. "Most folks wish it had never been written."

I can't say I blame them. I once told Allie that living in the Book's shadow felt like having a parent who committed murder. I'm guilty by association. Now imagine what that kind of attention could do to an entire town, its reputation, its property values. *House of Horrors* put Bartleby, Vermont, on the map for all the wrong reasons.

"And what about you?" I ask Dane. "What's your take on my father's book?"

"Don't have one. I never read it."

"So you're the one," I say. "Nice to finally meet you."

Dane grins again. This time it's genuine, which makes it so much nicer than his earlier effort. It shows off a dimple on his right cheek, just above the edge of his stubble.

"Not a fan, I take it," he says.

"Let's just say I have a low tolerance for bullshit. Especially when I'm one of the main characters."

Dane leans against the patch of stone wall next to the gate, his arms crossed and his head tilted in the direction of Baneberry Hall. "Then I guess you're not scared of staying all alone in that big house up there."

"You've been inside more than I have," I say. "Should I be?"

"Only if you're afraid of dust bunnies," Dane says. "You said you plan on fixing the place up. You have any experience with that?"

The irritated prickle returns, itching the back of my neck. "Yeah. A bit."

"That's a pretty big job."

There's more to the sentence, the unspoken part left dangling like an autumn leaf. I know what it is, though. Something vaguely sexist and patronizing. I get it all the time. Constant questions that would never be posed to a man. Am I skilled enough? Strong enough? Capable enough?

The rest of Dane's sentence, when it finally drops, turns out to be only slightly more egalitarian.

"For just one person, I mean," he says.

"I can handle it."

Dane scratches his chin. "There's lots to do inside. Especially if you really intend to trick it out for resale."

96

That's when I realize he isn't completely being a sexist jerk. He's also, in a round-about way, asking for a job.

"You have experience in home renovation?" I ask.

"Yeah," Dane says. "A bit."

Hearing my own answer thrown back at me is more amusing than annoying. Clearly, Dane Hibbets and I have underestimated each other.

"It's my main gig," he says. "General contracting. Home repair. Things like that. But business lately hasn't exactly been booming."

I take a moment to size him up, wondering if hiring Dane will be more trouble than it's worth. But Allie was right — despite my knowledge and skill, I will need some help. Dane's been inside Baneberry Hall. He knows the place better than I do. And if my father thought him good enough to keep paying him, then it might be wise to do the same.

"You're hired," I say. "I'll pay you a fair wage for working on the house. When I sell it, you can claim the lion's share of the work. Might help get you some new clients. Deal?"

"Deal," Dane says.

We shake on it.

97

"Good. We start tomorrow. Eight a.m."

Dane gives me a clipped salute. "Sure thing, boss."

The drive from the gate to the house itself is a series of expectations either met or subverted. I had assumed the spiral ascent would feel like climbing the lift hill of a roller coaster — all mounting dread and stabs of regret. Instead, it's just a calm drive through the woods. Uneventful. Peaceful, even, with twilight adding a hazy softness to the surrounding forest.

The only thing that gives me pause is an abundance of spiky-leafed plants along the side of the road. Sprouting from them are tight clusters of red as bright as stage blood in the glare of the truck's headlights.

Baneberries.

They're everywhere.

Spreading deep into the woods. Swarming around tree trunks. Running all the way up the hillside. The only place they're not growing is at the top of the hill, almost as if they're intimidated by the presence of Baneberry Hall.

Again, I had steeled myself for the moment it rose into view. Since I have no actual memories of it, I expected a heart-in-throat fear of a house I'd known only through my father's writing. The pictures in the Book make Baneberry Hall look like something out of a Hammer horror film. All dark windows and storm clouds scudding past the peaked roof.

But at first glance, Baneberry Hall doesn't resemble a place one should fear. It's a just a big house in need of some work. Even in the thickening twilight, it's clear the exterior has been neglected. Strips of paint hang off the windowsills, and moss stipples the roof. One of the second-floor windows has a crack slanting from corner to corner. Another has been broken entirely and now sits covered with plywood.

Yet the place isn't without appeal. It looks solid enough. There don't seem to be any immediately noticeable structural issues. The porch steps don't sag, and no cracks appear in the foundation.

Dane was right. It's got good bones.

Before I left Boston, I made sure to check that the house was still hooked up to the necessary utility lines. It was, which in hindsight should have tipped me off that my father had been doing more than just holding the house for safekeeping. Baneberry Hall has all the utilities of an average home. Running water. Gas. Electricity. The only thing it doesn't have is a phone line, which is why I remain in the truck and use my cell phone to call my mother. I deliberately waited to come here until she and my stepfather left for Capri. By the time my mother listens to this voicemail, she'll be half a world away.

"Hey, Mom. It's me. Just wanted to let you know that, while I really do appreciate your offer to buy Baneberry Hall, I've decided to fix it up and sell it on my own." Hesitation thickens my voice as I tiptoe into the part she's *really* not going to like. "In fact, I'm here right now. Just wanted to let you know. Enjoy your trip."

I end the call, shove the phone into my pocket, and retrieve my luggage from behind the pickup's passenger seat. With two suitcases in my grip and a large duffel bag strapped to my back, I make my way to Baneberry Hall's front door. After a moment spent fiddling with the keys, the door is unlocked and opened with an agitated creak of the hinges.

I peer inside, seeing an unlit interior painted gray by twilight. A strange smell tickles my nostrils — a combination of stale air, dust, and something else. Something more unpleasant.

Decay.

As I stand there breathing in the unwelcoming odor of Baneberry Hall, it occurs to me that maybe I *should* be scared. Fans of the Book would be. Wendy Davenport and tens of thousands more. They'd be terrified right now, worried about all the horrors lying in wait just beyond this door.

I'm not.

Any trepidation I feel is related to more mundane matters. Mostly what's causing that whiff of decay. Is it wood rot? Termite damage? Some woodland animal that found its way inside during the winter and died here?

Or maybe it's my imagination. A remnant of my expecting to find a house in utter disrepair. Not a place that still has a caretaker and a cleaning woman. Definitely not a place my father continued to occupy one night a year.

I step into the vestibule, drop my bags, and flick a switch by the door. The light fixture above my head brightens. Inside it is a trapped moth. Silhouetted wings beat against the glass.

I'm not sure what I expect to see as I move deeper into the house. Squalor, I suppose. Twenty-five years of neglect. Cobwebs strung like party banners from the corners. Holes in the ceiling. Bird shit on the floor. But the place is tidy, although not spotless.

A thin coat of dust covers the vestibule floor. When I turn around, I see footprints left in my wake.

I keep moving, pulled along by curiosity. I had thought being here again would spark at least some memories, no matter how faint. Faded recollections of me on the front porch, sitting in the kitchen, climbing the stairs before bed.

There's nothing.

All my memories are of reading about such things in the Book.

I trace the path my parents took during their first tour. The one my father had written about in detail. Past the staircase. Under the chandelier, which does have a few zigzags of cobwebs strung through its arms. Into the great room. Pause at the fireplace, where the grim countenance of William Garson should be staring down at me.

But the painting's not there. All that's above the fireplace is an expanse of stone, painted gray. Which means either Mr. Garson's portrait never existed or my father had it covered up during one of his unmentioned visits.

After that it's on to the dining room and the subterranean kitchen, with its wall of bells that once must have gleamed but are now dull from tarnish. I touch one — the tag above it reads PARLOR — and it lets out a tinny, mirthless sound.

I cross to the other end of the kitchen, glancing at the ceiling as I go. Over the butcher-block table is a rectangular area not part of the original ceiling. The paint doesn't quite match the rest of the kitchen, and there's a visible seam surrounding the patch that had been replaced. In the center is a grayish oval where the ceiling has started to bulge.

A water stain.

Even though it looks to be decades old, the stain means something in the ceiling had been leaking at some point. Definitely not ideal.

At the kitchen's far end, I don't bother descending into the stone-walled cellar. The whisper of a chill and the strong smell of mold wafting from the doorway tell me that's a place best explored in the daytime and with protective gear.

So it's back to the first floor and into the circular parlor, which is smaller than I imagined. The whole house is. My father's descriptions of Baneberry Hall made it seem bigger — a cavernous place usually only found in Gothic fiction. Manderley on steroids. The reality is less grand. Yes, it's large, as houses go, but cramped in a way I hadn't expected, made even more so by dark wood trim and fusty wallpaper.

The parlor is cluttered with furniture covered by drop cloths, making it look like a roomful of ghosts. I yank them away, creating plumes of dust that, when cleared, reveal pieces so finely made they belong in a museum.

Probably Garson family furniture. Items like this would have been well above what my parents could have afforded at the time. Especially the cherrywood secretary desk sitting near the curved wall of windows at the front of the room.

Taller than me and twice as wide, the desk's lower half consists of a shelf that can be lowered to form a writing surface and several sets of drawers. The top half contains a pair of doors that, when spread open like wings, reveal apothecary drawers for ink jars and pens, a small oval mirror, and wooden slots for mail — a feature that went unused by my father. He simply stacked the mail atop the lowered writing surface. Scanning the dusty pile, I spot unopened bills, old flyers, and faded grocery store circulars, some dating back a decade.

Next to them is a gold picture frame. I pick it up and see a photograph of me and my parents. I assume it was from before we came to Baneberry Hall, because we all seem happy. My parents especially. They were a good-looking couple. My mother, willowy and pert, contrasted nicely with my father's scruffy handsomeness. In the photo, my father has an arm snaked around my mother's waist, pulling her close. She's looking at him instead of the camera, flashing the kind of smile I haven't seen from her in years.

One not-so-big, happy family.

Until we weren't.

In the photo, I stand in front of my parents, sporting pigtails and a missing front tooth that mars my wide grin. I look so young and so carefree that I hardly recognize myself. I lift my gaze to the desk's oval mirror and spend a moment comparing the woman I am with the girl I used to be. My hair, slightly darker now, hangs loosely around my shoulders. When I smile widely, copying my look in the photo, it feels forced and unnatural. My hazel eyes are mostly the same, although there's now a hardness to them that wasn't present in my youth.

I set down the frame, turning it so the picture's no longer visible. I don't like looking at this younger, happier version of myself. It reminds me of who I once was — and who I might be now if the Book hadn't happened.

Maybe Allie was on to something. Maybe I'm not ready for this.

I shake off the thought. I'm here, and there's a lot to do, including resuming my examination of the desk. Sitting among the stacks of mail is a silver letter opener that looks as old and ornate as the desk itself. That's confirmed when I pick it up and see a set of initials floridly engraved on the handle.

W.G.

Mr. William Garson, I presume.

I place the letter opener back on the desk, my hand moving to a sheet of paper beside it. Once folded in half, it now rests facedown on the desktop. Flipping it over, I see a single word written in ink, the letters wide, capitalized, emphatic.

WHERE??

Such a terse question, which raises several more. Where is what? Why is someone looking for it? And, above all, who wrote this? Because it's certainly not my father's handwriting.

I hold the page close to my face, as if that will help me better make sense of it. I'm still staring at those emphatic question marks when I hear a noise.

A creak.

Coming from the room next door.

The Indigo Room.

I whirl around to the doorway that separates it from the parlor, and for a split second I expect to see Mister Shadow standing there. Stupid, I know. But growing up with the Book has trained me to think he's real, even though he's not. He can't be.

Mister Shadow isn't there, of course. Nothing is. Just beyond the doorway, the Indigo Room sits dark and silent and still.

It's not until I turn back to the desk that I hear another creak.

Louder than the first.

I shoot a glance at the desk's oval mirror. Reflected in the glass, just over my shoulder, is the doorway to the Indigo Room. Inside, it's still dark, still silent.

Then *something* moves.

A pale blur passing the doorway.

There and gone in an instant.

I rush to the Indigo Room, trying not to think of Mister Shadow, when all I can do is think of Mister Shadow, even though three words echo through my head.

He. Doesn't. Exist.

Which means it's something else. An animal, most likely. Something that knows this place is unoccupied 364 days a year. Something I definitely don't want hanging around now that I'm here.

Inside the Indigo Room, I hit the light switch by the door. Nothing happens to the chandelier dangling from the ceiling. Either the wiring is shot or the bulbs have all burned out. Still, the light spilling in from the parlor allows me to make out some of the room's details. I notice kelly-green walls, parquet floors, more furniture dressed like ghosts.

What I don't see is Indigo Garson's portrait over the fireplace. Just like in the great room, the stone is painted gray.

I turn away from the fireplace, and something lurches at me from a pitch-black corner of the room.

Not an animal.

Not Mister Shadow.

An old woman, startlingly pale in the half-light.

A scream leaps from my throat as the woman draws near. She stumbles toward me, her arms outstretched, slippered feet threatening to trample the hem of her nightgown. Soon she's upon me, her hands on my face, the palms pressing hard against my cheeks, my nose, my mouth. At first, I think she's trying to smother me, but then her hands drop to my shoulders as she pulls me into a desperate embrace.

"Petra, my baby," she says. "You've come back to me."

JUNE 26
DAY 1

Moving from the apartment in Burlington to Baneberry Hall was easy, mostly because there wasn't much to move beyond my many books, our clothes, and a few assorted knick-knacks we'd accumulated over the years. We decided to use most of the furniture that came with the house — more out of budgetary concerns than anything else. The only furnishings we didn't keep were the bedroom sets.

"I will not force my daughter to sleep in a dead girl's bed," Jess insisted. "And I definitely won't sleep in the bed of the man who killed her."

Another thing she insisted on was burning a bundle of sage, which was supposed to clear the house of negative energy. So while Jess roamed around with a fistful of smoldering herbs, trailing smoke like a walking stick of incense, I stayed in the kitchen and unpacked the extensive set of dishes she had also inherited from her grandfather.

Helping me was Elsa Ditmer, who lived in the cottage outside the front gate not occupied by Hibbs and his wife. Like her mother and grandmother before her, she cleaned houses for a living, including Baneberry Hall. And while Jess and I couldn't afford a full-time cleaning lady, we were all too happy to hire her for a few days to help us move in.

A stout woman in her early forties, Elsa had a soft-spoken demeanor and a wide, friendly face. She arrived bearing a housewarming gift — a loaf of bread and a small wooden box of salt.

"It's tradition," she explained. "It means you'll never go hungry in your new home."

She said little else as we worked, speaking only when spoken to. After Jess passed through the kitchen in a cloud of sage smoke, I said, "I assure you we're not always this strange. You must think we're the most superstitious people on earth."

"Not at all. Where my family is from, everyone is superstitious." Elsa held up a dessert plate that had recently been freed from its newspaper wrapping. "In Germany, it would be customary for me to break this. Shards bring luck. That's how the saying goes."

"And do they?"

"That hasn't been my experience." She gave a wistful smile. "Perhaps I haven't broken

111

enough plates yet."

Elsa set the plate gently back on the table. As she did, I noticed the wedding band on her right ring finger. Barely in her forties and already a widow.

"Pick it back up," I said, before quickly unwrapping a matching plate and clinking it against Elsa's. "Shall we?"

"I couldn't," she said, blushing slightly. "Such pretty plates."

They were indeed pretty. And plentiful. Two broken ones wouldn't be missed.

"The sacrifice will be worth it if it brings a little luck to this place."

Elsa Ditmer grudgingly agreed. Together, we tossed the plates onto the floor, where they shattered into pieces.

"I feel lucky already," I said as I fetched a brush and dustpan and began sweeping up the shards. "At least luckier than Curtis Carver."

The smile on Elsa's face dimmed.

"I'm sorry," I said. "That was cruel of me. You probably knew them."

"A little, yes," Elsa said with a nod. "I did some cleaning here when they needed it."

"What were they like?"

"They seemed happy, at first. Friendly."

"And Curtis Carver? Was he —"

I paused, choosing my words carefully. Elsa

Ditmer had known the man. She even might have liked him, and I didn't want to offend her if she had. It was a surprise when she finished my sentence for me.

"A monster?" she said with undisguised venom. "What else could he be? A man who could do such a thing to his own child — to any child — would have to be a monster. But he was very good at hiding it. At least in the beginning."

The dutiful husband I was trying to be wanted to ignore the remark. After all, I'd promised Jess not to drag the past into our present. But the journalist in me won out.

"What happened?" I asked, keeping my voice low just in case Jess was approaching in a cloud of sage smoke.

"He changed," Elsa said. "Or maybe he was always like that and it just took me some time to notice it. But in the beginning, he was very nice. Charming. Then the last few times I saw him, he seemed nervous. Jittery. He looked different, too. Tired and very pale. At the time, I thought it had something to do with his daughter. She was ill."

"Was it serious?"

"All I know is what Mr. Carver said. That she was sick and needed to stay in her room. My girls were crushed. They liked coming here to play."

113

"You have daughters?"

"Yes. Two. Petra is sixteen, and Hannah is six." Elsa's eyes lit up when she said their names. "They're good girls. I'm very proud."

I finished sweeping up the broken plates and dumped the shards into a nearby trash can. "It must have been hard for them, losing a friend in such an awful way."

"I don't think Hannah quite understands what happened. She's too young. She knows Katie is gone, but she doesn't know why. Or how. But Petra, she knows all the details. She's still shaken up by it. She's very protective. Strong, like her father was. I think she thought of Katie as another little sister. And it pains her to know she couldn't protect her."

I risked another question, knowing Jess would be angry if she ever found out. I decided that no matter what I learned, I wouldn't tell her.

"What exactly did Curtis Carver do? We weren't told any of the details."

Elsa hesitated, choosing instead to focus on carefully stacking the remaining plates.

"Please," I said. "It's our home now, and I'd like to know what happened here."

"It was bad," Elsa said with great reluctance. "He smothered Katie with a pillow while she was sleeping. I pray that she stayed asleep through the whole thing. That she never woke up and realized what her father was doing to her."

She touched the crucifix hanging from her neck, almost as if she was reassuring herself that such an unlikely scenario had actually happened.

"After that, Curtis — Mr. Carver — went up to the study, put a trash bag over his head, and sealed it shut with a belt around his neck. He died of asphyxiation."

I let that sink in a moment, unable to understand any of it. It was, quite frankly, incomprehensible to me how a man could be capable of both acts. Not the tightening of a belt around his neck until he couldn't breathe, and certainly not the smothering of his daughter while she slept. To me, madness was the likely culprit. That something broke inside Curtis Carver's brain, leading him to murder and suicide.

Either that or Elsa Ditmer was right — he had been a monster.

"That's very sad," I said, simply because I needed to say *something*.

"It is," Elsa said as she gave her crucifix another gentle touch. "It's a small consolation knowing sweet Katie's now in a better place. 'But Jesus said, Suffer little children, and forbid them not, to come unto me: for of such is the kingdom of Heaven.' "

Behind us, one of the bells on the wall let out a single ring. A surprise, considering their age and lack of upkeep. I didn't think any still worked. Elsa also appeared taken aback. She continued to caress the crucifix as a worried look crossed her face. That expression grew more pronounced when the bell rang again. This time, it kept ringing — a weak, wavering tinkle that nevertheless filled the otherwise silent kitchen.

"It's probably Maggie," I said. "I knew it was only a matter of time before she discovered those bells. I'll go upstairs and tell her to stop."

I checked the brass tag over the still-ringing bell — the Indigo Room — and hurried up the steps. The air on the first floor was thick with the scent of burning sage, telling me Jess had just passed through. Perhaps I had been too quick to blame my daughter and it was my wife who was responsible for the ringing bell.

I headed to the front of the house, expecting to find Jess roaming the parlor and Indigo Room, yanking on random bellpulls as clouds of sage smoke gathered around her. But the parlor was empty. As was the Indigo Room.

All I saw was furniture that had yet to be freed from their canvas drop cloths and the lovely painting of Indigo Garson over the fireplace. The only logical explanation for the ringing I could think of was the wind, although even that seemed unlikely, seeing how the room contained no detectable draft.

I was about to leave the room when I spotted a flash of movement deep *inside* the fireplace.

A second later, something emerged.

A snake.

Gray with parallel rust-colored stripes running down its back, it slithered from the fireplace, undulating quickly across the floor.

Thinking fast, I grabbed the drop cloth from the closest piece of furniture and threw it on top of the snake. A hissing, squirming bulge formed in the fabric. With my heart in my throat, I snatched up the edges of the drop cloth, gathering them until it formed a makeshift sack. Inside, the snake flapped and writhed. I held it at arm's length, the canvas swinging wildly as I hurried to the front door.

As soon as I was off the front porch, I tossed the cloth into the driveway. The fabric fell open, revealing the snake. It was on its back, flashing a bit of bloodred belly before flipping over and zipping into the nearby woods. The last I saw of it was the flick of its tail as it disappeared in the underbrush.

Turning back to the house, I found Elsa Ditmer on the front porch, a trembling hand over her heart.

"There was a snake in the house?" she said

with palpable alarm.

"Yes." I studied her face, which retained the fraught expression I'd noticed in the kitchen. "Is that bad luck?"

"Maybe I'm too superstitious, Mr. Holt," she said. "But if I were you, I'd break a few more plates."

FOUR

The woman is Elsa Ditmer, which only becomes clear to me once both the police and her daughter arrive within a minute of each other.

First is the police, summoned by a frantic 911 call I'd made five minutes earlier. Rather than some rookie cop, I'm sent the police chief, a woman named Tess Alcott, who seems none too pleased to be here.

She steps into the house with a scowl on her face and the cocksure gait of a movie cowboy. I suspect both are affectations. Things she needs to do to be taken seriously. I do the same when I'm on the job. In my case, though, it's a no-nonsense demeanor and clothes that appall my mother.

"I think I already know which one of you is the intruder," Chief Alcott says.

She doesn't get the chance to say anything else, because that's when Mrs. Ditmer's daughter rushes through the still-open door. Like her mother, she's in nightclothes. Flannel pajama bottoms and an oversize Old Navy T-shirt. Ignoring Chief Alcott and me, she heads straight to her mother, who sits in the parlor, slumped in a chair still covered by a drop cloth.

"Mama, what are you doing here?"

The old woman reaches out for me, her fingers stretched, as if that might bridge the two-foot gap between us. "Petra," she says.

That's when I understand who she is. Who all of them are. Elsa Ditmer, her daughter, Chief Alcott — all are characters in the Book. Only they're not characters. They're living, breathing people. Other than my parents, I've never met someone mentioned in the Book, and therefore I must remind myself of their existence in real life.

"That's not Petra, Mama," her daughter says. "That's a stranger."

Mrs. Ditmer's face, which had contained a kind of beatific hope, suddenly collapses. Grim understanding settles over her features, darkening her eyes and making her bottom lip quiver. Seeing it hurts my heart so much that I need to turn away.

"As you can see, Mrs. Ditmer gets confused sometimes," Chief Alcott says. "Has a tendency to wander off."

120

"I was told she wasn't well," I say.

"She has Alzheimer's." This is spoken by her daughter, who's suddenly at our side. "Sometimes she's fine. Almost as if nothing is wrong. And at other times her mind gets cloudy. She forgets what year it is, or else wanders off. I thought she was asleep. But when I saw the chief drive by, I knew she had come here."

"Does she do that a lot?"

"No," she says. "Usually the gate is closed."

"Well, it's all over now," Chief Alcott says. "No harm meant, and no harm done. I think it's best if Elsa gets home and back into bed."

Mrs. Ditmer's daughter doesn't move. "You're Maggie Holt," she says, in a way that makes it sound like an accusation.

"I am."

When I offer my hand, she pointedly refuses to shake it.

"Hannah," she says, even though I'd already inferred that. "We've met before."

I know, only because it was in the Book. Although my father had written that Hannah was six at the time, she looks a good decade older than me. She's got a rawboned appearance. A woman whose soft edges had been scraped away by life. The past twenty-five years must have been a bitch.

"I'm sorry about your mother," I say.

Hannah shrugs. A gesture that seems to say, *Yeah, you and me both.*

"Petra's your sister, right?"

"*Was* my sister," Hannah says. "Sorry if my mom scared you. It won't happen again."

She helps her mother out of the chair and guides her carefully to the door. On their way out, Elsa Ditmer turns and gives me one last look, just in case I've magically turned into her other daughter. But I'm still me, a fact that's met with another crestfallen look on Mrs. Ditmer's face.

After they're gone, Chief Alcott lingers in the vestibule. Above her, the moth in the light fixture has gone still. Maybe just for a moment. Maybe forever.

"Maggie Holt." The chief shakes her head in disbelief. "I guess I shouldn't be surprised you're here. Not with your father's passing and all. My condolences, by the way."

She notices my bags, still on the vestibule floor.

"Looks like you intend to stay awhile."

"Just long enough to fix this place up and sell it."

"Ambitious," Chief Alcott says. "You plan on turning it into a vacation home for some

Wall Street type? Or maybe a bed-and-breakfast? Something like that?"

"I haven't decided yet."

She sighs. "That's a shame. I was hoping you'd come to demolish the place. Baneberry Hall deserves to be nothing but rubble."

The pause that follows suggests she's expecting me to be offended. I'm not.

"I assume my father's book has been a problem," I say.

"It was. For a year or so, we had to post officers outside the front gate. That was a hoot. Some of those guys weren't so tough once they realized they had to spend a shift outside the house of horrors. I didn't mind it, though. Someone had to keep the ghouls away."

"Ghouls?"

"Ghost tourists. That was our name for them. All those folks coming by, trying to climb the gate or hop the wall and sneak into the house. I won't lie — some of them made it pretty far."

My back and shoulders tense with unease. "They got inside?"

"A few," the chief says nonchalantly, as if it's nothing to be concerned about. "But those days are long gone. Sure, a couple of drunk kids try to sneak onto the property every so often. It's never a big deal. Dane Hibbets or Hannah Ditmer usually sees them coming and gives me a ring. It's mostly quiet now, which is just the way I like it."

Chief Alcott fixes me with a hard stare. It feels like a warning.

"Like I said, my time here is temporary. But I do have a question. What happened to Petra Ditmer?"

"She ran away," the chief says. "That's the theory, at least. No one's been able to track her down to confirm it."

"When?"

"Twenty-five years ago." Chief Alcott narrows her eyes into suspicious slits. "I remember because it was around the same time your father told me this place was haunted."

So she's the one. The cop who filed the report that started the whole *House of Horrors* phenomenon. I don't know whether to thank her or curse her. The only thing I *do* know is that one of the Book's original sources is idling in the vestibule, and I'd be a fool not to press her for information.

"Since you're here, Chief," I say, "would you like a cup of coffee?"

It turns out that despite the many things

tstill left inside Baneberry Hall, coffee isn't among them. We have to settle for tea made from bags so old I suspect they were here before my parents bought the place. The tea is terrible — those leaves had long ago lost their punch — but Chief Alcott doesn't seem to mind. As she sits in the kitchen, her earlier annoyance softens into a state of bemused patience. I even catch her smiling when she sees me grimace after tasting my tea.

"I gotta admit, when I started my shift, I never expected I'd end up here," she says. "But when the call came through saying something was going on at Baneberry Hall, I knew I needed to be the one to check it out."

I arch a brow. "For old times' sake?"

"Old times indeed." She removes her hat and sets it on the table. Her hair is silver and cut close to her scalp. "God, that feels like ages ago. It *was* ages ago. Hard to believe I was once that young and naive."

"In his book, my father referred to you as Officer Alcott. Were you new to the force back then?"

"A total rookie. Green in every way. So green that when a man started talking about how his house was haunted, I wrote down every word."

"I'm assuming you didn't believe him."

"A story like that?" Chief Alcott lifts her mug to her lips, thinks better of it, and places it next to her hat. "Hell no, I didn't believe him. But I took his statement, because that was my job. Also, I figured something weird had gone on here if you were all staying in the Two Pines."

The Two Pines was the motel just outside town. I'd passed it on my way here, the twin trees on the neon sign out front blinking into brightness as I drove by. I remember thinking it was a sad little place, with its L-shaped row of sun-bleached doors and a parking lot that contained more weeds than cars. I have a hard time picturing my family and Chief Alcott crammed inside one of those boxlike rooms, talking about ghosts.

"What exactly did my father tell you that night?"

"Pretty much what's in that book of his."

"You read it?"

"Of course," the chief says. "It's Bartleby. Everybody here has read it. If someone says they haven't, then they're lying."

As I listen to the chief, I look to the wall opposite the bells. It's partially painted, with streaks of gray primer covering up the green.

I'm hit with a memory — one as sudden as it is surprising.

Me and my father. Side by side at that very wall. Dipping our rollers into a pan of gloppy gray and using it to erase the green. I can even remember accidentally putting my hand in the primer, and my father telling me to make a handprint on the wall.

That way you'll always be part of this place, he said.

I know it's an actual memory and not something from the Book because my father never wrote such a scene. It's also vivid. So much so that I half expect my father to stroll into the kitchen, wielding a paintbrush and saying, "You ready to finish this, Mags?"

Another crack of grief forms in my heart.

"You okay there, Maggie?"

I tear my gaze away from the wall and back to Chief Alcott, who regards me with concern.

"Yeah," I say, even though I'm now dizzy and slightly unmoored. Not just by the memory and its accompanying grief but from the fact that I'm able to remember anything at all about this place. I didn't think that was possible, and it leaves me wondering — in equal parts anticipation and dread — what I might recall next. Because that memory of my father isn't entirely warm and fuzzy. It's tainted by all the years of deceit that came after it.

"Have you ever —" I turn the mug of tea in my hands, trying to think of the best way to pose my question to Chief Alcott. "Have you ever wondered why my father told you those things that night? You said yourself you didn't believe him. So why do you think he did it?"

The chief gives the question ample consideration. With her head tilted back and an index finger tapping her angular chin, she brings to mind a quiz show contestant reaching for an answer that's just beyond her grasp.

"I think it was a long con," she finally says. "That your father — maybe your mother, too — was laying the groundwork for what was to come. And naive me was their patsy. I'm not saying they knew it was going to become as popular as it did. No one could have predicted that. But I do think they hoped that tall tale of theirs would get noticed. If I had blown them off, they probably would have gone straight to the *Bartleby Gazette* next. Thanks to me, that rag went straight to them."

"After you talked to my parents, did you come out here to investigate?"

"Sure I did. The gate was wide open, and the front door was unlocked."

"Did you see anything strange?"

128

"You mean ghosts?" The chief lets out a low chuckle, making it clear she finds the very idea ridiculous. "All I saw was a house with no one in it. Your things were still here, making it clear you'd left in a hurry. But there were no signs of struggle. Nothing to suggest something had attacked you or your parents. You'd cut yourself, though. There was a Band-Aid on your cheek, just under your eye. I remember because I said it made you look like a football player."

I absently touch my left cheek, my index finger sliding along the inch of raised skin there.

"What happened after you checked the house?"

"I went back to the Two Pines and told your parents that everything was in order," Chief Alcott says. "I said whatever was there had left and that you all were free to return. That's when your father told me he had no intention of coming back here. I gave Walt Hibbets a call, asked him to lock up the place, and took my leave."

"And that was it?"

"You're asking an awful lot of questions for someone who lived through it," the chief says. "Care to tell me why?"

I take a gulp of foul-tasting tea and tell her everything. No, I don't remember my time here. No, I don't think Baneberry Hall is haunted. Yes, I think my parents were lying. No, I don't know why. Yes, I definitely think they've been hiding something from me for the past twenty-five years. And, yes, I completely intend on finding out what it is.

The only thing I leave out are my father's dying words. They're too personal to share.

When I'm finished, Chief Alcott runs a hand through her silver hair and says, "So that's why you wanted to sit and chat."

"It is," I admit. "I want to talk to as many people mentioned in my father's book as possible. I want to hear their version of things, not his. Maybe then I'll have a better idea of why my parents did it and what they're hiding."

"Call me crazy," the chief says, "but did you ask your parents?"

"I tried. It wasn't helpful."

"Well, getting folks here to tell their story isn't going to be easy, seeing how some of them are dead."

"I already heard about Walt Hibbets," I say.

"And Janie June," Chief Alcott adds. "Brian Prince is still around, though."

I know that name. It's hard to forget the man who wrote the article that changed the course of your family's life.

"He still writes for the *Bartleby Gazette*?"

"He does. Only now he's the owner, editor, and sole reporter. I have a feeling you'll be hearing from him the moment he learns you're back here."

"Is there anything else you can remember from that night?" I say. "Anything you think I should know?"

"I'm afraid that's all I've got." Chief Alcott grabs her hat. "Sometimes, though, I think about that night. How your dad looked. How all of you looked. You know that phrase? 'You look like you've just seen a ghost'? That applied to all three of you. And from time to time I wonder if there's a kernel of truth to that book of his."

My hands go numb with surprise, forcing me to set my mug on the table. "You think Baneberry Hall is really haunted?"

"I wouldn't go that far," she says. "I don't know what went on in this house that night. But whatever it was, it scared the shit out of you."

With that, Chief Alcott takes her leave. I walk her to the door and lock it behind her. Between Elsa Ditmer's surprise appearance and hearing that *House of Horrors* fanatics had actually gotten inside, it seems like a good idea.

Alone again, I resume the tour that had been so suddenly interrupted. I notice something strange as soon as I return to the parlor. The winglike doors in the top half of the secretary desk are closed, even though I'm almost certain I left them open.

But that's not the only thing that's weird. The letter opener — the one with William Garson's initials that I'd lain atop the desk — is now gone.

JUNE 27
DAY 2

Our first full day at Baneberry Hall began bright and early, mostly because none of us slept well the night before. I chalked it up to being in a new place with its own set of night noises. The clicking of the ceiling fan. The eerie scratching of a tree branch against the bedroom window. An endless chorus of shifts and creaks as a summer storm rocked the house.

I even heard noises in my dreams. Strange ones that seemed to be coming from both above and below. I dreamed of doors slamming shut, drawers being yanked opened, cupboards closing and opening and closing again. I knew they were dreams because every time I woke up, certain there was an intruder in the house, the noises would end.

Maggie had them, too, although I suspect it was more her imagination than actual dreams. She entered our room a little past midnight, clutching her pillow as though it were a beloved teddy bear.

"I heard something," she said.

"So did I, sweetie," I said. "It's just the house. Remember how I told you the apartment sings a song at night? This house does, too. It's just a different song than the one we're used to."

"I don't like this song," Maggie said. "Can I sleep here tonight?"

Jess and I had already discussed the likely possibility that Maggie wouldn't want to sleep in her room. She was young and unaccustomed to change.

"We'll allow one night in our bed," Jess had said. "I know it sounds a little harsh, but she'll need to learn to sleep in her own room."

Since Jess was sound asleep — my wife could sleep through an earthquake and an alien invasion happening at the same time — the decision was mine. Tonight would be the night.

"Sure you can," I said. "But just for tonight. Tomorrow you've got to stay in your own room."

Maggie snuggled in next to me, and I tried once more to sleep. But the dreams returned. All those noises. I couldn't tell where they were coming from. And they'd always be gone when I woke.

The only instance when the noise seemed

to be more than a dream happened just as dawn was beginning to break. I was fast asleep when I heard it.

Thud.

It came from the floor above. So loud that the ceiling shook. And forceful. Like something heavy hitting the floor.

Jolted from sleep, I sat up, gasping. I cocked my head, my ear aimed at the ceiling, listening for any additional sounds. All was silent. It had been a dream after all, just like the others.

Just to make sure, I looked to Maggie and Jess, wondering if they, too, had heard it. Both were still fast asleep, Jess curled around our daughter, their hair intertwined.

I looked at the clock. It was 4:54 a.m.

I tried to go back to sleep, but the dreams had made me jittery and fearful that, as soon as I closed my eyes, the noises would begin again. By the time five a.m. rolled around, I gave up and went downstairs.

As I descended the staircase to the first floor, I saw that the chandelier had been left on overnight and was glowing oppressively bright in the faint grayness of early morning. So there *was* a wiring problem. I made a mental note to ask Hibbs if he could take a look.

Reaching the first floor, I went to the light

135

switch just off the vestibule and flicked it off.

That was better.

I continued on my way to the kitchen, where I made coffee. Jess was up an hour later, groggily kissing me on the cheek before going straight for the pot of java.

"You wouldn't believe the strange dreams I had last night," she said.

"I would," I said. "I had them, too."

"And Maggie? I assume there's a good reason she's still in our bed."

"She was scared."

"We can't let her make a habit of it," Jess reminded me.

"I know, I know. But this is a huge change for her. Think about it — that cramped apartment is all she's ever known. Now we bring her here, to a place with ten times the space. Think how intimidating that must be for her. Even I'm intimidated. All night, I dreamed that I was hearing things."

Jess looked up from her mug, suddenly uneasy. "What kind of things?"

"Just random noises. Doors. Cupboards. Drawers."

"That's what I dreamed about, too," Jess said. "Do you think —"

"Those sounds were real?"

She responded with a nervous little nod.

"They weren't," I said. "I'm sure of it."

"Then why did we both hear them? Maggie probably did, too. That's why she was scared." A stricken look crosses Jess's face. "Shit. What if there was an intruder? Someone could have been inside our house, Ewan. Did you check to see if anything is missing?"

"Half our stuff is still in boxes. As for everything that came with the house, I wouldn't know what's missing and what's not. Besides, the front gate was closed and the door was locked. No one could get in."

"But those noises —"

I pulled Jess into a hug, her body rigid with tension and her coffee mug hot against my ribs. "It was nothing. We're just not used to so much house, and it allowed our imaginations to go wild."

It was a solid explanation. A logical one. Or so we thought. Although Jess's fears would later come to be fully justified, at the time I believed what I was saying.

Yet another hint of wrongness, of something amiss about the place, occurred a few hours later, when Elsa Ditmer arrived for a second day of unpacking. This time, she brought her daughters.

"I thought Maggie might like to make some new friends," she said.

Both girls were the spitting image of their mother. Same open, expressive face. Same friendly eyes. It was in personality where they differed.

The younger, Hannah, possessed none of her mother's reticence. When Maggie came downstairs, Hannah sized her up in that way only the very young can get away with. Apparently finding my daughter acceptable, she said, "I'm Hannah. I'm six. Do you like hide-and-seek? Because that's what we're going to play. There's lot of good places to hide here, and I know them all. I'm just warning you now, so you won't be surprised when I win."

Petra, the older Ditmer girl, was quieter. Unlike with her mother, I didn't detect any shyness about her. She was more aloof. Appraising everything — me, Jess, the house — with a cool detachment.

"I'll keep an eye on them," Petra said as Maggie and Hannah ambled off to play hide-and-seek. "To make sure they don't fall down a well or something."

At sixteen, she was already taller than her mother and as thin as a beanpole. Her clothes — a pink tank top and khaki shorts — made her limbs seem all the longer. She reminded me of a deer, gangly but fleet. Her hair had been pulled into a ponytail, revealing a gold crucifix similar to the one her mother wore.

"They'll be fine with Petra," Elsa said. "She's a good babysitter."

As I watched Petra hurry off to catch up with Maggie and Hannah, I couldn't help but recall what Elsa had told me the day before about her daughter being strong and protective. In the wake of an uneasy first night in our new home, it made me feel better.

So, too, did the idea of Maggie hopefully finding a new friend in Hannah. In the past year, Jess and I had grown increasingly worried about our daughter's lack of friends. She was, we suspected, lonelier than she let on. Maggie was a quiet girl. Not shy, exactly. Observant was more like it. Content to sit back and watch, just like Petra seemed to be.

With the girls off on their own, we adults split up. Jess and Elsa went to the Indigo Room, which after the day before was hopefully snake-free. I returned to the kitchen, where I sorted through all the plates, utensils, and gadgets the Carvers had left behind. Despite what happened here, it was still hard for me to fathom why Mrs. Carver hadn't wanted to keep anything. Maybe she was afraid that every single item in the house retained memories she'd rather forget. If that was the case, I was all too happy to sort through the chipped teacups and tarnished silverware, keeping some, packing away others.

Halfway through the task, one of the bells on the wall rang. A different one than yesterday. This time it was one of the numbered bells indicating former guest rooms from the bed-and-breakfast days. The ringing bell belonged to No. 4. Also known as Maggie's bedroom.

At first, I ignored it, thinking it was just the girls playing. I braced myself for a chorus of rings as the girls explored various rooms, trying out the bellpulls in each. But Maggie's room was the only one that rang.

And rang.

And rang.

They were frantic rings, too. Strong. This wasn't a group of girls lightly pulling on a rope. This was a full-on tug.

Curious, I left the kitchen and made my way to the second floor. Up there, I no longer heard the bell itself. Just the ragged slide of the rope as it kept being yanked from the wall.

Maggie was the one doing the yanking, which I learned when I entered her room, catching her in mid-pull.

"There was a girl in here," she said, her eyes shining with fear.

"Are you sure it wasn't just Hannah?" I asked. "You're supposed to be playing hide-and-seek, remember?"

Elsa Ditmer had joined us by then, drawn by the ruckus. She remained in the hallway, seemingly unwilling to enter the room.

"It could have been Petra," she said.

"No," Maggie told us. "They're hiding."

Hearing their names, Hannah and Petra emerged from their hiding places elsewhere on the second floor. Both stood with their mother in the doorway.

"We're right here," Hannah said.

Petra peeked into the room. "What's going on?"

"Maggie said there was someone in her room," I said.

"There *was*," Maggie said, stomping her foot.

"Then where did she go?"

Maggie pointed to the armoire, that great wooden beast plunked down directly across from the bed. The doors were closed. I flung them open, revealing the armoire's empty interior. Maggie, though clearly caught in a lie, doubled down.

"But I saw her!" she cried.

By this time, Jess had joined the scene. With the frazzled patience only a mother could possess, she steered Maggie out of the room. "Let's get you some lunch and then a nap. After last night, you're probably exhausted."

I followed them out of the room, only to be stopped in the hallway by Elsa, who said, "Your daughter. She's sensitive, yes?"

"Aren't all girls that age?"

141

"Some more than others," Elsa replied. "Katie was also sensitive."

"The Carver girl?"

Elsa gave a quick nod. "Girls like that can sense things the rest of us miss. When that happens, it might be wise to believe them."

She left then, retreating quietly down the hall.

At first, I dismissed what she told me. Maggie was my daughter, not hers. And I wasn't about to pretend to believe made-up things just to appease her. But that night, I couldn't stop replaying Elsa's words in my head.

Especially when the noises returned.

Not just the usual sounds of a house settling in for a long summer night, but the dreams as well. The bumps and thumps of doors, cupboards, closets opening and closing. The cacophony filled my sleep, silencing itself only when I woke a few minutes before midnight.

Sitting up in bed, I looked to the bedroom door, listening for the slightest hint the noises were real. All I heard were sleep-heavy breaths from Jess and a chorus of crickets in the woods outside.

I immediately thought of Maggie and how Elsa Ditmer had — quite rightly — pegged her as sensitive. It dawned on me that her advice about believing Maggie in reality meant seeing things through my daughter's eyes. To understand that, even though I knew these were the sounds of a house settling, they could seem quite menacing to someone so young. And if they were keeping me awake, then it was possible Maggie also couldn't sleep. Which is why I decided it wouldn't hurt to check on her.

Sliding out of bed, I crept out of the room and down the hallway to Maggie's room. As I approached, I saw the door — which, at Maggie's insistence, had been left open after we kissed her goodnight — suddenly close with a soft click.

So she *was* awake.

I opened the door a crack, expecting to see Maggie climbing back into bed, preparing to read one of her picture books by moonlight. Instead, I saw that she was already in bed, covered by her sheets from toe to shoulder. She was also, it seemed, fast asleep. By this point, both Jess and I could recognize when she was faking sleep. The shallow breaths. The flickering eyelids. The exaggerated, stone-heavy stillness of her limbs. This was the real deal, which prompted a single, worrisome question: Who had just closed her bedroom door?

The girl. The one Maggie said she saw.

That was my first thought. A crazy notion,

143

immediately dismissed. There was no girl. As for the bedroom door, that had closed on its own, be it from a draft or from loose hinges or from the simple fact that it had been hung wrong when it was installed all those decades ago.

But then I looked to the armoire. The place where Maggie said this imaginary girl had disappeared.

Both of its doors were wide open.

FIVE

The armoire doors are closed.

No surprise there. It probably hasn't been opened in twenty-five years.

What does surprise me is that someone — my father, I assume — has nailed the doors shut with a pair of two-by-fours. The boards crisscross the split between doors, giving it a distinctly forbidden look. Like a haunted house on a trick-or-treat bag.

Appropriate, I guess.

Also ridiculous.

Then again, the same could be said of my choosing to sleep in my old bedroom. There are plenty of other places where I could set up camp while I'm here. My parents' old bedroom being the largest and, presumably, the most comfortable.

But it's this room that speaks to me after I haul my luggage upstairs. No. 4 on the wall of bells in the kitchen. I'd like to think that's due to familiarity. In truth, I suspect it's simply because the room is nice. I can see why my dad chose it be my bedroom. It's spacious. Charming.

Except for the armoire, which is the opposite of charming. A hulking, ungainly thing, it dominates the room while also feeling like it belongs somewhere else. The parlor. The Indigo Room. Anywhere but here.

The way it's been boarded up doesn't help matters. I can only guess as to why my father felt the need to do it. That's why I go back outside, retrieve a crowbar from the truck, and pry off both boards in four quick pulls.

The wood clatters to the floor, and the armoire doors pucker open.

When I open them all the way, I see dresses.

They're small. Little-girl dresses in an array of Easter-egg colors. Flouncy and frilly and cinched at the waist with satin ribbons. Shit no self-respecting child should ever be forced to wear. I sort through them, the fabric slightly stiff, dust gathered on the shoulders. On one, a strand of cobweb runs from sleeve to skirt. That's when I realize these dresses are mine, meant for a much-younger me. According to the Book, my mother hung them here with the hope I'd one day want to dress like a Stepford Wife. To my knowledge, I never wore a single one. Which is probably why they've been left in the armoire, unused and unloved.

But when I move to the closet under the eaves and open its slanted door, I find more of my clothes inside. Clothes I'm certain I *did* wear. They're exactly my style. Sensible jeans and striped T-shirts and a pair of sneakers with a wad of gum stuck to the left one's sole. It's a lot of clothes. My whole five-year-old wardrobe, it seems, is contained in this room.

In the *60 Minutes* interview — the same one with shy little me and my awful bangs — my parents claimed we had fled Baneberry Hall with only the clothes we were wearing. I've watched it so many times the exchange is permanently etched in my memory.

"Is it true you've never been back to that house?" the interviewer said.

"Never," my father said.

"Ever," my mother added for good measure.

"But what about your things?" the interviewer asked. "Your clothes? Your possessions?"

"It's all still there," my father answered.

As with most things related to the Book, I

never believed it. We couldn't have left *everything* behind.

Yet as I stare into a closet filled with my old clothes, I start to think that maybe my parents had been telling the truth. That suspicion is heightened further when I go from the bedroom to the adjoining playroom. The floor is scattered with toys. Wooden blocks. Chunky Duplo bricks. A naked Barbie lies facedown in the carpet like a murder victim. It looks like a little girl had suddenly left the room mid-play, never to return.

I try to think of why my parents would have done such a thing. Why deny their only child her clothes? Her toys? Surely, I must have loved some of them. A favorite shirt. A beloved stuffed animal. A book I'd made my parents read to me over and over again. Why take that away from me for no good reason?

The best answer I can come up with is that it was for verisimilitude. That no one would have believed my parents if they had returned to grab that Barbie, for instance, or those gum-marred sneakers. That, in order for this long con Chief Alcott talked about to work, they needed to willingly abandon everything.

I guess my parents thought it was a sacrifice worth making. One they later made up for by lavishing me with things following the Book's success. My father was especially fond of spoiling me. I was the first girl in my school to have a DVD player. And a flat-screen TV. And an iPhone. When I turned sixteen, he gave me a new car. When I turned seventeen, he gave me a second one. At the time, I chalked up the gifts to post-divorce guilt. Now I think it was a form of atonement for making me live with the Book.

Call me ungrateful, but I would have preferred the truth.

I leave the playroom and head down the hallway, peeking into the other rooms on the second floor. Most of them had been guest rooms during Baneberry Hall's stint as a bed-and-breakfast. They're small and, for the most part, empty. One, presumably a remnant from the B&B days, contains a twin bed stripped of sheets and a tilted nightstand, the shadeless lamp on top of it leaning like a drunk man. In the room next to it are an old sewing machine and spools of thread stacked in tidy pyramids. On the floor sits a cardboard box filled with *Life* magazines from the fifties.

Since most of this stuff came with the house, it makes sense that my parents would leave a lot of it behind. None of it looks to be of any real value, and I can't imagine there was any emotional attachment to a broken nightstand or a mid-century Singer sewing machine.

It's a different story in my parents' old bedroom at the end of the hall. Although I assume this is where my father slept during his annual overnight stays here, the room looks like it hasn't been touched in twenty-five years. Just like my playroom, it's been frozen in time. My mother's jewelry from back then — far more subdued than what she wears now — litters the top of the dresser. Nearby is a striped necktie, coiled like a snake. A dress sits in a puddle in the corner. The heel of a black pump peeks out from beneath the fabric.

The room, in fact, is filled with clothes. The dresser, arranged with a His side and a Hers, is stuffed. Each pull of a drawer reveals socks and underwear and things my parents never wanted me to see. A box of condoms. A tiny bag of marijuana hidden inside an old Band-Aid tin.

More of my mother's clothes hang in the closet, including a floral sundress I remember only because she's wearing it in a framed photograph my father kept in his apartment. She looks happy in that photo, with my father beside her and baby me in her arms.

Thinking about that photo now, I wonder how it ended up at my father's place. Did it once grace Baneberry Hall? If so, did my father take it with him when we left? Or did he steal it away years later during one of his many secret visits here?

Then there's the biggest question: Why take just that photograph?

Because everything else has been left behind. My father's suits and jeans and underwear. A watch that still sits on the nightstand. My mother's wedding dress, which I find in the back of the closet, zipped into a plastic garment bag.

It's all still here. My father hadn't been lying about that. It makes me wonder what other aspects of the Book are true.

All of it.

The thought jabs into my brain, unprompted and unwelcome. I close my eyes, shake my head, will it away. Just because we left everything behind doesn't mean this place is haunted. All it means is that my father had been willing to sacrifice everything — his house, his possessions, his family — for the Book.

Back in my own room, I unpack my bags, stowing my adult wardrobe next to my childhood one. I strip off my jeans and work shirt, replacing them with flannel shorts and a faded *Ghostbusters* tee stolen from an old college boyfriend. The irony of it was too funny to resist.

I then climb into a bed that was slightly too big for five-year-old me and too small for present-day me. My feet stretch over the edge, and a good roll in either direction is likely to send me tumbling to the floor. But it will do for the time being.

Rather than sleep, I spend the next hour lying awake in the darkness and doing what I do with every house I work on.

I listen.

And Baneberry Hall, it seems, has plenty to say. From the whir of the ceiling fan to the creak of the mattress beneath me, the house is full of noise. Outside, a gust of warm summer air makes the corner of the roof groan. The sound joins the chorus of crickets, frogs, and night birds that inhabit the woods surrounding the house.

I'm almost asleep, lulled by nature's white noise, when another sound rises from outside.

A twig.

Snapping in half with a heavy crack.

Its sudden appearance silences the rest of the forest. In that newfound quiet, I sense a disturbance in the backyard.

Something is outside.

I slide out of bed and go to the window, which offers a sharply angled view of the night-shrouded yard below. I scan the area nearest the house, seeing only moonlit grass and the upper branches of an oak tree. I move my gaze to the outskirts of the yard, where forest replaces lawn, expecting to see a deer cautiously stepping into the grass.

Instead, I see someone standing just beyond the tree line.

I can't make out many details. It's too dark, and whoever it is stands in too much shadow. In fact, had they stayed a few feet deeper in the forest, I wouldn't have known they were there at all.

But I do know. I can see him. Or her.

Standing in statue-like stillness.

Doing nothing but staring at the house.

So far.

I think back to what Chief Alcott said about people trying to get inside. Ghouls, she called them. And some of them succeeded.

Not while I'm here.

Turning away from the window, I sprint out of the room, down the stairs, and to the front door. Once outside, I run around the side of the house, dew-drenched grass slick beneath my bare feet. Soon I'm in the backyard, heading straight to the spot where the figure stood.

It's now empty. As is the entire tree line.

I listen for the sound of retreating footsteps in the woods, but by now the crickets and frogs and night birds have started back up again, making it hard to hear anything else.

I remain there for a few minutes longer, wondering if I'd really seen someone lurking outside. There's a chance it could have just been the shadow of a tree. Or a trick of the moonlight. Or my imagination, stuck in paranoid mode after my chat with Chief Alcott.

All are possible. None are likely.

Because I know what I saw. A person. Standing right where I am now.

Which means I need to invest in a security system and install a spotlight in the backyard as a deterrent. Because despite the front gate and the forest and the stone wall that surrounds everything, Baneberry Hall isn't as isolated as it seems.

And I'm not as alone here as I first thought.

JUNE 28
DAY 3

After two days of unpacking and arranging our own furniture with what came before us, it was finally time for me to tackle the third-floor study — a thrilling prospect. I'd always wanted my own office. My entire writing career had taken place in white-walled cubicles, at rickety motel room desks, on the dining room table in the Burlington apartment. I hoped having a space of my own would once again make me feel like a serious writer.

The only hitch was that this room had also been the site of Curtis Carver's suicide, a fact that weighed on my thoughts as I climbed the narrow steps to the third floor. I worried his death would still be felt in the study. That his guilt, desperation, and madness had somehow infiltrated the space, swirling in the air like dust.

My fears were allayed once I finally entered the study. It was as charming as I remembered. All high ceilings and sturdy bookshelves and that massive oak desk, which I had no doubt once belonged to William Garson. Like Baneberry Hall itself, it had a grandeur that could be conjured only by a man of wealth and status. The whole room did. Instead of Curtis Carver, it was Mr. Garson's presence that loomed large inside the study.

But I couldn't ignore the brutal fact that a man had taken his own life within these walls. In order to make this space truly my own, I needed to rid it of any traces of Curtis Carver.

I started in the first of two closets, both of which had slanted doors like the one in Maggie's bedroom. Inside were shelves stacked with vintage board games, some dating back to the thirties. Monopoly and Clue and Snakes and Ladders. There was even a Ouija board, its box worn white at the corners. I remembered what Janie June had said about Gable and Lombard staying here and smiled at the thought of them using the Ouija board in the candlelit parlor.

Below the games, sitting on the floor, were two square suitcases, their surfaces feathery with dust. I slid both out of the closet, finding them not without some heft.

Something was inside each of them.

The first suitcase, I discovered upon opening it, wasn't a suitcase at all. It was an old record player inside a leather carrying case.

Fittingly, the other case contained LPs kept in their original cardboard sleeves. I sorted through them, disappointed by the collection of Big Band music and movie musical soundtracks.

Oklahoma. South Pacific. The King and I.

Someone had been a Rodgers and Hammerstein fan, and I was fairly confident it wasn't Curtis Carver.

I carried the record player to the desk and plugged it in, curious to see if it still worked. I grabbed the first record in the case — *The Sound of Music* — and let it spin. Music filled the room.

As Julie Andrews sang about the hills being alive, I made my way to the second closet, passing a pair of eyelike windows similar to the ones facing the front of the house. These two looked onto the backyard, beyond which sat woods that sloped sharply down the hillside. Peering outside, I saw Maggie and Jess round the corner of the house, hand in hand. Knowing I was up here, Jess shot a glance toward the window and waved.

I waved back, grinning. It had been a rough few days. I was sore from all that moving and unpacking, tired from restless nights, and concerned about Maggie's problems adjusting. That morning at breakfast, when I asked why she'd opened the doors to the armoire in the middle of the night, she swore she hadn't done it. But my stress melted away as I watched my wife and daughter enjoying our new backyard. Both looked happy as they explored the edge of the woods, and I realized that buying this place was the best decision we could have made.

I continued to the second closet, which was almost empty. The only things inside were a shoebox on the top shelf and, next to it, almost a dozen green-and-white packages of Polaroid film. The shoebox was blue with a telltale Nike swoosh across its sides. Inside was the reason for all that film — a Polaroid camera and a stack of snapshots.

First, I examined the camera, boxy and heavy. Pressing a button on the side raised the camera's lens and flash. A button on the top clicked the shutter. On the back was a counter telling me there was still enough film inside for two more pictures.

Just like with the record player, I decided to test the camera. I went to the back window, seeing that Maggie and Jess were still outside, heading toward the woods. Maggie was running. Jess trailed after her, calling for her to slow down.

I clicked the shutter as both entered the forest. A second later, amid much whirring, a square photograph slowly emerged from a slot in the camera's front. The image itself had just started to form. Hazy shapes emerging from milky whiteness. I set the picture aside to develop and returned to the snapshots stored in the shoebox.

Picking up the top one, I saw it was a picture of Curtis Carver. He stared straight at the camera with a blank look on his face, the light from the flash turning his skin a sickly white. Judging from the stretch of his arms at the bottom of the image, he had taken the picture himself. But the framing was off, capturing only two-thirds of his face and the entirety of his left shoulder. Behind him was the study, looking much the way it did now. Empty. Dim. Shadows gathered in the corner of the vaulted ceiling.

A date had been written in marker across the inch-high strip of white that ran across the bottom of the photo.

July 2.

I reached back into the box and grabbed another picture. The subject was the same — an off-center self-portrait of Curtis Carver taken in the study — but the details were different. A red T-shirt instead of the white one he wore in the previous photo. His hair was unkempt, and stubble darkened his cheeks.

The date scrawled under the picture read July 3.

I snatched three more pictures, bearing the dates July 5, July 6, and July 7.

They were just like the others. As were four more that lay beneath them, dated July 8, July 9, July 10, and July 11.

Flipping through them felt like watching a time-lapse video. The kind they showed us in grade school of flowers blooming and leaves unfurling. Only this was a chronicle of Curtis Carver, and instead of growing, he seemed to be receding. With each picture, his face got thinner, his beard grew longer, his expression more haggard.

The only constant was his eyes.

Staring into them, I saw nothing. No emotion. No humanity. In every photograph, the eyes of Curtis Carver were dark blanks that revealed nothing.

A saying I'd heard long ago came to mind: *When you stare into the abyss, the abyss also stares into you.*

I dropped the photos back into the box. Although there were more inside, I didn't have the stomach to look at them. I'd done enough staring into the abyss for one morning.

Instead, I grabbed the photo I'd taken, which was now fully developed. I liked what I saw. I'd managed to capture Maggie and Jess on the verge of vanishing into the woods.

Maggie was barely visible — just a brown-haired blur in the background, the flashing white sole of a sneaker indicating that she was running. Jess was clearer. Back turned toward the camera, head tilted, right arm outstretched as she pushed a low-hanging branch out of her way.

I was so focused on the two of them that it took me a moment to notice something else in the photo. When I did see it, my whole body jerked in surprise. My elbow knocked into the record player, ending the song that had been playing — "Sixteen Going on Seventeen" — with an album-scratching screech.

I ignored it and continued to stare at the photo.

There, standing just on the edge of the frame, was a figure cloaked in shadow.

I thought it was a man, although I couldn't be sure. Details were sparse. All I could make out was a distinctly human shape standing in the forest a few feet from the tree line.

Who — or what — it was, I had no idea. All I knew was that seeing it sent a cold rush of fear coursing through my veins.

I was still staring at the figure in the picture when a scream tore through the woods, so loud that it echoed off the back of the house.

High-pitched and terrified, I knew at once it belonged to Jess.

In an instant, I was out of the study and

hurtling myself down two sets of stairs to the first floor. Outside, I veered around the house and sprinted into the backyard, where more screaming could be heard.

Maggie this time. Letting out a loud, continuous wail of pain.

I picked up my pace as I entered the woods, bounding through the underbrush and dodging trees to where Jess and Maggie were located. Both were on the ground — Jess on her knees and Maggie lying facedown beside her, still screaming like a siren.

"What happened?" I called as I ran toward them.

"She fell," Jess said, trying to sound calm but failing miserably. Her words came out in a frantic tumble. "She was running, and then she tripped and fell and hit a rock or something. Oh, God, Ewan, it looks bad."

Reaching them, I saw a small pool of blood on the ground next to Maggie's head. The sight of it — bright red against the mossy green of the forest floor — sent me into a panic. Gasping for breath, I gently rolled Maggie over. She had a hand pressed against her left cheek, blood oozing from between her fingers.

"Be still, baby," I whispered. "Let me see how bad it is."

I pried Maggie's hand away, revealing a

gash below her left eye. While not very long, it appeared deep enough to require stitches. I took off my T-shirt and pressed it to the cut, hoping to slow the bleeding. Maggie screamed again in response.

"We need to get her to the emergency room," I said.

Jess, her maternal instincts kicking in something fierce, refused to let me carry Maggie. "I can do it," she said, hoisting our daughter over her shoulder as blood gushed onto her shirt. "I'll meet you at the car."

Off she went, a still-whimpering Maggie in her arms. I stayed behind just long enough to examine the spot where Maggie had hit her face. It was easy to find. A wet splotch of blood glistened atop a rectangular rock that jutted an inch or so out of the ground.

Only it wasn't a rock.

Its shape was too orderly to be caused by nature.

It was, to my complete and utter shock, a gravestone.

I dropped to my knees in front of it and brushed away decades of dirt. A familiar name appeared, the soil in the carved letters making them stand in stark contrast to the pale marble.

WILLIAM GARSON
Beloved father
1843–1912

Six

After seeing that person outside, it took two hours and one Valium before I was calm enough to get back in bed, let alone fall asleep. Even then, a night terror invaded my slumber. Me, in bed, the figure in the forest now suddenly hovering over me, its back against the ceiling.

I woke up gasping, my skin covered in a thin sheen of sweat that glistened in the moonlight coming through the window. I took a second Valium. It did the trick.

Now it's six in the morning, and even though all I'd like to do is stay in bed, I can't. There's work to be done.

Since there's no coffee in the house, I use a cold shower as a poor substitute for caffeine. I emerge wide awake, but in a sore and sorry way. It feels as though I've just been slapped, my skin pink and pulsing. When I glance in the bathroom mirror, I see how it makes my scar stand out in the faint light of dawn. A small slash of white on my otherwise rosy cheek. I touch it, the skin surrounding it puffy and tender from lack of sleep.

For breakfast, I have a protein bar — literally the only food I thought to bring along — washed down with another mug of horrid tea and a vow to get to the grocery store by the end of the day.

I check my phone as I eat, seeing a text from my mother. Its tone and subject matter tell me she's heard my voicemail.

So disappointed. Don't stay there. Please

My response is a master class in maturity.

Try and stop me

I hit send and go upstairs to roam the Indigo Room and parlor, looking for the letter opener I'm certain I misplaced last night during the unexpected drama with Elsa Ditmer and her daughter. It is the only explanation. Letter openers don't just vanish by themselves. But after several minutes of fruitless searching, I give up.

I tell myself it's here somewhere, likely buried under years of junk mail. It'll turn up at some point. And if it doesn't, so be it.

By seven, I'm outside and unloading my pickup truck before Dane arrives, even though it'd be easier with his help. I do it myself because, one, I'm already here and don't feel like wasting time and, two, I want him to see that I *can* do it myself. That he's here to assist, not carry most of the load.

When Dane arrives promptly at eight, half the truck has been emptied and equipment litters the front lawn. He eyes the drill case sitting next to the ladder, which leans against the tile saw. I think he's impressed.

He helps me finish unloading the truck as I go over the plan. Clear the house, keeping anything that might be worth saving and throwing out the rest. We'll start at the top, in my father's old study, and work our way down, room by room. I still don't know what I'm going to do with it all. I need more time in the house before I can come up with a proper design. But already I'm leaning toward taking a cue from what's already here. Rich woods, ornate patterns, jewel tones. If I had to put a label on it, I'd call it Victorian glamour.

With the truck unloaded, we grab some empty cardboard boxes and head inside. The house feels larger in the morning light. Warmer and brighter. Most people, if they didn't know its history, would describe the place as homey. But the past hangs heavy over Baneberry Hall. Enough for me to feel a chill when we pass a back window and I see the spot where last night's trespasser had been standing.

"You have a key to the gate, right?" I ask Dane as we climb the steps to the third floor.

"I wouldn't be a good caretaker if I didn't."

"You didn't happen to be strolling around the grounds last night? Around eleven?"

"At that hour, I was asleep in front of the Red Sox game. Why?"

"I saw someone in the woods. A few feet from the backyard."

Dane turns around on the steps to give me a concerned look. "Did they do anything?"

"As far as I know, they just stood there looking at the house before disappearing in the woods."

"It was probably a ghoul," Dane says.

"I guess that term isn't just cop talk."

"We all call them that. They're mostly local kids. I've heard they like to dare each other to sneak onto the property and get close to the infamous House of Horrors. They're harmless. But you might want to stop making it easy for them. The front gate was wide open this morning. That's like sending them an invitation to trespass."

Dane's mansplaining aside, I know he's right. I'd forgotten about the gate last night.

My lesson learned, I don't plan on doing it again.

"Duly noted," I say as I open the door to the study. It's hot inside, even though it's not even nine and the sun is still rising behind the woods out back. It's also dusty. Huge particles of it swirl around us as we enter, practically glowing in the light shining through the circular windows.

Dane looks around the room, impressed. "This is a great space. What do you plan on doing with it?"

"I was thinking guest bedroom," I say. "Or maybe an in-law suite."

"You'd need to put in a bathroom."

I grimace, because he's right. "Plumbing will be a bitch."

"So will the cost," Dane says. "I know this sounds crazy, but if you wanted to, you could get rid of the floor —"

"And make the room below a master suite with cathedral ceilings —"

"And a skylight!"

We stop talking, both of us slightly out of breath. We speak the same language. Good to know.

Dane zeroes in on the bookshelves along the wall. I go to my father's desk, getting uncomfortable flashbacks to when Allie and I emptied my father's apartment a week after his death. It was rough. The entire place smelled like him — a soothing combo of wool, aftershave, and old books. Every item dropped into a cardboard box felt as though a part of his existence was being locked away where no one could see it. Every tattered cardigan. Each worn-edged book. I was erasing my father piece by piece, and it gutted me.

Worse still was finding a box of manuscripts in his office closet, sitting with his old typewriter and a set of rarely used golf clubs. It turned out he had written five books after *House of Horrors.* All of them fiction. All unpublished. One included a letter from his longtime agent, saying no one wanted anything other than another ghost story.

Now I open the top drawer of my father's desk slowly, steeling myself for similar signs of his failure. There's nothing in it but pens, paper clips, and a magnifying glass.

The next drawer, though, holds a surprise.

A copy of the Book.

I pick it up and blow dust from the cover. It's a hardcover. First edition. I can tell because it's the only one not to feature the words all writers dream of having on their book jacket: *New York Times* bestseller. Every edition after this one wore them like a badge of honor.

The cover is a good one, which many say contributed to the Book's initial success. It's an illustration of Baneberry Hall as seen from an angle not attainable in real life. A bird's-eye view of a tall, crooked house on a hill. There's a light on in the third floor — the very same floor in which Dane and I now stand — the greenish glow seeping through the round windows, making it look like Baneberry Hall is watching you. The forest encroaches on the house from all directions, the trees bending toward it, as if waiting to do its bidding.

This is the edition I read, back when I was nine. I knew my father had written a book. I knew it was a big deal. I remembered the interviews and TV crews and studio lights that hurt my eyes.

What I didn't understand — not really — was what the book was about and why people treated my family differently from everyone else. I eventually found out from a classmate named Kelly, who told me she had to disinvite me from her upcoming birthday party. "My mom says your dad wrote an evil book and that I'm not supposed to be friends with you," she said.

That weekend, I snuck into my dad's office and took his first-edition copy down from the shelf. For the next month, I consumed it in secret, like it was a dirty magazine. By flashlight under the covers. After school, before my father got home from the writing class he taught just to stay busy. Once, when I'd brazenly shoved the book in my backpack and took it to school, I skipped third period to read it in the girls' bathroom.

It was thrilling, reading something forbidden. I finally understood why my classmates had been so giddy about stealing their older sisters' copies of *Flowers in the Attic.* But it was also deeply unsettling to see my parents' names — to see *my* name — in a book about things I had no memory of.

Even more disconcerting was how my father had turned me into a character that in no way resembled the real me, even though only four years separated us. I saw nothing of myself in the Book's Maggie. I thought I was smart and capable and fearless. I picked up spiders and scrambled to the top of the jungle gym. The Maggie in the Book was shy and awkward. A weirdo loner. And it hurt knowing it was my own father who had portrayed me that way. Was that what he thought I was like? When he looked at me, did he see only a scared little girl? Did everyone?

Finishing the Book left me feeling slightly abused. I had been exploited, even though I didn't quite understand that at the time. All I knew then was that I felt confused and humiliated and misrepresented.

Not to mention angry.

So fucking furious that my younger self didn't know what to do with it. It took me weeks to finally confront my parents about it, during one of their custody exchanges in which I was handed off like a relay baton.

"You lied about me!" I shouted as I waved the Book in front of them. "Why would you do that?"

My mother told me the Book was something we didn't discuss. My father gave me his scripted answer for the very first time.

"What happened, happened, Mags. I wouldn't lie about something like that."

"But you did!" I cried. "The girl in this book isn't me."

"Of course it's you," my mother said, trying hard to end the conversation.

"But I'm nothing like her!" I'd started to cry then, which made me all the more humiliated. I'd wanted to be stronger in the face of their resistance. "I'm either the girl in this book, or I'm me. So which one is it?"

My parents refused to provide an answer.

My mother left me with a kiss on the cheek, and my father took me out for ice cream. Defeated, I swallowed my anger, gulping it down like a bitter pill, thus setting the course for the rest of my adolescence. Silence from my mother, denial from my father, and me starting a yearslong secret search for more information.

A little of that nine-year-old's anger returns as I flip through the Book, scanning passages I've long committed to memory.

"I really hate this book," I say.

Dane gives me a curious look. "I've heard it's good."

"It's not. Not really."

That's another aspect of the Book I find so frustrating — its inexplicable success. Critics weren't kind, calling the writing pedestrian and the plot derivative. With reviews like that, it shouldn't have become as big as it did. But it was something different in a nonfiction landscape that, at the time, had been dominated by books about getting rich through prayer, murder in Savannah, and barely contained Ebola outbreaks. As a result, it became one of those things people read because everyone else was reading it.

I continue to page through the Book, stopping cold when a two-sentence passage catches my eye.

"**Maggie, there's no one here.**"

"**There is!**" **she cried.** "**They're all here! I told you they'd be mad!**"

I slam the Book shut and drop it on the desk.

"You can have this, if you want," I tell Dane. "In fact, you can take pretty much anything in this room. Not that it's worth anything. I'm not sure there's a market for household junk found in bogus haunted houses."

There are two closets, one on each side of the room, their doors slanted to accommodate the vaulted ceiling. We each take one, Dane's opening with a rusty creak.

"Nothing in here but suitcases," he says.

I cross the room and peer over his shoulder. Sitting on the closet floor are two square cases. We drag them out of the closet and each open one. Inside Dane's is a record player. Inside mine is an album collection. The record on top is a familiar title: *The Sound of Music.*

Seeing them gives me the same creeping sense of unease I felt last night when I realized my father hadn't lied about leaving everything behind. I do an involuntary shimmy, trying to shake it away. Just because they exist doesn't mean what my father wrote is true. I need to remember that. Baneberry Hall is likely filled with things mentioned in the Book.

Write what you know. My father's favorite piece of advice.

"It's junk," I say as I stalk back to my closet. "We should toss it."

Dane does the opposite and lifts the record player onto the desk. The case of records soon follows. "We should give it a spin," he says while sorting through the albums. "Showtunes or, uh, showtunes?"

"I prefer silence," I say, an edge to my voice.

Dane gets the hint and backs away from the desk, joining me at the second closet as I pull the door open.

Inside is a teddy bear.

It sits on the floor, back against the wall like a hostage, its once-brown fur turned ashen from years of dust. One of its black-button eyes has fallen off, leaving a squiggle of thread poking from its fur like an exposed optic nerve. Around the bear's neck is a red bow tie, the ends squashed, as if it had been hugged too tightly for too long.

"Was this yours?" Dane says. He gives the bear a squeeze, and a puff of dust rises off its shoulders.

"No," I say. "At least, I don't think so. I

176

have no memory of it."

A thought occurs to me. A sad one. It's possible this bear had once been Katie Carver's and was left behind, like so many of the family's belongings. My father, not knowing what to do with it, might have stuck it in the closet and forgotten about it.

I take the bear from Dane, set it on the desk next to the record player, and return to the closet. There's something else inside, perched on a top shelf.

A blue shoebox.

Just like the one my father claimed to have found in the Book. Filled with strange pictures of Katie's father.

My unease returns. Stronger now, and more insidious. With trembling hands, I take the box to the desk and open it, already knowing what I'll find inside: a Polaroid camera and a stack of photos.

I'm right on both counts.

The camera fills one end of the box, clunky and heavy. The photos — five of them in all — lie haphazardly beside it. But instead of Curtis Carver's vacant stare, the first photo I see is, shockingly, of me. Like the one in the parlor, it bears only the faintest resemblance to me.

I'm wearing jeans and a Batman T-shirt in the photo, which was snapped in front of

Baneberry Hall, the house lurking in the background like an eavesdropper. Its presence means I was five at the time. Because there's no scar on my cheek, I also assume it was taken in the first three days of our stay. There's not even a bandage.

It's also missing in the next photo, which shows me standing with two other girls, one roughly my age and the other much older. We're in my bedroom, lined up in front of the armoire, our eyes glowing red from the flash and giving us the look of demon children.

The younger girl I recognize. I saw the same features in the face of the woman I met last night. The only difference is a present-day hardness not evident in this younger version of herself.

Hannah Ditmer.

Which means the older girl in the photo is Petra.

She's so pretty it takes my breath away. Long limbs, creamy skin, blond hair that's been piled atop her head. Unlike Hannah and me, who stand stiff-backed with our arms at our sides, Petra strikes a playful pose. Hand on her hip. One leg bent in a backward kick. Flash of bare feet, toenails painted red.

We're dressed for sleep, Hannah and me

in pajamas, Petra in a large white T-shirt and Umbro shorts. She also wears a necklace — a tiny crucifix hanging from a slender gold chain.

I remember that night. Or at least the Book's version of it. The sleepover gone terribly wrong. It was one of the first things nine-year-old me obsessed about — how I had absolutely no memory of that horrifying night. I spent nights awake, scared that what I'd read was true. Because it was indeed scary. A kind of nightmare-in-a-horror-movie scenario that no one would want to experience. But I had and couldn't recall any of it, which meant that something must have been terribly wrong with me.

After several sleepless nights staring at the ceilings in both of my bedrooms in both of my parents' separate homes, I began to realize that the reason I couldn't remember the events in the Book was because they never happened.

I had assumed that included the sleepover.

But according to this Polaroid, I was wrong. There was, at some point in our twenty days at Baneberry Hall, a time when Hannah and Petra had spent the night.

At least part of it.

Petra's in the next photo as well, standing

in the kitchen with my mother. The two of them stare up at a giant hole in the ceiling in a pose of unintended synchronicity. Both in profile, their heads tilted back and their throats exposed, they could pass for mother and daughter. It makes me wonder if my mother ever saw this photograph and, if so, how it felt to see herself pictured with a younger woman of a similar nature. A girly girl. The kind of daughter she'd never have.

There are two other people in the photo, overlapping in the background. In front is an older man in flannel and jeans making his way up a ladder. Behind him is someone younger, barely visible. All I can make out is a crescent of face, a bent elbow, half of a black T-shirt, and a sliver of denim.

Walt Hibbets and my father. Two days after the kitchen incident.

Like the sleepover, it's one of the most famous passages in the Book. And, if this photo is to be believed, also similarly rooted in truth.

I hold both Polaroids side by side, studying them, my stomach slowly filling with a queasiness that began the moment I found the shoebox. It's the sinking feeling that comes with bad news, dashed hopes, sudden heartbreak.

It's the feeling of realizing what you

thought was a lie might be true.

Part of me knows that's completely ridiculous. The Book is fiction, despite having the words *A True Story* slapped on its cover, right below the title. My mother said as much. Yet a tiny voice in the back of my head whispers that maybe, just maybe, I could be wrong. It's the same voice that last night, right before Elsa Ditmer made her presence known, suggested the person inside the Indigo Room could have been Mister Shadow.

I hear it now, hissing in my ear.

You know it's true. You've always known.

What makes it so unnerving is that I recognize that insistent whisper.

It's my father. Sounding just like he did right before he died.

I hear it again when I fish the last two photos out of the box. The first is a shot of my father performing a prototypical selfie. Arm extended. Chin lowered. Swatch of bare wall in the background over his left shoulder. He stares straight at the camera, which makes it seem as if he's looking beyond it, into the future, his eyes locking on mine through a distance of twenty-five years.

Never go back there, his voice says. *It's not safe there. Not for you.*

181

Hoping my father's whisper will go away if I'm not longer looking at his face, I flip to the last Polaroid. It was taken at a vertiginous angle from one of the windows that overlook the backyard. On the ground are two people entering the woods.

One of them is my mother.

The other is me at age five.

It's exactly like the photo my father described in the Book. The one he took when he found the Polaroid camera. My gaze drifts against my will, moving to the left of the frame, simultaneously knowing and fearing what I'll find there.

Sure enough, hugging the edge of the frame is a dark shape hiding among the trees.

It could be a tree trunk, darkened by shadow.

It could also be a person.

I can't quite tell because the picture quality is so poor. It's grainy and slightly out of focus, giving everything a jittery blur. Despite that, the dark form bears a distinct human shape.

But the worst part about the figure is that it's standing near the same spot as the person I saw last night. That could be a coincidence. But the churning unease in my stomach tells me it's not.

182

My father's imaginary whisper pipes up again.

It's Mister Shadow. You know it's him.

But Mister Shadow isn't real. Just like the Book isn't real.

I continue to stare at the photo, thinking about what happened moments after it was taken. My hand flutters to my cheek, my fingertips touching the slash of smooth skin under my eye. I realize the scar is yet another bit of proof that the Book — fantastical though it may be — contains strands of truth.

I drop the pictures on the desk, where they spill across its surface. The one on top is the selfie of my father, his eyes looking right into mine, as if he already knows what I'm about to do next.

Exit the office, leaving Dane alone.

Head outside, past the truck, weaving through the equipment on the lawn, and moving around to the back of the house.

Pass the exterior wall overtaken by ivy, their tendrils climbing all the way to a second-floor window.

Push into the shadow-shrouded woods in a one-woman re-creation of my father's photograph and hurtle down the hillside, swishing through weeds, passing bright red swaths of baneberries, tripping over tree roots.

Finally, I come to a stop at a cluster of marble blocks jutting from the earth like rotten teeth.

The cemetery.

Yet another thing my father wasn't lying about.

Behind me, Dane calls my name. He's in the woods now, too, catching up to me. He freezes when he sees the gravestones.

"Whoa," he says.

"My thoughts exactly."

I kneel in front of the nearest stone, wipe the dirt away, see a name carved into the marble.

Then I begin to laugh.

I can't believe I thought — even for just a moment — that the Book was true. It shows how good of a liar my father was and how greatly I'd underestimated his talent. Of course he sprinkled *House of Horrors* with real-life events and places. If there's an honest-to-God cemetery on your property, it's only natural to mention it. When you throw enough facts into your fiction, tangling them together like a nest of snakes, some people are bound to believe it. Politicians do it all the time.

And for a second there, I did believe. It

was hard not to after encountering so many things mentioned in the Book. The record player. The photograph of me and my mother. The sleepover and the kitchen ceiling and the graveyard. All of it made me think the Book was real.

But now I look at the name on the gravestone and realize I was right all along — the Book is bullshit.

ROVER
He was a good dog

Dane, now at my side, stares at the stone and says, "This is a freaking pet cemetery?"

"Looks like it," I say. "If not, the Garsons were one seriously messed-up family."

We stroll through the rest of the cemetery. While certainly old and admittedly creepy, it's nothing compared to the place my father wrote about. There are stones for several dogs, too many cats to count, and even a pony named Windy.

Pointing to its grave, Dane says, "Maybe it was a ghost horse your family encountered."

"Ghosts don't exist," I reply. "Equine or otherwise."

"Hey, now. Don't be so quick to dismiss ghosts."

"You don't believe all that stuff, do you?"

Dane's expression grows contemplative. "Do I believe in ghosts? Not really. At least, not in what people think of as supernatural. But I do believe that things happen. Things we can't explain away, no matter how much we try. The uncanny. That's what my maternal grandmother called it."

"She was a believer?"

"Oh, yes. She was old-school Irish. Grew up hearing stories of sprites and banshees. I always thought it was silly, how she believed in such things." His voice goes quiet now. No more than a whisper. "But then I saw one when I was ten. Maybe not a ghost. But something."

"Something uncanny?" I say.

He blushes a little and scratches the back of his neck. A boyish gesture that's oddly endearing. Of the many versions of Dane Hibbets I've encountered in the past twenty-four hours — cockily handsome caretaker, eager employee, font of information — this is the one I like the best.

"We were living in an old house a few towns away," he says. "It was tall and narrow. My bedroom was on the top floor, kind of isolated from the rest of the house. I didn't mind it too much. I was ten. I wanted privacy. But then one night in October, I woke up to the sound of my bedroom door being opened. I sat up in bed and saw my grandmother poke her head into the room. 'I just wanted to say goodnight, Boy-O,' she said. That was her nickname for me. Boy-O. Then she left, closing the door behind her. Before going back to sleep, I checked the clock on the nightstand. It was one thirty-two a.m.

"In the morning, I went downstairs and found my parents sitting at the kitchen table. My mother was crying. My father just looked dazed. I asked them where Nana was and why no one had told me she was visiting. That's when they told me. My grandmother had died during the night. At exactly one thirty-two a.m."

We stand in silence after that. To speak would be to break the sudden, strange connection between us. It's similar to our exchange in the office, although this time it feels more potent because it's personal. In that silence, I think of Dane's story and how it's more sweet than scary. It makes me wish my father had said something similar before he died. Instead, I got a vague warning about Baneberry Hall and an apology for something he never got around to admitting, both of which led me here.

187

"I have a confession to make," I eventually say.

"Let me guess," Dane says, deadpan. "Your real name is Windy."

"Close. I didn't come back just to renovate Baneberry Hall. My real reason for returning is to try to figure out why we left this place the way we did."

"You think there's more to the story?"

"I know there is."

I tell him everything. My checkered history with the Book. My father's cryptic last words. My certainty that my parents have been withholding the truth from me for twenty-five years.

"I know my father was a liar," I say, giving a nod toward Rover's grave. "Now I want to know just how much he lied about. And why."

"But you already know it wasn't the truth," Dane says. "Why go to all this trouble just to learn the specifics?"

"Because —" I pause, trying to find a way to articulate a gut feeling that can't be expressed in words. "Because for most of my life, I've been defined by that book. Yet my parents refused to tell me anything about it. So I grew up lonely and confused and feeling like a freak because everyone

188

thought I was the victim of something un-canny."

Dane nods approvingly at my use of his grandmother's term. "It's a good word."

"It really is," I say, smiling even though tears are gathering in my eyes. I wipe them away with the back of my hand before one can escape. "But I never experienced it. It never happened. Now I just want to know the real story. There's your rambling, embar-rassingly personal answer."

"Thank you for your honesty," Dane tells me. "That couldn't have been easy."

"It wasn't," I say. "But Baneberry Hall has been the subject of so many lies, I figured it's time someone started telling the truth."

JUNE 29
DAY 4

The next day, I was back in the woods, this time with Hibbs. Jess was inside with Maggie, attempting to ease our daughter's pain with some child aspirin and cartoons. Our trip to the emergency room had ended up being better than I expected. It was still slow — more than three hours from arrival to departure — and still expensive. But Maggie hadn't needed stitches, which was good news all around.

The bad news was that we had a graveyard on our property, which was why I'd asked Hibbs to tag along. I needed someone to help me count the headstones.

"I'd heard rumors they were out here, but never believed them myself," Hibbs said as we scanned the ground, looking for more graves. So far, I'd found three. Two presumably for William Garson's eldest son and grandson — William Jr. and William III, respectively — and one too weathered to read.

"No one knew about this place?" I said.

"Someone did, once upon a time," Hibbs replied. "But time passed, the place changed hands, and the forest kept on growing. It's sad, when you think about it. The final resting place of a once-great family now sits in a forest, forgotten. Here's another, by the way."

He pointed to a fourth brick-like stone rising from the earth. Carved into its top was a name and a date.

INDIGO GARSON
Beloved daughter
1873–1889

"She was a beauty, that one," Hibbs said. "That portrait of her up in the house? That's true to life, or so I've been told."

"Do you know a lot about the Garsons?"

"Oh, I've heard plenty over the years."

"Do you know what happened to Indigo? She died so young."

"I've heard her story," Hibbs said. "My grandfather knew her. Back when he was just a boy. Told me she was the spitting image of that portrait. So it should come as no surprise that the artist who painted it fell madly in love with her."

That had been my first impression upon seeing it. That the only reason an artist would have rendered Indigo Garson in such an

angelic fashion was that he had been enam-
ored of her.

"Did she love him in return?" I asked.

"She did," Hibbs said. "The story goes that
the two planned to run away and get married.
William Garson was furious when he found
out. He told Indigo she was far too young to
get married, even though at that time being a
bride at sixteen was quite common. He forbade Indigo from ever seeing the artist again.
Despondent over her lost love, Indigo killed
herself."

I shuddered at the realization that another
former resident of Baneberry Hall had committed suicide.

"How?"

"Poisoned herself." Hibbs pointed farther
down the hill, where a cluster of plants sat,
their spindly branches covered with scarlet
berries. "With those."

"She ate baneberries?" I said.

Hibbs gave a solemn nod. "A true tragedy.
Old Man Garson was heartbroken about it.
The rumor is he hired that same artist to come
back and paint his portrait on the other side of
that fireplace. That way he and Indigo would
always be together in Baneberry Hall. The
painter didn't want to, but he was flat broke
and therefore had little choice."

Now I understood why the portrait of William

Garson in the great room was so sneakily unflattering. The painter had despised him, and it showed.

I walked to Mr. Garson's gravestone, the smear of Maggie's blood still there, now dried to a dark red.

"How widely known is that story?" I asked. "Does the rest of the town know it?"

"I suppose most do." Hibbs gave me a gold-tooth-flashing grin. "At least all us old-timers do."

"What else do you know about this place?"

"More than most, I'd say," Hibbs said with noticeable pride.

"The day we met, you asked if Janie June had told us the whole story," I said. "At the time, I thought she had. But now —"

"Now you suspect Janie June was holding out on you."

"I do," I admitted. "And I'd appreciate it if you filled in the blanks for me."

"I'm not sure you want that, Ewan," Hibbs said as he pretended to scour the ground for more graves. "You might think you do, but sometimes it's best not knowing."

Anger rose in my chest, hot and sudden and strong. It only got worse when I looked down and saw my daughter's blood staining William Garson's grave. I was so mad that I stalked across the wooded cemetery and grabbed

Hibbs by his collar.

"You told me I needed to be prepared for this place," I said. "But I'm not. And now my daughter's hurt. She could have been killed, Hibbs. So if there's something you're not telling me, you need to spit it out right now."

Hibbs didn't push me off him, which I don't doubt he could have done. Despite his age, he looked to be as strong as a bulldog. Instead, he gently pried my fingers from around his shirt collar and said, "You want the truth? I'll give it to you. Things have happened in that house. Tragic things. Indigo Garson and the Carver family, yes. But other things, too. And all those things, well, they . . . linger."

The word sent a chill down my back. Probably because of the way Hibbs said it — slowly, drawing out the word like it was a rubber band about to snap.

"Are you telling me Baneberry Hall is haunted?"

"I'm saying that Baneberry Hall *remembers*," Hibbs said. "It remembers everything that's happened since Indigo Garson gulped down those berries. And sometimes history has a way of repeating itself."

It took a moment for that information to sink in. It was so utterly absurd that I had trouble comprehending it. When it all eventually settled in, I felt so dizzy I thought I, too, was going to fall and whack my head on William Garson's grave.

"I'm not saying it's going to happen to you," Hibbs said. "I'm just telling you it's a possibility. Just like your house getting struck by lightning is a possibility. My advice? Be as happy as you can in that house. Love your family. Hug your daughter. Kiss your wife. From what I've heard, that house hasn't witnessed a lot of love. It remembers that pain. What you need to do is make it forget."

I returned from the woods to find Maggie on the sofa in the parlor, her head resting in Jess's lap. Half her cheek was covered by a large bandage. The skin surrounding it was colored an angry red that I already knew would darken into a nasty bruise.

"How many are there?" Jess said.

"About a dozen. That we could find, anyway. I wouldn't be surprised if there are more graves out there, their stones either completely crumbled or buried by plant life."

"I want to strangle that Janie June. She should have told us there was a goddamned cemetery in our backyard."

"Maybe she didn't know," I said. "They're pretty hidden."

"She's a Realtor," Jess snapped. "It's her job to know what's on the property. I think she knew telling us about it would freak us out and then she'd have to find another gullible couple to swindle."

"We weren't swindled," I said, even though I was starting to think we were. If not swindled, then at least misled. Because Jess was right — surely a Realtor would know about a cemetery on the property.

"What did Hibbs have to say about it?"

On the walk back to the house, I'd decided not to tell Jess about Indigo Garson's tragic death. She was already on edge knowing about two deaths inside Baneberry Hall. A third would likely send her running from the house, never to return. And, to be brutally honest, we couldn't afford for that to happen. Buying the house had cost us almost everything we had. There was nothing left over for a down payment on a new home or a rental.

We were, for better or worse, stuck there.

Which meant I needed to follow Hibbs's advice and make our time there as happy as possible. Even if it meant not being honest with my wife. In my mind, there was no other choice.

"Nothing much," I said before scooping Maggie from the couch. "Now let's go for some ice cream. Three scoops for everyone. I think we've all earned it."

Considering everything Hibbs had told me that afternoon, I was surprised by how exhausted I felt when bedtime rolled around. I had assumed I'd be awake half the night, worrying about all I'd heard about the cemetery, Indigo Garson, the way Baneberry Hall *remembers.* Instead, I fell asleep the moment my head hit the pillow.

It didn't last long.

At five minutes to midnight, I awoke to a strange sound.

Music.

Someone, somewhere, was singing.

A man. His voice soft and lilting. Drifting from a distant part of the house.

I looked to the other side of the bed to see if Jess had also been awakened by the music, but she remained fast asleep. Hoping she'd stay that way, I slid out of bed and crept out of the room.

The music was slightly louder in the hallway. Loud enough for me to recognize the song.

"You are sixteen, going on seventeen —"

The music was coming from upstairs, a fact I realized when I reached the other side of the hall. I could hear it echoing down the steps that led to my study. Accompanying the music was a chill strong enough to make me shiver.

"Baby, it's time to think."

I started up the stairs slowly, nervously. With each step, the song got louder and the chill got worse. At the top of the stairs, it had grown so cold that, had there been more light there, I'm certain I would have seen my breath.

"Better beware —"

When I opened the study door, the song practically boomed out of the room. Inside, it was pitch-black. The kind of darkness that gave one pause. And cold. So freezing that goose bumps formed on my bare skin.

"— be canny —"

I stepped into the study, hugging myself for warmth. I flicked the switch by the door, and light flooded the room.

"— and careful —"

Sitting on the desk, right where I had left it, was the record player. The album on top of it spun at full speed and at top volume.

"Baby, you're on the —"

I plucked the needle from the record, and silence fell over the house like a wool blanket. The cold went away as well — an instant warming that swept through the room. Or so I thought. As I stood in that newfound silence and warmth, it occurred to me that it might have been my imagination.

Not the music.

That had been all too real.

The album still spun atop the turntable, its grooves catching light from the fixture overhead. I switched it off, not looking away until the record came to a complete stop. I assumed it was Jess's doing. That in a fit of insomnia she had made her way up here and listened to some music before getting tired.

The only excuse for the cold was that I'd somehow imagined it. Any other explanation — a draft, a gust of freezing air from the open window — seemed unlikely, if not downright impossible. Therefore it must have been my imagination, prompted by what Hibbs had told me earlier. Here was the irrational fear I'd been expecting, arriving a few hours late.

And that's exactly what it was — irrational.

Houses didn't remember things. The supernatural didn't exist. I had no reason to fear this place.

By the time I returned to bed, I had convinced myself it was all in my head.

That everything was normal.

That nothing strange was going on at Baneberry Hall.

It turned out I was wrong.

So utterly wrong.

SEVEN

I send Dane home for the day after our talk in the cemetery. It feels like the right thing to do, despite the fact that we accomplished next to nothing. After revisiting our possibly haunted pasts, both of us deserve an afternoon off.

For me, that involves heading into town for much-needed groceries.

My drive to the store brings me onto Bartleby's main thoroughfare. Maple Street, of course. I pass clapboard houses as sturdy and unbending as the people who surely live inside them, storefronts with large windows and signs hawking authentic maple syrup, the obligatory church with its ivory steeple stretching toward the sky. There's even a town square — a small patch of green with a gazebo and flagpole.

Although quaint, there's a slight dinginess to Bartleby not present in similar towns. A sense that time has passed it by. Still, I notice small attempts at modernization. A sushi restaurant. A vegetarian bistro. A consignment shop specializing in designer brands with a diaphanous Gucci dress prominently displayed in the window.

And I see a bakery, which makes me slam on the brakes in the middle of Maple Street. In my experience, where there are baked goods, there's also coffee. Usually good coffee. Considering my under-caffeinated state, that's worth slamming the brakes.

I park on the street and step into a space decorated in a manner that's both trendy and timeless. Copper fixtures. Tile-top tables with mismatched chairs. Midnight-blue walls filled with vintage illustrations of birds inside ornate frames. At the rear of the shop, an old-fashioned display case stretches from wall to wall, filled with gorgeously decorated cakes, delicate pastries, and pies with elaborate crusts worthy of Instagram. As far as visuals go, the owner certainly knows what she's doing.

I walk to the display case, ready to tell the woman adjusting pastries inside it how much I like the design. The compliment dies on my lips when the woman rises from behind the counter and I see who she is.

Marta Carver.

I recognize her from the pictures I saw

when I was a *House of Horrors*–obsessed tween who hoped Google would help fill the gaps in my knowledge. She's older and softer now. Fiftyish, brown hair graying at the roots, slightly matronly in her yellow blouse and white apron. Her glasses don't help — the same unflattering spectacles she wore in all those photos.

I'm apparently not the only one who's done some Googling, because it's clear she knows who I am. Her eyes widen just enough to register her surprise, and her jaw tightens. She clears her throat, and I brace myself for an angry tirade about my father. It would be justified. Of the many people in Bartleby who hate the Book, Marta Carver has the biggest reason for doing so.

Instead, she forces her lips into a polite smile and says, "What can I get for you, Miss Holt?"

"I —"

I'm sorry. That's what I want to say. *I'm sorry my father exploited your tragedy in his book. I'm sorry that because of him the whole world knows what your husband did.*

"Coffee, please," is what I end up saying, the words tight in my throat. "To go."

Marta says nothing else as she pours my coffee and hands it to me. I muster a weak "Thank you" and pay with a ten-dollar bill.

The change goes into a tip jar atop the counter, as if that seven dollars can make up for twenty-five years of pain.

I tell myself there's no need to apologize. That it was my father, not me, who wronged her. That I'm just as much a victim as she is.

But as I leave that bakery, I know two things.

One, that I'm a coward.

And, two, that I hope to never see Marta Carver again as long as I live.

I return from the grocery store with a dozen paper bags in the back of my pickup. Because Baneberry Hall's kitchen leaves a lot to be desired, I stocked up on food that's easy to prepare. Canned soups, cold cereal, frozen dinners that can be zapped in the ancient microwave.

When I pull up to the house, I find a Toyota Camry also parked in the circular drive. Soon a man appears from the side of the house, as if he's just been roaming the grounds. He's in his early fifties, trim, with a tidy beard, a checked sport coat, and a matching bow tie. The outfit makes him look like an old-timey salesman. All that's missing is a straw hat and a bottle of snake oil. As he approaches with one hand extended and another gripping a reporter's notebook, I realize exactly who he is.

Brian Prince.

I can't say I wasn't warned.

"Good to see you, Maggie," he says, as if we're old friends.

I hop out of the truck, scowling. "You're trespassing, Mr. Prince."

"My apologies," he says, doing a half bow of attrition. "I heard you were back in town, so I decided to drive out here and see for myself. When I saw the front gate open, I realized the rumors were true. Hope you don't mind the intrusion."

I grab a grocery bag from the truck and carry it to the porch. "Will you leave if I say yes?"

"Grudgingly," he says. "But I do intend to come back, so you might as well get it over with now."

"Get what over with?"

"Our interview, of course," he says.

I return to the truck and grab two more bags. "I'm afraid I'm not very newsworthy, Mr. Prince."

"Oh, I beg to differ. I think the community would be very interested to know that a member of the Holt family has moved back to Baneberry Hall."

"I'm not moving in," I say. "In fact, I'm

moving out. There's your article in two sentences."

"What are your plans for the house?"

"Fix it up, sell it, hopefully walk away with a profit," I say, nodding toward the equipment on the lawn as I make my way to the porch. First the table saw. Then the electric sander. Then the sledgehammer.

"The fact that Baneberry Hall will soon be back on the market is newsworthy in itself," Brian says.

Deep down, I know Brian Prince is blameless. He heard a juicy story about a haunted house, interviewed my father, and wrote down what he said. He had simply done his job, just like Tess Alcott had done hers. The only two people responsible are my parents, and even they had no idea the story of Baneberry Hall would grow into the unruly phenomenon it became. That still doesn't keep me from wanting to grab the sledgehammer and chase Brian Prince off my property.

"Newsworthy or not, I don't *want* to talk to you," I say.

"Your father did," he says. "Sadly, he never got the chance."

I lower the bags on the porch, my legs wobbly with surprise. "You communicated with my father?"

"Not often," Brian says. "But we continued to correspond on and off over the years. And one of the things we discussed shortly before his illness took a turn for the worse was him coming back here to do an interview with me."

"Your idea, I suppose."

"Actually, it was your father who suggested it. He pitched it as an exclusive interview. Him and me talking inside this house, twenty-five years later."

It's yet another thing my father never mentioned, probably because he knew I would have tried to talk him out of it.

"Did he tell you what the gist of this conversation would have been?" I say, toying with the possibility it might have been an attempt to finally come clean after all these years. A confession, of sorts, taking place at the scene of the crime.

That idea is immediately shot down by Brian Prince.

"Your father said he wanted to reaffirm what he had written in his book."

"And you were just going to go along with it?" I say, my opinion of Brian Prince swiftly changing. Maybe he's not as blameless as I first thought. "Listen to my father tell a bunch of lies and write it down as fact?"

"I wasn't planning on going easy on him,"

Brian says as he fussily adjusts his bow tie. "I was going to ask some tough questions. Try to get at the truth of the matter."

"The truth is that he made it all up," I say. "Everyone knows that."

"I don't think it's as simple as that," he says.

Because Brian Prince shows no sign of leaving anytime soon, I take a seat on the porch steps. When Brian sits next to me, I'm too tired to shoo him away. Not to mention a tad curious about what he thinks is the real reason we abandoned Baneberry Hall.

"Did you investigate his claims?" I ask.

"Not back then," Brian admits. "I didn't have access to this house, for one thing. Plus there was other news to deal with."

I roll my eyes. "It must not have been too important. The *Gazette* put my father's bullshit story on the front page."

Which, I wanted to add, was the reason other news outlets paid so much attention to it. If Brian's article had been buried inside the paper, no one would have even noticed it. But by splashing it across the front page, along with a particularly sinister photo of Baneberry Hall, the *Gazette* had provided validation for my father's lies.

"If our deadline had been a day later, your

family's story probably wouldn't have even made the paper. But I didn't hear about the Ditmer girl's disappearance until the morning after that issue had gone to press."

My body goes rigid at the mention of Petra. "I thought she ran away."

"I see you've already talked to Chief Alcott," Brian says, flashing me an unctuous smile. "That's the police's official line, by the way. That Petra Ditmer ran away. I guess it sounds better than saying a sixteen-year-old girl vanished under mysterious circumstances and they were too inept to find out what really happened to her."

"What do you think happened?"

"That's one of the things I wanted to ask your father."

An uneasy feeling floods my gut. Although I'm unsure where Brian is going with this, his tone of voice already suggests I'm not going to like it.

"Why ask him?" I say. "My father didn't make Petra run away —"

"Vanish," Brian interjects.

"Vanish. Disappear. Whatever." I rise, heading back to the truck, no longer wanting to hear what else Brian has to say. "My father wasn't involved in any of that."

"I thought that, too," Brian says, still on the porch steps, still smiling, still acting like this is just a friendly visit when it's clearly not. "It wasn't until later — long after your father's book came out — that I began to suspect they could be related."

"How?"

"For starters, Petra Ditmer was last seen on July 15 — the same night you and your family left this place. That's a bit too strange to be a coincidence, don't you think?"

The news hits me hard. There's a dizzying moment in which I think I'm going to faint. It comes out of nowhere, forcing me to lean against the truck to keep from falling.

Petra Ditmer vanished the same night we fled Baneberry Hall.

Brian is right — that does feel like more than just a coincidence. But I don't know what else it could be. Petra certainly didn't run away with my family. That's something I would have remembered. Besides, Chief Alcott was inside our hotel room at the Two Pines that night. Surely she would have noticed if a sixteen-year-old girl had also been there.

"I think you're overreaching," I say.

"Am I? I've read your father's book many times. In it, he had lots to say about Petra Ditmer. Considering their age difference, they seemed quite *close.*"

He puts a lascivious spin on the word that

209

makes my blood boil. Yes, Petra was mentioned frequently in the Book, often at key moments. That can't be denied, especially when I now have the photos to prove it. But that doesn't mean she and my father were, to use Brian's euphemism, close.

I knew my father better than he did. Ewan Holt was a lot of things. A liar. A charmer. But he wasn't a creep or a womanizer. I know that as sure as I know that my mother, had she been cheated on, would have taken my father for every cent he was worth. Since she didn't, I have to believe we left Baneberry Hall for other reasons.

"Most of what's in my father's book is verifiably false. You can't trust a single thing he wrote. Including how much time he spent with Petra Ditmer. My father wasn't a stupid man, Mr. Prince. He certainly wouldn't have written so much about Petra — in a book that hundreds of thousands of people have read — if he was the one who caused her disappearance."

"Now you're the one who's overreaching. I never said he caused her disappearance. What I'm *suggesting* is that they're related. Your family fled Baneberry Hall at almost the exact same time Petra Ditmer vanished without a trace. That's not normal, Maggie. Not here in Bartleby." Brian stands and makes a show of wiping his pants, as if merely sitting on Baneberry Hall's porch steps has somehow dirtied him. "Something strange happened the night your family left, and I fully intend to find out what it was. Now, you can help me or hinder me —"

"I'm sure as hell not going to help you," I say.

Even though Brian Prince and I share the same goal, it's clear we're each looking for different results.

"Although that's not the answer I wanted to hear, I respect it nonetheless," Brian says. "But just so you know, I *will* uncover the truth about that night."

"You're going to have to do it off my property," I say. "Which means you need to leave. *Now.*"

Brian makes one last adjustment to his bow tie before getting into his car and driving away. I follow behind him, walking the long, curving road down the hillside to the front gate. Once I've made sure he's gone, I close the gate and lock it.

Then it's back to the house, where I'm finally able to carry my groceries inside. Burdened with bags heavy in both arms, I get just past the vestibule before noticing something wrong.

It's bright in here.

Way too bright.

I look to the ceiling and see the chandelier burning at full glow.

But here's the weird thing: when I left the house, it had been dark.

While I was gone, it had somehow been turned on.

June 30
Day 5

Thud.

Just like three nights before, the sound rattled the house and jerked me from sleep. Turning over, I looked at the digital clock on the nightstand, the numbers glowing green in the predawn darkness: 4:54 a.m.

The exact same time I'd previously heard the noise.

It was unnerving, yes, but also helpful, because it let me know that it hadn't been a dream. This sound was real, and coming from the third floor.

Despite the ungodly early hour, I slipped out of bed and made my way to the study upstairs. Inside, nothing seemed amiss. The doors to both closets were closed, and the record player was silent.

As for the noise, I had no idea what it was. I suspected the house was responsible. Most likely something to do with the heating system resetting itself at a designated time. Granted, just before five in the morning was an odd time for that, but I saw no other possibilities for what the noise could be.

Rather than go back to bed, I went downstairs before dawn for the second time since we moved in. Once again, the chandelier was lit. I would have continued to think it was the wiring if I hadn't heard the record player the night before. Clearly, both were the work of my unusually sleepless wife.

When Jess joined me in the kitchen after six, I greeted her by saying, "I never knew you were a *Sound of Music* fan."

"I'm not," she said, the second word stretching into a yawn.

"Well, you were last night. I don't mind you going into the study. Just remember to turn off the record player when you leave."

My wife gave me a sleepy-eyed look of confusion. "What record player?"

"The one on my desk," I said. "It was playing last night. I figured you'd had trouble sleeping, went up there, and listened to music."

"I have no idea what you're talking about," Jess said as she made her way to the coffeepot. "I was asleep all night."

It was my turn to look confused. "You weren't in my office at all?"

"No."

"And you didn't turn the record player on?"

Jess poured herself a cup of coffee. "If I had, I certainly wouldn't have picked *The Sound of Music.* Did you ask Maggie? She likes that movie. Maybe she was exploring?"

"At midnight?"

"I don't know what to tell you, Ewan," Jess said as she sat down at the kitchen table. "Did *you* have it on at some point?"

"I did," I said. "But that was two days ago. Right before Maggie hurt herself."

"Did you turn it off?"

I didn't know. All I could remember was hearing screams in the woods and bumping into the record player before running out of the study. Between taking Maggie to the emergency room and exploring the cemetery in the woods, I'd never had time to return there until the night before.

"Now that you mention it, I don't think I did."

"There you go." Jess drank heartily from her mug, proud of herself. "You left the player on, and something bumped the needle back onto the record. Then the house was alive with the sound of music."

"But what could have bumped it?"

"A mouse?" Jess suggested. "Maybe a bat? It's an old house. I'm sure there's something scurrying around inside these walls."

215

I winced. "I don't even want to think about it."

But think about it I did. It was possible that an animal could be living in the study. After all, there had been a snake in the Indigo Room. Although I found it highly unlikely any animal could accidentally play a record.

After breakfast, I returned to the third floor and examined the record player. Everything looked normal. Turned off, record on the turntable, no sign a rodent had been anywhere near it. I bumped the arm, just to see if it could easily be moved by man or mouse.

It couldn't.

So much for Jess's theory. That meant the culprit had to be Maggie.

Before leaving, I unplugged the record player. Just in case. Then I made my way to Maggie's wing, prepared to tell her she needed to ask permission before entering my study. It struck me as the only way to prevent it from happening again.

I found Maggie alone in the playroom next to her room. Only she didn't act like she was alone. Sitting on the floor with an array of toys in front of her, she appeared to be talking to an imaginary person across from her.

"You can look, but you can't touch," she said, echoing something Jess told her nearly every time we went shopping. "If you want to play, you'll need to find your own toys."

"Who are you talking to?" I asked from the doorway. In Burlington, Maggie hadn't shown any signs of having an imaginary friend. The fact she had one now made me wonder if it wasn't a by-product of having Elsa Ditmer's daughters here three days before. Now that she had finally experienced some companionship, maybe Maggie longed for more.

"Just a girl," she said.

"Is she a new friend of yours?"

Maggie shrugged. "Not really."

I stepped into the room, focused on the patch of floor where her imaginary not-friend would have been sitting. Even though no one was really there, Maggie had cleared a space for her.

"Does she have a name?"

"I don't know," Maggie said. "She can't talk."

I joined her on the floor, making sure I didn't invade the space of her imaginary friend. I still felt guilty about when I'd accused Maggie of lying about the girl in the armoire. She hadn't been lying. She was pretending.

"I see," I say. "So which one of you was in my study last night?"

Maggie gave me the same confused look I'd received from Jess in the kitchen. A slight tilt of the head. Right eyebrow raised. A scrunching of the face. The two were so alike, it was uncanny. The only difference was the bandage on Maggie's cheek, which crinkled as she scrunched.

"What study?" she said.

"The room on the third floor. You haven't been up there, have you?"

"No," Maggie said, in a way that made me think she was telling the truth. Her voice usually contained a note of hollowness when she was lying. It remained convincing when she turned to the empty space across from her and said, "You weren't up there, were you?"

She paused, absorbing a silent response only she could hear.

"She wasn't," Maggie informed me. "She spent last night in the wooden box."

Those two words, innocuous by themselves, took on a sinister new meaning when used together. It made me think of a coffin and a little girl lying inside it. I smiled at Maggie, trying to hide my sudden unease.

"What wooden box, sweetie?"

"The one in my room. Where Mommy hangs things."

The armoire. Again. I thought it strange how fixated she seemed to be on a simple piece of furniture. I told myself that Maggie was five and only doing things all kids her age did. Playing. Pretending. Not lying.

But then I remembered the sounds I kept

hearing in my dreams. And the thud that most definitely wasn't a dream. That got me thinking about what Hibbs had said about the house remembering. And the way Maggie's door had closed the other night, almost as if pulled by an unseen force. A sense of dread crept over me, and I suddenly no longer had the desire to indulge my daughter's imagination. In fact, all I wanted was to leave the room.

"I have an idea. Let's go outside and play." I paused, opting to make one small concession to Maggie's imagination. "Your new friend can come, too."

"She's not allowed to leave," Maggie said as she took my hand. Before we left the playroom, she turned back to the spot where her imaginary friend presumably still sat. "You can stay. But tell the others I don't want them here."

I paused then, struck by one word my daughter had used.

Others.

The unseen girl Maggie had been talking to and playing with — she wasn't her only imaginary friend.

"I'm worried about Maggie," I told Jess that night as we got ready for bed. "I think she's too isolated. Did you know that she has imaginary friends?"

Jess poked her head out of the master bathroom, toothbrush in hand and mouth foaming like Cujo. "I had an imaginary friend when I was her age."

"More than one?"

"Nope." Jess disappeared back into the bathroom. "Just Minnie."

I waited until she was done brushing her teeth and out of the bathroom before asking my follow-up question. "When you say you had an imaginary friend named Minnie, are you talking about Minnie Mouse?"

"No, Minnie was different."

"Was she a mouse?"

"Yes," Jess said, blushing so much even her shoulders had turned pink. "But they were different, I swear. My Minnie was my height. And furry. Like an honest-to-God mouse, only bigger."

I approached Jess from behind, took her into my arms, kissed her shoulder right next to the strap of her nightgown, the skin there still warm. "I think you're lying," I whispered.

"Fine," Jess admitted. "My imaginary friend was Minnie Mouse. I have a shitty imagination. I admit it. Happy now?"

"Always, when I'm with you." We crawled into bed, Jess snuggling against me. "Our daughter, I suspect, isn't. I think she's lonely."

"She'll be going to kindergarten in the fall," Jess said. "She'll make friends then."

"And what about the rest of the summer? We can't expect her to spend it cooped up in this house with imaginary friends."

"What's the alternative?"

I saw only one. And they lived just outside Baneberry Hall's front gate.

"I think we should invite the Ditmer girls over," I said.

"Like a playdate?"

That would have been the proper course of action, had their previous playdate gone well. But with Hannah being so bossy and Maggie so shy, they didn't gel as much as they should — or could — have. To truly bond, they needed something more than another half-hearted game of hide-and-seek.

"I was thinking more like a sleepover," I said.

"Both girls?" Jess said. "Don't you think Petra's a little old for that?"

"Not if we pay her to babysit. She could watch Maggie and Hannah, and we, my dear, could have a proper date night."

I kissed her shoulder again. Then the nape of her neck.

Jess melted against me. "When you put it that way, how's a girl supposed to say no?"

"Great," I said, drawing her tighter against me. "I'll call Elsa tomorrow."

The matter was settled. Maggie was going to have her first sleepover.

It turned out to be a decision all three of us would later come to regret.

EIGHT

In the evening, I get a text from Allie.

Just checking in. How's the house?

It has potential, I write back.
Allie responds with a thumbs-up emoji, and No ghosts, I presume.

None.

But there's lots about the place that doesn't sit well with me. The person standing behind the house last night, for instance. Or the chandelier that magically turned itself on. That one had me so spooked that I called Dane to ask if he'd been in the house while I was gone. He swore he hadn't.

Then there's everything Brian Prince told me, which has prompted me to sit in the kitchen with a copy of the Book and my father's Polaroids lined up on the table like place settings. I flip through the Book, looking for hints Brian might be onto something, even though his insinuation that my father engaged in some kind of improper relationship with Petra is both wrong and, frankly, gross.

Not long after my mother married Carl, my father and I took a trip to Paris. I hadn't wanted to go. I had just turned fourteen, an age at which no girl wants to be seen with one of her parents. But I knew my father hadn't reacted well to my mother's decision to remarry and that he needed the trip more than I did.

We departed a few months before I finally stopped asking questions about the Book, knowing I'd never get a straight answer. I asked about it only once during the trip — another one of my sneak attacks, this time in front of the *Mona Lisa* — and received my father's stock answer. That's why one of the things I remember most about the trip, other than croque monsieurs and a dreamy, flirty café waiter named Jean-Paul, was a rare moment of honesty during an evening picnic in the shadow of the Eiffel Tower.

"Do you think you'll ever get remarried like Mom?" I asked.

My dad chewed thoughtfully on a piece of baguette. "Probably not."

"Why?"

"Because your mother is the only woman I've ever loved."

"Do you still love her?"

"As a matter of fact, I do," my father said.

"Then why did you get divorced?"

"Sometimes, Mags, a couple can go through something so terrible that not even love can fix it."

He went quiet after that, stretching out on the grass and watching the sun sink lower behind the Eiffel Tower. Even though I knew he was referring to the Book, I dared not ask him about it. He'd already let his guard down. I didn't want to push it.

Maybe if I had, I finally would have received an honest answer.

I put down the Book and grab the Polaroids, paying extra attention to the ones that feature Petra. At first glance, they're innocent. Just a teenage girl being herself. But creepier undertones emerge the longer I look at them. In the picture taken in the kitchen, neither Petra nor my mother acknowledges the photographer's presence, giving the image an uncomfortable, voyeuristic feel. A photo snapped before the subject realized someone was there.

Worse still is the picture of the sleepover. Petra is front and center. So much so that

Hannah and I might as well have not even been there. Unlike the kitchen shot, Petra knows she's being photographed — and she likes it. Her hands-on-hip, one-leg-bent pose is something a forties pinup would strike. It almost looks like she was flirting with the photographer, which in this case had to have been my father.

I slap the photos facedown on the table, disappointed with myself for giving in to gossip.

Behind me, one of the bells on the wall rings.

A single, resounding toll.

The sound jolts me from my chair, which overturns and slams to the floor. I push myself against the table, its edge pressing into the small of my back as I scan the bells. The kitchen is silent save for the sound of my heart — an audible drumroll coming from deep in my chest.

I want to believe I heard nothing. That it was one of those weird auditory blips everyone experiences. Like ringing in the ears. Or when you think you hear your name being called in a crowd and it ends up just being random noise.

But my pounding heart tells me I'm not imagining things.

One of those bells just rang.

Which leads me to a single, undeniable fact — someone else is inside the house.

I edge around the table, never taking my eyes off the bells, just in case one of them rings again. Moving backward, I reach the counter, my hands blindly sliding along its surface until I find what I'm looking for.

A block holding six knives.

I grab the largest one — a carving knife with a seven-inch blade. My reflection quivers in the glinting steel.

I look scared.

I *am* scared.

Holding the knife in front of me, I creep out of the kitchen and up the steps to the main part of the house. It's not until I'm in the great room that I hear the music. A crisp, almost dreamy tune I'd have recognized even without the lyrics floating from somewhere above.

"You are sixteen, going on seventeen —"

My heart, which was still beating wildly a mere second ago, stops cold, making the song sound even louder.

"Baby, it's time to think."

I move through the great room on legs so numb with fear it feels as though I'm floating. When I reach the front of the house, I notice the chandelier is jangling. Almost as if someone is pounding the floor directly

227

above it.

"Better beware —"

I have two options here — run, or confront whoever's inside the house. I want to run. My body begs me to, twitching insistently. I opt for confrontation, even though it's not the wisest choice. Running only leads to more questions. Facing it head-on can only lead to answers.

"— be canny —"

Mind made up, I start to run, not giving my body a chance to protest. I rush up the stairs, across the second-floor hallway, up another set of steps. I'm still running when I reach the third floor, the study door shut and looming before me.

"— and careful —"

I hurtle toward the door with my grip tight around the knife, letting out a scream as I go. Part of it's self-defense. Trying to catch whoever's inside off guard. The rest is fear, bursting out of me the same way I'm bursting into the room.

"Baby, you're on the brink."

The study is empty, even though all the lights are on and the record player on the desk blares at full volume.

"You are sixteen —"

I flick the needle away from the turntable and, pulse still thrumming, survey the room, just to confirm it is indeed empty. Whoever had been up here must have left as soon as they started the record player, ringing the bell on the way out.

Which means it was a ghoul. Some punk-ass kid who'd read the Book, heard I was back here, and now wanted to reenact part of it.

The only wrinkle in my theory is that I'd closed and locked the gate after Brian Prince left. I also closed and locked the front door when I got back to the house. If it was a *House of Horrors* prankster, how did he get inside?

That question vanishes when I take another look at the desk and notice something off.

Just like the letter opener in the parlor, the teddy bear Dane and I had found in the closet is now gone.

July 1
Day 6

"He says we're going to die here."

Until then, the day had been notable for *not* being notable. No ringing bells or rogue snakes or new, unnerving discovery. If there had been a thud at 4:54 in the morning, I slept right through it. It had simply been a normal day. Our first at Baneberry Hall.

Then my daughter uttered those words, and it all went to shit.

I immediately fetched Jess, knowing this was a job best handled by the both of us. Even then, I wasn't sure what we should do. One of my daughter's imaginary friends was telling her she was going to die. That wasn't covered in any parenting handbook.

"Mister Shadow isn't real," Jess said as she climbed onto the bed and took Maggie into her arms. "And he's not a ghost. He's just a piece of your imagination with a mean voice telling you things that aren't true."

Maggie remained unconvinced.

"But he *is* real," she said. "He comes out at night and says we're going to die."

"Do your other friends say stuff like that?"

"They're not my friends," Maggie said in a way that broke my heart a little. Basically, she was telling us that she had no friends. Not even imaginary ones. "They're just people who come into my room."

"Just how many people have you met?" Jess said.

"Three." Maggie counted them off on her fingers. "There's Mister Shadow. And the girl with no name. And Miss Pennyface."

Jess and I exchanged concerned looks. Whatever this was, it wasn't normal.

"Miss Pennyface?" I said. "Why do you call her that?"

"Because she has pennies over her eyes. But she can still see. She's watching us right now."

Maggie pointed to the corner by the closet with the slanted door. I saw nothing but an empty space where the angled ceiling began its sharp descent. Jess didn't see anything, either, because she said, "There's no one there, honey."

"There is!" Maggie cried, once more on the verge of tears. "She's looking right at us!"

She was so convincing in her certainty that I continued to stare at the corner, searching the shadows there, looking in vain for something I couldn't see but that my daughter could, even if it was just in her mind's eye.

Then I heard a noise.

Tap.

It came from somewhere down the hallway. A single rap on the hardwood floor.

"What the hell was that?" Jess said.

"I don't know."

Tap.

The noise was louder that time. Like whatever was causing it had moved a few feet down the hallway, closer to Maggie's bedroom.

Tap-tap.

These were louder still, the second sounding nearer than the first.

"Do you think it's the pipes?" Jess asked.

"If it is, why haven't we heard it until now?"

Tap-tap-tap.

Three that time, growing in volume until they were right outside.

Maggie pressed against her mother, her wide eyes unblinking.

"It's Mister Shadow," she said.

Jess hushed her. "Maggie, stop it. He's not real."

Mister Shadow might not have been real, but the tapping certainly was. The only explanation I could think of was the most obvious one: an intruder had entered Baneberry Hall.

"Someone's inside the house," I whispered.

The noise was now an unbroken stream, so loud and so close. It seemed to pass right by the bedroom door, even though no motion accompanied it.

Tap-tap-tap-tap-tap-tap.

The sound began to recede as it continued down the hall, seemingly heading to the steps that led to the third floor.

I bolted from the bed, determined to follow it. "You and Maggie stay right here."

Jess protested. "Ewan, wait —"

If she said anything else, I didn't hear it. By then I was already running down the hallway, trying to locate the source of the —

Tap-tap-tap-tap-tap.

I looked up and down the hallway. Nothing was there. Certainly nothing that could have caused something as strange as that —

Tap-tap-tap-tap.

The sound had become quieter, almost as if it had moved to another section of the house. I heard one last *tap* before it died away completely, leaving me standing in a silent hallway.

It didn't last long.

Within seconds, I heard something else.

Music.

Coming from directly above me.

"You are sixteen, going on seventeen —"

I bolted up the steps to the third floor, taking them two at a time. When the door to my study edged into view, I saw that it was closed, a thin strip of light visible just beneath it.

"Baby, it's time to think."

I knew I should have turned back, but by then it was too late. Whoever was behind that door had heard me coming. Besides, momentum kept me moving. Up the rest of the steps, through the door, into the study.

"Better beware —"

Just like the other night, the study was empty. It was just me and the record player and the damn album spinning and spinning and spinning.

"— be canny —"

I turned it off, the song mutating as the turntable slowed to a stop. I then examined the study, wondering where the intruder had gone.

And how he had caused those taps.

And if it was going to happen again.

Because it had already happened once before. Two nights ago, when I'd first heard the record player. That hadn't been Jess or Maggie or a goddamn mouse.

The realization that our home had been broken into twice now rattled me. With shaking hands, I removed the record from the turntable and stuffed it into its cardboard sleeve. I saw no need to give the intruder a chance to play it a third time. I then unplugged the record player and put it back inside its case. Both cases were then put back in the closet where I found them.

Then I went downstairs to call the police.

The policewoman who came to our house, Officer Tess Alcott, was so young I at first didn't believe she was a cop. She looked like she had barely finished Girl Scouts, let alone a police academy. Officer Alcott probably got that a lot, for she presented herself with a gruffness that felt forced.

"Was anything taken?" she asked, her pen pressed to the tiny notebook in her hands. "Any missing valuables? Any cash that's unaccounted for?"

"Not that we know of," I said. "But a lot of this stuff wasn't ours. We inherited it when we bought the house. So something could be missing that we didn't know about."

The three of us were in the parlor, me and Jess perched on the edge of the couch, too nervous to relax. Officer Alcott sat across from us, surveying the room.

"Curtis Carver and his wife owned this place before you, didn't they?" she said.

"Yes," Jess said. "Do you think that could have something to do with the break-in?"

"I don't see any reason why it would."

I squinted at her, curious. "Then why did you ask?"

"So I can comb our records and see if there were any break-ins when they lived here. How did the intruder get inside? I'm assuming the front door was unlocked."

"It wasn't," I said. "I locked it before I went upstairs to tuck my daughter into bed, and it was still locked after the intruder had left."

"So, they came in through a window?"

"They were all closed," Jess said.

Officer Alcott, who had been writing this all down in her notebook, suddenly looked up, her pen paused against paper. "Are you certain there even was an intruder?"

"We heard noises," I said, understanding in that moment just how ridiculous I sounded. Like a child. Someone as scared and imaginative as Maggie.

"Lots of houses make noises," Officer Alcott said.

"Not this kind of noise." I tried to describe the tapping sound that had moved down the hallway, going so far as to knock on the parlor floor in an attempt to replicate it. When the officer seemed unconvinced, I added, "There was also music. Someone had turned on the record player in my study. That's happened twice now."

Officer Alcott turned to Jess. "Did you hear the record player?"

"I didn't." Jess gave me an apologetic look. "Neither of the times it was on."

The notebook and pen went back into the front pocket of Officer Alcott's uniform. "Listen, folks," she said. "If nothing was taken and there are no signs of a break-in and only one of you heard things —"

"We both heard the tapping," I interjected.

Officer Alcott raised a hand, trying to calm me. "I'm not sure what it is you want me to do here."

"You can believe us," I said testily.

"Sir, I do believe you. I believe you heard something and thought it was an intruder. But this sounds to me like whatever you heard wasn't what you *thought* you'd heard."

I understood then a little bit of Maggie's frustration whenever we talked about her imaginary friends. Not being believed was maddening. Only in my case, what I was saying was real. Those things *happened.*

"So we're just supposed to let it happen again?"

"No," Officer Alcott said. "You're supposed to be smart and vigilant and call us the next time you see anything suspicious."

Her choice of words didn't go unnoticed.

See anything suspicious. Not hear.

Officer Alcott departed with a tip of her hat and a nod of her head, leaving Jess and me to fend for ourselves. I did it the only way I knew how — by raiding the house for supplies to create a makeshift security system.

A pack of index cards.

Several spools of thread.

A box of chalk.

"What's all this for again?" Jess asked as I tore off a piece of index card.

"To see if someone's sneaking into the house." I stuffed the paper sliver between the door and its frame so that it would fall out if the door was opened. "If they are, this will tell us where he's getting inside."

I used the chalk to draw a thin line across the floor in front of the door. After that, I stretched the thread across the doorway, keeping it ankle-height. If anyone entered, I'd be able to tell. The thread would be snapped, and the chalk would be smudged.

"How many places are you going to do this?" Jess asked.

"The front door and every window," I replied.

By the time I went to bed, every openable window in the house had a length of thread across it and a small slip of index card stuck under its sill.

Whoever the intruder was, I was prepared for his next visit.

Or so I thought.

It turned out I wasn't prepared for anything that lay in store for us.

NINE

I'm still looking at that empty patch of desk
when something else catches my attention.
On the extreme edge of my vision, I detect
motion outside one of the study windows.
Rushing to the glass, I glimpse a dark figure
vanishing into the woods behind the house.

In an instant, I'm on the run again, revers-
ing my route up here. Down the steps,
across the hall, down more steps. On my
way to the front door, I pause long enough
to grab a flashlight from a box of supplies
sitting in the great room.

Then I'm outside, sprinting around the
house and crashing into the forest. It's
pitch-black here, the moonlight eclipsed by
the trees. I turn on the flashlight. The beam
jitters across the ground before me, catching random clusters of baneberries.

"I know you're out here!" I shout into the
darkness. "I saw you!"

There's no response. Not that I'm expecting one. I just want whoever it is to know I've seen them. Hopefully that alone will prevent a return visit.

I continue to move through the woods, the downward slope of the hill making me go faster. Soon I'm at the pet cemetery, the lumpy gravestones blurs of white in the flashlight's beam. Then I'm past the graves and approaching the stone wall at the base of the hill. It's intimidating in the darkness — ten feet high and as thick as a castle wall.

It dwarfs me when I stand next to it, which should be reassuring. No one's getting over that baby. Not without a ladder. But that realization prompts an uneasy question: How did this ghoul get on the property?

An answer arrives a minute later, when I decide to exit the woods by following the wall to the front gate. I get only about fifty yards before seeing a section of wall that has crumbled away. It's not a big gap. Just a foot-wide space cut through the wall, like someone using a finger to slice a stick of butter. To pass through it, I need to turn and sidestep my way across. Once I'm on the other side — and no longer officially on Baneberry Hall property — I glimpse the back of a cottage through the trees. Its exterior, yellow in the daytime, looks whitish in the moonlight. One window is aglow. Beyond it flickers the green-blue screen of a television set.

The cottage belongs either to Dane or the Ditmers. I'm not sure who lives on either side of the road. I suppose it's something I should find out, since an accidental side entrance to my property sits not far from their backyard.

Not that Dane or Hannah Ditmer would need to sneak onto the property. Each has keys to both the gate and the front door. They could walk right in whenever they wanted.

Which suggests that whoever was in the house had come and gone this way. All they needed to do was pass through the gap in the wall. The hardest part, as far as I can tell, is knowing about it. And it wouldn't surprise me if a lot of people in Bartleby and beyond had that knowledge.

I head back to the house, my pace hurried, suddenly convinced there are more ghouls on the way and that I need to head them off at the pass. Back inside, I grab the knife and do a search of Baneberry Hall. It's a nerve-shredding task. Opening each door, not knowing what I'll find behind it. Flicking each switch and anticipating the worst in that nanosecond of darkness before the lights come on.

Baneberry Hall ends up being empty.

For how long, I have no idea.

Which is why I take a page from my father's book.

Literally.

I rip the page straight out of the copy on the kitchen table and tear it into small pieces. It feels good. I've never defaced a copy of the Book before, and the satisfaction I get in doing so now makes me wish I'd started years ago.

I think of my father as I slip a scrap of paper into the crack of the front door, wondering if he'd be amused to see me doing something he wrote about in the Book. Probably not. If anything, I suspect he'd be disappointed that I broke my promise about never returning to Baneberry Hall.

I tried mightily not to disappoint him. Even though by age nine I'd pegged him as a liar, I still sought his approval at every turn. Maybe it stemmed from a sense that if I proved myself enough, he'd eventually deem me worthy of knowing the truth about the Book. Or maybe it was just typical broken-family rebellion. Since I knew I'd never live up to my mother's lofty standards, I aimed for the much-lower bar set by my father.

That doesn't mean he wasn't a good father. He was, in many ways, a terrific dad, and not just because he spoiled me rotten. He was attentive and kind. He never talked down to me, like my mother did. And he never, ever underestimated me.

Growing up, I was given lists of books to read, movies to see, albums to listen to. Things no one would suggest for a teenager. Bergman films. Miles Davis records. Tolstoy and Joyce and Pynchon. Each one was a sign he thought I was capable of opening my mind and expanding my horizons. And even though I had zero interest in jazz or *Gravity's Rainbow,* I tried my best to appreciate his tastes. My father believed in me, and I didn't want to let him down.

I disappointed him anyway. When I went to college and decided to study design and not journalism or English lit, dashing his dreams of having another writer in the family. When I quit the boring-but-stable design job I had since graduation to start the company with Allie.

That one began a period of ups and downs that lasted until my father's death. He once told me our relationship was like a rose. Beautiful, yes, but it came with thorns. I liken it to the weather. It was always changing. Icy seasons. Warm spells. Months

244

when we'd talk almost every day and long sections of radio silence.

Most of it was my doing, each phase dictated by my relationship to the Book. If I made it through a few months without being associated with *House of Horrors,* I'd treat my father like he was my best friend. But the moment the Book and I would inevitably be pushed together again — like the time I was ambushed by a tabloid reporter on its twentieth anniversary — I'd turn cool, even bitter.

Meanwhile, my father began his retreat from the world, cloistering himself in his apartment with his beloved books and classic films. Once a ubiquitous interview subject, willing to be quoted about anything from the supernatural to the publishing industry, he cut himself off from all media. For a long time, I thought he'd grown tired of living with the lie he had created and no longer wanted anything to do with it. His correspondence with Brian Prince suggests otherwise.

Our relationship changed when he got sick. His cancer was aggressive, sinking its teeth into him quickly and without reprieve. There wasn't time for any more pettiness on my part. I needed to be there for him, and I was, right to the very end.

By midnight, there's a scrap of the Book tucked into the front door and every window.

I go to my room.

I lock the door.

I put the knife I've been carrying on the nightstand next to the bed.

My final act for the night is to take a Valium, crawl under the covers, and try to sleep, even though I already know it's not going to arrive easily, if at all.

I didn't sleep all night. As the minutes ticked by, accumulating into hours, I lay awake, staring at the ceiling, wondering if, when, how someone could get inside. The night was full of noises, all of them innocent. Yet that didn't keep me from thinking each one was the intruder returning for another round. I thought about the stone wall and wrought-iron gate at the end of the driveway and how I had once scoffed at their existence. Now I wished they were higher.

By the time the darkness of night had started to soften into dawn, my thoughts turned to something else.

Thud.

There it was.

I looked at the clock: 4:54 a.m. Right on schedule.

Abandoning the notion of getting any sleep, I slipped out of bed — quietly, so as not to wake Jess and Maggie, who had spent another night with us. I crept downstairs and was immediately greeted by the site of the chandelier at full glow, a fact that seemed impossible. I'd made a point of making sure it was off before going to bed the night before.

Fearing an intruder had once again been inside the house, I hurried to the front door. The thread remained taut across it. The chalk line on the floor was undisturbed. The bit of index card was still wedged between door and frame.

Secure in the knowledge the door hadn't been breached, I went down to the kitchen, made a pot of extra-strong coffee, and poured it into a mug roughly the size of a soup bowl. After taking a few eye-opening gulps, I returned to the rest of the house and methodically checked all the windows. They were the same as the door — completely undisturbed.

No one was there.

No one but us chickens.

My grandmother had used that phrase, back when I was a boy and my cousins would play hide-and-seek in the hulking barn behind her house. Because I was the youngest and smallest, it was Gram who'd hide with me, pulling me into her arms and shrinking her surprisingly spry body behind hay bales or in dark cubbyholes that always smelled of leather and motor oil. When one of my cousins came looking, calling out to see if anyone was there, Gram would always reply, "No one but us chickens!"

Security check complete, I returned to the kitchen and grabbed my coffee mug. As I took a sip, I noticed white dust sprinkling the tabletop. Sitting among it were small chunks of gray rubble.

Then I felt it.

Something inside the mug.

Small and whip thin.

It lashed against my upper lip before scraping my front teeth, slimy and foul-tasting.

I jerked the mug away from my mouth. The coffee I hadn't been able to swallow streamed down my chin. The liquid I did swallow came back up in a gurgling, choking cough.

I peered into the mug. A circular ripple spread across the coffee's surface and splashed against the mug's rim. I tilted the mug, and the thing inside breached the surface — a slick shimmer of gray rising and falling in the mud-brown liquid.

I dropped the mug and backed away from the table as coffee rushed across its surface. Riding the wave, like some small sea serpent washing ashore, was a baby snake.

It squirmed along the table, tracing a sinuous path through the spilled coffee. I stared at it, dumbfounded and disgusted. My stomach roiled so much I had to clamp a hand over my mouth.

Looking up, I saw a hole in the ceiling's plaster that was roughly the size of a shot glass. Two more baby snakes slipped through it and fell onto the table. Their landing sounded like two fat raindrops hitting a windshield.

I scrambled to find something to contain them. A bowl. Tupperware. Anything. I was rooting through a cupboard, my back turned to the table, when something else landed with a sickening splat.

I turned around slowly, dreading to see what I already knew I'd find there.

A fourth snake.

Not a baby.

Fully grown and more than a foot long, it had landed on its back, exposing a belly as red as baneberries. It flipped over, and I saw twin stripes the color of rust running down its back, just like the snake I'd found in the Indigo Room the day we moved in.

This bigger snake slithered past the babies and went straight to the upturned coffee mug, trying to coil itself inside. It hissed. In anger or fear, I couldn't tell.

I was still staring at it, paralyzed with horror, when two more baby snakes rained down onto the table.

I looked to the hole in the ceiling, where a seventh snake — another adult — was winnowing its way out, headfirst. It tried to reverse course by bending its body back toward the ceiling, which only hastened its slide from the hole.

When it landed — another splat, like a water balloon hitting its target — the table shimmied. Flecks of plaster from the ceiling fluttered like confetti. By then, most of the baby snakes had dropped off the table's edge and were slithering in all directions. One came right toward me, prompting me to scramble onto the counter.

Above, a mighty tearing sound emanated from the ceiling. Cracks spread across its surface, zigzagging like lightning bolts. Standing on the counter, I threw myself against the row of cupboards as a massive chunk of ceiling smashed onto the table.

A rolling cloud of dust filled the kitchen. I closed my eyes and again covered my mouth, blocking the scream that had formed in my throat. The wave of dust hit me. It was gritty, like sand. Small granules stuck to my skin and coated my hair.

When I opened my eyes again, the dust was still settling, revealing the damage in gut-tightening increments. The rectangular hole in the ceiling. The matching chunk on the table, now broken into several smaller pieces.

And more snakes.

A dozen. Maybe more.

They had landed as a single unit — a writhing, hissing knot of snakes so big I worried the table would collapse under their weight. Within seconds, they were untangled and oozing outward.

Across the table.

Onto the floor.

A few more stragglers dropped from the ceiling, sending up their own individual puffs of dust.

The scream I'd been withholding finally broke free and echoed through the kitchen.

I screamed for Jess.

I screamed for help.

I screamed sounds I didn't know I was capable of just because there was no other way to express my panic and revulsion and fear.

When they died down — settling as surely as the ceiling dust — I realized no amount of screaming could help in this situation. I had to jump down from the counter and run. There was no other choice.

Letting out another scream, I jumped. My bare feet hitting the floor sent the snakes around me rearing up. One struck at me. Its fangs snagged the hem of my pajama bottoms, got caught in the fabric, tugged until it was freed.

Another went for my right foot. I sprang away just in time, missing its bite, only to have a third snake aim for my left foot. It also missed.

I crossed the kitchen that way, jackrabbiting over the floor. At one point I stepped on a snake when I landed. A baby. Its body wriggling sickeningly against the bottom of my foot.

Then I was at the steps, on my way up at the same moment Jess and Maggie were coming down. They'd heard my screams and came running.

I wished they hadn't.

Because it meant that they, too, caught a glimpse of the horror in the kitchen.

Maggie screamed when she saw the snakes, making sounds similar to my own. Jess let out a horrified gurgle. I thought she was going to be sick, so I took her arm and dragged her up the stairs before she had the chance. I used my other hand to grab Maggie, who'd been standing a few steps behind her.

Together, we climbed the steps and ran through the dining room. Jess and Maggie waited on the front porch while I went to the master bedroom to fetch my keys, wallet, and a pair of sneakers.

Then the three of us fled the house, not knowing where we were going but knowing we couldn't stay inside.

Two weeks later, we did the same thing.

That time, though, we didn't return.

TEN

It's the dead of night and I'm in bed, not quite asleep but not quite awake.

My father had a phrase for that.

In the gray.

That netherworld between deep sleep and full wakefulness.

So I'm in the gray.

Or at least I think I am.

I might be dreaming, because in that fuzzy grayness I hear the armoire doors crack open.

I open my eyes, lift my head from the pillow, look to the armoire towering against the wall opposite the bed.

The doors are indeed open. Just an inch. A dark slit through which I can see into the armoire itself.

Inside is a man.

Staring.

Eyes unblinking.

Lips flat.

Mister Shadow.

This isn't real. I repeat it in my head like a chant. *This isn't real. This isn't real.*

But Mister Shadow is still there, lurking inside. Not moving. Just staring.

Then the armoire doors open and he's suddenly by the bed, leaning over me, gripping my arms and hissing, "You're going to die here."

My eyes snap open — for real this time. I sit up in bed, a terrified yelp leaping from my throat. I cast a panicked glance toward the armoire. Its doors are shut. There's no Mister Shadow. It was all just a dream.

No, not a dream.

A night terror.

One that stays with me as I get out of bed and tiptoe to the armoire. Even though I know I'm being paranoid and ridiculous, I press my ear to one of the doors, listening for a hint of noise from within.

There's nothing inside.

I know that.

To think otherwise would make me just as gullible as Wendy Davenport and any of the other people who believe the Book.

Yet fear tightens my chest as I tug the doors open just a crack. I tell myself it's vigilance that makes me peer inside. Someone broke into the house last night, and it makes sense to make sure whoever it was hasn't come back.

But I know the score.

I'm looking for Mister Shadow.

Inside the armoire, I see nothing but the dresses that still hang there, draped in darkness. They brighten once I throw the doors completely open, allowing them to be hit with the gray light coming through the bedroom windows.

The armoire is empty. Of course it is.

Even so, the nightmare lingers. Enough for me to decide to start my day, even though it's barely dawn. In the shower, each groan of the creaky pipes seems to signal Mister Shadow's approach. Every time I close my eyes against the spray of water, I expect to open them and find him here.

What bothers me so much about the nightmare is that it didn't seem like one. It had the feel of something experienced. Something real.

A memory.

Just like the one I had of me and my father painting in the kitchen.

But it can't be.

I can't remember something that never happened.

Which means it's the Book I'm remembering. A sound theory, if my father hadn't written it in first person. The reader sees everything only through his eyes, and I've read *House of Horrors* too many times to know my father never wrote such a scene.

I survive the shower unscathed, of course, and make my way downstairs. The slip of paper is still jammed in the front door. It's the same with all the windows.

Nothing has been disturbed.

I'm all alone.

No one here but us chickens.

When Dane arrives at eight, I'm already on my third cup of coffee and twitchy from the caffeine. And suspicious. Deep down, I know Dane had no role in last night's events. Yet seeing him enter Baneberry Hall without my having unlocked the gate or the front door reminds me of the section of missing wall and the cottage just beyond it. There's also the record player to consider. No one else knew we had found it yesterday. Only me and Dane, who insisted on dragging it to the desk.

"Which cottage is yours?" I ask him. "The yellow one or the brown one?"

"Brown."

Which means the one I saw last night belongs to the Ditmers. Dane's sits on the other side of the road.

"Now I have a question," he says, eyeing

the coffee mug in my hand. "Is there more of that, and can I have it?"

"There's half a pot with your name on it."

When we go down to the kitchen, I pour a giant mug and hand it to Dane.

He takes a sip and says, "Why did you ask about my cottage? Were you planning on paying me a visit?"

I note the flirtation in his voice. It's impossible to miss. This time, unlike on the night of my arrival, it's not entirely surprising. Or unwanted. But his timing could definitely be better. I have more pressing issues.

"Someone broke in last night," I say.

"Seriously?"

"Seriously."

I relay the events of last night, sparing no detail. He hears it all — the bell, the music, the missing bear, me shouting at whoever it was as they fled through the woods.

"And you thought it was me?" he says.

"Of course not," I say, massaging the truth so as not to offend him. "I was just wondering if you saw anything suspicious last night."

"Nothing. Have you asked Hannah if she did?"

"Haven't had the chance. But do you know about the breach in the wall? There's a spot where it's crumbled away."

"That's been there for decades, I think. I wrote to your father last year asking if he wanted me to repair it, but he never got back to me."

That's because he was enduring aggressive rounds of chemotherapy, even though none of us had much hope it would help things. It was just a stalling tactic. A way to stretch out my father's life by a few more months.

"Well, someone used it to get on the property," I say. "They snuck into the house, although I don't know how."

Dane grabs a chair and sits down backward, his legs straddling the chair back. "Are you certain of that? The bear could have simply fallen behind the desk. We piled quite a bit of stuff on there."

"That doesn't explain the record player. It couldn't have turned on by itself."

"Not unless there's something funky going on with the wiring. Have you noticed anything else weird?"

"Yes," I say, recalling the night of my arrival. "The light switch in the Indigo Room doesn't work. Not to mention the chandelier being on when I got home yesterday."

"How about down here?" Dane looks to the kitchen ceiling and studies the light fixture, a chunky rectangle of smoked glass and gold trim that, like the rest of the kitchen, reeks of the eighties. His gaze soon moves to the bulging, stained swath of ceiling situated directly over the table.

"Looks like water damage," he says.

"I've already added it to the very long list of things that need to be done to this kitchen."

Dane climbs onto the table and stands beneath the bulge, trying to get a closer look.

"What are you doing?"

"Checking to see if the ceiling is compromised," he says. "You may need to fix this sooner rather than later."

He pokes the bulge with an index finger. Then, using his whole hand, he pushes on it. Seeing the ceiling give way slightly under his fingers unlocks another memory I know only from the Book. My stomach clenches as I picture the plaster opening up and snakes pouring out.

"Dane, don't." My voice is more anxious than I want it to be. "Just leave it alone for now."

"This plaster is weak as hell," he says as he keeps pushing. The ceiling expands and contracts slightly — like the rise and fall of a sleeping man's chest.

It's snakes, says the whispering voice I

261

heard yesterday. My father's voice. *You know they're there, Maggie.*

If there are snakes coiled inside that ceiling, I want to pretend they're not there, just like my parents pretended the Book didn't tear our family apart.

"Dane, I'm serious," I say, angry now. "Stop doing that."

"I'm just —"

Dane's hand bursts through the ceiling, punching into the plaster all the way up to his wrist. He curses and yanks away his fist.

The ceiling quivers as small chunks of plaster rain down around him.

The seams of the patch job darken, growing more pronounced. Puffs of plaster dust pop from newly formed crevices and spiral to the table.

A small groan follows.

The sound of the ceiling giving way.

Then it falls.

A rectangular section drops away like a trapdoor. It swings toward Dane, who tries to twist out of its path. The ceiling hits him anyway, knocking him over.

He lands hard and scoots backward, narrowly missing the swath of plaster as it fully rips away from the ceiling and breaks apart against the tabletop. Dust blooms from the rubble — a foul-smelling cloud that rolls through the kitchen.

I close my eyes and press against the kitchen counter, my hands gripping the edge, bracing for the snakes I'm certain will start raining down at any moment.

I'm not surprised when something drops from the ceiling.

I've been expecting it.

I don't even flinch when I hear it land on the table with a muffled thud.

When the dust clears, Dane and I both open our eyes to see a formless blob sitting on the table like a centerpiece.

Dane blinks in disbelief. "What. The. Fuck."

He jumps down from the table and backs away. I do the opposite, moving toward it.

It's a sack. Burlap, I think. Or maybe canvas. The dust covering it makes it hard to tell. I poke it with an index finger, and whatever's inside shifts, creating a sound I can only equate to Scrabble tiles inside their fabric pouch.

"Maybe it's hidden treasure," Dane says, his voice dazed so that I can't tell if he's being silly or serious.

Saying nothing, I lift the sack and tilt it. What's inside pours out in a dusty stream and lands on the table in a dull-gray heap.

They're bones.

263

Human ones.

I know because sliding out of the sack last is a skull, which rolls atop the pile. Leathery scraps of tissue cling to the bone, out of which sprout wiry strands of hair. Its eye sockets resemble twin black holes.

Transfixed and terrified, I stare into them, knowing deep down — in a place where only my darkest thoughts and fears reside — that this is why my family left Baneberry Hall.

"You tell us, right this goddamn instant, what other problems are hiding inside that house, or I swear to Christ I'll make sure you lose your Realtor's license."

Jess's voice, already loud whenever she got angry, grew in both rage and volume as she spoke on the phone to Janie June.

"You're damn right, I'm serious!" Jess yelled in response to something Janie June said. "Just like I'm serious about suing you for everything you're worth."

All were empty threats. There was nothing we could legally do. When we agreed to buy Baneberry Hall as is, all of its problems became our problems. We also had the house inspected, which found nothing to indicate there was a family of snakes living in the ceiling. This was simply a case of Mother Nature being an utter bitch.

Yet Jess continued to shout at Janie June for another fifteen minutes, her voice ringing off the wood-paneled walls of our room.

Even for a cheap roadside motel, the Two Pines Motor Lodge had seen better days. The rooms were minuscule, the lighting was poor, and an unpleasant combination of cigarette smoke and industrial-strength cleaner clung to every surface. Had there been anywhere else in Bartleby to call home for a night, we would have gone there. But the Two Pines was the only game in town. And since our house was overrun with snakes, we couldn't be picky.

Still, we tried to make the best of a bad situation. After checking in the day before, Jess left to raid the vending machines. She returned with an armful of stale crackers, candy bars, and lukewarm sodas. We ate them sitting on the floor, Maggie all too happy to be having candy for lunch. After dinner at a diner a half-mile down the road, we spent the night crowded onto one of the twin beds, watching a TV that flickered with static no matter what channel we landed on.

Now it was morning, and all attempts to make the best of things had completely gone out the window. Not that the windows in the Two Pines could be opened. They were sealed, making the room stuffy as well as loud as Jess continued her tirade.

I was relieved when Officer Alcott knocked

266

on our door right before we were due to check out, telling us the snakes had all been cleared and that we could return home.

"What kind of snakes were they?" Jess asked after hanging up on Janie June.

"Just a bunch of red-bellies," Officer Alcott said. "Completely harmless."

"You didn't have one swimming in your coffee," I replied.

"Well, they're gone now. Animal control rounded them all up. But I have to warn you — your kitchen now looks like a disaster area. Thought I should give you a heads-up before you return, just so you're prepared."

"I appreciate that," I said.

After Officer Alcott left, we said goodbye to the Two Pines and wearily went back to a house we weren't sure we wanted to return to. I drove us home in silence, feeling stupid for never considering how the reality of owning Baneberry Hall would be far different than the fantasy I'd created in my head. But now we were faced with nothing but reality. It had taken just over a week for the dream of Baneberry Hall to curdle into a nightmare.

And it did indeed feel like a nightmare when Jess and I descended the steps into the kitchen.

Officer Alcott had been wrong. The place didn't look like a disaster area. It felt more like a war zone. London during the Blitz. The snakes were gone, but the debris remained. Chunks of ceiling. Splinters of wood. Cottony bits of insulation that probably contained asbestos. I covered my nose and mouth and told Jess to do the same before we stepped into the thick of the mess.

A good idea, it turned out, for a strong and nasty odor filled the air. It stank of dust and rot and something vaguely sulfurous that hadn't been there the day before.

I walked through the rubble with a sinking feeling in my stomach. This would be a major cleanup. A costly one. I wanted to grab Jess by the arm, turn right around, and abandon Baneberry Hall for good. It was too big, with too many problems and far too much history.

But we couldn't. We'd sunk pretty much all our money into this place. And even though we didn't have the burden of a mortgage to deal with, I knew we wouldn't be able to sell it. Not this quickly and certainly not in this condition.

We were stuck with Baneberry Hall.

Yet that didn't mean we had to like it.

Jess summed up my feelings perfectly as she stared into the gaping hole that used to be our kitchen ceiling.

"Fuck this house," she said.

ELEVEN

I sit on the front porch, unsure if I'm allowed to go back inside Baneberry Hall. Even if I can, I don't want to, despite being in desperate need of cleaning up. My hair is powdered with dust, and my face is a grimy mess. I also smell. Like sweat. Like drywall. Like puke, because that's what I did a few minutes after seeing what slid out of that sack. Which was canvas, by the way. I learned that a few hours ago. A canvas duffel bag into which the body had been stuffed.

I've learned a lot of things in the six hours I've spent on this porch. I know, for instance, that Baneberry Hall is now considered a crime scene, complete with yellow tape stretched over the front door and a state police tech van parked in the driveway.

I know that when a skeleton plummets from the ceiling onto your kitchen table, you'll get asked a lot of questions. Some you'll be able to answer. Like, "What caused the ceiling to collapse?" Or, "After finding the skeleton, did you do anything to the bones?" Others — such as "How did a skeleton get into your ceiling in the first place?" — will leave you stumped.

And I know that if *two* of you happen to be present when bones inexplicably drop out of your ceiling, you'll be questioned separately to see if your stories match up. That's what happened to me and Dane, who was taken to the back of the house for his interrogation.

Now Dane is gone, having been sent home by Chief Alcott. I remain because this is technically my house. And when human remains are found inside a house, the police make sure the owner sticks around for a bit.

Chief Alcott, who has been entering and exiting the house for hours, emerges wearing rubber gloves on her hands and paper booties over her shoes. She joins me on the porch, snapping off the gloves and wiping her hands on the front of her uniform.

"You might want to start thinking about finding a place to stay for the night," she says. "It's going to be a while. The crime scene guys have finished gathering all the remains, but there are still rooms to be examined, evidence to be collected, reports to be filed. The usual red tape. Hopefully after all this, we'll be able to figure out who it is."

"It's Petra Ditmer," I say.

She's the only person it could be. The girl who's been missing for twenty-five years. The girl who never came home the same night my family left ours.

The girl who most definitely didn't run away.

"I'm not jumping to any conclusions," the chief says. "Neither should you. We won't know anything for a day or so. The remains will be going to the forensics lab in Waterbury. They'll sort through everything, check dental records, try to make a positive ID."

It would be nice to think I could be wrong. That those bones belonged to someone else and not a sixteen-year-old girl. A particularly loathsome member of the Garson family, maybe. An unknown victim of Curtis Carver.

But I'm sure it's Petra.

"Were you able to tell how the body got into the ceiling?" I say.

"From above," Chief Alcott says. "We found a section of loose boards on the first floor. Four feet by three feet. They could be lifted right up and put back into place without anyone noticing. Add in the rug

271

that covered it, and you have yourself a perfect hiding spot."

I know. My father had mentioned it in the Book. Until now, I thought he had made it up.

So many thoughts run through my head. All of them horrible. That there were human remains inside the house the entire time I've been here. That those remains used to be Petra Ditmer, Chief Alcott's wait-and-see approach be damned. That her body had been stuffed into a duffel bag and shoved under the floorboards. That I probably walked over her dozens of times without even realizing it.

"What room was this in?" I say.

"Second one from the front. With the green walls and the fireplace."

The Indigo Room.

The same place Elsa Ditmer was roaming when I returned to Baneberry Hall. Maybe she's not as confused as we all think. There's a chance that, despite her illness, she knows more than everyone else and is struggling to find the right way to tell us.

"Listen, Maggie," Chief Alcott says. "I'm going to be honest with you here. If this does turn out to be Petra Ditmer —"

"It is."

"*If* it's her, well, it's not going to look very

272

good for your dad."

She says it gently, as if I haven't been thinking the same thing for the past six hours. As if my father's last words haven't been repeating themselves in my skull the whole time, like an echo that refuses to end.

So. Sorry.

"I understand that," I say.

"I'm going to need to ask you this sooner or later, so I might as well do it now. Do you think your father was capable of killing someone?"

"I don't know."

It's a terrible answer, and not just because of how noncommittal it is. It's terrible because it makes me feel like a shitty daughter. I want to be like those children of suspected killers I've read about in tabloids and seen on *Dateline.* People who are certain of their parent's innocence.

My father wouldn't hurt a fly.

He's a gentle soul.

I'd have known it if he was capable of murder.

No one ever believes them. *I* never believe them.

I can't bring myself to be so adamant about my father's innocence. There was a body in our ceiling, for God's sake. Then there are his last words, which are so damning I'm glad I never mentioned them to Chief Alcott. I don't want her mentally convicting my father before we know all the facts. Especially when the facts we *do* know make him look guilty as sin.

But then I think about my conversation with Brian Prince, when he all but accused my father of causing Petra's disappearance. At that moment, I was more certain and quicker to defend. What I said then still holds up. We left Baneberry Hall together. That's indisputable fact. My father couldn't have killed Petra and hidden her body while my mother and I were inside the house with him, and he wouldn't have had a chance to return once we were ensconced at the Two Pines.

But he did return. Not then, maybe, but later, coming back on the same day year after year.

July 15.

The night we left and Petra disappeared.

I have no idea what to make of that.

I'm on the verge of telling Chief Alcott about those visits, hoping she'll have a theory about them, when the front door opens and state police investigators emerge with the body. Even though there's nothing left of its human form, the skeleton is removed from the house like any other murder victim — in a body bag placed on a stretcher.

They're carrying it down the porch steps when a commotion rises from the other side of the driveway. I turn to the noise and see Hannah Ditmer pushing her way through the crowd of cops.

"Is it true?" she asks everyone and no one. "Did you find my sister?"

She spies the stretcher with the body bag, and her face goes still.

"I want to see her," she says, heading straight for the body bag.

One of the cops — a doe-eyed kid who's probably working his first crime scene — puts both blue-gloved hands on her shoulders. "There's nothing left to see," he says.

"But I need to know if it's her. *Please.*"

The tone of that word — ringing with both determination and sorrow — pulls Chief Alcott from the porch steps.

"Open it up," she says. "It won't hurt to let her take a look."

Hannah makes her way to the side of the stretcher, one hand fluttering to her throat. When the doe-eyed cop gently unzips the body bag, the sound draws others like flies to honey.

Including me.

I stop a few yards away, aware of how

unwelcome my presence might be. But, like Hannah, I need to see.

The young cop opens the bag, revealing the bones inside, arranged approximately the same way they'd be if the skeleton had been intact. Skull at the top. Ribs in the middle. Long arms resting beside them, the bones still connected by pieces of blackened tendon. The bones are cleaner than when I'd found them, some of their grime having been wiped away in the kitchen. It gives them a bronze-like sheen.

Hannah studies the remains with intense concentration.

She doesn't cry. She doesn't scream.

She simply looks and says, "Did you find anything else in there?"

Another cop steps forward, dressed in civilian clothes and a state police baseball cap.

"These were in the bag the body was found in," he says as he holds up several clear evidence bags.

Inside them are pieces of clothing that time has turned to rags. A scrap of what appears to be plaid flannel. A T-shirt darkened by stains. A pair of panties, the strips of fabric barely clinging to yellowed elastic, and a bra that's mostly now wire. Chunks of rubber in another bag indicate they had once been a pair of sneakers.

"It's her," Hannah says with a swallow of grief. "It's Petra."

"How can you tell?" Chief Alcott asks.

Hannah nods at the smallest of the evidence bags.

Inside, as clear as day, is a gold crucifix.

JULY 4
DAY 9

Walt Hibbets's gold tooth was on full display as he stared openmouthed at the hole in our kitchen ceiling.

"Snakes did all *that*?" he said.

"You should have seen it yesterday," I replied. "It looked worse then."

With the help of Elsa Ditmer, Jess and I had spent the previous afternoon cleaning the kitchen. As Petra babysat Maggie, we shoveled debris, swept floors, scrubbed the table and countertops. We were exhausted by the time we were finished, not to mention dirtier than I think we'd ever been in our lives.

Now it was time to patch the formidable hole in the ceiling. For that, I enlisted Hibbs, who brought a boy from town to help because the task was too big for just him alone. Together, they moved the kitchen table out of the way and placed a ladder under the hole. Hibbs climbed it until his head and shoulders vanished into the ceiling.

"Hand me that flashlight," he said to his helper.

Light in hand, Hibbs swept the beam around the depths of our ceiling.

The rest of us watched, our faces raised. Me, Jess, Hibbs's helper, and Petra Ditmer, who'd ostensibly dropped by to see if we again needed someone to watch Maggie during the cleanup. It was clear that morbid curiosity had drawn her. She hadn't checked on Maggie once since her arrival.

I had taken the camera down from the study the day before, snapping a few pictures in case the insurance company needed proof of the damage. That morning, I picked it up and took a shot of Petra and Jess staring at Hibbs on his ladder. Hearing the click of the shutter, Jess looked my way, then at Petra, then back to me. She was about to say something, but Hibbs beat her to it.

"Well, the good news is that there doesn't seem to be any other damage," he announced. "Beams look good. Wiring is fine. Looks like there's still some nest up here, though."

He swept the remnants of the nest onto the floor. Dust mostly, although I also spotted cobwebs, crinkly strands of dried snakeskin, and, most disturbingly, the bones of a mouse.

"Now that's strange," Hibbs said. "There's

something else in here."

He descended the ladder holding a tin box that looked to be as old as the house itself. He handed it to Jess, who took it to the kitchen table and used a rag to wipe away the dust.

"It's a biscuit tin," she said, turning it over in her hands. "Looks like it's from the late 1800s."

The tin had seen better days, even before it somehow found its way into our ceiling. A prominent dent marred the lid, and the bottom corners were edged with rust. But the color was nice — dark green accented with golden curlicues.

"Do you think it's valuable?" Petra asked.

"Not really," Jess said. "My father sold ones just like it in his shop for five bucks a pop."

"How do you think it got up there?" I asked.

"Floorboards, most likely," Hibbs said. "What room is above this one?"

I spun in place, trying to pinpoint our exact location within Baneberry Hall. Since the kitchen ran the width of the house, that meant either the great room or the Indigo Room.

It turned out to be the latter, as Hibbs and I found out when we went upstairs to check. We had been roaming both rooms, tapping the floor with the toes of our shoes, when a section of boards in the Indigo Room made a hollow sound.

Both of us dropped to our hands and knees by the boards, which were partly covered by an Oriental rug placed in the dead center of the room. Together, Hibbs and I rolled the rug out of the way, revealing a section of boards about four feet long and three feet wide that wasn't connected to the rest of the floor. We each took an end and lifted. Inside was a clear view to the kitchen, where Jess and Petra remained huddled over the biscuit tin.

It explained a lot. Not just how the tin got into the ceiling but also how a snake had gotten into the Indigo Room our first day there. It had somehow slithered up through the loose boards.

Jess, startled to see us leering down at her from the ceiling, said, "Come back down. There's something inside this tin."

By the time Hibbs and I returned to the kitchen, the biscuit tin had been opened and its contents laid out on the table. Four envelopes, turned yellow with time.

Jess reached into one and removed a sheet of paper folded into thirds. The page made a crackling noise when she smoothed it out. Like the crunch of leaves in autumn.

"It's a letter." She cleared her throat and began to read. " 'My dearest Indigo. I write these words with a heavy heart, having just

281

spoken to your father.' "

Petra grabbed it from her hands, the paper crinkling. "Ho. Ly. Shit," she said. "These are love letters."

"It looks like they were sent to Indigo Garson," Jess said.

"*Dearest* Indigo," Petra said, correcting her. "Can I have them?"

I almost told her no. That I wanted to take a look at them first. I was stopped by Jess, who shot me a warning look, reminding me of the promise I'd made. The past is in the past.

"Pretty please?" Petra said. "I'm, like, obsessed with old stuff like this."

"I suppose that's fine," I replied, eliciting a satisfied nod from Jess. Still, I couldn't help but add a caveat. "Let me know if there's anything of historical significance in them."

Petra gave me a wink. "I promise to tell you if I find anything juicy."

That night, I dreamed of old envelopes sitting in front of me. Each one I opened contained a snake that slithered into my hands and curled around my fingers. Yet I kept opening envelopes, praying at least one would be empty. None were. By the time the last envelope had been opened, I was covered in snakes. A wriggling, hissing blanket I couldn't shake off.

I woke up in a cold sweat, just in time to

catch a familiar sound fill the house.

Tap.

I looked to Jess, fast asleep beside me.

Tap-tap.

I sat up, listening as the sound made its way up the hallway.

Tap-tap-tap-tap-tap-tap-tap

A flurry of them flew past our bedroom door.

Then it was gone, replaced by music, distant but unmistakable.

"You are sixteen, going on seventeen —"

I sat up in bed, all memories of that awful dream banished from my mind. All I could think about was that song, playing in spite of the fact I had put both the record player and the albums back in the closet.

"Baby, it's time to think."

What followed felt like a dream. A recurring one that wouldn't go away no matter how much I wanted it to.

I got out of bed.

I traversed the hallway, bare feet on hard-wood.

I climbed the steps to the third floor, rising into a confounding chill emanating from the study.

The déjà vu continued as I entered the study and saw the record player sitting on the desk, looking as though I had never moved it.

"Better beware, be canny and careful —"

I plucked the needle from the album and turned off the record player. I then stood there, completely still, wondering if it really was a dream and, if so, when it would finally end.

TWELVE

The sign outside the Two Pines Motor Lodge is already aglow when I pull into the parking lot, its neon trees casting a sickly green light that spreads across the asphalt like moss. When I enter the motel office, the clerk doesn't look up from her magazine. A blessing, considering I'm sweaty, disheveled, and still coated with dust.

"A room is fifty a night," she says.

I dig out my wallet and place two twenties and a ten on the front desk. I assume this isn't the kind of place that requires a credit card. Proving me correct, the clerk takes the cash, grabs a key from the rack on the wall next to her, and slides it toward me.

"You'll be in room four," she says, still not making eye contact. "Vending machines are at the other end of the building. Checkout is at noon."

I take the key, and a puff of dirt rises from my sleeve. Because the house was still crawling with cops when I left, I have no fresh change of clothes. Just a bag of travel-size sundries I bought at a convenience store on the way here.

"Um, are there any laundry facilities here?"

"Sorry, no." The clerk finally looks at me, her expression slanted and bewildered. "But if you rinse all that in the sink now, it might be dry by morning. If not, there's a hair dryer attached to the wall."

I thank her and shuffle to my room. As I unlock the door, I wonder if it's the same one my parents and I stayed in after fleeing Baneberry Hall. If so, I doubt much has changed between stays. The interior looks as though it hasn't been updated in at least thirty years. Stepping inside feels like entering a time machine and being zapped straight back to the eighties.

I head to the bathroom, turn on the shower, and, still fully dressed, step under the spray. It seems easier than using the sink.

At first, it looks like the shower scene from *Psycho* — stained water circling the drain. When enough grime slides off my clothes for me to deem them salvageable in the short term, I take them off piece by piece.

It's not until after all the clothes are off and draped over the shower curtain, dripping soapy water, that I plop down in the tub, knees to my chest, and begin to weep.

I end up crying for half an hour, too sad, angry, and confused to do anything else. I cry for Petra, mourning her even though I have no memories of meeting her. I cry for my father, trying to square the man I thought he was with the horrible thing he might have done.

Finally, I cry for all the versions of myself that have existed through the years. Confused five-year-old. Sullen child of divorce. Furious nine-year-old. Inquisitive me. Defiant me. Dutiful me. So many incarnations, each one seeking answers, leading me to right here, to right now, to a potential truth I have no idea how to handle.

I'd hoped the shower and crying jag would invigorate me — a cleansing blast of catharsis. Instead, it only leaves me weary and prune-fingered. Since I have nothing dry to wear, I wrap myself in a towel and use a comforter from one of the twin beds as a makeshift robe. Then I sit on the edge of the stripped bed and check my phone.

Allie called while I was in the shower. The voicemail she left is jarringly perky.

"Hey, handywoman. It dawned on me today that you've sent me exactly zero pictures of the interior of that house. Get on that, girl. I want details. Cornices. Friezes. Wainscoting. Don't leave a bitch hanging."

I want to call her back and tell her all that's happened in the past twenty-four hours. I don't, because I know exactly what she'll say. That I should leave. That I should come back to Boston and forget all about Baneberry Hall.

But it's too late for that. Even if I wanted to leave, I don't think I can. Chief Alcott will surely have more questions for me. Then there are my own questions — a list a mile long, all of them still unanswered. Until I learn more about what really happened in that house, I'm not going anywhere.

I text Allie back, trying to match her in perk.

Sorry! Been too busy for pictures. I'll try to send you sexy wainscoting snaps tomorrow.

That task over, I tackle a second — another call to my mother. Unlike the first one, this time I want her to pick up.

My hope is that my mother can shed more light on my father's association with Petra. Brian Prince was right — the two of them *did* seem close in the Book. That doesn't

288

mean it's true. Only my mother knows for sure. Only she'll be able to assure me that my father is innocent.

For the first time in my life, I need her opinion.

Which is why my heart sinks when the call again goes straight to voicemail.

"Hi, Mom. It's me. I'm still in Vermont, doing work at Baneberry Hall. And, um, we found something." I pause, struck by the awfulness of the euphemism. Petra wasn't a mere something. She was a person. A vibrant young woman. "We need to talk about it. As soon as possible. Call me back. Please."

I end the call and survey the room.

It's a dump.

The wood-paneled wall opposite the room's sole window has been faded by the sun. A ceiling tile in the corner bears a stain worse than the one that was in Baneberry Hall's kitchen, which doesn't engender good thoughts. I look at the carpet. Orange shag.

There's a knock on the door. Two tentative raps that make me think it's the desk clerk coming to tell me the state of Vermont has deemed the place a health hazard and ordered the premises vacated. Instead, I open the door to find Dane standing outside.

"I'm sorry I broke your ceiling," he says sheepishly. "To make up for it, I brought apology gifts."

He lifts his hands, revealing a bottle of bourbon in one and a six-pack of beer in the other.

"I didn't know how drunk you needed to get," he explains.

I grab the bourbon. "Very."

Dane correctly takes it as an invitation to join me. He steps inside and closes the door behind him. The presence of the alcohol momentarily masked just how damn good he looks. He's in jeans and a threadbare Rolling Stones T-shirt that fits tight across his chest. There's a hole in the shirt, right where his heart is located, revealing a patch of tanned skin.

"Nice shirt," I say when Dane catches me staring.

"I've had it since I was a teenager."

"It shows."

"Nice blanket," Dane says.

I twirl a corner of the comforter. "I'm pretending it's a caftan."

Dane uncaps a beer. I open the bourbon. There aren't any glasses in the room — it's not that kind of hotel — so I swig directly from the bottle. The first swallow does nothing but burn the back of my throat. The second proves to be a repeat of the first. The third gulp is the charm. Only then do I start to feel that welcome numbness creep over me.

"How did you find me?" I say.

"Process of elimination." Dane takes a sip of beer. "I went to the house first. The police were still there, which meant you were staying somewhere else. Which in Bartleby means here."

"Lucky me," I say before two more swigs of bourbon.

The two of us fall into a comfortable silence, Dane on one bed, me on the other, content with simply drinking and staring at the Red Sox game flickering on the twenty-year-old television.

"Do you really think it was Petra Ditmer in the ceiling?" Dane eventually says.

"Yeah, I do."

"God, her poor mother."

"Did you know her?" I ask.

"I might have met her one of the times I was here visiting my grandparents. But if I did, I don't remember it."

"You said you talked to my father when he came to the house each year," I say. "What did you talk about?"

291

Dane sips his beer a moment, thinking. "The house. The grounds. If anything had needed fixing."

"That's all? Basic maintenance stuff?"

"Pretty much," Dane says. "Sometimes we'd talk about the Red Sox or the weather."

"Did he ever mention Petra Ditmer?"

"He asked me about Elsa and Hannah. How they were doing. If they needed money."

An odd question to ask someone. I want to think it was my father being charitable. But I suspect it might have been something else — like a guilt-prompted desire to pay them off.

I gulp down more bourbon, hoping it will stop me from thinking this way. I should be certain of my father's innocence. Instead, I'm the opposite. Waffling and unsure.

"Do you think it's possible to believe two things at once?" I ask Dane.

"It depends on if those things cancel each other out," he says. "For example, I believe Tom Brady is the greatest quarterback to ever play the game. I also believe he's an asshole. One belief does not negate the other. They can exist at the same time."

"I was talking about something more personal."

"You're in New England. The Patriots *are*

personal."

On one hand, I'm grateful for the way Dane is trying to take my mind off things with the booze and the banter, but it's also frustrating — the same kind of avoidance tactics my parents used.

"You know what I'm talking about," I say. "I truly believe my father wasn't capable of killing anyone, let alone a sixteen-year-old girl. He was never violent. Never raised a hand to hurt me. Plus, I knew him. He was doting and decent and kind."

"You also think he was a liar," Dane says, as if I need reminding.

"He was," I say. "Which is why I can't stop thinking that maybe he *did* do something. That if the Book was a lie, then maybe everything about him was. The things he said. The way he acted. His entire life. Maybe no one really knew him. Not even me."

"You really think he killed Petra?"

"No," I say.

"Then you think he's innocent."

"I didn't say that, either."

The truth is that I don't know what I think. Even though all signs point to his being involved in Petra's death, I'm having a hard time seeing my father as a killer. Equally difficult is thinking he's completely innocent. He lied to me literally until the end of his life. And people don't lie unless they're hiding something.

Or want to spare someone the truth.

Whatever that truth is, I know Petra's death was part of it.

"One thing is clear," Dane says, interrupting my thoughts. "Your reason for coming here has changed. Big-time."

My plans for the house have, that's for certain. Even if the police let me back into Baneberry Hall to renovate it, I'm not sure I still want to. From a brutally practical standpoint, it's foolish. That house will sell for a wisp of what it's worth, if it can be sold at all after this new tragic development.

But I look at the project through a more human lens. Petra Ditmer had spent more than two decades rotting inside Baneberry Hall. A horrible fate. When I think about it that way, it's easy to agree with Chief Alcott. Baneberry Hall should be reduced to rubble.

"I came here to learn the truth," I tell Dane. "That's still my goal. Even if I might not like what that truth turns out to be."

"And the house?"

"I'll be back there tomorrow." I throw my arms open, gesturing to the sun-bleached wall and stained ceiling and shag carpet that smells of mildew. "But tonight, I get to live in the lap of luxury."

Dane shifts on the edge of his bed until we're facing each other, our knees almost touching. The mood in the room has changed. An electricity passes between us, tinged with heat. Only then do I realize my arms-wide gesture has thrown the blanket from my shoulders, leaving me sitting in just a towel.

"I can stay here with you," Dane says, his voice husky. "If you want me to."

God, it's tempting. Especially with a quarter bottle of bourbon in me and Dane looking the way he does. My gaze keeps returning to that hole in his shirt and its tantalizing glimpse of flesh. It makes me want to see what he looks like without the shirt. It would be easy to make that happen. One tug of this towel is all it would take.

And then what? All my conflicting emotions and confusion will still be there in the morning, this time complicated further by the mixing of work and pleasure. Once you tie the two of them together, it's nearly impossible to untangle them again.

"You should go," I say as I pull the blanket back around my shoulders.

Dane nods once. No asking me if I'm absolutely, positively sure. No turning on the charm in the hope I'll change my mind.

"See you tomorrow, then," he says.

He takes the beer but leaves the bourbon. Another unwise companion to spend the night with. I want to finish off the bottle and pass out into sweet, drunken oblivion. Like sleeping with Dane, it would hurt more than help. So, with great reluctance, I tighten the blanket around me and take the bottle to the bathroom to pour the rest down the sink.

JULY 5
DAY 10

"Are you fucking with me?"

Even though I knew it was the worst possible way to greet my wife in the morning, I couldn't help it. Discovering the record player back on the desk and playing that infernal song had put me in a mood so dark that I'd spent the night tossing and turning, worried that as soon as I drifted off, the music would return.

When the thud from upstairs arrived at exactly 4:54, I knew sleep would never arrive.

My agitation was only heightened when I went down to the first floor and found the chandelier glowing as bright as the sun.

By the time Jess entered the kitchen, I couldn't help but confront her.

"What are you talking about?" she said, her expression a mix of hurt and confusion.

"You know damn well what I'm talking about. The record player was on again last night."

"In your study?"

I huffed out a frustrated sigh. "Yes, in my study. I put it in the closet, but last night there it was, back on my desk and playing that stupid song. So, if this is some sort of prank, I need you to know it's not funny. Not anymore."

Jess backed against the counter, shrinking into herself. "I don't know why you think I had anything to do with it."

"Because you're the only person who could have done it."

"You're forgetting about our daughter."

Upstairs, the doorbell chimed. I ignored it. Whoever it was could wait.

"Maggie's not that crafty."

"Really?" Jess said. "I know you think she's Daddy's little girl and can do no wrong, but she's not as innocent as she looks. I'm pretty sure half of this imaginary-friend stuff is just to get your attention."

I barked out a laugh so bitter it surprised even me. "Is that your excuse for this record-player bullshit?"

By then, I knew the fight was about more than just a record player. It was about everything that had happened since we moved to Baneberry Hall. Ten days of headaches and regrets and tension that had gone unaddressed until that moment. Now it was out, flaring up with the heat and speed of a wildfire.

"I didn't touch your record player!" Jess

shouted. "And if I did, it would have been justified, considering you're the one who forced us to move into this godforsaken house."

"I didn't force you!" I yelled back. "You loved this house, too."

"Not as much as you. I saw it on your face the moment we stepped inside. That this was the house you wanted."

"You could have said —"

"No?" Jess said, cutting me off. "I tried, Ewan. It didn't work. It never works. You debate and cajole until you get your way. Always. And Maggie and I have no choice but to go along with it. Now we're in a house with a fucking graveyard out back and our daughter acting weirder than she's ever acted before and then this goddamn ceiling —"

She stopped, red-faced and sobbing. Tears streamed down her cheeks — a sight I couldn't bear under any circumstances. I was about to pull her into my arms, hug her as tight as I could, and tell her everything would be okay. But then she spoke again, and it stopped me cold.

"And don't even get me started on Petra."

My spine stiffened. "What about her?"

"I've seen the way you look at her, Ewan. I saw you take her picture yesterday."

"You were in the picture, too."

"Only because I happened to be standing there."

I was incredulous. I had as much sexual interest in Petra Ditmer as I did in Hibbs.

"She's a child, Jess. The idea that I have the hots for her is ridiculous."

"Almost as ridiculous as me getting up in the middle of the night to turn on a record player I've never even seen."

Jess wiped her eyes and left the kitchen. I followed, chasing her up the steps to the first floor.

"Jess, wait!"

She continued up the servants' steps just outside the dining room, storming upstairs. I stopped, caught short by the sight of someone standing in the great room, framed by the doorway that separated it from the dining room.

Petra Ditmer.

"I rang the doorbell," she said. "Maggie let me in."

"How long have you been here?" I said.

"Not long," Petra said, even though the flush on her cheeks made it clear she'd heard, if not everything, then at least a big chunk of our argument.

"This isn't a good time, Petra."

"I know, and I'm sorry." She looked at the floor, nervous. "But I read the letters last night.

The ones that were in the ceiling."

Petra dug into the backpack she was carrying and removed the envelopes, now individually sealed in plastic bags. Pressing them into my hands, she said, "You'll want to read these, Mr. Holt."

I dropped the letters onto the dining room table. At that moment, they were the least of my concerns. "I will, but —"

Petra scooped them up and pushed them back into my hands. "Now," she said. "Trust me."

The letters sat open on the floor of the Indigo Room, where Petra and I had retreated after she demanded I read them. There were four of them, handwritten in a swooping, elegant script.

"All of them were written by someone named Callum," Petra said. "They're addressed to Indigo, which makes me think she hid them in the floorboards after she read them. You know, for safekeeping."

"Why would she need to hide them?"

Petra pointed to the first letter. "The answer's right there."

I picked it up, the paper as rigid as parchment, and began to read.

July 3, 1889

My dearest Indigo,
I write these words with a heavy heart,
having just spoken to your father. As we
both feared, my darling, he has unconditionally refused to give me permission to
ask for your hand in marriage. The
reasons for his decision were exactly the
ones we had anticipated — that I lack
the means to provide you with the life-
style to which you are accustomed and
that I have proven myself not a whit in
the world of business or finance. Although I pleaded with him to change his
thinking, assuring him that if you become my wife you will want for nothing,
he refused to entertain the matter. Our
plan to join our lives as husband and
wife the proper way — with your father's
blessing, before the eyes of God, and
witnessed by those closest to us — has
come to a shattering end.

Yet I retain hope, my beloved, for there
is another way in which we can become
man and wife, although it is one I wished
with all my heart to avoid. Since your
father has made it abundantly clear his
opinion won't be swayed, I boldly suggest we defy his wishes. I know of a

reverend in Montpelier who has agreed to join us in marriage without the consent of your family. I know full well that elopement is a drastic undertaking, but if your love for me is as strong as you claim, then I beseech you to consider it. Please reply immediately, telling me of your decision. Even if it is no, I assure you I will remain, always and forever —

Your faithfully devoted,

Callum

I lowered the letter, my gaze moving to the painting above the fireplace. Hibbs had told me the story about Indigo's failed attempt to run off with the man who'd lovingly created that portrait, and I wondered if he and the letter writer were one and the same.

Standing, I approached the painting, once again amazed at the amount of detail on display. The joyful spark in Indigo's eyes. The hint of a smile in her ruby lips. The individual strands of fur on the rabbit she was holding. Other than the cracked paint around the rabbit's eyes, the work was flawless. I wasn't surprised one bit when I looked to the bottom right corner and found the artist's name.

Callum Auguste.

"It was him," Petra said, suddenly beside me. "He's the dude who wrote the letters."

"Yes," I said, chuckling at her word choice. "The very same dude."

We returned to the letters on the floor, where I proceeded to read the rest, beginning with one dated three days after the first.

July 6, 1889

My darling Indigo,

My heart has been singing with joy since receiving your reply, and will continue to rejoice for the rest of my days. Thank you, my dearest one, for agreeing to my plan, despite how much it pains you to disobey your father's wishes. I know the bond between you is stronger than what most fathers and daughters share. You are the apple of his eye, and one cannot blame him for wanting only the best for you. It is my greatest hope that he will soon come to understand and accept what we already know — that all you and I require is our undying love.

I have spoken again with the reverend who has agreed to marry us in secret. He would like to perform the ceremony within the next two weeks. While I'm aware that doesn't provide you with ample time to prepare for such a life-changing event, it's better to do this sooner than later. To delay our nuptials any longer would be to risk your father discovering what we are planning. I have already made arrangements to have a carriage waiting outside Baneberry Hall's gate at the stroke of midnight in nine days' time. At the reins will be a trusted friend of mine who has already agreed to take you to the place where we will exchange vows. A place that I am reluctant to disclose in this letter, for fear it will somehow get into the wrong hands. Prepare as much as you are able as discreetly as possible. When the clock strikes midnight, make your escape, hoping that someday your father's opinion of our marriage will have changed and you will be allowed to return to the home you so love, this time as my wife.

Forever yours,
Callum

July 10, 1889

My beloved Indigo,
Your most recent letter has me concerned, more than I care to admit. Do you suspect your father has somehow received word of our plan? If so, what reason do you have to believe he knows?

I pray this suspicion is merely the result of nervousness about what we are about to do, for no good can result from your father's knowledge. I urge you once again to go about this with the utmost secrecy.

Yours in devotion,
Callum

July 15, 1889

Fear grips me as I write these words — a deep, bone-rattling fear that your father plans to stop our impending marriage by any means necessary. I gather from your last letter than he does indeed know what we have planned, even though he has yet to admit as much. Do not trust him, my dearest. The only thing preventing me from storming the doors of Baneberry Hall and stealing you away is the knowledge that mere hours stand between now and the stroke of midnight. Remain strong and safe until then, my love.

Yours for eternity,
Callum

I lowered the last letter in a state of sadness, knowing that Indigo never did join poor, besotted Callum at the altar. Petra, sensing my grief, said, "She never married him, did she?"

"No," I said. "The story I heard is that her father found out, stopped her from eloping, and forbade her from ever seeing Callum again."

Petra let out a low whistle. "Damn. What did Indigo do?"

"She killed herself."

"Damn." Her expression grew pensive. "Indigo was how old when she died?"

"Sixteen," I said.

"So am I. And trust me, if I was in love with someone, nothing would stop me from seeing him. Not even my mother. And I definitely wouldn't kill myself."

She sorted through the letters, ignoring their delicate state. When she stabbed at one with an index finger, tiny chips fell from the page.

"Right here," she said, reading aloud. *" 'Your father plans to stop our impending marriage by any means necessary.' "*

She passed the letter to me, and I read it again, paying close attention to Callum's warning about William Garson.

Do not trust him, my dearest.

"What if —" Petra stopped herself, her cheeks flushing again, as if she knew what she was about to say was stupid. "What if

Indigo Garson didn't commit suicide? What if she was murdered by her father?"

I was thinking the same thing. I'd always thought the official story I got from Hibbs was missing a key element that tied it all together. This, I realized, could be it.

"I think you might be onto something," I said. "The question is, what can we do about it?"

Petra arched a brow, as if the answer was obvious.

"We do some research," she said. "And see if we can prove that William Garson was a killer."

THIRTEEN

In the morning, I spend an hour blow-drying my still-damp clothes before checking out of the motel. It says a lot about the accommodations in Bartleby that I'd rather return to an allegedly haunted house that had a skeleton in the ceiling than spend another night at the Two Pines.

But it's more than just the sad state of the motel that brings me back to Baneberry Hall. I return because I need to. The truth — about why we left, about why my father kept coming back, about what happened to poor Petra — is getting closer. Now it's just a matter of finding it.

I even get a police escort, courtesy of Chief Alcott, who stops by the motel as I'm checking out to give me the all-clear to return home. She insists on steering her battered Dodge Charger ahead of me the whole way home. When we reach Baneberry Hall, I understand why.

The front gate is blocked by reporters from both print and television. Several news vans have set up camp on the side of the road, their back doors open and beefy cameramen waiting inside like bored children. They leap from their vans when we pull up to the gate, cameras swinging my way. The reporters crush around my truck, including Brian Prince, his bow tie giving his I-told-you-so expression an extra veneer of smugness.

"Maggie!" he shouts. "Do you think your father murdered Petra Ditmer?"

I keep driving, inching the truck forward until I'm at the gate. Chief Alcott climbs out of her cruiser, armed with the keys I handed to her before we left the Two Pines. She ambles through the crowd and unlocks the gate.

"Come on now," she says to the scrum of reporters, clearing them with several sweeps of her arms. "Let her through."

Brian Prince is the last to move. He raps on the truck's window, begging me for a quote.

"Talk to me, Maggie. Tell me your side of the story."

I pound the gas pedal and the truck surges forward, leaving Brian flailing in a cloud of dust. I don't slow until I'm up the hill and in front of Baneberry Hall. It looks more sinister now than it did this time yesterday, even though I know that's impossible. The only things that have changed are what I now know about the place and the length of broken police tape dangling from the front door.

Chief Alcott pulls into the driveway behind me. She gets out of her Charger, and I hop out of the truck. We stand at a distance, facing each other like movie cowboys before a gunfight, both of us fully aware that we might not be on the same side. It all depends on how guilty I think my father is, something that changes by the minute.

"I was hoping we could talk," she says. "The folks in Waterbury did a preliminary examination of the remains last night."

"It's Petra, isn't it?"

"Not officially. They still need to check dental records. But the bones belonged to a female in her late teens. So, it's looking pretty likely that it's her."

Even though I'm not surprised, the news leaves me feeling unmoored. I go to the porch and sit on the steps, my damp jeans chafing my thighs. I'd feel more comfortable in a change of clothes, but I'm not quite ready to enter Baneberry Hall.

"Do they know her cause of death?"

"Not definitively," Chief Alcott says. "Her skull was fractured. That's the only damage they could positively identify. They can't conclude that's what killed her. That'll be hard to do, considering the condition those bones were in."

"Why did you think Petra ran away all those years ago?" I say.

"Who says I did?"

"Brian Prince."

"Figures," she mutters. "The truth is that I *did* suspect something might have happened to Petra."

"Why didn't you do anything about it?"

"I wasn't in charge, so I didn't call the shots. That was three chiefs ago. No one else on the force gave two shits about a teenage girl. I did, but I stayed quiet anyway, which is something I've regretted every damn day for the past twenty-five years." Chief Alcott takes a deep breath to collect herself. "But now I *do* get to call the shots. And I want to know what happened to that poor girl. So, let's talk suspects. Other than your father, who else do you think could have put that body under your floorboards?"

"I should be asking you that," I say. "Come to think of it, should we be discussing this at all?"

The chief removes her hat and runs a

hand through her short silver hair. "I don't see any harm in us talking. I'm just trying to cover all the bases. You shouldn't consider me the enemy, Maggie."

"You think my father murdered someone."

"You haven't given me any reason to think otherwise."

Had my mother called me back, I might be better equipped for this conversation. But she didn't, even after I called her again this morning. Now I can only blindly toss theories like darts in a dive bar.

"I know my father looks guilty," I say. "And, for all I know, he might have done it. But if he did, then it doesn't make sense why he mentioned Petra so much in his book. If he had some kind of affair with her, like Brian Prince thinks, or he killed her, like probably everyone thinks, it would have made more sense not to mention her at all."

"Maybe that's what he was hoping we'd think," Chief Alcott suggests.

"Or maybe someone else did it."

The chief jerks her head in the direction of the front door. "There wasn't a whole lot of people with access to that house."

"Walt Hibbets," I say. "He had keys to the place."

"True," Chief Alcott says. "But what would his motive have been? Petra lived

313

across the road from him all her life. He would have had plenty of chances to kill her. Not that old Walt was the killing type. But if he was, why wait until then?"

"Maybe he knew Baneberry Hall was empty," I say, grasping. "And he put the body there to frame my father."

"Hiding a body isn't the best way to frame someone. But it's interesting you mentioned someone from the Hibbets family." The chief's tone is loaded, making me squirm in discomfort. My jeans squeak on the steps. "I was surprised to see Dane here yesterday."

"He's helping me work on the house," I say. "Why is that a surprise? He's a contractor, after all, although he said business was light."

"Did you ever stop to wonder why?"

I hadn't. I didn't give it any thought whatsoever. I needed help, Dane was there, we made a deal.

"What are you getting at?" I ask.

"I'm saying that most folks here aren't too keen on hiring an ex-con," the chief says.

My breath catches in my throat. This bit of news isn't quite as shocking as yesterday's events, but few things are.

"What did he do?"

"Aggravated assault," the chief says. "This

was in Burlington. About eight years back. There was a bar fight. Dane got overzealous and beat the other guy until he was unconscious. Cut him up real bad, to boot. His victim spent a month in the hospital, and Dane spent a year in prison."

My mind seizes on an image of Dane in a dive bar, slamming his fist repeatedly into a stranger's dazed, bloody face. I want to think he isn't capable of such violence, but I'm unsure of everything, at least when it comes to the men in my life.

Chief Alcott senses this and says, "I wouldn't fret over it, if I were you." She stands, but not before giving my knee a friendly pat. "You have bigger things to worry about."

She puts her hat back on, returns to her cruiser, and drives away, leaving me alone on the steps to consider three things. One, that Dane — the man I came *this* close to sleeping with last night — has a violent streak. Two, that I never did come up with a good reason as to why Chief Alcott shouldn't suspect my father. And three, that it's possible she brought up the former to prevent me from doing the latter.

This prompts one last thought — that despite her assurances to the contrary, maybe Chief Tess Alcott has her own agenda.

I don't enter the house until thirty minutes after Chief Alcott departs. Part of that time is spent talking to an understandably pissed-off Allie.

"Why didn't you tell me a dead girl was found inside Baneberry Hall?" she says as soon as I answer the phone.

"I didn't want you to worry."

"Well, I am," she says. "Especially because I had to see it on Twitter. 'Body found in *House of Horrors* mansion.' That's what the headline said. And for a second, I thought it was you."

My heart sinks, for multiple reasons. I hate the fact that Allie, even for a moment, thought something bad had happened to me. Then there's the matter of Baneberry Hall once again being national news. Because if Allie saw it, lots of people have as well.

"I'm sorry," I say. "I should have told you."

"Damn right, you should have."

"But everything is crazy right now. I found the body of that poor girl, and the police think my father did it, and someone broke into the house."

"There was an intruder?" Allie says, unable to conceal her alarm. "When?"

"Two nights ago. They didn't do anything. Just roamed through the house a little."

"That sounds like something," Allie says.

"I'm not in any danger."

"Yet." Allie pauses to take a calming breath I can hear through the phone. "Maggie, I get that you need answers. I really do. But this isn't worth it."

"It will be," I say. "Something happened in that house the night we left. And I've spent most of my life wondering what it was. I can't leave now. I have to see this through."

Allie says she understands, even though it's clear she doesn't. I don't expect her to. Most people faced with such a fucked-up situation would be content to go home, let the police handle it, and wait for answers. But cut-and-dried answers about how Petra died will tell me only half the story.

I need context.

I need details.

I need *truth*.

If my father killed Petra, I want to know about it, mostly because then I'll know how to feel about him.

I came here hoping to forgive my father.

I won't be able to forgive a murderer.

Which is why I also can't let go of the idea that he's innocent. I am my father's daughter. We chose different paths and we had our share of disagreements, but I had more in common with him than I do with my mother. He and I were far more alike than we were different. If he's a killer, what does that make me?

After ending the call with Allie, it takes me ten more minutes before I get the courage to enter Baneberry Hall. On my way in, I yank off the remnant of police tape, which flutters away like a windblown leaf. I pause in the vestibule, tentative. A replay of my arrival. The only difference is that now Baneberry Hall actually feels haunted.

I tread quietly deeper into the house. Out of respect to Petra, I suppose. Or maybe a subconscious fear that her spirit still lingers. In the Indigo Room, the area rug's been rolled against the wall. The police took the floorboards that used to lie under it as evidence. Now there's a hole in the floor roughly the same size and shape as a child's coffin.

I peer through it to the kitchen below, which has been cleared of all ceiling debris. That's likely also evidence now, swept into cardboard boxes and carried out of the house.

I go to the parlor next. Sitting on the hulking secretary desk is the photo of my family in its gold frame. I turn it around and face the image of us together and happy and completely oblivious about what was to come. My handsome, charming father. My smiling mother. Gap-toothed me. All of them strangers to me now.

I spend a moment gazing wistfully at the picture.

Then I slam it against the desk.

Again.

And again.

And again.

I keep slamming until the glass is broken into a hundred pieces, the metal is bent, and the image of my family is creased beyond recognition.

A more accurate depiction.

My actions, though cathartic, have left the desk littered with glass shards. I try to sweep them together with the nearest piece of paper I can find, which turns out to be the folded note bearing that single, quizzical word.

WHERE??

I'd forgotten about it in the turmoil of the last few days. At the time, I had no idea

319

what it meant. Seeing it again brings a flash of understanding.

Petra.

Someone had been looking for her, even if the police weren't. And they came right to the source — my father.

I search the desk, looking for similar messages. I find them in a lower drawer. Stuffed inside, in no discernible order, are dozens of sheets of paper. Some are folded. Others lie flat. Some bear edges made crisp by time. Others are as white as down.

I pick one up, its message written in a wide, messy script.

WHY?

I grab another page. A yellow-edged one. The handwriting is the same, albeit slightly neater. The lines aren't as wobbly. The script less frenzied.

TELL ME WHERE SHE IS

I scoop up every page that's been shoved into the desk, arranging them in a flat pile. I then shuffle through them, reading each one. They all bear similar messages.

WHAT DID YOU DO TO HER????

I sort through the stack again, slapping the pages on top of one another like a bank teller counting out cash.

There are twenty-four of them.

One for every year since Petra Ditmer disappeared.

And the last one I see tells me exactly who wrote them.

WHERE IS MY SISTER?

The interior of Bartleby's library bore an uncanny resemblance to Baneberry Hall. Large and charmingly Gothic, it was a riot of arched windows and carved cornices. Stepping inside literally felt like coming home. I wasn't surprised when I saw the bronze plaque just inside the door announcing that the library had been paid for by William Garson.

A portrait of him hung on the other side of the hallway. I recognized his face from the one in the great room, although this portrait's painter had been far more kind. Mr. Garson's features were softer, his eyes not as dark. With his top hat and white beard, he looked more like a kindly old man than someone capable of killing his daughter.

The library's main reading room was a wood-trimmed octagon in the middle of the building. The circulation desk sat in the center of the room — the library's beating heart. Fanning outward from the desk like spokes on a wheel were wooden bookshelves that stretched from floor to ceiling on two separate levels. Staircases flanking the door swept upward to the second floor.

That's where I found Petra.

She had commandeered an entire table, which was covered with books about Bartleby history and several bulky file folders. "You're here," she said when she saw me. "I didn't think you were going to show."

I almost didn't, for Jess's sake. Although she had apologized for what she said yesterday — an exhausted "I'm sorry about the Petra stuff. I was just being jealous and ridiculous" — I knew she wouldn't like the idea of my meeting alone with Petra. Especially when our intention was to dig into Baneberry Hall's history, something I promised my wife I wouldn't do. But my curiosity about Indigo Garson's fate overrode any apprehension I had about our meeting. It always won out over common sense.

"Looks like you've been busy," I said as I took a seat next to Petra.

"I had help." Petra patted the stack of folders. "The reference librarian gave me this. Said they get a lot of people coming in wanting to know more about your house. Does it feel weird living in a place that's famous?"

"I haven't been there long enough," I said, leaving out how Baneberry Hall feels weird for a bunch of other reasons. "Does it feel weird living almost literally in its shadow?"

Petra snagged a lock of blond hair and absently twirled it. "Not really. I haven't lived anywhere else to know the difference, but my mom gets weird sometimes."

"How so?"

"She always prays before she goes up there. Kisses her crucifix. Stuff like that. She told me once that it was haunted."

"She really thinks that?"

"She's just superstitious," Petra said as she grabbed one folder and handed another to me. "It's the German in her. Very strict. *Very* Christian. Like, if she knew I was doing this, she'd tell me no good could come of it. That it will only lead to me being haunted by William Garson's evil spirit or something."

The folder she'd given me was filled with newspaper clippings. Most of them came from the local paper, the *Bartleby Gazette,* which looked to be almost as old as Baneberry Hall. The first clipping was a photocopy of a ragged front page dated September 3, 1876. The top story — bearing the headline OPEN HOUSE AT GARSON MANSE — was about the evening William Garson invited the entire town to visit his grand estate.

Many other articles in the folder had a similarly fluffy bent. Headlines about balls and birthdays and famous visitors to Baneberry Hall. I especially got a kick out of one from 1940. *HOLLYWOOD ROYALTY SUMMERS IN BARTLEBY.* The article included a blotchy photo of Clark Gable and Carole Lombard having cocktails in the Indigo Room.

But tales of death also lurked among the stories of glamour and frivolity. Far more than I had been led to believe. A string of tragedies that began with the death of Indigo Garson. A car accident in 1926 that killed another member of the Garson clan. A drowning in the bathtub in 1941. Two bed-and-breakfast guests dying mysteriously, one in 1955 and the other a year later. A fatal fall down the steps in 1974.

Sorting through them made me think of what Hibbs had said.

Baneberry Hall remembers.

It also made me wonder why he never bothered to tell me about all the other deaths that happened there. It was impossible to think he simply didn't know about them. His family had worked those grounds for generations. Which meant there was a reason he omitted those other deaths.

Maybe he didn't want to scare us away.

Or maybe he never wanted us to know.

I came to the *Gazette* article about Curtis and Katie Carver, the most recent tragedy to occur there. The writer wasted no time in getting to the grisly details.

A man and his young daughter are dead in what Bartleby police have called a bizarre murder-suicide at Baneberry Hall, one of the town's oldest and most infamous addresses. Police say Curtis Carver, 31, smothered his six-year-old daughter, Katie, before killing himself — a crime that has sent shock waves through the normally quiet community.

The photo that ran with the article was the same picture Jess had found during our tour of the house. Marta Carver and young Katie in matching dresses and smiles, Curtis keeping his distance, looking simultaneously handsome and sinister.

I put the clipping on a pile of articles about the other Baneberry Hall deaths. I wanted to read more — about all of them. But we were there to learn about William and Indigo Garson. The others would have to wait.

"I'm going to make copies of these," I told Petra. "I'll be right back."

The library's only photocopier sat large and heavy just outside the door of the octagonal reading room, offering copies for a dime apiece. Digging out change from my pocket, I got to work, making copies of each article.

My final copy — a reproduction of the article about the Carver family, the photo of them splotchy and dark — was sliding out of the machine when a woman passed by and entered the reading room. The mood inside the library shifted at her presence. It was like an electric pulse sparking across the entire place, silent yet keenly felt by all. People glanced up from books. Whispered conversations came to a sudden stop.

Turning around, I saw the same face that was on the photocopy.

Marta Carver.

Trying to ignore the unwanted attention, she browsed a shelf of new releases, her head held high. But then she caught me staring, and I had no choice but to approach her. Nervously, I said, "Excuse me. Mrs. Carver?"

She blinked at me from behind her spectacles. "Yes?"

"I'm Ewan Holt."

Her posture straightened. It was clear she knew who I was.

"Hello, Mr. Holt."

We shook hands. Hers was small and contained the slightest tremble.

"I'm sorry to bother you, but I was wondering if there was anything still at Baneberry Hall that you'd like to keep. If so, I'd be happy to deliver it to you."

"I have everything I need, thank you."

"But all that furniture —"

"Is yours now," she said. "You paid for it."

Although her voice wasn't unkind, I sensed an unspoken *something* humming just beneath her words. It was, I realized, fear.

Marta Carver was terrified of Baneberry Hall.

"It's not just the furniture," I said. "I've found other things that I think belong to you. A camera. A record player. I think there are some photographs still there."

At the mention of photographs, Marta Carver glanced at the freshly made copies still clutched in my hand. The top one, I realized, was the article about her husband murdering her daughter. I flipped the copy inward against my body, but it was too late. She'd already seen it, and reacted with an involuntary flinch.

"I need to go," she said. "It was nice meeting you, Mr. Holt."

Mrs. Carver slipped past me and quickly left the library. All I could do was mumble an apology at her back, feeling not only stupid but rude. I returned, vowing never to bother her again.

"Look at this," Petra said when I came back to the table.

She was reading a *Gazette* article about Indigo Garson's death, written a few months after it happened. I looked over her shoulder at the headline.

GARSON DEEMED INNOCENT IN DAUGHTER'S DEATH

"According to this, a maid told the police that on the night of Indigo's suicide, she saw Mr. Garson in the kitchen putting what looked like a bunch of baneberries in a bowl. She was coming up from the cellar, so he didn't see her. She said he took the berries and a spoon upstairs. An hour later, Indigo was dead. I just know he killed her, Mr. Holt."

"Then why wasn't he put on trial for her murder?"

"That's what this whole bullshit article is about. How there wasn't any evidence and how even if there was, a man like William Garson would never do such a thing. 'An exemplary member of the community.' That's a direct quote from the police." Petra pointed out the words with a stab of her index finger. "I know things were different back then, but it's like they didn't even try. 'Oh, a teenager is dead. Who cares?' But you can be damn sure that if it was the other way around — if Indigo had been seen bringing a freaking bowl of baneberries to her father — she would have been hung in the town square."

She slumped in her chair and took a deep breath, her rant over. I understood her anger. We'd reached a dead end. Even though both of us believed William Garson had killed his daughter, there was likely no way to prove it.

"I'm going to go," Petra said. "I'm too riled up. I need to get ice cream. Or scream into a pillow. I haven't decided. See you tomorrow."

I looked at her, confused. "Tomorrow?"

"The sleepover. We're still coming, right?"

After all the ceiling chaos and fighting with Jess, I'd forgotten about the plan to have Hannah and Petra spend the night at Baneberry Hall. It wasn't a good time for a sleepover. It felt like the worst time, actually. But Maggie was in desperate need of friends. I couldn't deny my daughter that.

"It's still on," I said as I tucked the articles under my arm, preparing to leave the reading room. "Maggie can't wait."

FOURTEEN

The reporters are still at the front gate.

I see them when I reach the end of the driveway, milling on the other side of the wrought iron, waiting for me to emerge. Now that I have, they surge forward, shoving their microphone-clutching hands through the gate's bars like a horde of undead in a zombie movie.

Among them is Brian Prince, his bow tie askew as he elbows others out of the way, angling for prime position.

"Maggie!" he shouts. "Talk to me! What are your plans now for Baneberry Hall?"

Behind him, flashbulbs pop into firecracker brightness. Caught in their glare, I retreat, slowly at first, shuffling backward before turning my back to the crowd. Soon I'm running up the driveway, winding my way up the hillside toward Baneberry Hall.

In order to leave this place, I'm going to need a different escape route. Lucky for me,

I know of one. Also lucky: Brian Prince and the other reporters haven't found it yet.

Veering off the driveway, I plunge into the woods and start to descend the hill again, this time under the cover of the trees. I push through the forest until I reach the stone wall that surrounds the property. A walk alongside the wall leads me to the section that's crumbled away. I pass through it and, five minutes later, find myself emerging from the woods behind Elsa Ditmer's cottage.

Because there could also be reporters waiting out front, I stick to the backyard, crossing it quickly before hopping onto the rear porch. The back door swings open before I get a chance to knock. Hannah stands just inside, her jaw clenched.

"What do you want?" she says.

"To say I'm sorry. For your loss."

"That's not going to bring my sister back."

"I know," I say.

Hannah bites the inside of her cheek and asks, "You've got anything else to say?"

"Actually, yes." I reach into my purse and pull out the notes, all twenty-four of them. "I was wondering if you could explain these."

She steps out of the way, allowing me entry into the cottage. I follow her to the kitchen. On the way, we pass the living room, where a game show blares from a console television. I get a glimpse of Elsa Ditmer cocooned in a recliner, a knit blanket pulled to her chin.

I wonder if Hannah has told her that Petra's been found. If so, I wonder if Elsa understands.

In the kitchen, I'm hit with the smell of cigarette smoke and cooking oil. We sit at a kitchen table with one leg that's shorter than the others. The table tilts when Hannah grabs a cigarette and lights up. It tilts back when I place the notes in front of her.

Hannah doesn't bother giving them a glance. It's clear she's seen them before.

"I started writing them a year after you guys left and Petra vanished," she says. "That damn book your dad wrote had just come out, and I was mad."

"That the three of you were in it?"

Hannah gives me an incredulous look. "That he did something to Petra and got away with it. When your dad showed up out of the blue — literally a year to the day after Petra disappeared — well, I couldn't deal with it anymore."

She reaches for the notes, sorting through them until she finds the one that led me to her door.

"I was so angry when I wrote this," Hannah says, flattening the note against the tilting table. "I thought it would be therapeutic or something. To finally write down the question I'd been thinking about for an entire year. It didn't help. It only made me angrier. So angry that I marched up to Baneberry Hall and left it on the front porch. It was gone after your father left the next day. That's when I knew he had seen it."

"And then it became an annual tradition," I say.

Hannah exhales a stream of smoke. "I thought that if I did it enough times, I might finally get an answer. And after a few years, I think your father had come to expect it."

"Did he ever confront you about it?"

"Nope," Hannah says. "He never talked to us. I guess he was afraid of what I would say."

"But he still paid your mother?" I asked.

"Every month." Hannah taps her cigarette against a ceramic ashtray and takes another long puff. "He paid a little more every year, directly deposited into my mom's account. Out of guilt, most likely. Not that I cared what his reason was. When you've got a sick mother to take care of, it doesn't matter where the money comes from. Or why."

"Even if it's from a man you think killed your sister?"

Hannah leans back in her chair, her eyes narrowed to slits. "Especially then."

"I was told most people thought Petra had run away. Why did you think my father had anything to do with her disappearance?"

"Because I saw him come back to Baneberry Hall," Hannah says.

"When?"

"About two weeks after Petra was gone."

Shocked, I lean on the table, which does another jolting tilt. "Two weeks? Are you sure?"

"Positive. I had a lot of trouble sleeping in those first few weeks Petra was gone. I'd lie awake all night, waiting for her to come back. One morning, I got up at the crack of dawn and went walking in the woods, thinking that I could still find her if I kept looking hard enough." Hannah lets out a sad, little laugh. "So, there I was, roaming the woods behind our house. When I reached the wall around your property, I followed it to the front gate. I had almost reached the road when I saw a car pull up."

"My father," I say.

"Yes. I saw him clear as day. He got out of

335

the car, unlocked the gate, and drove on through."

"Did he see you?"

"I don't think so. I was still in the woods. Besides, he seemed pretty focused on getting inside as fast as possible."

"How long was he there?"

"I don't know. I had gone home by the time he left."

"What do you think he was doing?"

Hannah stubs out her cigarette. "At the time, I had no idea. Now, though? I think he was dumping Petra's body."

Chief Alcott told me she went to Baneberry Hall the night we left, finding nothing out of the ordinary. If my father had killed Petra and stuffed her body in the floor, that means he either did it well before the chief searched the house or well after.

Maybe two weeks after.

In which case Petra's body would had to have been kept somewhere else. Something I don't want to think about.

"Did you tell anyone that you saw him back at the house?" I ask Hannah.

"No, because I didn't think anyone would listen to me," she says. "The police weren't really interested. By then your dad's story about Baneberry Hall being haunted was spreading. We'd already started to see looky-loos driving up to the front gate, trying to get a look at the place. As for Petra, they were convinced she'd run away and would return when she felt like it. She never did."

"That's what your mother thought as well, right?"

"She did," Hannah says. "Because that's what I told her had happened."

She lights another cigarette and inhales. One long, hungry drag during which she decides to tell me everything she knows.

"Petra had a boyfriend. Or something."

Hannah lets the word hang there, insinuating. It makes me wonder if Brian Prince had shared his theory about my father with her.

"I don't know who it was or how long it had been going on," she says. "But she snuck out at night. I know because we shared a bedroom. She'd wait until she thought I was asleep before climbing out the window. When I woke up in the morning, she'd be right back in bed, asleep. I asked her about it once, and she told me I had been dreaming."

"Why the need to sneak out?"

"Because my mother didn't allow dating. Or boys. Or anything that would displease God." Hannah holds up her cigarette as an example and takes another devilish puff.

"The thing you need to know about my mother is that she was strict. As was her mother. And her grandmother. The Ditmer women were hardworking, God-fearing people. There's a reason they all became housekeepers. Cleanliness is next to Godliness."

A bit of ash drops from Hannah's cigarette onto the kitchen table. She doesn't brush it away. A small act of rebellion.

"Growing up, Petra and I weren't allowed to do anything. No school dances. No going to the movies with friends. It was school and work and prayer. It was only a matter of time before Petra was going to rebel."

"How long had she been sneaking out?"

"Only a week or two, as far as I could tell. The beginning of July was when I first watched her do it."

My heart sinks. I'd been hoping it had started weeks before my family moved into Baneberry Hall. But, no, we were there by the beginning of July.

"The night Petra disappeared, did you see her leave?"

Hannah gives a quick shake of her head. "But I assumed she did, because she was gone the next morning."

"And that's when you told your mother she had run away?"

"Yes."

"Why?"

"Because Buster was also gone."

Hannah sees the confusion on my face and elaborates.

"He was Petra's teddy bear. She got it years before I was born and still slept with it like she was my age. If she spent the night somewhere, Buster went with her. You don't remember this, but she had him when we went to your house for that sleepover."

Hannah gets up and leaves the kitchen. She returns a minute later with a photograph, staring at it as she resumes talking.

"She'd never leave home without him. Ever. When we realized Buster was also gone, we assumed she'd run away. Most likely with this boy she'd been seeing."

That boy could have been my father, a possibility that makes me as wobbly as the kitchen table. The feeling gets worse when Hannah finally shows me the photograph. It's her and Petra, presumably in their bedroom. Petra sits on a bed. Next to her is a disturbingly familiar teddy bear.

Brown fur.

Button eyes.

A red bow tie circling its neck.

It's the very same bear Dane and I found in my father's office. Now it is gone. While I don't know — and likely will never know — who took it, I can think of only two reasons it was in Baneberry Hall.

"You mentioned that Petra brought Buster that time you spent the night," I say.

"Yes," Hannah says. "Even though we never made it the full night."

I'm well aware of that, thanks to the Book.

"Is there a chance Petra left it behind?" I say, hoping I'm not revealing too much. Hannah doesn't need to know that, until a few nights ago, Buster was still inside Baneberry Hall. "Maybe it got lost."

"She brought him home with her," Hannah says. "I'm certain of it."

That leaves only the other reason Buster could have been in the house. The one I'd been hoping wasn't true.

Petra brought the bear with her because she thought she was leaving for good. Probably with my father. The idea sucks all the air from my chest.

Short of breath, there's nothing left for me to do but stand and leave the cottage in a daze. Hannah follows me past the living room, where the television has changed from a game show to a sitcom. Forced laughter blares from the TV.

It's not until I'm at the back door that I turn around to ask Hannah one more thing.

340

A question prompted not just by that picture of Petra and her bear but by the memory of yesterday morning. Mister Shadow in the armoire, staring at me, creeping closer.

"You seem to remember a lot about the night you two came to Baneberry Hall for that sleepover."

"It was pretty hard to forget." Hannah huffs out a humorless laugh, as if she can't believe that, with everything else going on, this is what I want to talk about. It makes perfect sense to me. She was there. She remembers. I don't.

"The things my father wrote about that night," I say. "That was bullshit, right?"

"I don't think so," Hannah says.

I study her, seeking a tell that she's lying. She levels her gaze at me, indicating she's dead serious.

"So, what my father wrote about that night —"

"It's all true," Hannah says, without a moment's hesitation. "Every damn word."

JULY 7
DAY 12

The day of the sleepover began like any other at Baneberry Hall.

Thud.

I got out of bed without looking at the clock — there was no need — and went downstairs, where the chandelier was aglow. I flicked it off with a heavy sigh and descended to the kitchen to brew a pot of extra-strong coffee. It had become my usual morning routine.

By then, exhaustion was a fact of life at Baneberry Hall. Almost as if the house was purposefully denying me a full night's sleep. I counteracted it as best as I could with mid-afternoon catnaps and going to bed early.

But on this day, there would be no napping. The afternoon was spent preparing for two extra people in the house. Grocery shopping, cleaning, and making the place look like a happy home, which it definitely wasn't.

The whole point of having the sleepover be supervised by Petra was to give Jess and me some much-needed relaxation time alone. But when Hannah and Petra arrived bearing backpacks, sleeping bags, and a tray of cookies from their mother, I realized their presence only added to our stress. Especially when Maggie asked to speak to Jess and me alone in the middle of dinner.

"Can't it wait?" I said. "You have guests."

"It's important," Maggie told us.

The three of us went to the great room, leaving Hannah and Petra to eat their spaghetti and meatballs in awkward silence.

"This better be good," Jess said. "It's rude to leave your friends like that."

Maggie's expression was deadly serious. The cut on her cheek had healed enough that she no longer needed a bandage. Now exposed, it gave her a weathered, wizened look.

"They need to leave," she said. "Miss Pennyface doesn't want them here. She doesn't like them. She's been angry all night." Maggie pointed to an empty corner. "See?"

"Now's not the time for this," Jess said. "Not with your friends here."

"They're not my friends."

"But they could be," I said in my most encouraging voice. "Just give it one night. Okay, kiddo?"

Maggie considered it, her lips a flat line as she weighed the pros and cons of friendship with Hannah.

"Okay," she said. "But they'll probably be mad."

"Who'll get mad?"

"All of the ghosts."

She went back to the table, leaving Jess and me speechless. Maggie, however, was chattier than ever, and remained that way through the rest of dinner. And the ice-cream sundaes made for dessert. And the board games played after that. When Maggie emerged victorious after a game of Mouse Trap, she ran around the dining room cheering like she'd just won the World Cup.

It was so nice to see her having fun with other girls. For the first time since we came to Baneberry Hall, Maggie looked happy, even when she shot occasional glances to the corners of the room.

Those fearful looks grew more pronounced when the girls got ready for bed. While Petra engaged in a half-hearted pillow fight instigated by her sister, Maggie merely sat there, her gaze flicking to the corner by her closet. And when I lined them up to take a picture with the Polaroid camera, she appeared more focused on the wall behind me than the camera's lens.

"They're down for the night," I announced to Jess after I'd turned out the lights in Maggie's room and retired to my own. "Whatever else they need, Petra can take it from here."

I collapsed on the bed, an arm flung over my eyes. I would have plunged immediately into sleep if something hadn't been weighing on my mind since dinner.

"I think we should take Maggie to see someone."

Jess, who had been applying moisturizer at her vanity, gave me a look in the mirror. "As in a shrink?"

"A therapist, yes. Clearly, something's going on with her. She's struggling with this move. She has no friends and doesn't seem to want to make any. And all this talk of imaginary friends — it's not normal. And it's not a plea for attention, either."

In the mirror, Jess's face took on a wounded look. "Do you plan on throwing that back at me every time we discuss our daughter?"

"That wasn't my intention," I said. "I was just making a case for why we should send her to someone who might be able to help."

Jess said nothing.

"Either you have no opinion on the matter," I said, "or you don't agree with me and just don't want to say it."

"Therapy's a big step," she finally said.

"You don't think Maggie has a problem?"

"She has imaginary friends and trouble making real ones. I don't think we should punish her for that."

"It's not punishment. It's getting her the help she needs." I sat up and moved to the edge of the bed. "These aren't typical imaginary friends, Jess. Miss Pennyface and Mister Shadow. Those are scary names, given to them by a scared little girl. You heard what she called them — ghosts. Imagine how terrified she must be."

"It's a phase," Jess insisted. "Brought on by this move and all the things that have happened with this house. I worry that sending Maggie to a shrink will make her feel like an outcast. To me, that's a far bigger concern than something she's going to grow out of as soon as she gets used to this place."

"And what if she doesn't grow out of it? What if this is a legitimate mental disorder that —"

A scream cut me off.

It came from Maggie's room, shooting down the hallway like a bullet. By the time the second scream arrived, Jess and I were already out of our bedroom and running down the hall.

I was first to reach Maggie's room, colliding with Petra, who had burst into the hallway. She wrapped her thin arms around herself, as if trying to ward off a sudden chill.

"It's Maggie," she said.

"What's wrong?" Jess asked as she caught up to us.

"I don't know, but she's freaking out."

Inside the bedroom, Maggie began to shout. "Go away!"

I ran into the room, confounded by what I saw.

The armoire doors were wide open, and all the dresses Jess had hung there were now scattered about the room. Hannah was up to her neck in her sleeping bag, mute with fear, scooching backward like an inchworm.

Maggie stood on her bed, shrieking at the open armoire.

"Go away! Go *away*!"

In the hallway, I heard Petra telling Jess what had happened.

"I was asleep," she said, the words tumbling out. "Hannah woke me up yelling, saying Maggie had just pulled her hair. But Maggie said she hadn't. That it was someone else. And then I heard the wardrobe door open and things flying out of it and Maggie screaming."

Maggie remained on the bed. Her shouts had devolved into an earsplitting wail that refused to die down. In the corner, Hannah's hands shot out of the sleeping bag and clamped over her ears.

"Maggie, there's no one here."

347

"There is!" she cried. "They're all here! I told you they'd be mad!"

"Sweetie, calm down. Everything's okay."

I reached for her, but she slapped my hand away.

"It's not!" Maggie cried. "He's under there!"

"Who?"

"Mister Shadow."

It wasn't until her voice died down that I heard an unidentifiable noise coming from under the bed.

"There's nothing down there," I said, hoping to convince myself as well as Maggie.

"He's there!" Maggie shrieked. "I saw him! And Miss Pennyface is right there!"

She pointed to the corner behind her closet door, which I saw had also been opened. I didn't remember it being that way when I came into the room, even though it had to have been.

"And then there's the little girl," she said.

"Where is she?" I asked.

"Right next to you."

Even though I knew it was my mind playing tricks on me, I still felt a presence beside me. It was the same way you could tell someone was sneaking up behind you. A disturbance in the air gave them away. I longed to look at my side, but I feared doing so would make Maggie think I believed her.

So, I didn't look, even when I felt — or thought I felt — someone brush my hand. Instead, I glanced across the room to Hannah, hoping her reaction would tell me if something was there. But Hannah's eyes were shut tight as she continued to slide backward into the corner where Maggie said Miss Pennyface was standing.

She wasn't, of course. There was no Miss Pennyface. But when Hannah reached the corner, she began to shout.

"Something touched me! Something touched me!"

In between her screams, I again heard the noise under the bed.

A muffled skittering.

Like a giant spider.

Without thinking, I dropped to my knees.

Above me, Maggie had resumed shrieking, matching Hannah in volume. More noise started up from the doorway. Jess asking me what the hell I was doing.

I ignored her.

I ignored everything.

I was focused solely on the bed. I needed to see what was under there.

With trembling hands, I touched the bed skirt, brushing it aside.

Then I peered into the dark under Maggie's bed.

Nothing was there.

Then the bedsprings sank — a jarring sight that made me yelp and jump away from the bed. I looked up and saw it was Hannah, out of her sleeping bag and now standing on the bed. She tugged at Maggie's arms, trying to snap her out of whatever spell she was under.

"Make it stop, Maggie!" she yelled. "Make it *stop*!"

Maggie stopped screaming.

Her head snapped in Hannah's direction.

Then she punched her.

Blood sprayed from Hannah's nose, flying across Maggie, the bed, the floor.

A stunned look crossed Hannah's face as she tilted backward and dropped off the edge of the bed. She hit the floor hard, wailing the moment she landed. Jess and Petra ran to her.

I stayed where I was.

Also on the floor.

Staring up at my daughter, who seemed not to have realized what she'd just done. Instead, she looked to the corner by the closet. The door was now shut, although I had no idea how or when that could have happened.

It was the same with the armoire. Both doors were completely closed.

Maggie looked to me and, in a voice thick with relief, said, "They're gone."

FIFTEEN

I close my father's copy of the Book, having just read the chapter about the sleepover. As I stare at the aerial view of Baneberry Hall on the cover, what Hannah said about that night plays on repeat in my head.

It's all true.

But it isn't. It can't be. Because if the part about the sleepover is true, then so is the rest of the Book. And I refuse to believe that. The Book is bullshit.

Right?

I shake my head, disappointed by my own uncertainty. Of course it's bullshit. I've known that since I was nine.

Then why am I still here at the dining room table with the Book in front of me? Why did I feel compelled to sit down and read the chapter about the sleepover in the first place? Why am I on the verge of reading it a second time?

I want to think it's because doing a deep

dive into *House of Horrors* is easier than facing the idea that my father might have killed Petra. It's a much-needed distraction. Nothing more.

But I know better. I've seen too many similarities between real life and the Book to dismiss it outright, and I can't shake the feeling that something eerie is happening. Something strange enough to make my hands tremble as I open the Book.

Then close it.

Then open it again.

Then throw it across the dining room, where it hits the wall in an angry flutter of pages.

I grab my phone, checking to see if my mother returned my call while I was reading. She hasn't. I call again. When it goes straight to her voicemail, I hang up without leaving a message. What am I going to say? *Hi, Mom, did you know about the body in the ceiling, and did Dad do it, and did I really see ghosts as a child?*

I drop the phone onto the table and reach for my dinner — a bag of tortilla chips and a can of mixed nuts. Although there's enough food in the house for several meals, cooking isn't in the cards. After what happened in the kitchen, I want to spend as little time there as possible. So I stuff some chips into my mouth and wash them down with a beer. That's followed by some nuts, which I chomp while eyeing the Book, now splayed on the floor. I'm tempted to pick it up. Instead, I grab the Polaroids I found in my father's study.

The first one is the picture of my mother and me entering the woods. On the far side of the frame is that dark shape I thought might have been a person but is clearly a tree in shadow.

Next is the one from the sleepover, with me and Hannah as minor players in the Petra Show. I study her pose — the hand on her hip, the bent leg, the lips parted in a flirty smile. I can't help but think she was putting herself on display for my father.

Petra had a boyfriend, Hannah had said. *Or something.*

Could that have been my father? Was he capable of betraying my mother like that? Even though he once told me my mother was the only woman he'd ever loved, sometimes love has nothing to do with it.

I move to the next photo — the ceiling repairs in the kitchen, which has a new, morbid significance after the events of the past few days. Now it's a picture of a sixteen-year-old girl looking directly at the spot where her remains would be discovered twenty-five years later. Seeing it makes me quiver so hard the chair shakes.

I push that Polaroid away and look at the one of me standing in front of Baneberry Hall, struck by something interesting. I don't have a bandage under my left eye, which led me to assume it had been taken immediately after we moved in. But when I take another look at the picture from the sleepover, there's no bandage there, either. Nor is there a cut, bruise, or any other sign of damage, even though according to the Book, the sleepover happened *after* I'd hurt myself on the gravestone in the woods.

I gather all the Polaroids and slide them around the table like mahjong pieces, putting them in chronological order based on the events in the Book.

First is me outside Baneberry Hall, smiling and guileless. The girl I never thought I was but now worry I might truly have been.

Second is my mother and me stepping into the forest behind the house.

Third is the sleepover, and fourth is the shot taken in the kitchen.

The fifth, the selfie of my father, could have been taken at any time, although it strikes me as being toward the end of our stay. He looks haggard. Like something had been weighing on his thoughts.

I know there was a bandage at some point because Chief Alcott told me she noticed it when interviewing my father at the Two Pines. Also, I have the scar to prove it.

If it wasn't on our third day here, which is what the Book claims, then when did it happen?

And how did I get it?

And why did my father fudge the facts?

A rhetorical question. I already know the answer. He did it because the Book is bull —

I'm stopped mid-thought by a voice from elsewhere in the house, singing a song that roils my stomach.

"You are sixteen, going on seventeen —"

I grip the table's edge, buzzing with fear. Hannah's words again streak into my thoughts: *It's all true. Every damn word.*

The song keeps playing, louder now, as if someone's just cranked the volume.

"Baby, it's time to think."

Bullshit. That's what I think.

There's no ghost in this house.

But there *is* a ghoul.

"Better beware, be canny and careful —"

I bolt from the dining room and pass through the great room. The chandelier is on again, even though I'm certain I haven't touched its switch in days.

When I reach the front door, I find it's

355

still locked. The slip of paper I stuck in the doorframe when I returned from the Ditmers' remains in place.

"Baby, you're on the brink."

The windows are also locked. I checked them earlier. If this is a ghoul — and of course it is — how did they get inside?

There's only one way to find out.

The song continues to play as I tiptoe up the stairs, trying hard not to make a sound. If I'm going to catch whoever's doing this, I need surprise on my side.

The music gets louder when I reach the second floor, which actually works to my advantage. It covers the sound of my footsteps as I pad into my bedroom and take the knife from the nightstand.

I move down the hallway, gripping the knife so tight my knuckles turn white. They remain that way as I climb the steps to the third floor. On the other side of the closed study door, the song continues to pulse.

I throw open the door and burst inside, announcing my presence with a primal scream and a jabbing knife.

The study is empty.

Almost.

On the desk, suddenly back again, is Buster.

■ ■ ■ ■

I stand in the driveway, hugging myself against the evening chill as Chief Alcott finishes her sweep of Baneberry Hall. I called her immediately after finding Buster and met her at the front gate. All the reporters had dispersed for the night, thank God. Had they stayed, they would have seen me unlocking the gate with trembling hands, pale as a ghost.

Upon her arrival, Chief Alcott checked the outside of the house first, circling it with a flashlight swept back and forth across the exterior walls. Now she's inside, checking the windows. I see her from the driveway — a dark figure framed in an eyelike window on the third floor.

When she's done, she steps onto the porch and says, "There's no sign of a break-in."

It's exactly what I don't want to hear. Something that pointed to forced entry — say, a broken window — would be a much better alternative to the reality I now face. Which is that there's no rational explanation for the record player turning on, or the sudden reappearance of Buster.

"Are you sure what you think happened actually, you know, happened?" she asks.

I hug myself tighter. "You think I'm making this up?"

"I didn't say that," the chief replies. "But I'm not discounting the possibility that your imagination is running a little wild right now. It wouldn't surprise me, considering what you found in the kitchen the other day. That would make anyone jumpy."

"I know what I saw," I say. "And I know what I heard."

"Maggie, I looked everywhere. There's absolutely no way an intruder could have gotten inside this house."

"What if —" I try to stop myself, knowing it will sound absurd. But it's too late. The words are already rolling off my tongue. "What if it's not an intruder?"

Chief Alcott squints at me. "What else can it be?"

"What if the things my father wrote were true?"

This time I can't even try to stop what I am saying. The words surprise even me. Chief Alcott appears less surprised than angry. I notice her nostrils flare.

"You're telling me you now think Baneberry Hall is haunted?"

"I'm telling you that something deeply weird is happening here," I say. "I'm not lying to you."

At first, I think I sound just like my father did in the later chapters of *House of Horrors*. Confused and scared and borderline crazy from sleep deprivation. But then it hits me — realization as disorienting as a sucker punch.

I sound like the me my father wrote about.

I've become the Maggie from the Book.

"I like you, Maggie," Chief Alcott says. "You seem smart. Good head on your shoulders. That's why I'm giving you the chance to stop this now and not take it any further."

"Stop what?"

"Doing the same thing your father did," the chief says. "He hurt this town. He hurt the Ditmers. And I'm certain he killed Petra Ditmer. He got away with it because he told that stupid ghost story of his and enough people were distracted by it. Including me. But I won't let you do the same thing. Now that we're on to what he did, I won't have you muddying the waters again with stories about this house being haunted. I refuse to let you write a fucking sequel."

She storms to her cruiser and is gone seconds later, the car's taillights glowing an angry red as they disappear down the hill.

I follow her down the long, winding driveway and lock the gate, wondering if that alone is enough to keep whatever the hell is going on from continuing to happen. I hope so, even though I doubt it. Right now, the Book is more real than it's ever been.

And I don't want to relive it.

I don't want to be that scared girl my father wrote about.

When I return to the house, the only other preventative measure I can think of is to march to the third floor, grab the record player, and carry it onto the front lawn. I then fetch the sledgehammer from the nearby pile of equipment. I lift it onto my shoulder, my triceps quivering from the strain.

Then, with a mighty swing, I bring the sledgehammer down and smash the record player into pieces.

JULY 8
DAY 13

Jess and I sat in the waiting room, not speaking. Something we'd done a lot of in the previous twelve hours. There wasn't a whole lot to say. We both already knew that something was profoundly wrong with our daughter.

The only words I had said to my wife since the fiasco the night before were, "I found a child psychologist who can see Maggie today. The appointment's at eleven."

"Great," Jess replied, the third of three words she'd spoken to me. The other two were after Elsa Ditmer had picked up her daughters amid a flurry of apologies from both of us. "They're gone," she had said, unintentionally repeating the same thing Maggie uttered after punching Hannah Ditmer.

Those words repeated themselves in my head long after both Maggie and Jess had spoken them. I still heard them — in both my wife's and daughter's voices — as I glumly looked around the waiting room of Dr. Lila Weber.

Because she was a child psychologist, I had expected Dr. Weber's office to be more child-friendly than it was. Toys by the door and the Wiggles playing in the background. Instead, the waiting room was as beige and bland as a dentist's office. A disappointment, seeing how I needed something to take my mind off the fact that Maggie had been speaking to Dr. Weber for almost an hour and that in mere minutes we'd find out just how messed up she truly was. A girl who behaved the way she did during the sleepover would have to be. And I wondered if Jess and I were to blame.

Maggie was an accident. A happy one, it turned out, but an accident nonetheless. One of the reasons Jess and I got married as quickly as we did was because she got pregnant. Since I loved Jess completely and we'd planned to wed eventually anyway, we saw no reason to delay the inevitable.

Yet the idea of being a father was terrifying to me. My own father was, by his own admission, a rotten cuss of a man. He drank too much and was quick to anger. Even though I knew he loved my mother and me, he rarely showed it. I worried I'd become exactly like him.

But then Maggie was born.

Jess's final month of pregnancy had been hard on her, and the difficulty continued in the delivery room. When Maggie emerged, she announced her arrival with silence. There was no crying. No delighted looks from nurses. I knew then that something had gone wrong.

It turned out that the umbilical cord had been wrapped around Maggie's neck, nearly strangling her to death at her moment of birth. That fraught moment of silence while the nurses worked to save Maggie was the most frightening moment of my life. Unable to do anything but wait — and hope — I gripped Jess's hand and prayed to a God I wasn't sure I believed in. I made a promise to him that if Maggie pulled through, I'd be the best father I possibly could.

Then at last Maggie began to cry — a full-throated wail that filled my heart with joy. My prayer had been answered. Right there and then, I vowed to do whatever it took to protect her.

As I waited in Dr. Weber's office that morning, I worried my protection wouldn't be enough and that whatever was wrong with Maggie was beyond my control. Yet she looked normal when she emerged from Dr. Weber's inner office, sucking on a lollipop and showing off a sticker on her hand.

"You've been so good today, Maggie," the

psychologist said. "Now I need you to be good for just a few more minutes while I chat with your parents, okay?"

Maggie nodded. "Okay."

Dr. Weber gave Jess and me a warm smile. "Mom and Dad, come this way."

The two of us stepped into her office and took a seat on the beige couch reserved for patients. Dr. Weber sat across from us, her face a mask of calmness. I searched it for signs that our daughter was severely damaged and it was all our fault.

"First, Maggie is fine," she said.

"Are you sure?" I asked.

"One hundred percent. She has an extraordinary imagination, which is a wonderful gift. But it also comes with its own set of difficulties."

The main one, as laid out by Dr. Weber, was an occasional inability to distinguish between what was real and what wasn't. Maggie's imagination was so vivid that sometimes when she interacted with her imaginary friends, she truly believed they were there.

"That's what seems to have happened last night," the doctor said. "She thought those imaginary friends —"

"Ghosts," I interjected. "She called them ghosts."

Dr. Weber nodded in response, squinting

ever so slightly to show how hard she was listening. I found it insufferable.

"We'll get to that," she said. "Back to last night. She thought — truly thought — there were others in the room, and her behavior followed suit."

"Is that why Maggie hit the neighbor girl?" Jess asked.

"It is," Dr. Weber said. "From the way Maggie described it, I think it was more a reflex than any innate sense of violence or attempt to cause harm. The best way I can describe it is like a dog snapping at someone when he's cornered and terrified. In that moment, Maggie simply didn't know what to do and lashed out."

That didn't explain everything. The closet door, the armoire, Hannah screaming that something had touched her.

And that noise.

The one under the bed.

That wasn't just Maggie's imagination. I had *heard* it.

"I want to know more about the ghosts," I said.

Dr. Weber's smile grew strained. "They're not really ghosts, of course. Going forward, I think it would be best to refer to them as imaginings."

"Maggie thinks they're real," I said.

"Which is something we'll have to work on," Dr. Weber said.

"Did she tell you about them?"

"She did, yes. She has three consistent *imaginings.*" She put extra emphasis on the word for my benefit. "One is a little girl she occasionally talks to. Another is a young woman she calls Miss Pennyface."

"Don't forget Mister Shadow," I said, because Maggie sure couldn't.

"He's the one she fears the most," Dr. Weber said.

"If these are all just —" I stopped myself before saying *imaginary friends,* choosing instead Dr. Weber's preferred term. "If these are *imaginings,* why is Maggie so afraid of them?"

"Children have dark thoughts, too," Dr. Weber said. "Just like adults. They're also good listeners. They pick up a lot more than we think they do. When problems like this occur, it's because the child is having a hard time processing what they've heard. Something bad happened in your home. Something tragic. Maggie knows that, but she doesn't know how to grapple with it."

"So what should we do?" I said.

"My advice? Be honest with her. Explain — in terms that she can understand — what happened, how it was a sad thing, and how that won't ever happen again."

That night, we took Dr. Weber's advice and sat Maggie down at the kitchen table, armed with some of her favorite treats. Hot chocolate. Sugar cookies. A pack of sour gummy worms.

Also on the table, at a slight remove from everything else, was the *Gazette* article about Curtis and Katie Carver I'd photocopied at the library.

"Before we moved in," Jess said, "something happened in this house. Something bad. And very sad."

"I know," Maggie said. "Hannah told me."

I groaned. Of course.

"Did she tell you exactly what happened?" I said.

"A mean man killed his daughter and then killed himself."

Hearing those words come out of my daughter's mouth almost broke my heart. I looked across the table to Jess, who gave me a small nod of support. It wasn't much, but it meant everything to me. It told me that, despite our recent clashes, we were still in this together.

"That's right," I said. "It was terrible and made everyone very sad. Bad things happen sometimes. But not all the time. Not often at all, in fact. But we know that what happened

might scare you, and we want you to understand that it's all in the past. Nothing like that
is going to happen while we're here."

"Promise?" Maggie said.

"I promise," I replied.

Jess reached across the table for our hands
and gave them a gentle squeeze. "*We* promise."

"If you have any questions about what happened, don't be afraid to ask," I told Maggie.
"We can talk about it anytime you want. In
fact, I have a newspaper article about it, if
you want to see it."

I waited until Maggie nodded before sliding
the article in front of her. Since her reading
skills were still limited, her gaze immediately
went to the photograph.

"Hey," she said, pressing a finger to the
photocopied face of Katie Carver. "That's the
girl."

I tensed. "What girl, honey?"

"The one I play with sometimes."

"Hannah?" Jess said hopefully.

Maggie shook her head. "The girl who can't
leave my room."

She then looked to the other side of the
photo and Curtis Carver's scowling face. Immediately, she began to whimper.

"It's him," she said, climbing into my lap and
pressing her face against my chest.

"Who?"

Maggie shot one last, frightened look at Curtis Carver.

"Him," she said. "He's Mister Shadow."

Sixteen

The reporters return bright and early. I know because I've been awake all night. Sometimes pacing the great room. Other times checking the front door and all the windows, making sure for the second, third, fourth time that they're secure. Most of the night, though, was spent in the parlor, sitting at attention with the knife in my hand, waiting for more weirdness.

That nothing happened didn't make it any less nerve-racking. Every shadow on the wall sent my pulse galloping. Each creak of the house prompted a startled jump. At one point, while pacing the room, I caught sight of myself in the secretary desk's mirror, startled not by my sudden presence there but by how crazed I looked.

I'd always assumed I was nothing like the fearful child in my father's book. Turns out it was me the whole time.

Now I'm at the third-floor windows, peek-

370

ing through the trees at the line of news vans arriving at the front gate. I wonder how long they'll be there before giving up. I hope it's just another few hours and not days.

Because I need to leave again, and this time going through the broken stone wall won't cut it. For this journey, I need a car.

I consider the idea of simply hopping into my truck and driving it right into the crowd, casualties be damned. But the thought is more revenge fantasy than actual plan. One, I'll need to get out of the truck to unlock and open the gate — giving Brian Prince and his ilk ample time to pounce. Second, even if I can drive away in peace, there's nothing to stop them from following me.

My only way to make a quiet getaway is to catch a ride with someone else. That means a phone call to Dane, even though we haven't spoken since he left the Two Pines. It is clear we are avoiding each other, although the reasons couldn't be more different. I suspect Dane is embarrassed I rejected his advances and wants to put some space between us.

My excuse is that I'm still trying to process what Chief Alcott told me about his time in prison. I believe that people make mistakes. But I also can't help but feel deceived. Until he convinces me he's not the same man who entered that prison, my trust in Dane will be limited to a ride into town.

"I need a favor," I tell him when he answers the phone. "Can you give me a lift in your truck?"

"Sure," he says. "I'll be right up."

"That's exactly what I don't want you to do. Take your truck a half mile from your place and wait for me on the side of the road."

Dane, to his credit, doesn't ask me why. "I'll be there in ten."

Just as he promised, his truck is idling on the roadside when I emerge from the woods, having passed through the gap in the wall.

"Where to, lady?" he says as I climb inside.

I give him the address to Dr. Weber's office, which I found online. Surprisingly, she's still practicing, and still in Bartleby.

The reason for my visit is simple: to ask her if I was indeed a patient of hers and, if so, what I said. Because I have few memories of Baneberry Hall that weren't influenced by the Book, I need the recollections of a third party to help me make sense of what's going on. Yet part of me already knows what's happening.

It's all true. Every damn word.

It's not safe there. Not for you.

"How's everything going?" Dane asks after driving in silence for several minutes.

"Fine," I say.

He shoots me a sidelong glance. "That's all I get? Fine? The other night, you couldn't stop talking."

"Things have changed."

More silence follows. A long, tense pause made all the more unbearable by the fact that Dane is right. I couldn't stop talking that night at the Two Pines. Because he was easy to talk to, back when I didn't know what he'd done and what he still might be capable of doing. Now I just want to get through this trip by saying as little as possible.

Dane refuses to let that happen.

"Is this about the other night?" he says. "If I made you uncomfortable, I'm sorry. I was just responding to the vibe in the room. Otherwise I never would have suggested it. The last thing I wanted was to make this —"

"Why didn't you tell me you were in prison?" I ask, unable to keep the question bottled up.

Dane doesn't react, save for a slight clearing of this throat. He's clearly been anticipating this moment.

"It never came up."

"So you're not denying it?"

"Not when it's the truth," Dane says. "I spent a year at Northern State Correctional. The food was bad, the company was worse, and don't even get me started on the showers."

The joke — not good to begin with — withers amid the strained mood inside the truck.

"And is it true you almost killed a man?" I say.

"Not intentionally."

I think Dane expects that to make me feel better. It doesn't.

"But you did intend to hurt him," I reply.

"I don't know what I intended," Dane says, his voice strained. "Everything got out of hand. The other guy started it, okay? Not that it matters, but that's a fact. Was I drunk? Yes. Did I go too far? Absolutely. And I regret every goddamn punch. I've served my time and changed my ways, but people are always going to judge me for that one awful mistake."

"Is that why you didn't tell me?" I say. "Because you thought I'd judge you?"

Dane sniffs. "That's what you're doing, isn't it?"

"I wouldn't if you had been honest with me. I know all too well what it feels like when people think they have you pegged. I would have understood."

"Then why are you acting so hurt about it?"

"Only because I deserved to know. I hired you for a job, Dane."

"So we're just boss and employee now?"

"That's what we've always been," I say, in a voice eerily like my mother's. I hear it — that clipped formality, the passive aggressiveness — and cringe.

"It didn't feel that way the other night," Dane says. "Hell, it never felt that way."

My mother's tone again seeps into my voice. "Well, that's how it's going to be now."

"Just because you found out I was in prison?"

"No, it's because of everything I'm dealing with right now. The Book, my father, what he might have done. I don't need another liar in my life."

We've entered Bartleby proper, the town still waking up. People emerge from their houses with sleepy expressions and steaming travel mugs of coffee. A block away, a church bell chimes out the hour — nine a.m.

Dane pulls up to the curb and gives me an impatient look. "You can get out here.

Consider it my resignation. Find someone else to mess up with your daddy issues."

I hop out of the truck without hesitation, giving Dane a mumbled "Thanks for the ride" before slamming the door and walking away.

Dane calls to me. "Maggie, wait."

I turn around and see his head stuck out the truck's window. A hundred thoughts seem to go through his head, all of them unspoken. In the end, he settles for a quiet, concerned "Will you need a ride back?"

I almost tell him yes. That I need more than a ride — I need him to help me understand just what the hell is going on and what, if anything, I can do about it. But I can't bring myself to say it. It's better to end things now.

"No," I say. "I can find my own way home."

I can also find my own way to Dr. Weber's office, which sits a block off Maple Street, on a tidy thoroughfare that looks residential but is mostly commercial. Craftsman-style homes sit amid compact yards, most bearing signs for the businesses contained within them. A dentist. A law office. A funeral home. Dr. Weber's is no different.

Inside, the office is soothing to the point

376

of blandness. Everything's colored either cream or beige, including a woman leaning over a desk to check the calendar. Creamy skin. Beige skirt. Off-white blouse. She looks up when I enter, her eyes kind but curious. Definitely Dr. Weber. It's the sort of expression that can only come from decades of intense listening.

"I didn't think I had an appointment first thing this morning," she says. "Are you a parent?"

"There's no appointment," I say. "I was hoping we could talk."

"I'm afraid I don't take walk-ins. Nor do I work with adults. But I'd be happy to give you the names of more appropriate thera-pists."

"I'm not seeking therapy," I say. "Been there, done that."

"Then I'm not sure how I can help you," Dr. Weber says kindly.

"I'm a former patient," I say. "We had one session. That I know of."

"I've had lots of patients over the years."

"I'm Maggie Holt."

Dr. Weber remains completely still. Her expression never changes. The only thing hinting at her surprise is a hand that makes its way to her heart. She notices and tries to

377

cover by adjusting the top button of her blouse.

"I remember you," she says.

"What did we talk about?" I say, immediately following it up with another, more pressing question. "And what was I like?"

Dr. Weber gives her calendar another quick glance before leading me into an inner office filled with more beige and cream, including the college degrees hanging on the wall in tasteful frames. It makes me wonder if the doctor has her own phobia — fear of color.

"I assume this visit was prompted by the recent incident at Baneberry Hall," Dr. Weber says as we sit, she in her doctor's chair and me in the one reserved for patients. "I imagine that was quite a shock for you."

"That's putting it mildly," I say.

"Do you think your father killed that girl?"

"I can't think of anyone else who could have done it."

"So that's a yes?"

"More like an I-don't-know." An edge creeps into my voice. The argument with Dane has left me feeling defensive. Or maybe the defensiveness stems from sitting under Dr. Weber's watchful gaze. "I was hoping you could help me fill in the blanks."

"I'm honestly not sure how much help I can be," Dr. Weber says. "We only had that one session your father mentioned in his book."

That's a surprise. I didn't expect Dr. Weber to have read it.

"What did you think of *House of Horrors*?" I say.

The doctor folds her hands in her lap. "As literature, I found it lacking. From a psychological standpoint, I thought it was fascinating."

"How so?"

"While on the surface it was about a haunted house and evil spirits, I saw the book for what it really was — a father's attempt to understand his daughter."

It sounds like something Dr. Harris would have told me. Typical analytical bullshit.

"I was five," I say. "There wasn't too much for him to try to understand."

"You'd be surprised by the complexity of young minds."

I start to rise from the chair, gripped by a sudden urge to leave. This is going nowhere. Certainly not in the direction I want it to. What keeps me here, hovering over the chair's beige upholstery, is the need for answers.

"All that book did was make life very hard for my family," I say. "Me, especially."

"Then why did you return to Baneberry Hall?"

"I inherited it. Now I have to get it ready to be sold."

"You don't *have* to," the doctor says. "Not really. Everything regarding the house could be taken care of remotely. Movers and designers and so forth."

"I *am* a designer," I say, bristling. "I needed to see the condition of the house."

"That's the key word, I think."

"House?"

Dr. Weber gives me a patient smile. "See. You needed to *see* the condition of the house. It's very similar to that phrase 'I'll believe it when I see it.' Which makes me think you came back not to see the condition of the house but to find out if, just maybe, your father was telling the truth in his book."

I lean forward in the chair. "What did I tell you during that session?"

"So you're a designer," Dr. Weber says, ignoring my question. "Of what?"

"Interiors."

"Fascinating."

I knew she'd glom on to that bit of information. Dr. Harris certainly had. She said

Baneberry Hall is the reason I do what I do. That the story of my family's brief time there has led me to seek out other stories in other houses. A constant quest for truth.

"What do you really hope to accomplish by renovating that house?" Dr. Weber says.

"To make a profit."

"Are you sure it's not really an attempt to change your experience there? Flip the house, flip your past."

"I think it's a little more complex than that," I say.

"Is it? You just told me that house made life very hard for you."

"No, I said my father's book did. That house has nothing to do with it."

"It absolutely does," Dr. Weber says, the newfound sparkle in her eye signaling she thinks she's got me all figured out. "It's all tied together, Maggie. The house. The book. Your family. I'm not surprised you say your father's book hurt you. I can only imagine how strange it must have been, growing up with such a burden. Now here you are, renovating Baneberry Hall. Don't you think this project is, in essence, now an attempt to rewrite that story?"

"I'm not here to be analyzed," I say, struck once more by the urge to leave. This time, I stand. Dr. Weber remains in her seat. Our sudden difference in height emboldens me. "If you don't want to tell me what I said during that session we had, fine. But I'm not going to let you waste my time in the process."

I take a step toward the door, stopping only when Dr. Weber says, "Your parents contacted me, saying you were having trouble adjusting to your new house. When I learned where you lived, I wasn't surprised."

She gestures for me to return to the chair. Seated once more, I say, "Because of what happened with the Carver family?"

"And other things," Dr. Weber says. "Stories. Rumors. Every town has a haunted house. In Bartleby, that's Baneberry Hall. And it was that way long before your father's book existed."

I think of the passages in the Book about the house's history. All those articles my father had reportedly found about deaths that had occurred there beyond the Carver family's tragedy. I assumed he'd made them up.

"When your parents brought you to see me, I was prepared to talk to a little girl afraid of the dark. Instead, I met a smart, willful five-year-old convinced there were supernatural presences in her house."

"I mentioned ghosts?"

"Oh, yes. A little girl, Miss Pennyface, and Mister Shadow."

A thin sliver of fear shoots up my spine like a titanium rod. I sit up straighter in my chair.

"My father made them up."

"It's possible," Dr. Weber says. "Children are impressionable. If an adult tells them something, no matter how impossible it may sound, a child will tend to believe it. Take Santa Claus, for example. So, yes, your father could have planted the idea of these people in your head."

For the first time since we've sat down, I detect uncertainty in Dr. Weber's voice.

"You don't think that's what happened," I say.

"I don't." The doctor shifts in her chair. "I can tell when a child's thinking has been manipulated. That wasn't the case with you. It's why I remember that session so vividly after all these years. You spoke with complete conviction."

"About ghosts?"

Dr. Weber nods. "You said they came into your room at night. One of them whispered to you in the darkness, warning you that you were going to die."

"They were probably night terrors. I've

had them since I was a little girl."

"I don't recall your parents mentioning anything about that," Dr. Weber says. "Do you still have them?"

"That's what it says on my Valium prescription."

Dr. Weber doesn't crack a smile at my admittedly bad joke. "The thing about people who suffer from night terrors is that they think they're real only when they're taking place. Once they wake up, they know it was just a bad dream."

I think about the night terror I'd had three nights ago. Me in bed and Mister Shadow watching me from the armoire. Even days later, it still makes me uneasy.

"So, those things I claimed to have seen — I thought they were real?"

"Even when you were wide awake," Dr. Weber says.

The chair seems to give way beneath me. Like I'm sinking into it, on the verge of sliding into nothingness. The sensation's so strong that I need to look down to confirm it's not really happening. Even then, the sinking feeling persists.

"So the stuff in the Book — the things you told my parents —"

"It's mostly true," Dr. Weber says. "I can't vouch for the authenticity of the rest of the

384

book, but that part happened. You truly believed these beings existed."

"But they didn't," I say, still feeling myself sinking. Down, down, down. Deeper into the rabbit hole.

"I don't believe in ghosts," Dr. Weber says. "But you *did* believe that something was coming into your room at night. Whether it was real or imagined, I can't say. But it did weigh on your mind. Something was haunting you."

I stand, relieved to be out of that chair. A backward glance confirms that the cushion is still there. That the sinking sensation had all been in my head.

I wish I could say the same about the ghosts I claimed to have seen as a child. But there's nothing to prove that they weren't made-up, either by me or my father.

All I know is that, at least to my young mind, those three spirits, including Mister Shadow, were absolutely real.

July 9
Day 14

Part of Jess's new job required her to teach summer school, which began that morning. Left to our own devices, Maggie and I went to the local farmers' market and then the grocery store.

It felt nice to get out of the house, even if it was just for errands. After what Maggie had said the night before, I wanted to spend as little time in Baneberry Hall as possible.

"Remember what Dr. Weber told us," Jess said before leaving for work, as if seeing a psychologist had been her idea. "This is just Maggie's way of processing what happened."

But I *was* concerned. So much so that I made Maggie sit at the kitchen table with some crayons and paper while I put away groceries. I was placing canned goods in a cupboard, my back turned to Maggie, when one of the bells on the wall suddenly chimed — a tinny half ring that stopped as suddenly as it started.

"Please don't do that, Mags."

"Do what?"

The bell chimed again.

"That," I said.

"I didn't do any —"

The bell rang a third time, cutting her off. I spun away from the cupboard, expecting to see Maggie at the wall, straining on her tiptoes to reach one of the bottom bells. But she remained at the table, crayon in hand.

The bell let out another ring, and this time I saw it move. The whorl of metal tilted ever so slightly, taking the bell with it until that familiar ring sounded again. That's when I knew it wasn't Maggie's doing and that the rope attached to that bell had purposefully been tugged.

I looked to the label above the bell, which now sat silent and still.

The Indigo Room.

"Stay right here," I told Maggie. "Do not move."

I took the steps to the first floor two at a time, hoping speed would help me catch whoever was doing this in the act. After rushing through the great room and to the front of the house, I burst into the Indigo Room.

It was empty.

An uneasy feeling overcame me as I spun slowly in the center of the room. A sense that something strange was going on. Something beyond Maggie's imaginings. As I continued to spin, making sure the room was indeed completely empty, one thing I *didn't* feel was surprise.

Deep down, I had *expected* the Indigo Room to be empty.

By then, the idea that someone continued to sneak into Baneberry Hall seemed more like wishful thinking than possible reality. People didn't break into homes only to ring bells and turn on record players. Nor were those things caused by mice or a draft or even snakes.

Something else was going on.

Something unexplainable.

Passing under the chandelier, I saw it was inexplicably lit, even though it hadn't been earlier that morning.

I hit the switch, darkening it once more, and continued to the kitchen. I was halfway down the steps when a chorus of bells rose from the kitchen, prompting me to run the rest of the way. Inside, I saw that every bell on the wall trembled, as if they had been rung at once.

Also trembling was Maggie, who no longer sat at the kitchen table. Instead, she crouched against the wall opposite the bells, pressing herself into a corner. Terror glistened in her eyes.

"He was here," she whispered.

"Mister Shadow?" I whispered back.

Maggie gave a single, solemn nod.

"Is he gone now?"

She nodded again.

"Did he say anything to you?"

Maggie looked from me to the wall of now-silent bells. "He said he wants to talk to you."

That night, I dropped the Ouija board on the kitchen table, where it landed with a thud so loud it startled Jess from the glass of wine she'd been staring into. We hadn't talked much about what happened with the bells because Maggie was always with us. But now that our daughter was in bed, I was able to give Jess a full report, followed by the retrieval of the Ouija board.

"Where did you get this?"

"I found it in the study."

"And what do you intend to do with it?"

"If Mister Shadow wants to talk, then I think we should try it."

Jess glanced at her wine, looking as though she wanted to down the whole glass. "Seriously?"

"I know it sounds stupid," I said. "And borderline ridiculous."

"I think it crosses that border, don't you?"

"You're the one who walked through this

place burning sage."

"That was different," Jess said. "It was just superstition. What you're talking about is —"

"Ghosts," I said. "Yes, I'm suggesting that Baneberry Hall is haunted."

There it was. The word we had tiptoed around for days. Now there was no way to avoid using it.

"You know how crazy you sound, right?"

"I do, and I don't care," I said. "Something strange is happening here. You can't deny that. Something we won't be able to stop until we know what we're dealing with."

Jess's face rippled with indecision as she stared at the box. When her mind was made up, she took a gulp of wine and said, "Fine. Let's do this."

The Ouija board was older than I had initially expected. Far different from the one I'd used as a teenager, when my friends and I would get high and try to scare one another. It was an actual board, for one thing. Solid wood that thunked against the table when I removed it from its box.

The varnish gave the wood an orange tint. Painted across it were two rows of letters, arced on top of each other like a double rainbow. In a straight line below them were numbers.

1 2 3 4 5 6 7 8 9 0

The upper corners each bore a single word. **YES** in the left corner, **NO** in the right. Two words ran across the bottom of the board.

GOOD BYE

Just like the board, the planchette also differed from my youth. It wasn't plastic, but real ivory, one end tapered to a point.

I lit a candle, set it on the table, and turned off the kitchen lights.

"Romantic," Jess commented.

"Can you please be serious about this?"

"Honestly, Ewan, I don't think I can."

We sat across from each other, taking opposite sides of the board. We then placed our fingers on the planchette, ready to begin.

"Is there a spirit present?" I said, addressing the area above the kitchen table.

The planchette didn't budge.

I asked again, this time intoning the words the way a medium would do in the movies. "Is there a spirit present?"

The planchette slowly began to move — a stuttering slide across the board to the word in the upper right corner.

NO

I looked across the table to Jess, who could barely contain her snickering. "I'm sorry," she said. "I couldn't help myself."

"Please keep an open mind," I pleaded. "For Maggie's sake."

Jess grew serious at the mention of our daughter. She knew as well as I did that this was about Maggie. If there were ghosts at Baneberry Hall, only she could see them. Which meant she'd continue to do so until they left.

"I will," she said. "Promise."

Once again, I asked if a spirit was present. This time, the planchette jerked forward — so hard I thought it was going to slide entirely out from beneath my fingers. They stayed with it, though, following it to the word in the upper left corner.

YES

"You need to be more subtle than that," I told Jess. "Stop pushing it."

"*You're* pushing it."

I looked to the board, where the planchette continued to circle **YES**, even though my fingers were barely touching it. It was the same with Jess. Her touch was so light it looked as if her fingers hovered over the ivory.

A chill entered the kitchen — a sudden drop

392

of temperature I felt in my bones. I hadn't felt cold like that since the night I first heard the music coming from the third floor. When I exhaled, I saw my breath.

Shivering, I spat out another question before the planchette could stop moving.

"Spirit, did you once reside in Baneberry Hall?"

The planchette continued to circle the word.

YES

"Spirit, what is your name?"

The planchette jerked again. So fast that Jess audibly gasped. I stared at it, dumbfounded, as it moved seemingly on its own to a letter in the center of the board.

C

Then another.

U

And another.

R

"Is this the spirit of Curtis Carver?" I asked.
The planchette did another lurch to the **YES**

in the upper left corner. Across the table, Jess gave me a worried look. She was about to lift her fingers from the planchette, but I shook my head, urging her to keep them there.

"Curtis, are you also who my daughter refers to as Mister Shadow?"

The planchette kept circling.

YES

"Our daughter said you've spoken to her," I said. "Is that true?"

More swooping and circling ensued around the word.

YES

"Do you have something to say to us?"

The planchette quickly slid back to the letter C. Six other letters followed, the planchette moving so hard I could hear it scritching across the board. Jess and I kept our fingers on top of it, our wrists jerking back and forth with each letter.

A

Then **R**.
Then **E**.
Then **F**.

Then **U**.

Then **L**.

"Careful?" I read aloud.

The planchette rocketed back to the **YES**, touching it briefly before returning to the double rainbow of letters and spelling out the same word.

CAREFUL

"What does that mean?" I asked.

The planchette never stopped moving, repeating the seven-letter pattern three more times.

CAREFUL

CAREFUL

CAREFUL

As soon as the planchette's narrowed tip hit the final **L**, it swung to the bottom of the board in a jarring swoop.

GOOD BYE

The chill left the kitchen. I felt it go — an instant warming.

"What the hell just happened?" Jess asked.

I didn't know. Nor did I have time to consider it, for at that moment a scream pierced the silence of the house.

Maggie.

Making the same siren-like wail she'd let out during the sleepover.

Jess and I ran upstairs, pounding up both sets of steps until we were on the second floor and in Maggie's room. Once again, she stood on her bed, screaming in the direction of the armoire.

Its doors were open.

"Mister Shadow!" she cried. "He was here!"

SEVENTEEN

After leaving Dr. Weber's office, I head back to Maple Street in search of Bartleby's public library. The doctor's mention of Baneberry Hall's history beyond the Carver family has me curious to find out more. As an added benefit, it will take my mind off Mister Shadow. Something I desperately need. I long for the quiet camaraderie only a library can provide.

Except Bartleby's library no longer exists — a fact I learn when I pop into a beauty salon to ask for directions.

"That closed years ago," the hairdresser says while not so subtly eyeing my split ends. "There was a fire, which destroyed almost everything. The town voted not to rebuild."

I thank her and move on, declining her offer of a trim. Without a library, there's only one place else I know to go for information — the *Bartleby Gazette*.

The newspaper's headquarters are located in an unassuming office building on the southern end of Maple Street. Outside, a newspaper box displays the latest edition. The headline running across the front page is in letters so bold they're practically screaming.

BODY FOUND IN BANEBERRY HALL

If the headline of every article was this sensational, then no wonder Allie was worried. I'd be alarmed, too.

A subhead sits below the main headline, not as large but equally as intriguing.

Remains discovered in notorious house allegedly girl missing for 25 years.

Included with the article, written by none other than Brian Prince, are three photos. One is an archive image of Baneberry Hall, probably taken around the time the Book came out. The other two are my father's old author photo and a faded yearbook shot of Petra Ditmer.

Seeing that front page makes me loath to enter the office. But the sad truth is that I need Brian Prince more than he needs me. So enter I do, finding myself in an office that's less like a functioning newspaper and more like a hobby. A solitary one. The newsroom, if it could even be called that, is filled with empty desks on which sit computers probably unused since the Clinton administration.

Sitting opposite the front door is a grandmotherly receptionist with the requisite bowl of hard candy. When she sees me, her mouth forms a tight *O* of surprise. "Mr. Prince is —"

I quiet her with a raised hand. "He'll want to talk to me."

Hearing my voice, Brian pops his head out of an office conspicuously marked EDITOR. "Maggie," he says. "This is certainly a surprise."

I can't argue there. I'm just as surprised as he is, especially when I say, "I need your help."

Brian's smirk is brighter than his bow tie. "With what?"

"I want to search your archives."

"Everything the *Gazette* has published in the past twenty years is archived online," he says, knowing full well that's not what I'm looking for.

We stare at each other a moment — a silent face-off. I blink first. I don't have much of a choice.

"Help me, and I'll give you an exclusive

interview," I say. "Nothing's off-limits."

Brian pretends to think it over, even though his mind's already made up. The ruthless glint in his eyes gives it away.

"Follow me," he says.

I'm led to a door in a back corner of the newsroom. Beyond it are a small hallway and a set of steps that go to the basement.

"This is the morgue," Brian announces as we descend the stairs. "All our old editions are here. Every single one."

He flicks a light switch when we reach the basement, brightening a room the size of a double-wide trailer. Running along the two longest walls are rows of metal shelves. Bound volumes fill them, each the height and width of a newspaper page. Printed on the spines are the years of publication, beginning with 1870.

I go straight for the one marked 1889. The year Indigo Garson died.

"What other years are you looking for?" Brian says.

I've read the Book so many times that I'm able to rattle off all the dates my father mentioned. Brian collects them all. Five volumes from four different decades — a load that leaves him red-faced and huffing.

"When are we going to do that interview?" he says as he plunks them down on a metal desk at the far end of the morgue.

I sit and open the first volume — 1889. "Now."

While a clearly flustered Brian Prince runs upstairs to retrieve a pen and notebook, I page through brittle copies of newspapers a hundred years older than I am. Because the *Gazette* has always been a weekly paper, it doesn't take me long to find an article about Indigo Garson — TOWN MOURNS GARSON HEIRESS.

I bristle at the headline's many indignities and implications. That heiress had a name, and it would have been decent of them to use it. Then there's how the headline pulls focus away from Indigo and directs it at Bartleby itself, as if a dead sixteen-year-old doesn't matter as much as the town's pain.

The article is equally frustrating. It reveals few details about how Indigo Garson died, yet takes great pains to mention that her father remained locked in his bedroom, inconsolable. The meat of the story doesn't arrive until a few issues later, with the shocking report that a maid at Baneberry Hall claimed to have seen William Garson carry the house's namesake berries up to his daughter. Two weeks after that was the headline my father had mentioned in the Book.

He hadn't been lying. All of this was true. I'm already moving to the next volume — 1926 — when Brian returns to the morgue. Leaning on a shelf with his pen and notebook, he says, "Are you ready to begin?"

I nod while flipping through pages filled with ads for ladies' hats, Model T cars, and the latest motion pictures playing at the town's Bijou Theater. It's not until I'm well into May that I see an article about a Garson family member killed in a car accident.

Truth number two.

"Do you think your father killed Petra Ditmer?" Brian asks.

"I hope he didn't."

"But you *do* think he did it?"

"If I do, you'll be the first to know." I open the collected newspapers from 1941. "Next question."

"Do you think Petra's death is why your family left Baneberry Hall so suddenly?"

"Maybe."

I find the article about the bathtub drowning that occurred that year. A third truth. The four and fifth ones come a few minutes later, while I scan the volumes from 1955 and 1956. Two bed-and-breakfast guests died, one in each of those years.

All the while, Brian Prince keeps lobbing questions at me. "Do you know of another reason you and your family fled the house?"

"It was haunted," I say while reaching for the papers from 1974. "Or so I've been told."

I've just found the article I've been looking for — *FATAL FALL AT BANEBERRY HALL* — when Brian slams an open palm across the page, blocking my view. It doesn't matter. Just seeing the headline confirms that my father hadn't been lying about any of the deaths at Baneberry Hall.

"You're not upholding your end of our deal," he says.

"You're interviewing me, aren't you?"

"It's not an interview if you refuse to answer my questions."

I get up and leave the desk, heading to another shelf of newspaper volumes. "I am answering them. I truly hope my father didn't kill Petra Ditmer. And, yes, maybe her death was why we left. If you want specifics, you'll need to talk to someone else."

"Just give me something I can use in next week's edition," Brian says as he follows me to a row of bound volumes spanning two decades ago. "A legitimate quote."

I grab two more volumes, one from twenty-five years ago, the other from the year before that, and carry them back to the desk.

"Here's your quote: Like everyone in Bartleby, I'm shocked and saddened by the recent discovery inside Baneberry Hall. My deepest condolences go out to the family of Petra Ditmer."

While Brian scribbles it down in his notebook, I open the volume from the year my family fled Baneberry Hall. The article about our departure is easy to find — it's splashed across the front page of the July 17 issue.

THE HAUNTING OF BANEBERRY HALL
Fearing for their lives, new owners flee historic estate.

The story that started it all.

I've seen it before, of course. Scans of the article are all over the internet. That tabloidy headline and photo of Baneberry Hall — eerily similar to the one currently on the front page of the *Gazette* — have been preserved forever.

So has the name of the man who wrote it.

"Still my finest hour," Brian Prince says

as he peers over my shoulder to see his byline.

"And my family's darkest," I reply.

I read the article for what's probably the hundredth time, wondering what my life would have been like had it never been written. I'd have had a more normal childhood, that's for damn sure. No being an outcast. No being teased and tormented. No Goth freaks trying to befriend me because they mistakenly thought I was one of them.

Maybe I would have become the writer my father wanted me to be. No article would have meant no Book, which is what steered me away from the profession in the first place.

And maybe my parents would have stayed happily married, our family intact, my holidays and summers not spent being tensely shuttled from one home to another.

But the article exists. Wishing otherwise won't change that. Until the day I die, I'll be associated with my father and what he claimed happened at Baneberry Hall.

I stop at a choice quote he gave to Brian.

"People will laugh," he said. "People will call us crazy. But I'm certain there's something in that house — something supernatural — that wants us dead."

Reading it, I can't help but think about

my conversation with Dr. Weber. She was convinced I had been telling the truth. That I believed what I saw inside that house.

Something was haunting you.

I slam the volume shut, no longer wanting to look at that article, even though I can probably recite it from memory.

I grab the second book I took down from the shelf. The previous year.

Again, it's not hard to locate the article I want. I know that date as well. When I get there, the first thing I see is a headline brutal in its simplicity.

MURDER-SUICIDE AT BANEBERRY HALL

Below it is a photograph of the entire Carver family — a regular sight during my obsessive teenage Googling. Only this time I'm struck by how similar the Carvers were to my family. Just alter the faces slightly and I could be looking at a picture of my parents and me during our time at Baneberry Hall.

But the real shock comes when I see the byline accompanying the article.

Brian Prince.

Two families with two vastly different experiences at Baneberry Hall. And Brian wrote about both of them.

406

I turn to the reporter still standing behind me. The interview is about to resume. Only now I'll be the one asking the questions.

July 10
Day 15

Jess shoved the Ouija board into the trash can, making a show of pushing it deeper against the garbage already inside the bin. She topped it with the remnants of our breakfast — runny oatmeal, scrambled eggs, and crumbs of toast scraped off plates.

"We're done with this, Ewan," she said. "No more talk of ghosts. No more talking *to* ghosts. No more pretending there isn't a logical explanation for all of this."

"You can't deny what's happening," I said.

"What's happening is that our daughter now spends every waking moment in this house terrified."

That I couldn't argue with. We'd spent most of the night consoling Maggie, who refused to go back to her room. Between crying jags and bouts of panicking, she told us she had been asleep when the armoire doors flew open. Then Mister Shadow stepped out of it, sat down on the edge of her bed, and told her she was going to die soon.

The story never changed, no matter how many times she told it.

My reaction was to be more concerned than ever before. I was convinced some form of ghostly entity was occupying our house, and I feared for the safety of our daughter.

Jess had a different reaction: denial.

"You can't keep entertaining the thought that any of this is real," she said as she prepared for a day of work on next to no sleep. "Until you stop, Maggie will continue to think Mister Shadow is real."

"But last night —"

"Was our minds playing tricks on us!" Jess shouted, her voice echoing off the kitchen walls.

"Our minds didn't move that thing all over the board."

"That was us, Ewan. Specifically *you*. I'm not an idiot. I know how Ouija boards work. It's all subtle direction and power of persuasion. Everything spelled out on that board was exactly what you wanted to see."

Jess was wrong about that. I didn't *want* any of it. But it was happening anyway. For instance, once she and Maggie managed to fall asleep, curled up together in our bed, I stayed awake, listening. First came a familiar sound in the hallway.

Tap-tap-tap.

It was followed by a snippet of music from the study above.

"You are sixteen, going on —"

The song was then cut off by the noise that always arrived at 4:54 a.m.

Thud.

Those sounds were real. They were happening. And I needed answers as to what was going on and how to stop it.

"We can't ignore this," I said. "We don't have a choice."

Jess took an angry sip of coffee and looked down at the mug clenched in her fist.

"There's always a choice," she said. "For example, I can choose to ignore my urge to throw this mug at your head. That would be the rational thing to do. It would keep the peace and prevent a big mess that one of us will have to clean up. That's how I *want* to handle this situation. But you continuing to think this house is haunted would be like this."

Without warning, she flung the mug in frustration. It sailed across the room, trailing dregs of coffee before exploding against the wall.

"The choice is yours," she said. "But you can be damn sure that if it's the wrong one, I'm not going to stick around to help you clean up the mess."

■ ■ ■ ■

Jess went to work. I cleaned up the broken mug and splashes of coffee. I had just dropped the glass shards, unlucky so far, into the trash when bells on the wall began to ring.

Four of them.

Not at once, but individually.

First was the Indigo Room. No surprise there. It was always the most active.

Following it was the fifth bell on the wall's first row — the great room.

After that came the last bell on the first row, which rang twice. Two short peals in quick succession.

The last bell to ring was the only peal from the second row. The third bell from the left.

The ringing continued in this manner. Four bells tolling a total of five times. Repeating itself in a distinct pattern. After watching the same combination of bells, I began to suspect that this wasn't just random ghostly ringing.

It seemed like a code. As if the bells — or whatever was controlling them — were trying to tell me something.

I dug the Ouija board out of the trash, wiping away a stubborn splotch of oatmeal before placing it on the kitchen table. As the bells continued their insistent pattern, I studied the

411

board in front of me. I realized that if I assigned a letter to each bell, I might be able to decipher what the bells were trying to say.

A wall-size Ouija board.

I began with the first bell on the first row. That was A. I continued matching bells to letters for the first row, which ended in L. Then I started in on the second row, beginning with M. The only wrinkle in this theory of mine was that the alphabet has twenty-six letters but the wall had only twenty-four bells. To solve that problem, I assigned the last bell on the second row the last three letters of the alphabet.

XYZ

I had no guarantee it would work. I assumed it wouldn't. It was ridiculous to think a ghost was spelling out words for me to decode. Then again, it was also ridiculous to believe in ghosts at all. Since I'd long ago gotten over that impossibility, I decided to keep an open mind.

The first bell rang. Eighth from the left on the first row.

H

The second bell was also on the first row, five spots from the left.

E

Next came the bell that always rang twice. Last one on the first row.

LL

By the time the sole bell in the second row rang, I'd already matched it to its corresponding letter, spelling out the full word.

HELLO

"Hello?" I said, ignoring the absurd fact that not only was I right about a spirit spelling out words, but I was now also speaking aloud to said spirit. "Who is this?"

The bells rang again, this time in a different configuration.

Third from the left on the first row.

C

Fourth from the right on the second row.

U

Various bells continued to ring, spelling out the name I'd already suspected.

CURTIS CARVER

"Curtis, did you speak to my daughter last night?"

The last bell on the second row chimed. Two more followed, one on the first and one on the second.

YES

"Did you tell her she was going to die here?"

The same three bells rang in the same order.

YES

I took a gulp, bracing myself for the question I didn't want to ask but needed to.

413

"Do you plan on killing my daughter?"

There was a pause that might have only lasted five seconds but felt like an hour. During that time, I thought of what Curtis Carver had done to his daughter. The pillow over her face while she slept. How horrible it must have been for her if she woke up, and I'm certain that before the end came, Katie Carver *did* wake up. I pictured the same thing happening to Maggie and became seized with panic.

Then a bell rang.

Second row.

Not at the very end but on the other side, second from the left.

N

The bell immediately to its right chimed next.

O

I exhaled — a long, heavy sigh of relief in which another question occurred to me. One I'd never considered because I thought I knew the answer since before we even moved into Baneberry Hall. But after seeing those two bells tilt out their song, I began to doubt that what I'd been told was true.

"Curtis," I said. "Did you kill your daughter?"

Again, there was a pause. Then two bells rang — the last sounds any of them would make for the rest of the day. But it was enough. Curtis Carver's answer was absolutely clear.

NO

EIGHTEEN

"I didn't know you wrote the original article about Curtis Carver," I say.

"I did." Brian Prince grins in a way that makes my stomach turn. He's *proud* of this fact. "It was my first big story."

I return my gaze to the article, preferring the picture of the Carver family over Brian's morbid smugness. "How much do you remember about that day?"

"A lot," Brian says. "Like I said, I was fairly new to the *Gazette,* even though I've lived in Bartleby my whole life. The paper was bigger then. *Every* paper was bigger in those days. Because a lot of the older, veteran reporters were still around, I was relegated to fluff pieces. Dog shows and baking contests. I interviewed Marta Carver a few days before the murder. She took me on a tour of Baneberry Hall and told me all the things she planned to do with the place. I wanted to do a similar story with your

416

mother, but your family wasn't there long enough for me to get the chance."

"I'm guessing you didn't see any ghosts on your tour," I say.

"Not a one. Now *that* would have been a story."

"What was Marta Carver like when you interviewed her?"

"She was nice. Friendly. Talkative. She seemed happy." Brian pauses, a thoughtful look settling over his features. For the first time today, he looks almost human. "I think about that day a lot. How it might have been one of the last happy days she ever had."

"She never remarried? Or had another child?"

Brian shakes his head. "Nor did she ever leave town, which kind of surprised everyone. Most people thought she'd move someplace where no one knew who she was or what had happened to her."

"Why do you think she stayed?"

"She was used to the town, I guess," Brian says. "Katie's buried in the cemetery behind the church. Maybe she thought that if she moved, she'd be leaving her daughter behind."

I look to the photo on the page in front of me — Curtis Carver standing apart from his family. "Curtis wasn't buried with her?"

"He was cremated. At Marta's request. The rumor is that she dumped his ashes in the trash."

The urn carrying my father's ashes sits in the back of a closet at my apartment in Boston, still in the box the funeral home handed to me as I left his memorial service. The plan was to scatter them in Boston Harbor at some point this summer. If it's proven that he killed Petra Ditmer, I might abandon that idea and take a cue from Marta Carver.

"It's got to be hard on her," I say. "Even all these years later."

"Every town has that one person something bad happened to. The one everyone else pities," Brian says. "In Bartleby, that's Marta Carver. She handles it with dignity. I'll give her that. What she endured would have crushed most other people, and the town admires her for it. Especially now."

It's something I hadn't thought of — how the current news surrounding Baneberry Hall also affects Marta Carver. Another dead girl was discovered in the very house where her own daughter died. That's got to dredge up a lot of bad memories.

"My father wrote that she left most of her belongings inside Baneberry Hall," I say. "Is that true?"

"Probably," Brian says. "She never went back to that house, I know that. After she found her husband and daughter dead, Marta called the police in hysterics. When the cops got there, they found her in a daze on the front porch and took her to the hospital. One of her friends told me she's never set foot inside Baneberry Hall since."

I lean in, getting close to the photo, studying Marta Carver's face. There isn't much to see. Her features are blurred. Nothing but dots of aged ink. But she has a story to tell.

"I need to go," I announce as I get up from the desk, leaving behind all the bound volumes of newspapers from the past. "Thanks for your help."

"Thanks for the *interview*," Brian says, putting air quotes around the word to underscore his sarcasm.

I pretend not to notice. I have a more pressing issue. One I'd hoped to avoid. But there's no getting out of it.

I need to talk to Marta Carver.

About Baneberry Hall.

And how I suspect her story is closer to my father's than anyone realizes.

Because it's lunchtime, there are quite a few people out and about. A man enters the sushi restaurant on Maple Street as, next door, a woman exits the vegetarian place with several takeout bags. But it's Marta Carver's bakery that draws most of the attention. Outside, people crowd café tables, checking their phones while sipping iced coffees. Inside, a line forms just beyond the door and snakes past the wall of birds.

When it's my turn at the counter, Marta greets me with the same polite formality as before. "What can I get you, Miss Holt?"

It dawns on me that I should have devised a plan before coming here. Or at least thought of something to say. Instead, all I do is hesitate awkwardly before saying, "I was wondering if we could talk. Somewhere private."

I don't tell her what, exactly, I want to talk about, and Marta doesn't ask. She already knows. The big question is if she'll agree to it. The Book has given her every reason to say no. Which is why I'm thrown off guard when she gives a quick nod.

"I'd like that."

"You would?"

I must look as surprised as I feel, for Marta says, "We're a lot alike, Maggie. Both of us have been defined by Baneberry Hall."

The guest in line behind me clears his throat, announcing his impatience.

"I should go," I say. "I can come back later. After the bakery's closed."

"I'll come to you," Marta replies. "After all, I know the way. Besides, it's time I faced that place again. I'll feel better knowing you're right there with me."

I leave the bakery feeling relieved. That went better than I expected.

I also feel fortunate that, after my sudden exit from the *Gazette* newsroom, Brian Prince hadn't decided to follow me. He would have stumbled upon another massive story if he had.

Marta Carver is about to return to Baneberry Hall.

After Jess left for work that morning, I convinced Petra Ditmer to babysit Maggie for a few hours. She was reluctant to do so. Understandable, considering what had transpired the last time she was at Baneberry Hall. She agreed only after I doubled her usual sitting fee.

With Petra watching Maggie, I went to the bakery Marta Carver owned downtown. I found her behind the counter, where she plastered on a polite smile and said, "How can I help you, Mr. Holt?"

"I need to talk," I said.

Marta nodded toward the customer standing behind me. "I'm sorry, but I'm very busy at the moment."

"It's important," I said. "It's about your time at Baneberry Hall."

"I really don't like to talk about that place."

Her shoulders were slumped, as if she were literally weighed down by grief. I wanted to leave her in peace. She had enough troubles, and I wasn't eager to add to them. It was only my need to know more about what was happening at Baneberry Hall that kept me talking.

"I'm worried about my daughter," I said. "She's experiencing things. Things I'm trying to understand but can't."

Marta's spine suddenly straightened. After another glance at the waiting customer behind me, she whispered, "Meet me in the library in ten minutes."

I retreated to the library and waited in the reading room. Marta arrived exactly ten minutes later, still in her apron and with a smear of icing on her forearm. A few bits of flour dusted the lenses of her spectacles, making it look as though she'd just run through a snowstorm.

"Tell me more about your daughter," she said. "What's she experiencing?"

"She's seeing things. When you and your family lived in Baneberry Hall, did anyone witness anything strange?"

"Strange how?"

"Unusual occurrences. Unexplained noises."

"Are you suggesting the house is haunted?"

"Yes." It was pointless to deny it. That was exactly my suggestion. "I think there are supernatural entities inside Baneberry Hall."

"No, Mr. Holt," Marta said. "I never saw

423

anything to suggest there were ghosts in that house."

"What about Katie and Curtis?"

Marta gave a hard blink at the mention of her family, as if their names were a gust of air she needed to brace against.

"I don't think so," she said. "My husband claimed to have heard a tapping in the hallway at night, but I was certain it was just the pipes. It's an old house, as you well know."

I assumed it was the same sound I'd been hearing in the hall.

Tap-tap-tap.

I had thought it was the restless spirit of Curtis Carver, but the fact that he also had heard it meant it was something else. Or *someone* else. Because I still didn't think the pipes were to blame.

"Back to your daughter," Marta said. "Is she sick?"

"Physically, no. Mentally, maybe. Was —" I managed to stop myself from saying Katie's name. From the way Marta had reacted to the first mention, I figured it was best not to do it again. "Was your daughter ill?"

"She had been sick, yes," Marta said. "Quite a lot. Constant weakness and nausea. We didn't know what was causing it. We took her to doctor after doctor, hoping one of them would be able to tell us what was wrong. We even went to an oncologist, thinking it might have been some form of cancer."

Having a sick child and being helpless to do anything about it is a nightmare for any parent. I'd already experienced the slightest hint of it with Maggie and her visit to Dr. Weber. But what Marta described was far worse.

"Every test came back negative," she said. "Katie was, on paper at least, a perfectly healthy child. The closest thing we got to a potential diagnosis was a doctor's suggestion that there might have been mold in the house. Something she was allergic to that didn't affect the rest of us. We arranged to have the house tested. It never happened."

She said no more, letting me infer the reason for that.

"I understand this is extremely difficult for you to talk about," I said. "But I was wondering if you could tell me what happened that day."

"My husband murdered my daughter, then killed himself." Marta Carver looked me square in the eye as she said it, daring me to turn away.

I didn't.

"I need to know how it happened," I gently said.

"I really don't see how describing the worst day of my life will help you."

"This isn't about helping me," I replied. "It's about helping my daughter."

Marta responded with a slight nod. I had convinced her.

Before speaking, she shifted in her chair and placed her palms flat against the table. All emotion left her face. I understood what she was doing — retreating to a safe place while she recounted the destruction of her family.

"I found Curtis first." Her voice had also changed. It was lifeless, almost cold. Another coping technique. "He was on the third floor. In that room of his. A man cave. That's what he called it. No girls allowed. I would have considered it ridiculous if Baneberry Hall hadn't been so big. There was enough space for each of us to have several rooms.

"That morning, I was awakened by a noise coming from Curtis's man cave. When I saw that his side of the bed was empty, I immediately got worried. I thought he might have fallen and hurt himself. I hurried up the steps to the third floor, not realizing that the life I had known and loved was about to end. But then I saw Curtis on the floor and knew he was dead. There was a trash bag over his head and that belt around his neck, and he wasn't moving. Not even a little. I think I screamed. I'm not sure. I do remember shouting for Katie to call 911. When she didn't respond, I ran back down to the second floor, yelling that she needed to get out of bed, that I needed her help, that she couldn't under any circumstances go up to the third floor.

"I really didn't think about why she wasn't responding until I was a few inches from her bedroom door. That's when it hit me. That she was dead, too. I knew it right before I got to the doorway. And when I did, I saw that it was true. She was lying there, so still. And a pillow —"

Grief cut through her voice like a hatchet. The masklike expression on her face shattered. In its place was a heart-wrenching combination of pain and sorrow and regret.

"I can't do this anymore," she said. "I'm sorry, Mr. Holt."

"I'm the one who's sorry," I said. "I shouldn't have insisted on it."

Yet there was one more thing I needed to know. Something I was reluctant to ask about because I knew it would only further Marta's pain.

"I have one last question."

"What is it?" Marta replied with understandable exasperation.

"You said you were awakened by a sound from the third floor."

"Yes. I realized later it was the sound of Curtis's body hitting the floor. A loud, horrible thud."

"Do you happen to know what time this was?"

"I looked at the clock when I realized Curtis wasn't in bed. It was four fifty-four a.m."

I had already assumed that. Yet it still didn't prevent the full-body shiver I felt upon hearing it.

Baneberry Hall remembers, Hibbs had said. And so it did.

It remembered key events and repeated them. What I'd been trying to understand was why. There had to be a reason I heard that dreadful thud upstairs every morning. Just like there was a reason for the ringing of the bells and Maggie's near-constant visits from the man she knew as Mister Shadow.

He says we're going to die here.

Coming secondhand from my daughter, it sounded like a threat. That the unruly spirit of Curtis Carver planned to do us harm.

Then why hadn't he done it yet? Instead, he continued to try to communicate with us. Which made me think he wasn't threatening us at all.

He was trying to warn us.

"Other than the tapping your husband heard, was there anything else he might have experienced that was suspicious?" I asked Marta.

428

"I already told you that he didn't," she said.

"And he never talked about feeling uneasy in the house?"

"No."

"Or that he was worried in any way about your family's safety?"

Marta crossed her arms and said, "No, and I'd appreciate it if you told me what you're suggesting, Mr. Holt."

"That someone else — or something else — killed your husband and daughter."

Marta Carver couldn't have looked more stunned if I had slapped her. Her body went still for a moment. All color drained from her face. Her appearance was so alarming that I worried she was going to pass out in the middle of the library. But then everything righted itself just before she snapped, "How dare you?"

"I'm sorry," I said. "It's just that I'm starting to suspect that what happened that day isn't what you *think* happened."

"Don't you tell me what I know and don't know about the destruction of my family," Marta said with pronounced disgust. "How would you know better than me about what happened?"

I hesitated, knowing I was about to say something that sounded colossally stupid. Insane, even. Not to mention completely insensitive to the plight of the woman who sat across from me.

"Your husband told me."

Marta shot out of her chair like an arrow. She looked down at me, her face twisted by both anger and pity.

"I knew you were naive, Mr. Holt," she said. "That was clear the moment I learned you'd bought Baneberry Hall. What I didn't know — not until right now — is that you're also cruel."

She turned her back to me and started walking. Away from the table, out of the reading room, and, finally, out of the library.

I remained at the table, feeling the full, guilty weight of Marta's words. Yes, it was cruel of me to burden her with my questions. And, yes, maybe I was also naive about the intentions of Curtis Carver. But something was about to happen at Baneberry Hall. Another remembering and repeating. Naive or not, I believed Curtis Carver was trying to save us from the same fate that befell his family. In order to avoid it, I needed to know who was responsible.

After ten more minutes spent stewing in guilt and worry, I left the library. On my way out, I passed the plaque dedicated to William Garson and, across from it, the kinder, gentler portrait than the one in Baneberry Hall.

Pausing at the painting, I noticed that Mr.

Garson's softer appearance wasn't the only difference between the two portraits.

In this one, gripped in his right hand, was a walking cane.

I zeroed in on it, taking in every detail. The ebony staff. The silver handle. The tight way William Garson gripped it, his knuckles knotted, as if he never planned on letting go. Seeing it brought to mind a sound I'd heard several times in the prior days.

Tap-tap-tap.

Coldness shot through my body. As frigid as the night I first heard the record player.

No, I thought. *You're being ridiculous. The ghost of William Garson isn't roaming Baneberry Hall, his cane tapping up and down the halls.*

Yet the cold stayed with me, even as I stepped outside into the July heat, the tapping sound echoing through my thoughts the entire way home.

NINETEEN

Marta Carver arrives just before sunset, bearing a shy smile and a cherry pie.

"It's from the bakery," she explains. "We bake fresh every morning, so I like to give leftovers to my friends."

I accept the unexpected gift, genuinely touched. "Are we friends?"

"I hope we can be, Maggie. We have —" She pauses, unsure how I'm going to react to whatever's coming next. "We have more in common than most."

I take that to mean she thinks my father is guilty. She may be right, although I'm starting to doubt it. The fact that the Book has proven itself to be true at almost every turn suggests someone else caused Petra Ditmer's death.

Or *something* else.

Something that frightens me to my core.

Had someone told me last week that I'd start to believe the Book, I would have said they were crazy. But for the first time in my life, I suspect my father knew something that I'm only now on the cusp of understanding.

I'm hoping Marta Carver can help me cross that line.

"It looks delicious," I say, gazing at the pie. "Come on in and we'll have a slice."

Marta doesn't move. She stares at Baneberry Hall's front door. Behind her round spectacles, her eyes burn with fear. In a guilt-inducing way, seeing her apprehension makes me feel better. It justifies my own fear.

"I thought I'd be able to go in there," she says. "I *want* to go in there. To show this house that I'm not afraid. How are you able to do it, Maggie?"

"I told myself what happened here wasn't real."

"I don't have that luxury."

"Then we'll talk out here," I say. "Just let me take this inside."

I carry the pie downstairs to the kitchen and return with two bottles of beer. Although I don't know if Marta drinks, it's clear she needs something to get her through this visit. Back on the porch, she accepts the bottle and takes a tentative sip. I notice the rings on her right hand — an engagement ring and a wedding band — and remember how Brian Prince told me she never remarried. I can only imagine how lonely she's been the past twenty-five years.

"I'm sorry about earlier," Marta says after another, longer sip of beer. "I thought I was brave enough to go inside. But this house has a power to it. I can't stop thinking about it, even though all I want to do is forget everything that happened here."

I raise my beer in a grim toast. "I know that feeling well."

"I thought you would," Marta says. "It's why I was glad you stopped by the bakery today. In fact, I was expecting it. I almost reached out to you, but after everything that's happened in the past few days, I didn't know if you'd want to talk. There's much to discuss."

"Let's start with my father," I say.

"You want to know if that book of his is true. At least my role in it."

Marta gives me a sidelong glance, checking to see if I'm surprised to learn she's read the Book. I am.

"I read it on the advice of my attorney," she says.

"Is your part of the story accurate?"

"To a degree, yes. I met with your father, in exactly the same way it takes place in the book. He came to the bakery, and then I met him at the library."

"What did you talk about?"

Marta holds the beer bottle with both hands, cradling it against her chest. It makes her look like a wallflower at a frat party. Timid and shy. "A lot of what eventually ended up in the book. Our time at the house. What happened that horrible day. He told me he was working on a book about Baneberry Hall, which is why I agreed to talk. I wanted him to know the truth. I was very honest about everything, from Katie's illness to how I discovered her and Curtis's bodies."

"And all that stuff about thinking your husband didn't do it?"

"We never discussed it," Marta says. "That part is entirely fiction."

I stare into my beer bottle, too ashamed by my father's actions to look Marta in the eye.

"I'm sorry my father did that. It was wrong of him."

What my father wrote about Curtis Carver is one of the many reasons I've struggled with the Book's legacy. It's one thing to make up an outlandish story and say it's real. Tabloids do it every week. Rewriting someone else's history isn't as easy to ignore. By openly claiming that Curtis Carver hadn't killed his daughter and himself, my father twisted Marta's true tragedy until it started to resemble fiction. The fact that she's here now shows a level of forgiveness I'm not sure I possess.

That's why it pains me so much to now think there's an inkling of truth to what my father wrote. Not just about Baneberry Hall being haunted.

About everything.

It's not safe there. Not for you.

"Did my father ever mention ghosts?" I say.

"Of course," Marta says. "By then, your family's story had been all over the news."

"You two didn't talk until *after* we left Baneberry Hall?"

"It was about two weeks after," Marta says. "I remember because it was the only thing people talked about when they came to the bakery. They worried I was distressed by seeing Baneberry Hall in the news so much."

"Were you?"

"At first," she admits. "But I was also curious about what your family had experienced here."

"Why?"

"Because it wouldn't surprise me if this

436

place is haunted." Marta steps off the porch to gaze up at the front exterior of Baneberry Hall. A reflection of the house fills the lenses of her spectacles, hiding the fearful curiosity I'm sure is in her eyes. "I don't believe in ghosts. But this house — and what's happened here — well, it could make me change my mind."

I remain on the porch, watching her watch Baneberry Hall. What I need to ask next is a make-or-break moment. One that might cause Marta Carver to think I'm exactly like my father.

Cruel.

"Did you ever wonder — even just for a second — if my father was right?" I say. "About those things he suggested in the Book. What if your husband didn't kill your daughter?"

I expect Marta to be angry. She ends up being the opposite. Returning to the porch, she pulls me into a fierce hug.

"Oh, Maggie, I know what you're feeling right now. I've been there, too. Wanting to believe anything other than what's right in front of you. For months — even years — I harbored this kernel of hope that Curtis didn't do it. That he couldn't have been that much of a monster. But he did do it, Maggie."

"How are you so sure?"

"He left a note," Marta says. "It was kept out of the official police report, which is why it wasn't in any articles about the crime. Curtis suffered from depression, which wasn't talked about as much then as it is now. Katie's illness sent him into a spiral. He wrote that he couldn't handle it anymore. That all he wanted to do was end the suffering he and Katie were experiencing. The police confirmed it was his handwriting, and forensics evidence proved he killed both Katie and himself."

She pauses, as if just saying those words has knocked the air out of her. That's what hearing them has done to me. I can scarcely breathe.

"It's hard coming to terms with the fact that someone you loved was capable of such cruelty," she eventually says.

I'm not ready to start that process. How can I, when so much of what happened that night remains unknown?

But Marta's mind is already made up, for she says, "I always wondered why your father wrote that book. It always troubled me why someone would go out of his way to spread such lies. It wasn't until I heard you found the Ditmer girl inside Baneberry Hall that it all made sense. It was his way of

438

justifying it."

"Justifying what?"

"Killing her," Marta says. "By exonerating my husband in the pages of his book, your father was also trying to exonerate himself. It's just that, until recently, none of us knew what his crime was."

I can't fault her thinking. In hindsight, much of the Book feels like a secret confession. My father went so far as to point out the spot in the floor where Petra's body had been hidden, almost as if daring someone to look there.

"I don't blame you for any of this, Maggie," Marta says. "Not the things your father said. Or the things he wrote. I can even understand why you're doing that thing on the auction sites."

For what feels like the twentieth time during our conversation, I give Marta a look of utter confoundment. "What thing? On what auction sites?"

"You've been selling things online. Items from Baneberry Hall. Authentic Baneberry Hall artifacts. That's what you've been calling them."

"But I haven't."

"Someone has," Marta says. "Several people have brought it to my attention, including my lawyer. He advised me to sue for part of the profits on the grounds that it's exploiting my tragedy."

I yank my phone from my pocket and open the web browser. Three search words later — *Baneberry Hall artifacts* — brings me to an auction site listing at least a dozen items claiming to be from what the seller calls "the most haunted house in America." I swipe through the wares on offer, seeing a fountain pen, several plates, a pair of candlesticks, and, the most recent addition, a silver letter opener.

I tap the image to enlarge it, paying close attention to the handle. It's not until I see two familiar letters engraved in the silver — *W.G.* — that I realize the seller isn't lying. This letter opener is the same one that went missing from Baneberry Hall.

And I know exactly who took it.

"I'm sorry," I tell Marta. "I need to go."

"Did I say something wrong?"

"Not at all. In fact, you helped me more than you know."

Marta wears a confused expression as I walk her to her car. I thank her for the pie and tell her I'll explain everything later. Because right now, I need to talk to a ghost.

Or, to be more precise, a ghoul.

JULY 12
DAY 17

I didn't tell Jess about the bells or my talk with
Marta Carver or my fear that something terrible was brewing inside Baneberry Hall. I
knew she wouldn't want to hear it. She'd made
up her mind that everything happening there
was, if not normal, then at least benign. Denial
was a powerful force, and Jess was fully
caught in its grip.

Once Jess left for work, I walked with Maggie to Elsa Ditmer's cottage to again convince
Petra to babysit. But instead of Petra, it was
Elsa herself who answered the door. We
hadn't spoken since the night of the sleepover, and I detected residual traces of anger
in her pinched expression.

"Do you need something, Mr. Holt?" she
said, looking not at me but at my daughter.

I explained that I needed to do some work
in my study and wondered if Petra could
watch Maggie for a few hours.

"Petra's being punished," Elsa said, not

elaborating why. But it was clear *how* she was being punished. Petra's voice, coming from somewhere deep inside the house, drifted out the open door.

"Lord have mercy on me," I heard her murmur. "Do not look upon my sins, but take away all my guilt."

Elsa pretended not to hear it. Instead, she finally looked my way and said, "I can watch Maggie, if you'd like. But only for an hour."

"Thank you," I said. "I really appreciate it."

Elsa retreated inside the house for a minute before returning. As she closed the front door, I could still hear Petra's feverish prayer.

"Create in me a clean heart, and renew within me an upright spirit."

Together, the three of us left for Baneberry Hall, strolling up the twisting, wooded drive in relative silence. Elsa spoke only when the roof of the house popped into view.

"Your daughter is still seeing things, yes?"

"She is," I replied. "Her doctor says she has a very active imagination."

"If only that were true."

I looked to Elsa, surprised. "You think Maggie's lying?"

"On the contrary. I think she can see things most of us aren't able to."

Ghosts.

That's what Elsa was talking about. That

Maggie was seeing ghosts. I already knew that. What I didn't know — and what I had failed to learn from Marta Carver — was if I needed to be worried. As we reached the house, it was clear I had talked to the wrong person. I should have gone to Elsa Ditmer all along.

"Do you think my daughter's in danger?"

Elsa gave a solemn nod toward Baneberry Hall. "In this house, all daughters are in danger."

I thought about the articles I'd found at the library. "You know its history, then?"

"I do," Elsa said. "My mother worked here. As did her mother. We're well-acquainted with the tragedies that have taken place inside these walls."

"What should I do?"

"You want my honest opinion?"

"Yes."

"I would leave as quickly as you're able," Elsa said. "Until then, watch your daughter closely. And be as careful as possible."

Rather than go inside, Elsa suggested that she and Maggie play in the backyard. After what I'd just been told, I thought it was a great idea. Part of me wanted to forbid Maggie from ever entering that house again, even though I knew that was impossible.

While they played, I went to the study and

sat at my desk, sorting through the articles I'd photocopied at the library. Not just the ones about the deaths of Indigo Garson and Katie Carver, but all the others, too. Those unnerving incidents no one had bothered to tell us about.

The accident in 1926 happened when a car curving its way down the hillside suddenly veered off the driveway into the woods. The driver claimed a white blur had streaked in front of the car, forcing him to swerve to miss it. The car hit a tree, killing the passenger — William Garson's fourteen-year-old granddaughter.

The man behind the wheel was her father.

In 1941, the person who drowned in the bathtub was the daughter of the Hollywood producer who had bought the place from the Garson family.

She was four, far too young to be in a bathtub on her own.

Which is why her father had been there with her.

He told police he had, for no ascertainable reason, suddenly blacked out. He woke up to the sight of his daughter's lifeless body floating in the tub. The police had considered pressing charges, but there hadn't been enough evidence.

Then two deaths in two years, after Bane-

444

berry Hall became a bed-and-breakfast. One guest, a fifteen-year-old, inexplicably climbed out a second-floor window and fell to her death. Another — a thirteen-year-old girl — was found dead in her bed, the victim of an unknown heart condition.

Both girls had been staying with their fathers.

The death in 1974 was another apparent accident. The victim, the only daughter of the family who bought the house after its bed-and-breakfast days had ended, tumbled down the main staircase.

She was five.

The same age as Maggie.

The only witness was her father, who couldn't provide a good reason why his daughter, who had gone up and down those steps hundreds of times, would fall.

Adding in Indigo Garson and Katie Carver, seven people had died in or near Baneberry Hall.

All of them girls.

All of them sixteen or younger.

All of them in the presence of their fathers.

Something entered the room just then. I sensed it — an additional presence imperceptibly felt.

"Is this Curtis Carver?"

Silence.

"If it is you, give me a sign."

The record player next to me switched itself on. I watched it happen, my eyes not quite believing what they were seeing. One moment, the turntable was still. The next, it was spinning, the grooves on the album atop it blurring as it picked up speed.

Even more incredible was when the record player's arm moved by itself, as if pushed by an unseen hand. The needle dropped on the usual spot, and the music began to play.

"You are sixteen, going on seventeen —"

I scanned the room, looking for a glimpse of Curtis Carver himself. If Maggie could see him, then it seemed reasonable I could, too.

I saw nothing.

Still, Curtis was there. The record player confirmed it.

"Did you kill your daughter?" I asked him.

The music continued to play.

"Baby, it's time to think."

I took it to mean his answer was no. Maybe because I had started to believe he was innocent. After all, he hadn't been around for all those other deaths. But William Garson had been. He had been at Baneberry Hall since the very beginning, even if for most of that time it was just literally in spirit.

"Was it William Garson?"

"Better beware, be canny and careful —"

The record began to skip, a single word repeating itself.

"careful"

"careful"

"careful"

Curtis's message was clear. William Garson was making fathers murder their daughters, just as he had.

And if I couldn't find a way to stop him, Maggie was going to be next.

TWENTY

Hannah Ditmer doesn't appear surprised when she finds me pounding on the back door of her mother's cottage. She seems more impatient than anything else, shooting me a look that says, *What took you so long?*

"Since I arrived, how many times have you been inside Baneberry Hall?" I say. "And how long have you been stealing from us?"

"It's not stealing if no one wants it," Hannah says.

"Just because that house sat empty didn't mean those things were yours to take."

Hannah gives an agree-to-disagree shrug. "I can give you back the stuff that hasn't sold. But most of what I took from that house is long gone. And good luck trying to get it back."

She drifts away from the open door, giving me the choice to enter or not. It's obvious she doesn't care. I opt to follow her, past the living room — the TV now blaring a cooking show — and into the kitchen.

"You never answered my question," I say. "How long has it been going on?"

"A couple years." Hannah sits at the kitchen table and reaches for her pack of Marlboro Lights. "Since my mom got sick."

That also answers my second question — why. And I get it. Elsa Ditmer was sick, they needed money, and Baneberry Hall was just sitting empty. A house-shaped treasure trove at the top of the hill.

"And how many times did you sneak in since I've been there?"

I know now it was her who kept entering Baneberry Hall and not some random ghoul from town. She's the shadowy figure I saw outside the night I arrived. And the one I saw fleeing the house the night after that. The ringing bells and the chandelier and the record player — all of it was Hannah.

She lights a cigarette. Smoke curls from her parted lips. "Enough that I'm surprised you didn't catch me earlier."

"Why'd you do it?" I say. "I don't care about most of the junk in that house. If you wanted it, all you needed to do was ask. You certainly didn't need to distract me with ringing bells and a record player."

"It wasn't a distraction," Hannah says. "It was more of an attempt to get you to leave.

That house has been a gold mine. I didn't want to risk losing it."

"So all of this was just some *Scooby-Doo* trick to scare me away?"

"I figured I'd give it a shot." Hannah exhales a stream of smoke, pleased with herself. "And I would have gotten away with it if it wasn't for you meddling kids."

"I assume that's why you also told me what my father wrote about that sleepover was true."

"Some of it was," Hannah says. "You really did think someone was in that wardrobe and started freaking out. And you did punch me. Although I was being a little bitch that night and probably had it coming. So, yeah, your father made up a lot of it, but the result was the same — we left early, and my mother was so pissed that she forbade us from going to your house again."

"You didn't need to lie about that," I say. "Nor did you need to do all that haunted-house shit. The record player and that stupid teddy bear."

Hannah stubs out her cigarette. "What bear?"

"You know what bear," I say. "Buster."

"I haven't seen Buster since the night Petra vanished."

I stare at her, looking for signs she's lying.

But Hannah's face is now like a mask, hiding all emotion.

"I think it's best if you give me your keys," I say. "To the gate and to the house itself."

"If you insist," Hannah says.

She leaves the kitchen and disappears upstairs, her footfalls heavy on the steps. Moments later, a shadow slides across the kitchen wall, darkening the Formica countertop. I spin around to see Elsa Ditmer in the doorway, wearing the same nightgown she had on the night I returned to Baneberry Hall. The crucifix around her neck glints in the kitchen light.

"You're not Petra," she says, shuffling toward me.

"I'm not," I say. "I'm Maggie Holt."

"Maggie." Elsa's upon me now, her hands cold on my cheeks as she stares into my eyes. "Don't stay in that house. You're going to die there."

Hannah enters the kitchen, a key ring in her hand. Her face drops when she sees her mother.

"Mama, you should be resting," she says, gently pulling Elsa away from me.

"I want to see Petra."

"I told you, Petra's gone."

"Where?" Elsa's voice is so full of heartbreak it makes me want to cover my ears.

451

"Where has she gone?"

"We'll talk about it tomorrow." Hannah looks my way, concerned I'm going to judge her for not telling her mother the truth. I wouldn't dare. I know full well how much the truth can hurt. "Now let's get you into bed."

The two women leave the kitchen. A few minutes later, Hannah returns and collapses into her chair. I can't help but pity her. She's a thief. She's a liar. But she's also had a much harder life than I have. I often forget that, despite all the grief it's brought us, my family's time at Baneberry Hall made us rich.

When Hannah slides the keys toward me, I push them back across the table.

"Listen," I say, "I don't plan on keeping most of the stuff inside that house. Next week, if you want, you can come over and take whatever you want to sell. There's a shitload of antiques in there. And a lot of money that could be made."

"All of it's yours," Hannah says.

"Not really. Most of it came with the house. It doesn't belong to anyone. So consider it yours."

"I'll think about it." Hannah takes the keys and, with a grateful nod, shoves them back in her pocket. "But just so you know, I haven't used these to sneak inside since you came back."

I cock my head. "What are you saying?"

"That there are other ways into that house."

"Where?"

Hannah reaches for another cigarette but decides against it. Instead, she stares at her hands and quietly says, "I got in through the door at the back of the house."

"There isn't a back door to Baneberry Hall."

"It's hidden," she says. "My mother showed it to me years ago."

Once again, I look for signs that she's lying. I don't see any. In that moment, Hannah Ditmer looks the most sincere I've ever seen her.

"Please. Tell me where?"

"Back of the house," Hannah says. "Behind the ivy."

July 13
Day 18

That morning, I was awakened by a series of blows to my face and chest. Lost in the gray between dreams and wakefulness, I at first thought it was the ghost of William Garson, beating me with his cane. But when I opened my eyes, I saw it was Jess, pummeling me with both fists.

"What did you do?" she screamed. *"What the fuck did you do?"*

She sat on top of me, red-faced and furious. Although I was able to buck her off me, Jess managed to land a haymaker before falling sideways. Pain pulsed across my jaw as we reversed positions — me straddling her thrashing legs and gripping wrists that vibrated with rage.

"What the hell is wrong with you?" I yelled.

"Me? What's wrong with *you?"*

Overpowered and overwhelmed — with rage, with despair, with exhaustion — Jess gave up the fight. It shattered my heart to feel

454

her body go limp beneath mine, to see her sink into the bed, moaning. I would have preferred a thousand punches to that.

"How could you do that, Ewan?" she moaned. "How could you hurt Maggie?"

The mention of our daughter sent me into a full-blown panic. I jumped off the bed and scrambled to Maggie's room, thinking of Katie Carver and Indigo Garson and all those other girls who'd died within these walls.

When I reached her room and saw Maggie sitting up in bed, the relief I felt was stronger than anything I'd experienced before or since. My daughter was safe. William Garson hadn't gotten to her.

Then I saw her neck, and my panic returned.

It was circled with marks so red they looked as though they'd been seared into her skin. Making it worse was how they resembled handprints. I could make out the ovals of palms and crimson columns left by fingers.

Maggie looked at me from the bed, terrified, and began to wail. I started to go to her but felt something swoop up behind me — a sudden force as strong as a wind gust. It was Jess again, her anger returning to full boil. In an instant she shoved me to the floor.

"Don't you dare touch her!" she shouted.

I scrambled backward along the floor, just in case Jess tried to kick me. She looked so angry I expected one at any moment. "What happened to her?"

Jess stared down at me with an unspeakable look of hatred on her face. There was nothing else it could have been. In that moment, my wife despised me.

"Maggie woke me up with her crying. I came here and found her gasping for breath. Her face was purple, Ewan. And then I saw those marks on her neck —"

"Jess, you know I would never hurt her. You have to believe me."

"Our daughter's pain is what I believe," Jess said. "And since I didn't hurt her, that leaves you."

Maggie had started to wail even more, the sound so loud I at first thought Jess couldn't hear me when I said, "It doesn't."

She heard. It just took her a second to react. When she did, it was with a snarled "Of course it was you!"

"Think about it, Jess," I said. "I was asleep. You're the one who woke me up."

"You weren't asleep," she said. "You'd just crawled back into bed the second before I heard Maggie crying."

Panic poured into me — an all-consuming wave. I remained on the floor, my head in my hands, feeling terrified and guilty. I'd hurt my daughter, and I hadn't even been aware of it.

"It wasn't me, Jess," I said. "I need you to believe that."

"Ewan, I saw you get back into bed."

"It might have been me, but it wasn't intentional," I said, knowing I sounded crazy. "William Garson made me do it."

He'd come for Maggie, just as he'd come for the others. Each method was different — baneberries for his daughter, a pillow over Katie Carver's face. Drownings and falls and accidents. Each death brought about by their fathers, even though they had no control over their actions.

"He's been killing people throughout the history of this house. All of them girls. All of them sixteen or under. He killed his daughter, Jess. And now he's making other fathers kill theirs. He's been doing it for years."

Jess looked at me like I was a stranger. I couldn't blame her. In that moment, I was unrecognizable even to myself.

"Listen to yourself, Ewan," she said. "Spouting this gibberish, trying to excuse what you've done. You're lucky I don't call the police."

"Call them." That would have been one way out of the situation — locking me away where I couldn't get to Maggie and William Garson couldn't get to me. "Please call them."

"You're sick, Ewan," Jess said before

snatching Maggie off the bed and leaving the room.

I followed them down the hall to our bedroom, my body getting more numb with each step. I couldn't believe that my biggest fear was about to come true. I was about to lose my family.

"I didn't mean to do it."

Jess slammed the bedroom door in my face. I reached for the handle and, finding it locked, began to pound on the door.

"Jess, please! You have to believe me!"

All I heard on the other side of the door was the sound of drawers being opened and closet doors slamming shut. Ten minutes later, Jess emerged with a packed suitcase, which she dragged behind her while still carrying Maggie. They veered into Maggie's room to repeat the process.

Slam.

Lock.

Pack.

I paced the hallway, wondering what to do. The answer hit me when Jess finally left Maggie's room with another, smaller suitcase.

Nothing.

Let them leave. Let Jess take Maggie as far away from Baneberry Hall as possible. It didn't matter that she was angry with me and might be for a very long time. Maybe forever. What mattered was that Maggie wouldn't be inside these walls.

"Just tell me where you're going," I said as I followed them down the stairs.

"No," Jess said with a ferocity I didn't think was possible.

I caught up to them at the bottom of the steps and pushed in front of Jess, briefly halting their escape.

"Look at me, Jess." I stood before her, hoping she still recognized the real me. Hoping that some small traces of that man remained. "I would never intentionally hurt our daughter. You *know* that."

Jess, who'd been keeping up a brave face for Maggie's sake, let it crumble. "I don't know anything anymore."

"Know that I love you. And I love Maggie. And I'm going to fix this while you're gone. I promise. This house won't hurt Maggie anymore."

Jess looked into my eyes, a thousand emotions shifting across her face. I glimpsed sadness and fear and confusion.

"It's not the house I'm afraid of," she said.

She stepped around me, weighed down with our daughter and two suitcases. All three were placed on the floor just long enough for her to open the front door. Jess picked up her suitcase. Maggie lifted hers. Then together the two of them, still in their nightclothes, left Baneberry Hall.

I watched their departure from the vestibule, not blinking as the car vanished from view. Under any other circumstances, I would have been devastated. My wife and child had left me. I didn't know where they were going. I didn't know when they'd return. Yet I felt nothing but relief after they were gone. It meant Maggie was far from Baneberry Hall.

It wasn't safe there. Not for her.

And it would never be safe with the spirit of William Garson still present. Although I knew I needed to rid him from the place, I had no idea how. In fact, there was only one person I could turn to for advice.

And he wasn't even alive.

Without any other options, I made my way to the kitchen and sat facing the bells on the wall.

Then I waited.

TWENTY-ONE

In my line of work, I've crossed paths with plenty of landscapers. Some are true artists, crafting elaborate groundscapes with attention paid to color, shape, and texture. Others are basic laborers, trained only to yank weeds and shovel mulch. But all of them have told me the same thing: plant ivy at your own peril. Gone unchecked, it spreads and climbs and persists more than any other vine.

The ivy behind Baneberry Hall has done all three for decades. It's thick — jungle thick — and scales the back of the house in a verdant swath that climbs past the second-floor windows. If there is a door back there, the ivy hides it completely.

At first, I try swiping at some vines, hoping they'll fall away from the wall. If only it were that easy. When that doesn't work, I shove my hands into the thick of it and blindly feel around, my fingers brushing

461

nothing but exterior wall.

But then I feel it.

Wood.

I do more tugging and brushing until a door begins to take shape deep within the vines. Short and narrow, it's less a door and more like a flat board where a proper door should be located. There's not even a handle — just a rusted bolt that I slide to the side.

The door cracks open, and I give it a pull, widening it until there's a gap big enough for me to fit through. Then, like a diver about to submerge, I take a deep breath and push through the curtain of ivy.

Once inside, I can barely see. There's no overhead light that I can find, and the ivy outside allows only dapples of moonlight to pass through. Luckily, I anticipated this and came prepared with a flashlight.

I switch it on and am greeted by a brick wall slick with moisture. A millipede scurries across it, fleeing the light. To my left is more wall. To my right is inky darkness that stretches beyond the flashlight's glow. I move through it, arriving shortly at a set of wooden steps.

The sight confounds me.

How did I never know this was here?

It makes me wonder if my parents knew about it. Probably not. I'd like to think that had my father been aware of a secret stair-case in the back of Baneberry Hall, he would have put it in the Book. It would have been too appropriately Gothic to resist.

I climb the steps slowly, taking them one at a time. I have no idea where they lead, and that makes me nervous. So nervous that the flashlight I'm gripping trembles, casting a jittery glow on the stairwell walls.

After a dozen steps, I reach a landing that could be right out of a Hammer film. It's small and creaky, with a skein of cobwebs in the corner. I pause there, disoriented, with no clue how far I've climbed or where I am inside the house.

I get a better idea once I ascend twelve more steps and a second landing, which would put me firmly on the second floor. There's a door here as well — similar to the one hidden behind the ivy. Smooth and featureless, save for another bolt keeping it shut.

I slide the bolt.

I pull the door.

Beyond it is a closet of some sort.

The flashlight's beam lands on several little white dresses hanging inside. Behind them is a thin slice of light.

More doors.

Reaching past the dresses, I push them

463

open and see a bedroom.

My bedroom.

I stumble through the doors and rotate around the room, seeing my bed, my suitcases, the knife sitting atop my nightstand.

Then I see the armoire.

The doorway through which I've just emerged.

Shock overwhelms me. I stare at the armoire, uncomprehending, when in truth the situation is easy to understand.

There is a direct route from outside into the bedroom.

It's why my father had felt it necessary to nail those boards across the armoire doors.

It's how Hannah Ditmer got into the house unnoticed and without disturbing the doors and windows.

It's how anyone with knowledge of the passageway can get inside.

Another wave of shock strikes. A real wallop that leaves me tilting sideways, on the verge of being bowled right over.

This entrance into Baneberry Hall isn't new. It's been around for decades. Likely since the place was built.

Someone had access to this room back when we lived here.

When I slept here.

It wasn't Mister Shadow who crept into

464

my room at night, whispering to me.

It was someone else.

Someone real.

July 14
Day 19

The first bell didn't ring until shortly after two p.m.

The sound of it snapped me out of the waking stupor I'd been in and out of since sitting down the day before. In all that time, I'd barely moved. I hadn't eaten. I certainly hadn't showered. When I did leave my post, it was only to relieve myself. By midmorning, I'd even stopped doing that, fearful I'd miss an all-important bell chime. Now two bottles of my urine sat in a corner of the kitchen.

I understood — as best as one could in a state of such extreme exhaustion — that I was probably going crazy. These weren't the actions of a sane man. But each time I was on the cusp of leaving the kitchen, something happened to remind me that I wasn't insane.

Baneberry Hall was.

During my twenty-hour vigil in the kitchen, the house had been alive with noise. Sounds no home should make under normal circumstances. Sounds that I had nonetheless grown accustomed to hearing.

Music trickling down from the third-floor study and quietly drifting through empty rooms above.

"You are sixteen, going on seventeen."

The sound of William Garson walking up and down the second-floor hallway, punctuating each step with a strike of his cane.

Tap-tap-tap.

And at 4:54 in the morning, a familiar noise from the study, so loud it reverberated through the house all the way down to the kitchen.

Thud.

Curtis Carver, I now knew. Hitting the floor when life left his body. An action his spirit was doomed to repeat every day for as long as Baneberry Hall was still standing.

But no sound caught my attention more than that single ring at two p.m. It was, after all, what I had been waiting for.

"Hello?" I said.

The same bell rang again. The Indigo Room.

Other bells began to chime a total of four times, repeating the pattern that made me understand the ringing in the first place.

HELLO

More bells rang. Four of them. One on the first row. One on the second. Back to the first, where the first bell in the row rang. Then again at the second with the chiming of the row's second bell.

Together, it spelled out my name.

EWAN

"Hi, Curtis." I coughed out a rueful chuckle. Yes, I was now on a first-name basis with a ghost. "I've been waiting for you."

One bell.

I

Four more bells from all over the wall.

KNOW

"Then you also know I need your help."

The last bell on the second row chimed — the start of a three-ring answer I knew well.

YES

"Then help me, Curtis," I said. "Help me stop William Garson."

One bell rang.

N

Then another.

O

I waited for more, inching forward in my chair. After ten seconds passed without the sound of any other bells, I said, "Why not?"

The same two bells rang again.

NO

"But he killed your daughter."

I got those same two rings in response.

NO

"He didn't?"

One ring. Two rings.

NO

"Then who did?"

Three bells rang a total of four times, the second one chiming twice on the second row.

LOOK

"At what?" I said, growing frustrated. "What should I be looking at?"

There was a pause during which I sat staring at the wall, waiting for a response. When it came — six bells ringing throughout the wall, two of them chiming twice — I could barely keep up. It was only after they had quieted that I had time to match the bells to their corresponding letters.

The word it spelled was PORTRAIT.

"William Garson's portrait?" I asked.

The second and third bells on the second row rang one last time.

NO

I was about to respond, but then the bells sprang to life again. Three rings followed by the shortest of pauses and then the same run of six bells and eight letters I'd just seen. Again, it took me a moment to figure it out.

When I did, I let out a gasp so loud and sudden that it echoed off the kitchen walls.

HER PORTRAIT

I rushed upstairs and moved through the great room. When I reached the front staircase, I looked up to see the chandelier aglow, even though it had been dark the last time I passed beneath it.

A sign that spirits were active. I felt foolish for not realizing it sooner.

I kept moving. Past the staircase. Into the Indigo Room. I didn't stop until I was at the fireplace, looking up at the portrait Curtis had been referring to.

Indigo Garson.

I stared at the painting, wondering what I was supposed to be seeing. Nothing seemed amiss about it. It was a portrait of a young woman painted by a man who had been in love with her.

I didn't find anything strange about that.

But then I looked to the white rabbit Indigo held in her hands. I'd previously noticed the chip of missing paint at the animal's left eye. Considering it was the portrait's only flaw, it was hard to miss. But it also drew the eye away from the fact that the rabbit had been rendered in a slightly different manner than everything else. It wasn't as detailed as the rest of the painting, as if it had been the work of an entirely different artist.

I moved close, studying the rabbit's fur, which lacked the individual brushstrokes of Indigo's shining hair. The paint there was thicker as well. Not overtly so. Just raised slightly higher than everything else. When I zeroed in on the rabbit's missing eye, I saw within its socket another layer of paint behind it.

Someone had painted over the portrait.

Using a thumbnail, I scraped at the paint surrounding the rabbit's eye. It fell off in tiny flecks that dusted the fireplace mantel. Each piece that was chipped away revealed a little bit more of the original portrait. Grays and red and browns.

I kept scraping until a sliver of paint lodged itself under my thumbnail — a needle prick of pain that shot through my entire hand. After that, I switched to a putty knife fished out of the utility drawer in the kitchen and kept scraping.

Slowly.

Methodically.

Careful not to also scrape the paint below, which emerged not unlike a freshly taken Polaroid. Color appearing from an expanse of white until the full picture was formed.

It wasn't until the rabbit had been completely chipped away that my body succumbed to exhaustion. It began with dizziness, which overtook me at alarming speed. I staggered backward, the room spinning.

Everything went gray, and I realized I was falling. I hit the floor and remained there, sprawled on my back, the gray that swarmed my vision darkening into blackness.

Before I passed out, I caught one good look at the original portrait, now freshly exposed.

Indigo Garson, looking as angelic as she always had. Same alabaster skin and golden curls and beatific expression.

But it was no longer a rabbit held in her daintily gloved hands.

It was a snake.

TWENTY-TWO

"I need your help."

There's silence on Dane's end — an uncertainty evident even over the phone. I don't blame him. Not after the things I've said. I'd understand if he wanted nothing more to do with me.

After tonight, he just might get that wish.

"With what?" he eventually says.

"Moving an armoire."

I don't tell him that the armoire needs not to be moved, but disassembled completely. And that the hole in the bedroom wall it will leave behind needs to be sealed shut. And that there's a door in the back of the house that will also need to be boarded up so no one will be able to enter Baneberry Hall without a key. All of that can wait until he gets here. Otherwise he might hang up.

"Can't it wait until tomorrow?" Dane says.

"It can't. I *need* your help. Please. I can't

do it alone."

"Fine," Dane says with an epic sigh. "I'll be there in ten."

"Thank you."

Dane doesn't hear that part. He's already ended the call.

I shove my phone into my pocket and prepare for the job ahead. The plan is simple — block off the secret passage to the bedroom, gather up my things, and leave Baneberry Hall.

This time, I won't be returning.

Once I'm back in Boston, I'll list the house and sell it as is for whatever offer I get, no matter how small it might be. I no longer want anything to do with this place. Nor do I want the truth about what happened here.

I just want to be gone.

It's not safe here. Not for me.

In the dining room, I gather the five Polaroids on the table and my father's copy of the Book, still splayed spine-up on the floor. They'll be going right back where I found them. Soon to be someone else's problem.

My hands full, I march to the third-floor study and go straight to the desk, where I drop the Book and the photos. I then grab Buster and toss him into the closet where he'd first been discovered.

Much like Baneberry Hall, I never want to see that bear again.

I turn back to the desk, where the Book sits open.

It was closed when I dropped it there.

I'm certain of it.

Yet there it is, flopped open, as if someone has just been reading it.

I approach the Book slowly, considering all the ways it could have opened on its own. I can't think of any. At least nothing that doesn't border on the supernatural. Or, to borrow a term from Dane's grandmother, the uncanny.

Bullshit, I think.

I then say it aloud, hoping that uttering the word will make it true.

"Bullshit."

But it isn't. I know that the moment I see the page the Book is open to. It's the chapter that takes place on the Fourth of July. The day the kitchen ceiling was patched. I scan the page, one passage in particular leaping out at me.

Now it was time to patch the formidable hole in the ceiling. For that, I enlisted Hibbs, who brought a boy from town to help because the task was too big for just him alone.

My heart beats faster as I read it again and let the full weight of the words sink in.

A boy from town.

Who was in this house the same time as Petra.

Who likely knew her.

Who could have been her boyfriend. Or something.

Who might have persuaded her to sneak out her bedroom window.

Who might have suggested they run away together and became violent when Petra got second thoughts.

Who then broke into Baneberry Hall and dumped her body under the floorboards because he knew there was a hiding place there.

A boy, I realize, who's in one of the Polaroids my father took.

I snatch the photo off the desk. When I first saw it, I'd thought it was my father standing behind Walt Hibbets and his ladder. I should have realized my father was likely behind the camera — and that it was someone else lurking in the back of the image.

I can't see too many details, even after I bring the picture close to my face and squint. Just a narrow slice of clothing and an even smaller sliver of face poke out beyond the ladder. The only way I can get a bigger, better view is if I had a magnifying glass.

Which I realize with a delighted jolt that I do.

There's one in the top desk drawer. I saw it there during my first trek into the study. It's still there now, sitting among pens and paper clips. I grab it and hold it in front of the Polaroid, the mystery man now exponentially larger. I see dark hair, half of a handsome face, a sturdy arm, and a broad chest.

And I see his T-shirt.

Black and emblazoned with an image that's only half visible.

The Rolling Stones logo.

My mind flashes back to that dingy room at the Two Pines. Dane stepping inside, looking so good that I couldn't help but stare. When he caught me, I complimented his shirt. I hear his voice loud in my memory.

I've had it since I was a teenager.

And I hear his voice now, coming from the study door, where he stands with his arms at his sides and a dour look on his face.

"I can explain," he says.

JULY 15
DAY 20 — BEFORE DARK

I woke up on the floor.

Where in the house, I didn't know.

All I knew when I regained consciousness was that I was somewhere inside Baneberry Hall, flat-backed on the floor, my joints stiff and my head pounding. It wasn't until I opened my eyes and saw the portrait of Indigo Garson staring down at me that everything came rushing back.

Me in the Indigo Room.

Scraping at the painting.

Seeing the snake in Indigo's hands.

A snake that, the longer I looked at it, the more unnerved I became. I wanted to believe Indigo's pose with the snake was one of those Victorian-era eccentricities. Like death masks and taxidermied birds on hats. But my gut told me there was something far more sinister behind it.

That the snake represented Indigo's true nature.

A predator.

I assumed it was William Garson who'd ordered it painted over. An attempt to hide the truth about his daughter. I suspected he couldn't bear to paint over the whole portrait. The artist — poor, besotted Callum Auguste — had done too good a job for that. So the rabbit replaced the snake, an ironic reversal not found in nature.

Now the snake was exposed again. With it came grim understanding that I'd been wrong about so much.

It wasn't William Garson making fathers kill their daughters inside Baneberry Hall.

It was Indigo.

I understood it with icy clarity. Just like the snake in her hands, she slithered her way into the minds of men who lived here, making them obsessed with what happened to her. I didn't know if she died by her own hand or her father's. In the end, it didn't matter. Indigo was dead, but her spirit remained. Now she spent her days seeking vengeance for what her father had done. She didn't care that he, too, was long gone. To her, every father deserved punishment.

So she made them kill their daughters.

Six times that had happened.

There wasn't going to be a seventh.

I made my way back to the kitchen slowly,

too sore from my night on the floor to move quickly. After hobbling down the steps, I found myself in front of the bells once more.

"Curtis," I whispered, fearful Indigo was also nearby. Lurking. Listening. "Are you there?"

Three familiar bells rang.

YES

"It was Indigo, wasn't it? She made you kill Katie."

Another three rings.

YES

"What can I do?" I said. "How can I stop her? How can I tell if she's here?"

Five bells rang a total of six times. At the final chime — the first bell on the first row — I realized he had spelled a word new to this weird form of communication.

CAMERA

I knew what he was referring to. The Polaroid camera in the study.

"Thank you, Curtis." As I whispered it, I realized I was never going to hear from him again. He'd told me everything he could. The rest was up to me. So before leaving the bells, I added a somber, sincere "I hope this frees you from this place. I really do. I hope you find peace."

With that, I made my way up three sets of stairs, my joints creaking the entire climb. In the third-floor study, I found what I was looking for in the closet.

A blue shoebox full of Polaroids.

I sorted through them, seeking the ones I'd neglected to look at the day I discovered the box. Photo after photo of Curtis Carver's increasingly haunted face. I wondered if, when he took them, he felt as helpless as I did. If he was as worried and racked with the same guilt that weighed on me.

The images of Curtis were so similar that I needed to look at the dates scribbled below them to indicate which ones I hadn't already seen. July 12th. That was one was new. As were pictures from July 13th and 14th.

The last Polaroid sat facedown at the bottom of the box. Flipping it over, I saw that, like the others, the date it had been taken had been written across the bottom of the photo.

July 15th.

A year to the day since Curtis Carver killed himself.

My gaze moved from the date to the image itself. At first, it looked like the others. But a second glance revealed something different from the rest of the photos. Something deeply, deeply wrong.

Someone else was in the room with Carver.

A dark figure tucked into a far corner of the study.

Although Maggie had called her Miss Pennyface, I knew her by another name.

Indigo Garson.

She looked exactly like the woman in the portrait. Same purple dress and ethereal glow. The only difference between her painting and her ghost was her eyes.

They were covered by coins.

Yet it was clear she could still see. In the photograph, she stared at the back of Curtis Carver's head, almost as if she could read his thoughts.

I was still studying the picture when a presence entered the room, invisible yet palpably felt.

"Curtis, is that you?"

I received no response.

Yet the presence increased, filling the room with a heat so strong it was almost suffocating. Inside that menacing warmth was something even more disturbing.

Anger.

It burned through the room like fire.

I grabbed the camera from the desk and took a self-portrait similar to the ones Curtis had taken.

The shutter clicked.

The camera hummed.

A picture slid out, its pristine whiteness slowly giving way to an image.

Me.

Arms extended. Staring at the camera. Expanse of study behind me.

Also behind me was Indigo Garson, edging into the frame. I saw a slender arm, the curve of her shoulder, stringy strands of blond hair.

She was there.

And she was waiting.

Not for me.

For Maggie.

"Keep waiting, bitch," I said aloud.

I raised the camera and took another picture.

Click.

Hum.

Slide.

In that photo, Indigo had moved to the other side of the study. She pressed against the wall, slightly hunched, her coin-covered eyes peering at me through a veil of hair. Her lips were twisted into a grin so sinister it turned my blood cold.

The only thing that kept me from fleeing the house was the knowledge that she didn't want to hurt me. Not yet, even though that moment would surely arrive. But for the time being, she needed me to get to Maggie.

Convinced I was out of harm's way for the short term, I moved to the closet, grabbed all the packages of film sitting inside, and carried them back to the desk.

I remained there as the pale light of morning changed to the golden sun of afternoon. Every so often, I'd take another picture, just to keep track of Indigo's whereabouts in the room. Sometimes she was in a far corner, facing the wall. Other times she was just a sliver of purple on the edge of the frame. In a few photos, she wasn't visible at all.

But I knew she was still there.

I felt the angry heat of her presence.

I continued to feel it until the daylight outside the office widows had given way to the lonesome blues of twilight. That's when Indigo suddenly vanished — an instant cooling.

I grabbed the camera and took another picture.

Click.

Hum.

Slide.

I snatched the Polaroid from the camera and held it in front of me, watching the image take shape.

It was just like all the others — me and a woman standing in the background.

Only this time it wasn't Indigo.

It was Jess. Standing just inside the study. Every muscle in her body tensed. Confusion streaking across her features like lightning.

I turned around slowly, hoping she was just an imagining brought about by hunger, thirst, and a need for sleep. But then Jess spoke —

"Ewan? What are you doing up here?" — and my heart sank.

It meant she was real and that Indigo's patience had paid off.

Maggie had come home.

TWENTY-THREE

Dane takes a step into the study. I take a
step back, pressing against the edge of the
desk.

"It's not what you think," he says.

I hold up the Polaroid. "You knew her."

"I did," Dane says. "I was living with my
grandparents that summer. My parents
thought it would do me some good. I was
seventeen and a fuckup and needed to get
away from them for a while. So I came
here."

"And met Petra. You're the reason she
snuck out at night."

A nod from Dane. "We'd meet in the
woods behind your house and mess around.
It wasn't anything serious. Just a summer
fling."

He's moved farther into the room while
talking, hoping I won't notice. I do.

"If it wasn't serious, why did you kill her?"

"I didn't," Dane says. "You have to believe

486

me, Maggie."

That's not going to happen. Especially when I recall the way we'd found Petra. Dane pushing on the stained ceiling, testing it. Pushing and pushing until it gave way, which — I now suspect — was exactly what he wanted to happen. I think he knew Petra's remains would be discovered at some point during the renovation and decided it would look better if he was the one to find them. That way all suspicion would shift to my father.

Dane edges forward again until mere feet separate us.

"Take one more step and I'm calling the police," I warn.

"You can't do that, Maggie," he says. "That'll send me instantly back to jail. No one will believe me. They'll just see an ex-con who almost killed a man. I won't stand a chance."

"Maybe you don't deserve one."

Dane swoops in close. I try to yank my phone from my pocket, but he slaps it out of my hands. It hits the wall and drops to the floor several yards away.

He grips my shoulders, shaking me. "Listen to me, Maggie. You need to pretend you never found out about me and Petra."

He stares at me with a mean scowl and

even meaner eyes. There's anger in them. A darkness that makes me wonder if it's the last thing Petra ever saw. I look away, spot the knife I brought with me still on the desk, and reach for it.

Dane sees it, too, and lunges for it.

That's when I run.

It starts with a push off the desk, followed by a quick arc around Dane. When he comes at me, I shove him in the chest.

Hard.

He lurches backward into one of the bookshelves, his arms flailing, loose books tumbling around him.

I run.

Down the steps.

Into the second-floor hallway, where I can hear Dane coming after me, his footfalls fast and heavy down the stairs from the third floor.

I keep moving. Breath hard. Heart hammering.

I hit the main staircase at a full run, pounding down it, trying to ignore the sound of Dane barreling across the hallway behind me. And how fast he's moving. And how he's surely gaining on me.

He's also at the stairs now. I hear his boots slam the top step and feel the shimmy of the staircase as he thunders after me.

I up my speed, my eyes on the vestibule and, just beyond it, the front door. In the slice of time it takes to move down the last two steps, I try to gauge if I can make it to that door before Dane catches up to me.

I decide I can't.

Even if I can get through that door — which is debatable — I'll still need to elude Dane's grasp long enough to get off the porch and into my truck.

That's not enough time. Not with the way he's storming up behind me.

I change tactics. A split-second decision that, at the bottom of the stairs, jerks me away from the vestibule and into the parlor.

Dane doesn't break stride as he veers in the same direction, panting my name so hard and so close I feel his breath on the back of my neck.

I ignore him as I propel myself through the parlor and into the Indigo Room.

It's dark inside.

Good.

I need it that way.

There's just enough light for me to see the hole where a length of floorboards used to be. Even then, a person would need to know it's there to avoid missing it entirely.

Dane doesn't.

I skip over the gap in the floor and jerk to

a stop before whipping around to face him.

Dane slows but keeps on coming.

One step.

Two.

Then he drops, plunging through the hole and vanishing so thoroughly that the only sign he was ever there at all is the sound of his body hitting the kitchen floor far below.

July 15
Day 20 — After Dark

"We need to leave," I told Jess. "Right now."

"Why? What's going on?"

"Maggie's not safe here."

I snatched the camera off the desk, along with two boxes of film. Then I hustled Jess out of the study and down the steps.

"I don't understand what's happening," she said.

We reached the second floor, and I turned around, snapping a picture of the stairs behind us.

Click.

Hum.

Slide.

"There is a ghost in our house," I said while waiting for the picture to develop. "Indigo Garson. She's been making fathers kill their daughters. Curtis Carver didn't murder Katie. Indigo forced him to do it."

I thrust the Polaroid at Jess, making sure she saw the figure of Indigo caught hobbling down the steps, the coins over her eyes reflecting the camera's flash. Jess clamped a hand over her mouth, trying to suppress a scream. It leaked out anyway, squeaking between her fingers.

"Where's Maggie?" I said.

Jess, her hand still covering her mouth, cast her wide, shocked eyes in the direction of Maggie's bedroom. Behind us, a volatile heat drifted from the third-floor stairs. Indigo announcing her presence.

"We need to get her out of there," I whispered. "Fast."

We both ran down the hallway, Indigo's presence hot on our backs. Inside the bedroom, Maggie sat on her bed, her knees to her chin. Flames of fear danced in her eyes.

"You'll have to carry her," I told Jess. "I don't — I don't trust myself to do it."

There was no second-guessing on Jess's part. She went straight for the bed and scooped Maggie into her arms.

"Mommy, I'm scared," Maggie said.

Jess kissed her cheek. "I know, honey. But there's nothing to be frightened of."

It was a lie. There was plenty to be afraid of.

Especially when the armoire doors flew open. A blast of hot air burst from inside, sending Jess reeling backward. Maggie rose from her arms, as if lifted by the scalding wind. She was then pulled toward the armoire, riding through midair, a screaming, crying tangle of limbs and hair.

Indigo had our daughter.

I reached the armoire just as Maggie vanished into it. When the doors began to close, I threw myself between them. The wood squeezed my ribs as I reached into the armoire — now a dark, fathomless space. I screamed Maggie's name and flailed my arms until one of my knuckles brushed her ankle.

I clamped my fingers around it and began tugging, hand over hand up her leg. When I reached her knee, I pulled harder until Maggie abruptly broke free from the armoire. We fell to the floor, Maggie on top of me, still screaming, still crying.

Behind us, Jess began to move the bed, shoving it against the armoire to block the doors. While it wasn't enough to trap Indigo inside, I hoped it would at least let us escape in the next few minutes.

That job done, we left the room and ran down the hall. Jess with Maggie, me with the camera, snapping off a shot of the empty hallway behind us.

Click.

Hum.

Slide.

I checked the photo as it spread into view. Nothing.

Down the steps we went, Jess in the lead. Maggie had gone limp in her arms, frozen with shock. At the bottom of the stairs, I took another photo.

Click.

Hum.

Slide.

Still nothing.

"I think she's gone," I announced.

"Are you sure?" Jess said.

"I don't see her." I held up a hand, seeing if I could feel Indigo's white-hot presence. "I don't feel her, either."

I took one last picture — Jess holding Maggie at the base of the stairs.

Click.

Hum.

Slide.

"We can't stay here," Jess said. "We need to pack up and leave before she comes back."

"I know."

I checked the photo still developing in my hands, the image of Jess and Maggie emerging from the whiteness.

Behind them — hovering right at Jess's back — was Indigo Garson.

I looked from the picture to my wife and daughter, still in that same position.

Then Maggie flew to the ceiling.

It happened in a blink.

One second she was in Jess's arms. The next she was on the ceiling, being dragged across it by an unseen force.

Jess and I could only watch in terror as Maggie thrashed against the ceiling, screaming as she continued to be moved against her will. When she came within arm's reach of the chandelier, she grabbed it and held on with all her might. The chandelier rocked back and forth. A few of its glass globes shook loose and crashed to the floor around us, the shards scattering.

Above us, Maggie had been wrenched free from the still-swaying chandelier and was once again being pulled across the ceiling. Jess kept screaming her name, as if that could free her.

But I knew there was only one way to make Indigo let go of Maggie. Since her goal was to hurt me as much as her father had hurt her, I needed to remove myself from the equation.

Or at least pretend to.

I dropped to my knees, surrounded by pieces of glass from the broken chandelier.

Shards bring luck.

Grabbing the largest glass piece I could find, I pressed it to my neck and shouted to the ceiling, "Indigo, let her go or I'll kill myself!"

Jess looked at me, horrified. "Ewan, no!"

"Trust me, Jess," I whispered. "I know what I'm doing."

Indigo wouldn't let it get that far. If she wanted Maggie dead, then she needed me to do the deed. That wouldn't be possible if I was already dead.

"I'm serious!" I yelled. "You know you can't do this without me!"

I pressed the shard deeper against my neck, twisting it slightly until the tip of glass pierced my skin. A thin line of blood ran down my neck.

Maggie dropped without warning, her descent dizzyingly fast. Jess and I both lunged for her, our arms entangling, forming an accidental cradle into which our daughter landed.

She had been in our arms for barely a second when a wave of heat bore down on us from above. Hotter than earlier. A full blast of fury.

Noise rose all around us — a sudden, violent hissing that seemed to come from every corner of the house. A moment later, snakes began to fill the room.

Red-bellies.

They appeared instantly, emerging from darkened corners and out from under the floorboards. I saw them on the second floor as well, slithering across the landing on their way down the stairs.

Within seconds, we were surrounded, the snakes sidewinding their way toward us. Quite a few hissed their displeasure, their open mouths exposing teeth as sharp as razor blades.

I pushed Maggie into Jess's arms, still fearful of what I might do if I continued to hold her. I then began to fight off the snakes, trying to clear a path toward the vestibule. I kicked. I stomped. Some snakes backed away. Others struck at my feet.

One lunged for Jess. I kicked it out of the way before it could make contact.

"We need to hurry," I said. "Run!"

That's exactly what we did. The three of us ran through the vestibule. Toward the front door. Onto the porch.

The snakes followed, pouring forth from the open front door in a writhing, teeming mass.

Indigo Garson was with them, unseen but definitely felt. White-hot air burned at my back as I guided Jess and Maggie down the porch steps and into the car.

"What about our things?" Jess asked as she climbed into the back seat with Maggie.

"We need to leave them," I replied. "It's too dangerous. We can't ever come back here."

I started the car and peeled down the driveway. Behind me, Maggie knelt on her seat and stared out the back window.

"She's still following us!" she cried.

I glanced in the rearview mirror, seeing nothing. "Miss Pennyface?"

"*Yes!* She's right behind us!"

Just then, something rammed into the back of the car. A hard, shocking jolt.

Jess screamed and reached for Maggie. I gripped the steering wheel, trying hard not to run off the road and into the woods, which is exactly what Indigo wanted. I slammed my foot down on the gas pedal and continued to speed down the twisting drive, tires squealing all the way.

The car was hit by another invisible force, this time on the passenger-side door. For a brief moment, I lost control of the car. It skidded onto the grass alongside the drive, perilously close to the trees. It was only through sheer force of will that I was able to right us and continue down the drive.

Jess, thankfully, had left the front gate open when she and Maggie returned, allowing me to drive right through it. As soon as we were off the property, I leaped from the car and slammed the gate shut.

Heat bore down on me as I fumbled with the keys, frantically trying to lock the gate. It burst through the gate's wrought-iron bars, turning them hot. If hell does exist, I suspect it feels a lot like the angry heat I experienced the moment I turned the key and locked the gate.

That was the moment the vengeful spirit of Indigo Garson realized she had failed.

We'd escaped Baneberry Hall, our family still intact.

And there was nothing she could do to lure us back there.

Others might one day pass through that gate, travel up that winding drive through the woods, and enter Baneberry Hall. If so, I wish them nothing but luck. They'll need it to survive such a place.

As for me and my family — my sweet Jessica, my beloved Maggie — we have yet to return. Nor do we intend to ever set foot inside that place.

For us, Baneberry Hall is a house of horrors. One that none of us may dare enter again.

TWENTY-FOUR

Half a dozen emergency vehicles sit outside Baneberry Hall, their flashing lights painting the house in alternating shades of red and white. In addition to Chief Alcott's cruiser, there's an ambulance, three more police cars, and, just in case things really get out of hand, a fire truck.

I watch from the porch as Dane is loaded into the ambulance. He's strapped to a stretcher, a brace around his neck. His fall through the floor didn't do much damage, all things considered. As the EMTs wheeled him out, I heard murmurs of broken bones, maybe a concussion. Whatever happened to him, he was injured enough to allow me to flee the house and call the police.

Now Dane is on his way to the emergency room and then, presumably, jail. He stares at me as the stretcher is pushed into the back of the ambulance, his expression pained, his eyes accusing.

Then the ambulance doors are slammed shut and Dane vanishes from view.

As the ambulance departs, Chief Alcott emerges from the house and joins me at the porch railing.

"Did he confess?" I say.

"Not yet. But he will. Give it time." The chief removes her hat and runs a hand through her silver hair. "I owe you an apology, Maggie. For saying those things about your father. For thinking he did it."

I can't be mad at her for that. I thought the same thing on and off throughout this whole ordeal. If anyone should be ashamed, it's me.

"We're both guilty on that front," I say.

"Then why'd you keep looking?"

I've been asking myself that same question for days. The answer, I suspect, lies in something Dr. Weber told me. That it was my way of writing my own version of the story. And while I did it for completely selfish reasons, I realize now the story isn't solely mine.

Petra's a part of it, too. It doesn't change what happened. Elsa's still without her older daughter, and Hannah no longer has a sister.

But they have the truth. And that's valuable.

I should know.

Chief Alcott departs with the rest of the emergency vehicles. They form a line down the driveway, their sirens on mute but their lights still flashing.

Another car arrives before they fully vanish down the hill, its headlights unexpectedly popping over the horizon. For a brief, blinding moment, it's a kaleidoscope of lights as the two cars slow down and pass each other. Blue and red and white. All flashing through the trees in spinning, disco-like fury. The emergency lights disappear. The headlights grow brighter as the car rounds the driveway and comes to a gravel-crunching stop.

I can't see who's inside. It's too dark, and my eyes are still stinging from the lights of the emergency vehicles. All I can make out is a person behind the wheel, sitting in complete stillness, almost as if they're tempted to start driving again.

But then the driver's-side door swings open, and my mother steps out of the car.

"Mom?" I say, shocked. "What are you doing here?"

"I could ask you the same thing."

She remains in the driveway, looking exhausted in her travel clothes — white slacks, print blouse, a pair of strappy sandals. Shed of their sunglasses, her eyes are bloodshot. Dark half-moons droop beneath them. She carries no luggage. Just a purse that's about to slip from her shoulder.

"For God's sake, Maggie," she says. "Why did you come back here? What did you think that was going to accomplish?"

"I needed the truth."

"I *told* you the truth," my mother says. "But you couldn't leave well enough alone. Because of that, I had to fly halfway around the world, and then I get here and see all those police cars. What the hell have you been up to?"

I bring her inside. There's a moment's hesitation at the front door, making it clear she has no desire to enter Baneberry Hall, but she's too tired to put up a fight. Once inside, the only thing she insists on is going down to the kitchen.

"I don't want to be up here," she says. "Not on this floor."

Down we go, into the kitchen, taking seats across from each other at the butcher-block table. There, I tell her everything. Why I decided to come back. What happened when I got here. Finding Petra's body and suspecting my father and realizing the true culprit was Dane.

When I finish, my mother simply stares at

503

me. She looks so old in the harsh and unsparing light of the kitchen. It illuminates the ravages of time she usually tries so hard to cover up. The wrinkles and age spots and gray strands sprouting along her hairline.

"Oh, Maggie," she says. "You really shouldn't have done that."

Unease slams onto my shoulders, so forceful that all of Baneberry Hall seems to shake.

"Why?" I say.

My mother's gaze flits around the room, making her look like a trapped bird. "We need to leave," she says.

"What aren't you telling me?"

"We need to leave and never come back."

My unease grows, pouring into me, weighing me down. When my mother stands, it takes all the effort I can muster to also get up and push her back into her chair.

"We're staying right here. We're going to sit here and talk, just like normal families do." On the way back to my seat, I spot the cherry pie on the counter. "Look, there's even dessert."

I grab the pie and drop it onto the table. It's followed by two forks, which clatter across the tabletop. For show, I grab one, cut off a huge chunk of pie, and stuff it into my mouth.

"See?" I say, gulping it down. "Isn't this nice? Just a mother-and-daughter chat that's been a long time coming. Now talk."

I take another massive bite, waiting for my mother to speak. Instead, she picks up a fork and digs out a tiny piece of pie. She tries to take a bite, but her hands are shaking so much that the pie falls from her fork. A gelatinous blob the color of blood splats onto the table.

"I don't know what you want from me," she says.

"The truth. That's all I've ever wanted." I take a third bite of pie. Proving that I'm capable of doing something she can't. "You need to tell me every fucking thing you've been hiding from me for the past twenty-five years."

"You don't want to know the truth. You think you do, Maggie. But you don't."

My mother's birdlike gaze comes to a stop at the hole in the kitchen ceiling. That's when I realize I was wrong about Dane. I might be wrong about everything.

"Is this about Dad?"

"I don't want to talk about it."

"Did he kill Petra Ditmer?"

"Your father would never —"

"It certainly feels like he did," I say. "All this secrecy. All these lies. It makes me think he really did kill a sixteen-year-old girl and that you helped him cover it up."

My mother slumps in her chair. Her hand, placed palm-down on the table, falls away in a long, exhausted slide.

"Oh, baby," she says in a voice made jagged by a hundred different emotions. "My sweet baby."

"So it's true?" I say.

My mother shakes her head. "Your father didn't kill that girl."

"Then who did?"

She reaches into her purse and pulls out a large envelope, which she slides across the table toward me. I open it and take a peek. Inside is a stack of pages. The top one bears an unexpected heading.

To Maggie

"Your father and I prayed this day would never come," she says.

"Why?"

"Neither of us wanted to tell you the truth."

"Why?"

"Because it wasn't your father who killed Petra."

My eyes remain locked on the page in front of me. "Then who did?"

"You did, Maggie," my mother says. "You killed her."

To Maggie

I'm writing this for you, Maggie, although I hope to God you never see it. If you do, it means your mother and I have failed.

For that, we are profoundly sorry.

By now, you already know some of the truth about what happened the night we left Baneberry Hall. This is the rest of it. And while it is my greatest hope that you don't read beyond this paragraph, I already know you will. You are, after all, my daughter.

We never planned to leave Baneberry Hall the way we did. We never planned to leave at all. Maintenance issues and prior tragedies notwithstanding, it was a lovely home. And it could have been a happy one if I hadn't become fascinated with the history of the house.

I admit I had an ulterior motive when I convinced your mother to buy it. I wanted a house with a past that I could research and write about and, hopefully, end up with a nonfiction account about being a beleaguered freelance writer who restored the fixer-upper he unwisely purchased.

But once I learned the circumstances surrounding the death of Indigo Garson, I realized I had stumbled upon an even better idea for a book. I was going to be the beleaguered freelancer who solved a murder at the fixer-upper he unwisely purchased.

I ended up writing a far different book.

A word about *House of Horrors:* Much of it is true. A lot of it is not. We did discover letters written to Indigo Garson by the man who wished to elope with her. Petra Ditmer and I did research those letters, discovering other tragedies that had occurred in the house over the years.

But for every truth, there was a lie.

There were no ghosts, of course, although you did have several imaginary friends. Mister Shadow was one. Miss Pennyface was another. Although they were figments of your imagination, they seemed to frighten and fascinate you in equal measure. So much so that we sought out help from Dr. Weber.

There were also no portraits of William and Indigo Garson over the fireplace. Besides the deaths of Katie Carver and Indigo — who I do believe was killed by her father and was what I set out to prove in my book — all the other deaths at Baneberry Hall were simply tragic accidents and completely unrelated.

All of them but Petra Ditmer's.

The guilt I feel about what we did hasn't

509

lessened one bit in the twenty-four years since she died. She was a bright young woman. She deserved better.

I know I'll never forget that night, even though it's all I want to do. I suspect it will take my death to erase that horrible night from my memory. Even then, I'm not so sure. I know we leave our bodies when we pass on. I hope we can choose to leave certain memories behind as well.

That night was supposed to be a good one — a much-needed break from the daily strife of Baneberry Hall. The house and all its problems had taken its toll on your mother and me. We could feel ourselves drifting apart a little more each day. The spark had gone out of our marriage, and we desperately needed to get it back.

To do this, we decided to have a "date night," which is a polite way of saying we rented a room at the Two Pines with the intention of fucking like teenagers. We needed to be away from not just the house and its myriad issues but from you as well. Just for an evening. That sounds more harsh than it really is. You might be a parent yourself when you read this, in which case you'll surely understand.

To get away, we hired Petra Ditmer to babysit. Thanks to your antics on the night she and her sister came for a sleepover, Petra had been forbidden from visiting Baneberry Hall and told us she'd need to sneak out in order to babysit. Your mother and I debated the ethics of this, deciding that since it was only for a few hours, a little dishonesty on Petra's part was worth a night to ourselves. We needed it. Both of us agree about that. We needed time alone, to be us again.

Petra snuck out of her house and arrived shortly after eight. Your mother and I went to the motel, where our goal was achieved multiple times. We left the hotel at midnight, relaxed and happy. The happiest we'd been in weeks.

It ended the moment we entered Baneberry Hall and saw the body of Petra Ditmer.

She lay in a heap at the bottom of the steps, her arms and legs twisted under her like a pretzel. So twisted that at first I couldn't tell what were legs and what were arms. Nothing seemed to be in the right place.

I knew she was dead, though. It was obvious. Her neck was also twisted. Turned at an angle so unnatural that I feel sick just thinking about it. Her right cheek lay flat against the floor, and her hair lay across most of her face. But I saw her eyes peeking out between the strands. Two large, shocked, dead eyes.

I couldn't stop staring at them. It was too

horrible to look away. I had seen dead people before, of course. But not one so young. And definitely not one so assuredly dead. All the other corpses I'd seen looked like they could have been sleeping.

Petra definitely wasn't asleep.

You sat at the top of the stairs, gently sobbing. When we asked you what happened, you looked up at us and said, "It wasn't me."

You kept repeating it, almost as if you were trying to convince yourself as much as us.

"It wasn't me. It wasn't me. It wasn't me."

At first, I believed you. You were my daughter, after all. I knew you better than anyone, even your mother. You were sweet and kind. You wouldn't purposely hurt anyone.

But then I thought about how you had punched Petra's sister in the face during the sleepover. It shocked me then and shocked me again in recollection. It was proof that anger boiled just beneath your placid demeanor.

There was also physical evidence. Petra's shirt had been torn. There was a gap in the seam at her shoulder, exposing pale skin. Just above it were three scratch marks on her neck, as if she'd been attacked. You also had a cut — a bad one under your left eye. I could only assume it was caused by Petra, fighting you off.

512

Still, you kept denying it.

"It wasn't me. It wasn't me."

"Then who was it, Maggie?" I asked, wishing with all my power that you'd give us a logical response.

But you only looked us in the eyes and said, "Miss Pennyface."

I remember that moment like it just happened. It was the moment I realized that my fears were correct. Since Miss Pennyface didn't exist, that meant it was you who had killed Petra.

Things would have turned out very differently if Petra's mother knew she was at Baneberry Hall. We would have had no choice but to go to the authorities. But no one else knew she was there. No one but us.

So when your mother tried to call 911, I stopped her before she could dial.

I told her we needed to think long and hard before we did that. That it might not be in our best interest to get the police involved.

"A girl is dead, Ewan," she said. "I don't care about our best interest."

"What about Maggie's?" I asked. "Because whatever we do next, it's going to affect her for the rest of her life."

I explained that if we called 911, the police would take even less time than it took us to see that this wasn't an accident. Petra's torn shirt and the scratches on her neck indicated far worse.

It showed that you had pushed her down those stairs.

I didn't know what precipitated it. I didn't want to know. I realized that the less I knew, the better. But I knew I still loved you, in spite of what you had done. I thought there was nothing you could do that would make me love you less. But I worried that knowing the details of what happened had the potential to change that thinking. And I didn't want to see you as a monster, which is what everyone else would have thought if word got out that you had killed Petra.

It was that argument that finally convinced your mother to go along with my plan. I told her that perception is a tricky thing. When people think of you a certain way, it's almost impossible to put that genie back in the bottle. And when the world considers someone a monster, people treat them like one, and it isn't long before that person starts to believe it as well.

"Is that what we want for Maggie?" I said. "For her to be locked up in some juvenile detention center until she's eighteen? Then to spend the rest of her life being judged by people? No matter what she does, for the rest of her life, people will look at her and only see a killer. What do you think that will do to her? What kind of life will that be?"

I'm not proud of what I did that night. The shame I carry weighs on my heart and keeps me up at night. But I need you to know that we did it for you. We wanted to spare you from the brutal existence you certainly would have had if the police got involved.

So we decided to keep it a secret.

While your mother took you upstairs to dress the wound on your face, I disposed of the body. Even though writing those words just now made me nauseous, that's exactly what I did. This wasn't an act of burial. It was disposal, pure and simple. I put Petra's body in a canvas knapsack left over from my days as a traveling reporter. I dropped it into the hole in the floor where we'd found the letters to Indigo Garson, replaced the boards, and unrolled the carpet over them.

Just like that, Petra was gone.

It was your mother who demanded we leave Baneberry Hall. The two of you came downstairs, you with a bandage on your cheek and she carrying the teddy bear Petra had brought with her that night.

I suspect it was the bear that caused what happened next. It jerked your mother out of her shock, making her realize it wasn't just a random person we had buried beneath the floorboards, but a young woman. Someone smart and sweet who still slept with a teddy bear.

"I can't be here," your mother gasped as the full weight of our actions sunk in. "Not knowing she's here. Not after what we've done to her. I just can't."

I understood then that we had no choice but to leave. In a daze, I hid the bear in the closet of my study. We then piled into the car without packing a thing and went back to the Two Pines motel. Thanks to a shift change, there was a new clerk at the front desk. And since we'd paid with cash, there was no record we'd ever been there earlier that night.

"I'm never going back there," your mother said once we were in our room. "I can't, Ewan. I'm sorry."

I, too, felt it wise not to return. We'd gotten away with a heinous deed. Going back to Baneberry Hall would remind us daily of what we'd done. All I wanted to do was forget.

"We'll never go back," I told her. "None of us will ever go back there."

"But people will be looking for Petra," your mother said. "Once they realize she's missing, they're going to ask why we're here and not at Baneberry Hall. We need to give them a reason."

I knew she was right. We needed to come

516

up with an explanation for why we left. A solid one. An innocent-sounding one. But that wasn't easy. Especially once people started looking for Petra. I knew that the police would search the house to back up our claim. All it would take was a half hour and a search warrant.

But inventing another calamity in the house was out of the question. There couldn't be a burst pipe or another snake infestation. Our reason for leaving had to sound appropriately extreme while also being completely invisible.

It was you, ironically, who came up with the idea. Half-asleep in front of the muted motel TV, you said, "When are we going home?"

"We're not," your mother answered.

Your response prompted all that followed.

"Because Miss Pennyface scared us away?" you said.

At first, the thought of claiming we abandoned Baneberry Hall because it was haunted struck me as preposterous. No one would believe it. But the more I thought about it, the more sense it made. It would be impossible to prove that we were lying. Plus, by that point I knew enough of Baneberry Hall's history to spin a decent tale. Then there was the fact that, because the idea of a haunting was so ridiculous, it might distract from the bigger secret hidden inside the house.

We went with it. We had no other choice.

Not that there was much time to think about it. I knew that, in order to deflect suspicion from us, we needed to be on record claiming Baneberry Hall was haunted before word got out that Petra had vanished.

I called the police to report a disturbance at the house. Officer Alcott came to the motel soon after. And for the next hour, I told her about Mister Shadow and Miss Pennyface and the horrors we'd endured. I knew the officer didn't believe me, especially after she went to the house to check things out.

When she returned to say everything looked fine, I knew there was a chance that we would actually get away with it. We would move to another town. Settle in a place far away and pretend the incident at Baneberry Hall never happened.

What I didn't expect was everything that came after. The newspaper interview, which I felt compelled to give, lest the police think we weren't serious. That was the rub, Maggie. We didn't care if people believed us. We just needed them to think that *we* believed it.

So we kept up the ruse, even when the story started making news across the state and beyond. Then came the book offer, which was so unexpected and so lucrative that we had to take it.

Your mother didn't want me to write *House of Horrors.* Especially when I had to return to Baneberry Hall two weeks after the crime to fetch my typewriter. But I knew there was no way to avoid it. Your mother had stopped going to her teaching job, and I had no writing gigs lined up. We desperately needed money. I didn't think anything would come of it. I considered it a temporary job that would hopefully lead to other writing assignments. I never for a second thought it would blow up into this unruly thing we could no longer control. When it did, the die had been cast. Your mother and I were forced to spend the rest of our lives pretending the fictions in that book were the truth. It was a lie that ultimately tore us apart.

Through it all, your mother and I debated how to help you going forward. You had killed someone, be it in anger or accidentally, and we worried about how that would affect you and what kind of person you would become. I wanted to send you to therapy, but your mother — rightfully — feared you'd reveal what we had done during one of your sessions. She wanted to tell you the truth — something I desperately wanted to shield you from. I never, ever wanted you to feel the guilt I carried.

Since you seemed to remember very little about our time at Baneberry Hall and had no recollection of the night we left, your mother and I decided the best thing to do was let you forget. We chose to stay silent, be watchful of your mood and mind-set, and try to raise you as best we could.

I know it was hard on you, Mags. I know you had questions neither of us could truthfully answer. All we wanted to do was shield you from the truth, even though we knew the falsehood we'd created in its place was inflicting its own damage. That book hurt you. We hurt you as well.

We could have done better. We *should* have done better. Even though every time you asked for the truth was a reminder of the guilt all of us carried.

I suppose that's another reason I'm writing this, Maggie. To unburden myself of the guilt I'd felt for almost a quarter of a century. Consider it my confession as much as it is yours.

It's now five a.m. and the sun will be up soon. I've spent the whole night writing this in my office in Baneberry Hall. You may or may not know this by now, but we never sold the house. We never even considered it. Knowing what was under the floor, selling it was too much of a risk.

Guilt brings me back here every year on the anniversary of the night it happened. I come to pay my respects to Petra. To apologize for what we did to her. My hope is that if I do it enough times, maybe she'll forgive us.

Each time I'm here, I ask myself the same question: Did I make the right decision that night?

Yes, if you consider how you've grown up to be a smart, strong-willed young woman.

Will I be judged harshly for it in the afterlife?

Yes. I truly believe I will.

I suppose I'll find out soon enough.

All I know for certain is that you have always been my proudest accomplishment. I loved you before we set foot inside Baneberry Hall, and I loved you just as much after we left it.

You're the love of my life, Maggie.

You always have been, and you always will be.

TWENTY-FIVE

Reading my father's letter feels like plummeting through a thousand trapdoors. One after another. Drop after drop after jarring drop. And I can't stop the sensation. There's no fighting this fall.

"You're lying." My voice sounds warped, like I'm talking underwater. "You're lying to me."

My mother comes toward me. "I'm not, honey. This is what happened."

She wraps her arms around me. They feel like tentacles. Foreign. Cold. I try to push her away. When she refuses, I squirm out of her grip, falling from my chair. My hand skates across the table, taking the pages my father wrote with it. I hit the floor, paper fluttering around me.

"It's a lie," I say. "It's all lies."

Even though I keep repeating it, I know in my heart of hearts it's not. My father wouldn't make up something like that.

Neither would my mother. There's no reason they would. Which means what I read is true.

I want to scream.

I want to throw up.

I want to reach for the nearest sharp object and rip open my veins.

"You should have told the police," I say, hiccupping with grief. "You shouldn't have covered it up."

"We did what we thought was best for you."

"A girl was dead, Mom! She was just a child!"

"And so were you!" my mother says. "*Our* child! If we'd called the police, your life would have been ruined."

"And I would have deserved it," I say.

"You didn't!" My mother joins me on the floor, crawling toward me in the slow, cautious way one approaches a trapped animal. "You're sweet and beautiful and smart. Your father and I knew that. We *always* knew that. And we refused to destroy your life because you made one mistake."

"I killed someone!"

Saying it unleashes the flood of emotion I've been trying to hold back. It flows out of me. In tears. In snot. In saliva that drips from my mouth as I moan.

523

"You didn't mean to," my mother says. "I'm sure of it."

I look at her through tear-clouded eyes. "We have to tell the truth."

"We don't, Maggie. What we need to do is pack your things and leave. We'll sell this place and never come back. This time for good."

I stare at her, appalled. I can't believe she still refuses to do the right thing. That after all these years and all these lies, she still wants to pretend none of this happened. They tried that once, and it damn near destroyed us.

Something breaks inside me. Surprising, since I didn't think there was any part of me left unscathed. But my heart was still intact, just waiting for my mother to shatter it. I can feel it disintegrating — a shudder that makes my chest heave.

"Get out," I say.

"Maggie, just listen to me."

My mother reaches for me, and I recoil. When she comes for me again, I strike, my open palm whipping across her cheek.

"Get out!" I scream it this time, the words echoing off the wall of bells. I keep screaming until I'm red-faced and frothing.

"Get out! Get out of my fucking house!"

My mother stays frozen on the floor, her

hand to her cheek. The tears glistening in her eyes tell me her heart's also broken.

Good.

Now we're even.

"If you want to throw your life away, I can't stop you," she says. "But I refuse to watch you do it. Your father's not the only one who loved you unconditionally. I feel the same way he did. About everything."

She stands, smooths out her slacks, and leaves the kitchen.

I don't move until the sound of the front door closing makes it way down to the kitchen. By then I've already decided what I'm going to do.

I'll wait.

By now, Chief Alcott is probably grilling Dane about the night Petra died. Unlike me, she's going to realize it doesn't add up. That there's more to the story. Then she'll come back here, armed with questions.

I'll answer every single one.

With my mother gone, I stand and climb the kitchen steps. It's a struggle. Shock has made my legs heavy and my body sluggish. It doesn't get better on the first floor. The great room seems to shift with each step. The walls sway, as if buffeted by a stiff wind, rocking back and forth. Beneath my feet, the floor buckles. I trip, even though the

525

floor isn't really buckling. Nor are the walls truly swaying.

It's me who's doing the changing.

An internal shift in which everything I thought I knew about myself is suddenly upended.

I came here wanting to know the truth. Now I do.

I am a killer.

A fact I'll need to get used to. Because right now the realization is so heavy that I can no longer stand. I end up crawling up the stairs to the second floor. There's more crawling in the hallway. Even then I'm so dizzy I continually bump into the wall on the way to my bedroom.

Inside, I throw myself onto the bed, too exhausted to move. I want to sleep for a long time. Days and days.

Maybe forever.

Before closing my eyes, I look to the armoire opposite the bed.

It occurs to me how just a few hours ago I'd planned to demolish it. Yet here it is, still standing, a strange sound coming from within.

Hearing it cuts through my wooziness enough to make me sit up, startled.

The armoire doors slowly open, revealing someone standing inside.

I want to believe I'm dreaming. That this whole experience is nothing more than a night terror from which I'll wake any second now.

But it's not a nightmare.

It's reality, and there's nothing I can do to stop it.

The armoire doors continue to open, revealing more of the dark figure within its depths.

Mister Shadow.

He's real.

I know that now.

He's always been real.

Yet when the figure at last emerges from the armoire, I see that I'm wrong. It's not Mister Shadow stepping gingerly into the room.

It's Miss Pennyface.

She takes another step, and the coins fall away from her eyes. Only there are no coins. There never were. It was moonlight coming through the bedroom window and reflecting off a pair of spectacles.

Now that it's gone, I see Miss Pennyface for who she really is.

Marta Carver.

"Hello, Maggie," she says. "It's been a long time since we've met like this."

TWENTY-SIX

Marta stops at the foot of the bed, hovering over me, and I'm struck with a sense of déjà vu.

No.

It's more than that.

It's a memory.

Her standing just like this, only we're both younger. Twenty-five years younger. I'm five and trembling under my covers, pretending I'm asleep but secretly watching her through half-closed eyes.

Watching her watch me as moonlight again flashes against her glasses.

Even worse is that it happened more than once. The memories continue, piling up, one after another, like some horrible slideshow projected on the backs of my eyelids.

Miss Pennyface visiting me at night again.

And again.

And again.

Marta must see the recollection in my

eyes, for she says, "When Katie was alive, I'd come into this room almost every night, just to watch her sleep. I loved her so much, Maggie. So very much. I never realized how strong a mother's love could be until I became one myself. Then I knew. A mother's love is fierce."

She flashes me a maternal smile before inching closer to the bed.

"But then my husband took it all away. First Katie, then himself. And I no longer knew what to do with all that fierce love. Then your family arrived. 'They have a little girl,' Janie June told me. 'A beautiful little girl.' When I heard that, I knew I had to see you for myself."

She jerks her head toward the armoire, not only her hiding place but her secret passage in and out of Baneberry Hall. She'd lived here long enough to know of its existence. My family hadn't.

"I returned here night after night," she says. "Not to hurt you. I had no interest in causing you harm, Maggie. I just wanted to watch you sleep, just as I had done with my own daughter. It made it feel like she wasn't really gone. Just for a few minutes. I need you to understand that, Maggie. I never wanted to hurt anyone."

One last memory hits me like a slap.

Marta standing over me, watching. Only this time we're not alone. I hear someone in the hallway, tiptoeing into the room to check on me.

Petra.

She screams when she sees Marta, who rushes toward her.

"It's not what you think," she says.

Petra makes a move toward the bed, trying to reach me. Marta intercepts her, gripping her arms.

"What are you doing here?" Petra shouts.

"Let me explain."

"You can explain to the police."

Petra breaks from Marta's grip and runs from the room, heading downstairs to the only phone in the house.

Marta follows. I hear a scuffle in the hallway. Feet heavy on floorboards. A loud thump against the wall. Terrified, I slide out of bed and follow the sounds. Marta and Petra are at the top of the stairs, arguing. Marta has Petra by the shoulders, shaking her while saying, "Just listen to me. Please let me explain."

I run to them, terrified and yelling and begging them to stop. I grab Marta's right arm. She shakes it loose and swings it at me, the back of her hand connecting with my face. Her ring digs into the flesh beneath my eye — an inch-long scrape that instantly starts to bleed.

There's another scream, and Petra tumbles backward down the stairs.

The memory ends, and I fall back onto the bed, unable to stay upright. All my energy is gone. The bed sways like a boat that's been unmoored, at the mercy of the waves. When Marta sits on the bed's edge, it's at a canted angle not possible in real life.

"You killed Petra," I moan.

"I didn't mean to, Maggie. It was an accident. All a terrible accident." Marta reaches for my hand and holds it in hers. "After it happened, I didn't know what to do. So I ran. I knew the police would come for me eventually. It was only a matter of time. I spent that night waiting for them, feeling almost as scared as when I found my husband's body up in that study of his. But something strange happened. The police never arrived. That's when I knew your family hadn't told them."

She touches my forehead, which is wet with sweat. All of me is. A sudden leaking of perspiration that baffles me until my stomach begins to cramp. It's a sharp, stinging pain that leaves me gasping.

"You've had the pie," Marta says. "Good.

That makes this easier."

I try to scream. Nothing comes out but a few pained rasps.

"Hush, now," Marta says. "It's nothing to fuss about. Just a little pie with some baneberries mixed in."

I clutch my stomach and roll over, the room rolling with me. Marta stays by my side, rubbing my back in a motherly way.

"I never really understood why your parents hid Petra's death," she says. "Even after that book came out, I wondered what their thinking had been. It took me a long time to understand they thought you had done it, Maggie."

Her hand continues to circle on my back. I wonder if she did the same thing with Katie when she was feeling sick.

"I have to admit, I was relieved. God help me, I was. I felt terrible about what happened. That poor girl. She didn't deserve that. And there were a few times I thought about confessing. Just marching right up to Tess Alcott and telling her the truth. I didn't because no one would understand it was an accident. No one would see it that way. I would have been punished for what happened. But when you get right down to it, haven't I been punished enough?"

Marta pauses, as if waiting for me to agree.

I say nothing.

"I spent the past twenty-odd years secure in the knowledge that I was safe," she says. "That God had decided I'd suffered enough for one life. Then you came back. And Petra was found. And I knew it was only a matter of time before the truth finally came out."

Marta's hand stops at the small of my back and stays there. I tense beneath it, fearing what's to come.

"I can't let that happen, Maggie," she says. "I've suffered. Far more than most. I lost my daughter and my husband on the same day. Few people in this world will ever know that kind of pain. But I do. I know it all too well. Forgive me, but I'm not about to suffer more."

She flips me onto my back in one rough, startling motion. I'm too weak to fight it. Just a rag doll in her arms. The room stops tilting enough for me to notice the pillow hugged against her chest.

Marta pushes the pillow over my face. A sudden darkening. My breathing, already labored, becomes almost nonexistent. I gasp for air, sucking in pillowcase instead, almost choking on the fabric.

She scrambles on top of me, increasing the pillow's pressure. I try to buck beneath her, to thrash my legs. But I have no energy left. The baneberries have stolen it from me. The most I can do is roll again onto my side.

It works.

Marta is thrown off-balance and falls away from me.

I fall, too.

Off the bed.

Onto the floor.

I take a deep breath of blessed air, and adrenaline kicks in, giving me the strength to start dragging myself along the floor. I'm at the doorway when Marta grabs an ankle and pulls me back toward the bed.

I scream and thrust out my free leg in a crazed, desperate kick. My foot slams against Marta's face, which makes her start screaming, too. The sound of it rings off the walls as I resume my frenzied scramble down the hallway.

Marta doesn't catch up to me until I'm at the top of the stairs. When she snags my leg again, I expect another pull back to the bedroom. Instead, she lifts it, flipping me over.

For a moment, the whole house goes upside down.

Then I'm on the stairs.

Still flipping.

Now rolling.

Now bouncing.

The edges of steps pound at my back. My head knocks against wall. My eyes pop open to see banister rails blurring past my face.

When it ends, I'm on my back at the foot of the stairs. Far above me, Marta stands at the top of the staircase, bent forward a bit, looking to see if I'm dead.

I'm not.

But I *do* think I'm dying.

A bright light forms atop the staircase, blinding in its intensity. So bright I grimace and squint. With that narrowing of my eyes, I'm able to see someone inside the brightness — a young woman just behind Marta, hovering at her shoulder.

She looks like Petra Ditmer.

Still sixteen and beautiful, flashing a smile of deep satisfaction.

The light lasts no longer than a blink. Definitely not long enough to confirm if the glow was indeed Petra or just a trick of my poisoned mind.

All I know is that right before the brightness dims, Marta Carver jolts forward, as if she's been pushed. She tumbles down the steps, bones snapping like twigs. There's one final snap when she lands — a loud crack of her neck I feel in my bones.

Her body rests a foot from mine, her head

twisted like an elastic toy.

That's when I know she's dead.

And that I'm not.

And that all of this is finally over.

I roll my head, looking upward, my gaze sweeping up the staircase the two of us have just tumbled down.

That's when I see someone standing at the top of the steps.

The person who had shoved Marta to her death.

It's not Petra, as I had thought.

It's her mother.

Elsa Ditmer stares at me, her eyes wild and alert. It's clear she knows exactly where she is, what she's done, and, after twenty-five long years, what happened to her daughter.

EPILOGUE

Vermont is gorgeous in October. Nothing but cerulean skies and fiery leaves and the smell of woodsmoke in the air. In the mornings, I like to sip my coffee on the front porch of Baneberry Hall and take it all in.

It's my first Vermont autumn. It will likely also be my last.

There's not much left to do on the house. With occasional help from Allie, I spent the rest of the summer and most of the fall renovating the place. My original plan in everything but execution. Instead of the Victorian glamour I'd envisioned, I settled for modern blandness. Open rooms and laminate floors and white everything. It seemed like the best option. Some houses don't deserve to have their stories preserved.

It's unclear how much Baneberry Hall will sell for when it's listed. The house is once more all over the news — not always a good thing in the world of real estate.

Despite it being reported everywhere that the Book was all a lie to cover up what my parents thought I'd done, rumors persist that Baneberry Hall is haunted. People also continue to believe that my father was right and that Curtis Carver never murdered his daughter before killing himself. In fact, there's a growing suspicion that Marta herself might have done it, even though all the evidence suggests otherwise.

All of this has brought out the ghouls, who've returned with renewed vigor. It got so bad that Chief Alcott had to resume stationing a police cruiser outside the front gate. I bring the cops coffee each night.

But I no longer feel unsafe here. It helps that I had the crumbled section of wall rebuilt, even though it was only the Ditmers and Marta Carver who got onto the property that way. I also had the secret passage bricked over and a state-of-the-art home security system installed. No more slips of paper stuck in the door for me.

As for the armoire, I happily took a sledgehammer to it, relishing the crack of the wood that came with each blow. Even so, I no longer sleep in that room, having moved instead to my parents' old bedroom.

It turns out that Marta Carver wasn't the only person who snuck through that armoire to visit me during the night. Elsa Ditmer had, too. While only partially lucid when interviewed by Chief Alcott, she confirmed in a foggy, roundabout way that she had entered my bedroom at least twice when I was a child.

Only I knew her as someone else.

Mister Shadow.

Not a ghost but a superstitious woman who knew of Baneberry Hall's history and came at night to whisper a warning that almost came true.

You're going to die here.

But now Elsa and her daughter are gone. Mrs. Ditmer's Alzheimer's got to be too much for Hannah alone, and she was admitted to a care facility near Manchester. Hannah went with her, moving into a studio apartment so she could be near her.

Before they left, my mother apologized to Hannah, who chain-smoked while she listened. When my mother finished, Hannah simply said, "You caused my family twenty-five years of pain. No apology is going to make up for that."

It was the last time I saw her, although in the days leading to her departure, I noticed more and more items missing from Baneberry Hall, including Petra's teddy bear, Buster. Other than that, everything that's vanished from the house has ended up on her online auction site. Thanks to renewed interest in Baneberry Hall and the Book, a lot of the things sold for five times what they're worth.

Dane is also gone.

I stopped by his cottage shortly after we both got out of the hospital. To his credit, he listened to what I had to say, letting me spend a good ten minutes standing on his doorstep and rambling my apology.

He said nothing when I finished. He simply turned away and closed the door.

A week later, he moved out.

It strikes me as ironic that I'm the only one who's still here. Me, who was never supposed to return in the first place. But it's more than just work on the house that's kept me here. I want to remain in Bartleby until all the legal issues are over.

That should come next week, when my mother is going to be sentenced for her role in covering up the death of Petra Ditmer.

It turns out that what she told me in the kitchen was wrong. She *could* stop me from throwing my life away — by confessing to Petra Ditmer's murder, which is exactly what she tried to do immediately after leaving me alone in Baneberry Hall. While Marta Carver was rubbing my back and telling me how she accidentally killed Petra, my mother was talking to Chief Alcott.

After hearing my mother's story, the chief came by the house to also bring me in for questioning. Instead, she discovered Elsa Ditmer, lost once more in an Alzheimer's haze in the parlor, and Marta and me splayed out in front of the stairs.

Marta was dead.

I was on my way.

After having my stomach pumped, my fluids restored, and a fractured wrist bandaged, I told Chief Alcott everything. I even included the part about seeing Petra Ditmer right as Elsa pushed Marta down the stairs, although everyone agrees I was hallucinating.

I hope not.

I'd like to think it was Petra's spirit, helping her mother save my life.

Once Chief Alcott got everyone's story straight, it was time for my mother's formal confession. In July, she pleaded guilty to one count of concealing a dead body. Now it's up to the judge to decide her punishment. Although she could get up to three years in prison, her attorneys think she could escape jail time altogether.

Whenever I ask my mother if she's scared

about possibly going to prison, she tells me no.

"Even though we did what we thought was right, it was still wrong," she said on the phone yesterday. "I'll serve whatever time the judge sees fit. All I care about is that you forgive me."

I do.

I forgave her the moment I heard she confessed to what we both had thought was my crime. I wouldn't have let her go through with it, of course. If I had been the one to kill Petra, I would have admitted it. But the fact that my mother was willing to sacrifice herself like that told me I had been wrong about her. She wasn't a monster. Neither was my father. They were just two people thrust into an unfathomable situation who were terrified about what might happen to their daughter.

It doesn't excuse what they did.

But it sure does explain it.

Everything, it turned out, was for me. As for who that is, I am still figuring it out.

That the relationship between my mother and me is the best it's ever been is another irony. She likes to joke that all it took for us to get along was an impending prison sentence. Yet I still can't help but think about what might have been. So many years have been wasted on cover-ups and lies. Now all we can do is make up for lost time. I only wish I'd been able to do the same thing with my father. But I hope he knows, wherever he is now, that he has also been forgiven.

My mother and Carl have been in Bartleby a lot these past few months, for reasons relating to her criminal case. Although she's now fine with spending an afternoon in Baneberry Hall, she refuses to stay the night. She and Carl always book a room at the Two Pines, which, in my mind at least, is probably worse than jail.

When they're not in town, I spend my nights roaming Baneberry Hall, thinking about all that's happened within these walls. Sometimes, I just sit and wait for Petra to appear. Unlike everyone else, I don't think she was a hallucination brought on by ingested baneberries and approaching death.

I believe she was real, and I'd like to see her one more time before I leave.

I want to tell her I'm sorry, and to thank her for coming to my rescue.

Maybe she already knows these things. Maybe she's finally at peace.

Right now, I'm in the study on the third floor, standing at my father's desk. All that sits here now is his old typewriter. I've spent several evenings in front of it, my fingers tripping over the keys, debating whether or not I should actually press a few of them.

Tonight, I decide that the time is right. Just because my interior design includes no traces of Baneberry Hall's story doesn't mean I won't tell it. In fact, the same publisher who put out the Book all those years ago has already contacted me about writing a sequel.

At first I declined, despite the sizable advance they offered. I'm a designer, not a writer. But now I'm thinking about taking them up on their offer. Not for the money, although that will keep Allie and me in business for years to come.

I want to do it because it's what I think my father would have wanted.

I am, after all, his daughter.

So tonight I sit down at his typewriter and peck at the keyboard, writing what may or may not be the first sentence of what may or may not become a new version of the Book.

Every house has a story to tell and a secret to share.

HOUSE
OF
SECRETS

THE REAL STORY

MAGGIE HOLT

MURRAY-HAMILTON, INC.,
NEW YORK, NY

ACKNOWLEDGMENTS

Every book is a journey that begins with the germ of an idea and ends with a finished product reflecting the hard work of dozens of people. This includes everyone at Dutton and Penguin Random House, especially the fabulous Maya Ziv, who guides me through each book with warmth, support, and a keen editorial eye. A special shout-out goes to Alex Merto and Chris Lin for continuing to give my books covers that are never less than gorgeously creepy.

At Aevitas Creative Management, I owe a million thanks to my tenacious agent, Michelle Brower, and to Chelsea Heller and Erin Files, who help my books take flight around the world.

Special thanks goes to the Rodgers & Hammerstein Organization for granting me permission to use lyrics from "Sixteen Going on Seventeen." Being allowed to let their song drift through the halls of my haunted creation makes my heart sing.

Thank you, as usual, to Sarah Dutton for being an excellent first reader who pulls no punches, and to the Ritter and Livio families for their unflagging enthusiasm and support. Finally, I owe more than thanks to Michael Livio, who willingly accompanied me on this journey every step of the way. This is for you. Always.

ABOUT THE AUTHOR

Home Before Dark is the fourth thriller from *New York Times* bestselling author **Riley Sager,** the pseudonym of an author who lives in Princeton, New Jersey. Riley's first novel, *Final Girls,* was a national and international bestseller that has been published in more than two dozen countries and won the ITW Thriller Award for Best Hardcover Novel. Sager's novels *The Last Time I Lied* and *Lock Every Door* were *New York Times* bestsellers.